Adela would have turned away, but Roarke grasped her arm and forced her to face him

"Think you that I have no sincere passion?" he asked in outrage, and she allowed herself a small, condescending smile.

"Certain of it I am," she asserted firmly, lifting her chin to hold his regard.

"And wrong indeed you are," Roarke gritted out, his fingers flexing around her arm as though he could not check their move.

So abruptly that she gasped in surprise, he hauled Adela close, and she had but an instant to note the flame in his eyes. Her own eyes widened in alarm as she guessed his intention, and she would have bolted, but Roarke's arms locked around her, imprisoning her against the hard wall of his chest.

"Fight me not, Adela," he whispered, both the plea and the sensation of his breath against her lips her undoing....

Dear Reader,

Claire Delacroix's *Romance of the Rose* was part of our 1993 March Madness promotion featuring talented first-time authors. Since then, Ms. Delacroix has published four novels. This month's *Roarke's Folly* is the third title of the ROSE SERIES, which began with *Romance of the Rose*. A landless knight sets out to regain his family's honor in this story that *The Medieval Chronicle* describes as "An absolutely charming medieval romance."

Our other titles this month include *Desire My Love* from Miranda Jarrett, the next book in the continuing saga of the irrepressible Sparhawk family of Rhode Island; *Vows,* by Margaret Moore, part of the Harlequin continuity series WEDDINGS, INC., the story of a Welsh immigrant who gets involved in the Underground Railway; and *Betrayed,* another wonderful Regency from author Judith McWilliams, about an American heiress forced to spy on her British relatives.

Keep an eye out for all four titles, wherever Harlequin Historicals are sold.

Sincerely,

Tracy Farrell
Senior Editor

Please address questions and book requests to:
Harlequin Reader Service
U.S.: 3010 Walden Ave., P.O. Box 1325, Buffalo, NY 14269
Canadian: P.O. Box 609, Fort Erie, Ont. L2A 5X3

CLAIRE DELACROIX

ROARKE'S FOLLY

Harlequin Books

TORONTO • NEW YORK • LONDON
AMSTERDAM • PARIS • SYDNEY • HAMBURG
STOCKHOLM • ATHENS • TOKYO • MILAN
MADRID • WARSAW • BUDAPEST • AUCKLAND

ISBN 0-373-28850-6

ROARKE'S FOLLY

Books by Claire Delacroix

Harlequin Historicals

Romance of the Rose #166
Honeyed Lies #209
Unicorn Bride #223
The Sorceress #235
Roarke's Folly #250

*The Rose Trilogy

CLAIRE DELACROIX

An avid traveler and student of history, Claire Delacroix can be found at home when she has a deadline, amid the usual jumble of books, knitting needles and potted herbs.

For my comrade-in-arms, Margaret Moore

Prologue

Château Fontaine, June 1251

Roarke was restless, and his mood had naught to do with the sounds of distress coming from the solar. He braced his elbows on his knees and propped his chin in his hands, uncertain what he was going to do with the rest of his life.

Another scream rent the air in the hall, and Roarke noticed that this time Armand visibly cringed. The older knight shoved to his feet, the strain of listening to his wife's labor clearly etched in his every gesture.

Sad 'twas, really, Roarke concluded with a minuscule shake of his head. He met Hugues' sympathetic gaze on the other side of the barren hearth and rose to pour his old friend a stiff shot of *eau-de-vie*.

"Surely it cannot take much longer," Armand muttered as he accepted the drink without really seeing that he had.

"Each comes in his own time," Hugues contributed philosophically, his words prompting Armand's lips to thin in irritation.

Another scream carried from the solar, and Armand ran one hand agitatedly through his hair. He regarded the heavy glass clenched in his other hand with something akin to surprise, then carelessly tossed back the *eau-de-vie*. Roarke waited expectantly for him to flinch at the strength of the liquor, but he was oblivious even of that, laying the now-empty glass aside without further thought.

Tragic. To think that one who had once been unfettered and self-sufficient should be so reduced by a woman's scream. Roarke made a mental note to ensure that his heart never be given the opportunity to hold him in thrall like this.

"The worst is that there is naught I can do," Armand growled, restlessly taking his seat before the hearth once again.

"Ah, but of course there is," Roarke countered lightly, typically finding refuge from his troubles in humor. Armand glanced up hopefully, and Roarke tossed him a cocky grin. "Simply touch her no more, and this childbearing will surely cease."

Hugues chuckled reluctantly beneath his breath even as Armand threw Roarke a look that might have turned a lesser man to stone.

"'Twas but a joke," Roarke explained with outspread hands, but Armand was having none of it. The taller man shoved to his feet and paced the length of the room and back under Hugues' indulgent eye.

"One would think that the other two might have strengthened his endurance," the older man commented under his breath. Roarke could only nod in agreement.

"In truth, he seems to take it worse each time," he concurred, unable to keep from watching his friend's agitated pacing.

If this was what marriage did to a man, Roarke knew that he could well live without it. Armand, who never turned a hair, regardless of the magnitude of the foe arrayed against him, was quite simply a nervous mess.

"Fool woman," he muttered now, pausing his pacing to make an agitated appeal to Roarke and Hugues. "Michel and Eloise should well have been enough for her. Why does she persist in this madness?"

Another scream carried to their ears, as though Alex herself would emphasize his point. Armand closed his eyes against the sound, his complexion turning visibly paler, despite his tan.

Hugues waved an indulgent finger in Armand's direction. "Pace the floor again," he demanded softly. "Well enough does it improve your temper."

Something flashed in the tall knight's eyes before he turned and did Hugues' bidding. Armand's response gave Roarke an uneasy sense that that demand had been something Baudouin might have said, mischievous tease that he had been. He wished heartily that Hugues had made some other comment instead. Poor timing 'twas indeed to remind Armand of his recently passed sire, when he was so worried about his spouse's very survival.

Before Roarke could think of something to say to change the direction of his friend's thoughts, Sophie appeared at the top of the stairs. Roarke noted with displeasure that the healer had but to crook a beckoning finger in Armand's direction to have that man striding quickly to the stairs.

Pathetic. He shifted his posture anew, knowing full well that his restlessness had little even to do with his old friend's newfound dedication to family life. He frowned, trying to pinpoint exactly why he had not leapt at the opportunity to marshal here at Fontaine.

To be in charge of the knights and men-at-arms in Armand's employ was no small responsibility, and one that not many others would offer Roarke at his age. Rationally, he should have grasped the chance with both hands, and he had seen in Armand's eyes that he was not the only one surprised by his lack of enthusiasm at the idea. It was, after all, a logical step for a knight sworn to the service of none, especially one without the pending responsibility of an estate to manage.

Hugues pushed to his feet, and Roarke glanced up at the motion, following the older man's gaze to Sophie, who still lingered at the head of the stairs. She smiled as she beckoned to both of them, and Roarke realized belatedly that Alex's cries had ceased.

"Both of you does she want to see," Sophie called encouragingly when Roarke did not rise, having assumed this to be a family moment. He shrugged and followed Hugues up the narrow stairs, concluding that it would be rude under the circumstances to not take a peek at the undoubtedly red, wrinkled, bald and bawling arrival.

He was not prepared for twins.

Apparently, neither was anyone else, for the solar was in a joyous uproar as the women bustled around with the two baby boys. The infants looked much as Roarke had expected, as he had plenty of time to realize, having one child pressed into his arms as soon as he crossed the threshold.

It was red and wrinkled, to be sure, but rather than bald, its head was covered with a thick shock of dark hair. Blue eyes opened blearily, the child's vision obviously unfocused as his gaze swam over Roarke unseeingly.

Then the babe squirmed with vigor, and Roarke knew well enough what would come next. Before he could attract the attention of one of the women and hand off the child, it arched its neck and bellowed fit to wake the dead.

Impossible 'twas to imagine being responsible for the existence of one of these creatures, let alone its health and welfare. Roarke panicked at the very thought that he might have left some such souvenir behind after one of his many liaisons, and he could think of naught but relieving himself of the burden of this particular squawking babe.

Not only could he not stand the pitch of the child's cries, but he had no idea how to ease whatever troubled it. This only made an awkward moment all the worse. One of Alex's ladies appeared fortuitously by his side, and Roarke thanked the heavens above for sending him an angel of mercy in this hour of need.

"Suits you, it does, to hold a baby," she murmured warmly, the invitation in her eyes unmistakable as she lifted her gaze to his. Clearly she had no intent to take the child, and Roarke could not believe his fate.

Oh, nay, Roarke thought wildly. Not for him was this family life, with all its obligations and responsibilities. Roarke all but shoved the child into her arms, noting with annoyance that it ceased its bawling almost immediately. The woman looked up with a soft smile as she rocked the babe against her breast, and Roarke incoherently mumbled some excuse about congratulating the father as he made his escape.

"Promise me." Armand's low voice carried to Roarke's ears despite the activity in the solar, and he turned immediately to follow the sound.

His friend was leaning over a drowsy Alex, his hands braced on the bed on either side of her shoulders to support his weight. She smiled sleepily as Roarke watched, and reached up to touch her husband's stern face with evident affection.

"Are you not pleased with the boys?" she asked softly, and the tall knight nodded but once.

"A fine pair they are, but I will not have you doing this again," he growled, his evident concern seeming to make Alex smile a little more. Something writhed within Roarke that a woman should have such control over a man, and he vowed yet again never to find himself in such a fix. Unnatural 'twas, and he restrained his urge to shake some sense into his old friend, for no good could come of this, of that he was certain.

"Baudouin and Jean, they should be named," Alex mused sleepily, her eyes drifting closed, her face turning into the dark tangle of her loose hair. "In honor of their grandsires," she added softly, seemingly on the verge of drifting off to sleep.

A muscle rippled impatiently in Armand's jaw, and Roarke could almost feel the force of his friend's annoyance.

"Alex," Armand bit out now, and Roarke silently praised his control in the face of Alex's flat refusal to accommodate him. "Alexandria de Fontaine, *promise* me this now."

She sighed and opened her eyes anew, regarding her spouse with something that could have been amusement at his insistence. "Sophie brought a pennyroyal cutting," she murmured, and the tension eased out of Armand's shoulders at this mystifying piece of news.

"And you will use it?" he insisted in a growl.

"I promise," Alex vowed. The glow in her eyes, and the way she twined her arms around Armand's neck, told Roarke that his congratulations might not be welcomed at this precise moment.

Truly Armand had himself a family now, Roarke reflected as he tactfully· turned away. Three sons and a daughter, the reconstruction of Fontaine's new keep virtually completed, and the château's vassals apparently quite satisfied with Armand's administration. Everything a knight could hope for 'twas, and Roarke wondered anew why the position of marshal held so little appeal for him.

He should want it, this he well knew, but he knew just as fully that he did not have any desire for the task. The very idea of taking such responsibility for anything at all filled him with dread, and if the truth were known, he found the entire matter of warfare and defense hopelessly dull. To spend a lifetime overseeing the maintenance of weapons, the sharpness of steel, the worthiness of warriors, did indeed threaten a special kind of hell for Roarke.

But whither now, if not Fontaine?

That restlessness seized him again, and Roarke recognized its source. Should he not take the position and swear his blade to Armand, he really had no place here, though he knew Alex and Armand would make him welcome as a guest for as long as he desired. But his place did not lie here, nor at Pontesse, where Hugues would similarly welcome his hand, nor even at Avigny, and well enough did he know it.

To travel could have been a matter of curiosity for him, but the vows of chastity and the necessary hardships of pilgrimage or crusade held little appeal for one so enchanted with hedonistic pleasures. 'Twas not that he had any difficulty working, for he would willingly labor the length of the day and into the night if a matter could hold his lively interest.

And the trouble with being a knight was that it no longer did that. To Roarke's mind, there were already scores of able knights much more dedicated to the task and more than adequate to defend whatever happened to need defending in these relatively peaceful times. He, however, would rather do something else.

Unfortunately, he had little idea what that something else might be. For his two favorite pastimes, drinking and wenching, were scarcely adequate ways to make a living, pleasurable as they might be.

So, the question remained where to go. For the first time in years, Roarke thought of home, and simultaneously stifled a groan. Indeed, he had not crossed that threshold since he had been entrusted to Avigny to squire for Armand, for there had been little enough to look back on. His family had attended his knighting at Avigny, but nigh on fourteen summers had passed since he had been home. A nostalgic and uncharacteristic desire to look upon his homeland once more seized Roarke at that realization.

Domestic squabbles aplenty would he find at home in Flanders, he knew, but still the idea held a measure of appeal. He smiled and wondered what sort of nonsense his mother had managed to entwine herself in. His sister Rochelle had undoubtedly kept things together in her inimitable fashion, but a dose of his mother's dottiness might suit Roarke well.

And as good a time as any this was to make the journey to the Low Countries, with his blade unsworn to any house or lord. Perhaps adventure and discovery would be had on the road.

He glanced idly over the purposeful bustle of the room and caught the eye of that same maidservant once more. She smiled coyly, and Roarke smiled back, appreciating now the

lusciousness of her curves and wondering how quiet the
stables would be this night.

Pennyroyal, he recalled suddenly, and his grin widened
wickedly. Now, there was a piece of information a man disinterested in responsibilities would do well to recall.

Chapter One

Troyes, August

"The fair!" Roarke shouted jubilantly as the perimeter of the town came into sight and he suddenly realized why the roads had been so busy. Too perfect 'twas to happen across this event with this restlessness fueling his normally high energy even higher. His squire looked up uncomprehendingly, and Roarke gestured broadly toward the commotion, unable to even imagine the extent of the trouble he could make this night.

"Have you never heard tell of the Hot Fair?" he demanded impatiently.

When Yves continued to look blank, Roarke closed the space between their mounts to confide the appeal of the event. Too young Yves was, even for a lad of thirteen, and after the better part of a year together, Roarke often despaired that he would have to teach the boy everything of life. Tragically, Yves seemed to have no instinct at all for revelry or mischief.

"'Tis the biggest and best celebration in all of Ghent," Roarke enthused. "Wine and beer to be had aplenty, women from all over Christendom to be sampled." He rolled his eyes appreciatively, and Yves stifled an adolescent giggle, evidently as much because he thought it was expected as any indication of his own enthusiasm. Roarke shot him a side-long glance, suddenly tempted to see of what the boy was made.

"What think you of having your druthers this night?" he demanded in a mischievous undertone, not mistaking the light of anticipation in Yves' eyes, despite the ruddy flush suffusing his neck.

"B-but milord, but thirteen summers have I seen." He stammered his objection, but Roarke clapped him on the back undeterred.

"And plenty man enough to do the job," he concluded easily.

"But, milord . . ." the boy protested weakly, his ears fair bright enough to glow in the dark.

Roarke grinned and chucked Yves under the chin. "But a drink or two you need to bolster your confidence and loosen your wit," he confidently assured the doubtful boy. Good sport 'twould be, and a good enough excuse to have an audience for his own conquest.

Mayhap *conquests*, if this energetic mood endured. "Make no mistake, I shall show you this night how 'tis done."

And a little sport and frivolity might be just what he needed to take his mind off the indecision that had plagued him of late, Roarke concluded with a grin of anticipation.

The wine was indeed as good as he had expected, and Roarke had imbibed more than his fair share when he finally spotted his prey.

She was waiting in line at the Templars' wool-weighing stand despite the lateness of the hour, half a dozen bales of white fleece that even Roarke could see were of fine quality piled around her feet in the gathering dusk. She was of average build, he noted with the satisfaction of a true connoisseur, neither too tall nor too small, neither too fair nor too dark, her hands finely boned, her face heart-shaped. Though she was indeed pretty, 'twas her skin that pressed her looks toward beauty, for her complexion glowed with a rosy radiance, a healthy tone uncommon in Roarke's wide experience of women.

Though she had draped a veil over her hair, 'twas slipping, undoubtedly as a result of hauling those bales of wool, and he could see that she had blond hair. Indeed, he had well missed the blondes of the north, Roarke thought as his anticipation rose. Little wisps of hair curled around her brow, damp with perspiration, and revealed its curly nature. Her full, ruddy lips thinned in impatience as the brother manning the scales worked with a ponderously slow speed, and Roarke smiled to himself. He well liked women with a bit of fire in their veins.

"Watch," he bade Yves simply, winking broadly as he entrusted the boy with the almost empty wineskin. Roarke brushed off his tabard, ran one hand through his own unruly shock of dark hair and strode toward the woman who did not yet realize that she would share his bed this night.

"Good evening," he began smoothly, summoning his most irresistible smile as he reached her side.

The line inched closer to the scales in that moment, and the woman, completely oblivious of Roarke's presence, bent to gather her bales and move forward.

"Let me help you with that," he murmured gallantly, reaching for the two closest bales.

"These bales are *not* for sale," she informed him frostily, plucking the two bales from Roarke's hands with businesslike ease and returning them to her pile without even sparing him a glance.

Annoyance rose in Roarke's chest, but he checked its path, certain that the prize was well worth this short detour. So, she had thought he was assessing the fleece. He could work with that.

"Although they are indeed fine, I must confess that I had no intention of buying them," he commented amiably.

His words got her attention, though not with the response Roarke had anticipated, for when she finally looked to his face, her expression was one of shock. He had just enough time to note that her eyes were a lovely golden brown before she spoke.

"Truly, you would confess your intent to steal so openly?" she demanded with barely controlled outrage, her accusation catching Roarke so completely unawares that he momentarily knew not what to say. "Indeed I thought I had met every dreg of humanity managing to scrape a living from the leavings at this fair, but your boldness surpasses anything or anyone yet encountered."

She shot him an eloquent look of disdain, evidently daring him to respond, but Roarke could do naught but stare dumbly back at her in the wake of her speech. She was prettier than he had originally thought, he realized, a fact that did not seem to encourage his normally facile tongue to action.

"Well, no, I—," he began, hating to hear himself stammer. He silently cursed the wine that seemed to have completely unhinged his tongue, rather than simply loosening it, and struggled to regain some semblance of composure.

Unfortunately, the lady showed no signs of being struck speechless.

"Good coin have I proposed to pay for these bales," she pointed out acidly, shaking an admonishing finger in his face, "and no trouble will I have from the likes of you before the deal is even completed."

The likes of him? What did that mean? Fighting a sense that he was doomed to lose this battle, Roarke plunged back into the fray, unable to understand what compelled him onward. "In truth, I merely meant to assist you in moving them," he tried to explain, pleased that he sounded respectably articulate, but she waved his words aside with disgust.

"Spare me the sordid tale," she told him with a sneer. "Truly I am not so naive as to believe an excuse as old as that. *Assist me,*" she repeated, and shook her head disparagingly. "And no sooner would I bend to pick another than my 'assistant' would disappear into the crowd with a bale or two to make a tidy profit on his 'aid.' Well served indeed am I to refuse assistance of that sort." She turned her back on Roarke resolutely, mustering her bales and making a great show of counting that they were still all there that kindled his ire.

"No petty thief am I," Roarke protested indignantly, almost flinching at the sharp look she shot over one shoulder.

"Nay?" she enquired archly. "Then even less reason have I to talk to you, if you would aspire to stealing the entire lot."

She held his gaze for a long moment in silent challenge, and Roarke was further annoyed that no pretty words came to him with which to ease her suspicions. He simply stared back at her mutely, certain that she must think him quite thick when she finally turned away.

Not at all sure why it troubled him so much, he squared his shoulders in irritation when she flicked her chin away. The way the man behind her in line stifled a smile when Roarke met his gaze did little to ease his annoyance. Roarke fancied he heard a boyish snicker behind him, and recalled with embarrassment that Yves was watching this display.

Too late was it to let the matter die. So, she thought him a common thief. Well, Roarke intended to straighten her out on that matter, at least.

"Indeed you have misjudged my intention," he started anew. The woman sighed openly before she turned to face him with an expression of resignation.

"What do you want?" she demanded bluntly, folding her arms impatiently across her chest. "If indeed you feel obligated to make some explanation for your behavior, at least have the courtesy to do it quickly, that you might not waste my time."

'Twas an unencouraging opening, to say the least, and Roarke's glib tongue once again mercilessly abandoned him to an inarticulate fate. He met her eyes tentatively, knowing how ridiculous it would sound to say that he had merely intended to bed her, not steal her wool, and found himself painfully aware of the amused perusal of the others waiting in line.

"But a few moments of your time, mayhap over a sip of wine once your business is concluded, and I would gladly make my explanation to you in full," he offered gallantly, relieved to feel a vestige of his usual charm returning.

Roarke's pleasure with himself was short-lived, however, for his quarry simply rolled her eyes in disgust. "Have you ever heard the like?" she demanded of the others waiting in the line. A chorus of assenting murmurs greeted her question, but she had already turned that sharp gaze back on Roarke.

"Make your explanation now, and you would do well to make it a good one," she ordered, and Roarke struggled not to fidget like a child caught at some mischief. Unlikely it seemed indeed that she would take kindly to a confession of his true intentions.

"I but wanted to talk to you," he offered tentatively, but one of her fair brows rose skeptically.

"Indeed?"

At least she had not turned her back again. Roarke knew that he had to take advantage of the meager opportunity, for it was likely to be the only one he would get.

"Indeed," he confirmed firmly, frowning as though trying to recollect something. "Well it seems to me that we might have met afore, and I was wondering if you came oft to the Hot Fair—" He got no further before she interrupted him with a dry laugh.

"Indeed, you know all of the old lines, do you not?" she observed, and the others in the line chuckled openly at her observation. "Next you will tell me that I look like the Madonna in the church where you learned the Mass as a child, or ask if I have had a physician cast my horoscope, as you are certain you know the position of the sun at my birth."

She regarded Roarke indulgently, a flicker of humor in those topaz eyes, and shook her head slowly. "Truly, the world would be incomplete without your kind, though no doubt women everywhere would well tolerate that loss, to not be so harassed." She would have turned away, but Roarke grasped her shoulder, her last remark catching him on the raw.

"Harassed?" he demanded angrily. "First you would accuse me of thievery, and now harassment. Have you always such sweet words for those who would assist you?"

"Assist me?" she repeated, her ire evidently rising to meet his own. "Next you will tell me that 'tis your chivalrous duty to assist all women so in need as myself." Her eyes narrowed, and she jabbed one finger in the direction of Roarke's chest. "Save your breath, and spare me your talk of chivalry, for well enough do I know that among your kind, that touching little speech is the last defense."

The observers nudged each other and nodded knowingly as they turned their attention as one back to Roarke, expectantly watching for his response. He felt his color rise before his audience, all too aware that she had hit the nail on the head.

Chivalry *was* his last argument, and usually a successful one. His anger redoubled that she had so effectively eliminated it. The awareness that he was being made to look like a fool, and that she was doing so deliberately, pushed Roarke's tolerance over the top.

"Nay, the code of chivalry insists that one help *ladies* in distress," Roarke shot back. The way her eyes widened told him that he had hit his mark. The onlookers gasped and looked to the woman. Her chin lifted angrily, her eyes glittered, and Roarke knew well enough already to brace himself against her words.

"Why, you spiteful worm of a human being!" she spat, advancing on him in a most menacing way. "No shame is there to be had in making one's way with the labor of one's hands, as I have done. No doubt 'tis *noble* blood running in your veins, you who would assault and insult a woman in a manner more suited to the common trash who abide in the gutters. No such venom have I earned by refusing your lewd invitation!"

"No invitation did I make." As Roarke defended himself, he felt a twinge of unfamiliar guilt at his words.

"Oh, no?" she demanded skeptically. "Truly, you think me daft, if you expect me not to understand that a roll in the hay was what this was all about. And if *that* be your objective, you'd best find yourself a cheap tavern whore to accommodate your needs, not a decent woman like myself."

"Nay, 'twas the wool alone that interested me," Roarke argued. Her eyes grew cold, telling him that once again he had said the wrong thing.

"So, 'tis the wool indeed you find most fetching about me?" she charged, and he stifled a groan. No winning this argument was there. "Well, *there* is a compliment that a woman might clutch to her heart until her dying day."

Roarke made a small sound of frustration in the back of his throat, seeing with relief that he was momentarily to be spared from responding. The line was moving again, and he bent to pick up several bales.

"At least I will get the wool," he muttered, missing the warning flash in her eyes.

"Well enough I told you that the wool was not for sale," she insisted angrily, her rising voice drawing Roarke's attention. "And neither will I let you steal it!"

Roarke glanced up to see her fist just before it connected with his jaw with surprising force. The blow sent him sprawling backward, the bales tumbling out of his grip as he fell.

"My wool!" Her voice carried to Roarke's ears even as the world cavorted dizzily around him, and he felt that curious twinge of guilt once more before his head thwacked against the cobblestones. He heard Yves' running footsteps, and a man's voice called out.

"Adela! Did he harm you?"

Adela. Roarke savored her name as the world faded to black around him, and felt himself begin to smile.

He had always enjoyed a challenge, and a challenge Adela certainly promised to be.

Adela stormed through the market to reach her father's stall once more, the dutifully weighed bales of wool bouncing against her knees. She did not notice their bumping in her annoyance, nor did she note the children and dogs scurrying out of her path.

Scoundrel. Well enough she knew that she should have grown a thicker hide about such matters by now, but 'twas likely she would never learn.

To think she had actually wondered if he might truly be interested in her.

Adela groaned at her own stupidity and shoved her way through the thick crowd at the intersection of paths between the temporary stalls. 'Twas but another trick of the apprentices in the guild, she was painfully certain of that.

If only this one had not been so handsome, she knew she could have been more philosophical about it all. Adela stifled a sigh, recalling how her heart had leapt when she met those mischievous gray eyes and noted the knight's rakish good looks.

The twinkle in his eyes should have warned her.

She was troubled for a moment that he had obviously been of noble blood, but then his taunt rang in her ears anew. Undoubtedly he had thought the very idea of teasing a bourgeoise such sport that he had willingly gone along with the scheme of Georges and the others.

If only she had made a match sooner.

If only she were not confronting her twenty-sixth summer still without a spouse.

If only she had a decent prospect, at least. Adela grimaced, knowing full well how her refusal of Georges' attentions had earned her both his scorn and a reputation throughout Ghent as a frosty virgin.

She sighed anew as she gained her father's stall, wishing something had worked out differently in her life, wishing that Georges would find someone else to torment, wishing that her father hadn't needed her so much when she was younger and should have been making her match.

Wishing a handsome rogue like that knight would indeed offer seriously for her favor.

'Twas not the way of the world, though, she acknowledged sadly, shoving back the drape with one foot and summoning a cursory smile of greeting for her sire. And 'twas certainly not destined to be the way of Adela's world.

The moon was high in the midday sky when Roarke awoke groggily, and he groaned aloud at the pain in his head when he tried to move. He lay back against the hay and closed his eyes for a long moment, then slowly opened them again to look at the moon.

It was still there, the white crescent hanging open end down in the bright blue sky, as though it, too, found its surroundings unexpected and disorienting. Roarke felt a curious sympathy for the moon, finding himself feeling much the same way. He supposed he should be used to it by now, never having been much for mornings, but on this day his mind felt as dense as a bale of wool.

A bale of wool. Roarke gnawed on his bottom lip and frowned. A familiar sense of unease told him that phrase should mean something on this morn of morns, but, typically, he had no idea what.

Indeed, it seemed that he felt much worse than usual.

Roarke closed his eyes and concluded that wine alone could not have given him this headache. He ran his fingers through his tangled hair and encountered a hard lump on the back of his head. Roarke touched it and winced at the pain that shot through his skull.

Adela.

Her name and his recollection of the previous evening came back to him in a rush, and Roarke sat up purposefully. The stables cavorted wildly around him, and he braced himself on his elbows, willing the walls to stop spinning as he blinked slowly.

The world eventually righted itself, and Roarke exhaled slowly in relief. Mercifully, it seemed he would live after all.

"Milord!" Roarke turned too quickly at the sound of Yves' voice and winced again at the resulting din that erupted within his head. She had hit him, he recalled now, frowning anew as he tried to recall why.

"Are you all right?"

"Not so loud," he urged as he held up one hand, and the boy obediently whispered as he continued.

"Your head must hurt," he offered sympathetically, and Roarke managed to nod without disrupting his universe overmuch. He ran one hand over the day's growth on his chin, grimacing when he found the bruise where Adela's fist had landed on him.

"Adela," he murmured, the way his squire fairly bounced in excitement drawing his wary glance.

"Never have I seen a woman punch anyone," he enthused with glowing eyes, reenacting the embarrassing moment once more for Roarke. "Pow! Not the first time was it that she had done that, I wager."

Roarke frowned as he fought to recall the evening's events fully. She *had* hit him. He fingered the bruise anew and acknowledged a grudging admiration for the force of the blow she had dealt him. Surprise she had had on her side, to be sure, he reasoned with remarkable speed, but still. He was quite certain a woman had never hit him before.

"What happened after she hit me?" he demanded slowly, but Yves looked blank.

"You fell and hit your head," he supplied simply, and Roarke made an impatient gesture.

Had he taught this boy naught of what was of import in the world? Obviously the woman must have been distraught about what she had done, and equally obviously 'twas this that he wished to hear. Mayhap these were her family's stables, he thought suddenly, and the very idea cheered him at the prospect that she might have felt so guilty.

"Nay, to Adela," he clarified, but the boy merely shrugged.

"She weighed her wool and left."

Roarke stared at Yves incredulously. "After she ensured that I was all right, of course?" he demanded impatiently, but the boy shook his head.

"Nay, she did not even look to see where you fell." When Roarke fell silent in an attempt to assimilate this piece of news, Yves leaned closer and dropped his voice. "'Twas her turn at the scales, you know," he confided by way of explanation, and Roarke knew his astonishment showed on his face.

In fact, that revelation seemed so unlikely that after his first feeling of dismay and a mere moment of reflection Roarke determined that the boy must be telling tales.

"Indeed you cannot tell me that she did not look at what she had done," he asserted firmly, noting with satisfaction the boy's rising discomfiture.

Now he would have the truth of the matter. No woman could walk away and leave him lying there without shedding at least one tear of remorse. Roarke knew the merit of his own charm well enough to understand that.

"In truth, she stopped once her wool was weighed," the boy confessed heavily. Roarke leaned closer to him and waited expectantly to hear the tale.

"Aye..." he prompted impatiently, watching the boy's color rise yet more with satisfaction.

"A thief she called you and... and she spat on your tunic," Yves admitted in a low rush, his gaze flicking quickly to Roarke and away.

Roarke stared at him, unable to believe what he had heard. The boy grimaced and stretched one finger tentatively toward a splat on Roarke's tunic. Roarke looked down at the mark in amazement. He touched the saliva in turn, not doubting for a moment what it was.

Adela had spat on him. 'Twas impossible to comprehend, and Roarke tried to recall whether he had ever aroused such an indignant response from a potential conquest.

"Well I knew that you would not believe me, so I left it there," Yves explained softly, but truly, the knight was so astonished that he had not even thought to admonish the boy.

Roarke did not even hear Yves slip away as he stared disbelievingly down at the mark on his tunic.

She had spat on him. It seemed his clouded mind could make no sense of the assertion. Roarke touched the spot again gingerly, quite certain even in his admittedly muddled state that such a thing had never happened to him.

Could he be losing his legendary charisma?

Impossible. He frowned and used a handful of straw to wipe away the evidence of Adela's distaste with him. Offensive 'twas, and undoubtedly inappropriate. Roarke nodded in mute self-agreement. Aye, that was it. The problem here lay with Adela. 'Twas she who had the difficulty, not he. And this was an insult rendered that could not be left untended. He felt his ire rise and brushed off his chausses more deliberately as his scowl deepened.

After all, who did this Adela think she was? A wool buyer, and a woman, while he, Roarke d'Aalgen, was a full-fledged knight. Earned his spurs through hard work he had, and blessed he was with noble blood coursing through his veins.

What right had she to treat him thus?

Obviously the only possible recourse was to seek out this woman and set her straight. Roarke nodded firmly and shoved to his feet, ignoring the dancing of the world around him as he shouted for his horse.

*   *   *

"Adela? Oh, aye, I know Adela." The Templar grimaced eloquently as he packed up his scales with practiced ease.

The fair had closed, the vendors packed up, most either already on the road or lingering in informal groups to exchange a last bit of news or make that last deal. The abrupt transition in the scene had done little to ease Roarke's typical morning disorientation when he reached the fairgrounds to find vast empty stretches of trampled grass instead of stalls and people jammed together.

"Know you where she is?" Roarke asked, his destrier taking a few impatient steps. The Templar glanced up now, and his eyes narrowed speculatively.

"Are you not the one who made jest of her last eve?" he demanded, and Roarke drew himself up straighter in the saddle.

"I made no jest," he asserted flatly, but the Templar wagged one finger in his direction as a grin launched itself slowly over his heavy face.

"Aye, you were that, I recall." He chuckled under his breath and efficiently closed the case that carried his weights. "Punched you, she did, and—" he raised his gaze, and his grin widened as he met Roarke's regard "—and called you a thief."

He seemed to be struggling not to smirk, and Roarke knew full well that he, too, had seen Adela's salute. Roarke felt his color rise, but he stubbornly held the Templar's gaze.

"A matter have I to discuss with her," he insisted, and the older man chuckled anew.

"Aye, well enough I can imagine that," he muttered, shooting Roarke an assessing glance as he finished packing and propped his hands on his hips. "You, best of any, should expect to feel the bite of the north wind on seeking her out."

"I would speak with her," Roarke maintained stubbornly, and the Templar sergeant shrugged his shoulders.

"No charge have you that you were not warned," he concluded easily, fixing Roarke with a bright eye before he pointed the way. "In the third aisle yonder was their stall. Weavers of a fine stripe they are, and a wise man might do well to compliment the work afore making his appeal."

"I thank you, sir." Roarke acknowledged the information and the advice with a quick nod before he turned his steed in that direction.

The remnants of half-packed merchandise made the aisles that had been so crammed with souls the night before easy to count. When Roarke found the row, he asked again after Adela, though this time he made the excuse that he sought some of their wool. The wizened merchant before him nodded in understanding, turning to indicate a spot with one bony finger. Roarke noted its vacancy even as the man spoke, and his heart sank.

"There they were these past weeks, but packed away they were when I arose this morn. Barely a chance to say farewell had I, for they went with the first group to travel north," he supplied, bending back over his own packing once more. "Well enough do I recall that they sold the last of the stripe last night," he mused, almost to himself, and Roarke had to strain to catch the words. "Mayhap that could be why they left early."

"Aye, little point would there be in staying, then," Roarke acknowledged, curiously unwilling to ride away and leave the matter rest. He wanted to know who else was with Adela that all insisted on saying "they" when he asked after her, but he knew not how to ask without appearing to have an interest he was certain he did not.

"Know you whence they come?" The question fell from Roarke's lips before he knew he had any intention of asking it.

The older man glanced up with surprise. "Nay, I know not," he confessed. "Each year do I see them here, and 'tis not in my nature to pry." He pursed his lips and shrugged.

"Likely somewhere in Flanders, I wager, by the quality of the work."

"Aye, likely," Roarke agreed, feeling an odd sense of failure as he thanked the merchant and turned back to Yves.

'Twas no matter, and he knew it—an issue left unresolved, but an unimportant one. Long had they to ride this day and an insult rendered by a common woman was little enough, compared to the larger problems in his life. Roarke nodded firmly to himself, refusing to admit that his arguments rang hollow even in his own ears.

Time 'twas to go home, he reminded himself, summoning Yves with a nod as he turned to the road and dismissed all thoughts of a saucy blonde from his mind.

Chapter Two

"Roarke!" The delighted cry was as familiar as the old hall itself, and Roarke turned expectantly at the sound.

He barely had enough time to make out his mother's figure closing in before her arms locked around him and she embraced him tightly. He grinned crookedly at the welcome, and bent accommodatingly over her shorter form, hugging her plump figure closer as her favored scent of lavender filled his nostrils.

He was home. Surprisingly, it mattered more than he had expected.

"'Tis so good to see you," his mother declared into his chest, her voice muffled by his tunic, and Roarke pulled back. She reached up and patted his cheek proudly, then ruffled his hair as if he were but a tot, not a grown man towering over her.

"Not changed a bit are you," she asserted perkily, her words prompting Roarke to give her an assessing glance.

The years had been kind to Ermengarde, but there were new lines on her fair complexion, and he could see even in the relative darkness of the hall that she had made some attempt to conceal the silver threads in her hair. She was softer and plumper than she had been, and it seemed to Roarke that she was shorter than he recalled, as well, though her hazel eyes still twinkled with the devil's own mischief.

"And what have you been about while I've been gone?" he inquired indulgently, grinning at the way her giggle made her look like a young girl.

"Naught, but Rochelle is getting married!" she confided in a delighted whisper.

"Married?" Roarke repeated in shock. He pulled back and gave his mother a dubious appraisal, wondering how badly she had gotten the facts twisted around this time. "Quite certain, are you?" he demanded skeptically, earning a delightful trill of laughter from his mother.

"Of course I am *certain*, Roarke. From your manner, one would think that I oft confused matters," she chided. Roarke raised his brows eloquently, but declined to comment further. With a coquettish flick of her veil, his mother turned and fairly skipped across the hall, evidently expecting him to follow, if he meant to continue the conversation.

Or else she had headed off on another mental tangent and had already forgotten that she had only told him half of the tale. Roarke shook his head indulgently and trailed after his mother.

A conspicuous absence on the sideboard made him pause and frown in thought. There had always been a pair of brass candlesticks there, ever since he was a child, but now the sideboard stood glaringly empty. Roarke scowled more deeply, unable to understand why anyone would move them.

He would have to ask Denis. Perhaps that ever-efficient chatelain was merely having them polished. Roarke glanced up in time to catch but a glimpse of his mother's hem at the top of the stairs before she disappeared into the solar, and he groaned. A merry enough chase did she lead, as he now recalled.

And he had evidently gotten much too slow in his absence to keep up with his mother.

"*Maman!*" he shouted as he took the stairs three at a time, not really expecting her to pay attention. He darted into the solar to find her already engrossed in her embroidery, sitting on a chest in the dappled sunlight coming through the glass window.

"Maman," he said again, more softly this time, and she glanced up with genuine surprise, a smile dawning on her pretty features at the sight of him. 'Twas at moments like this that he wondered whether she truly could be as flighty as she seemed, for 'twas beyond belief that she could have already forgotten his presence.

"Come and sit with me, Roarke," she invited, patting the seat cushion beside her. "So long it has been since we have had a chat."

"Did you say that Rochelle was getting married?" Roarke inquired carefully as he took his seat, and his mother's smile broadened.

"Oh, that she is, and to the most charming man." She nodded to herself happily and took another careful stitch before favoring Roarke with a sharp look. "A very *wealthy* man, he is," she confided, holding his gaze for an instant as though that were of particular merit before returning to her work. "The nuptials are in a month, and you had best stay to attend, now that you are finally home."

Rochelle was getting married. It was almost unthinkable, and Roarke struggled to come to terms with the idea. So adamant Rochelle had always been that she would not take a spouse, and indeed, she had managed matters efficiently here for so long that it seemed unlikely that she had need of one.

"But why?" Roarke asked finally.

"All the usual reasons, I believe," his mother retorted impishly, unable to stifle a mischievous smile as she spoke. Roarke grinned back and shook his head.

"Well enough do you know what I mean," he chided gently. "The lands pass to Rochelle through your family's tradition, and always did she intend to administer them alone."

Ermengarde pursed her lips, tilting her head to one side as she thoughtfully considered her work. "I suppose—" she

finally asserted quietly "—that love has a way of taking one
by surprise."

Roarke would not know anything of that, he concluded
easily as he glanced around the familiar solar. And a mercy
that was, from his point of view.

Something was different about the solar, he realized suddenly, and he studied the room anew. The brass plate that
had hung over the fireplace was gone, and he recalled once
more his thought that Denis might be having the brass
cleaned this day.

But no, his mother's embroidery threads were no longer
housed in that delicately carved ivory box her sire had
brought home from the Crusades, their brilliant tangle now
contained by a mundane wicker basket instead of the casket she so treasured.

And the rosewood chest Ermengarde carefully folded her
veils into each evening was gone, as was the tapestry acquired by her grandsire that had adorned the west wall, the
one that usually blocked the chinks with its rich display.
Roarke's gaze swept assessingly over the room as he sought
to recall every little trinket and determine whether it was still
here before he turned to his mother.

"Where has everything gone?" he demanded without
preamble, and she glanced up from her work with something akin to shock.

"Everything?" she repeated in a small voice, a tremu-
lous voice that reminded Roarke of the days when his father's bellow had filled the hall. When that man had
shouted, "Ermengarde!" in frustration, she had responded in much this same manner, and the recollection
made Roarke suddenly very nervous.

"Yes, *everything,*" he repeated evenly, unwillingly hearing an echo of his sire's carefully restrained annoyance in his
own tone. "The candlesticks, the tapestry, your father's
ivory casket." He raised his brows and held her gaze stubbornly, even as her eyes filled with helpless tears.

"I, well, um." Ermengarde made a shaky stitch in her work. Her brows drew together momentarily before she lifted her chin defiantly. "I put them away for safekeeping," she asserted, her every gesture and very tone telling her son that she was lying.

"Show me," he challenged softly, and her bottom lip trembled. She stared at him reproachfully, as though she had just found him responsible for some particularly vile crime, and Roarke was dismayed to find himself feeling guilty for discovering her deception. "Where are they?" he demanded once again, as if to show that he would not back down, and Ermengarde glanced quickly away.

"We had some difficulties, so I had to sell a few things," she admitted in a voice so small as to be virtually inaudible.

"Difficulties?" Roarke repeated, knowing his anger showed in his eyes, but somehow managing to keep his tone level. "What sort of *difficulties?* And why did you not summon me?"

His mother plucked at her kirtle as one heavy tear shimmered and threatened to fall. Roarke told himself that he would not be swayed by her tears, even as he felt his resolve weakening.

"Financial difficulties, if you must know," Ermengarde admitted in a low voice. She gestured vaguely into the air. "It seemed such a good harvest, but Denis said the tithes just were not enough." She raised her troubled gaze to Roarke.

"I do not understand how this can be. Everything is so *expensive,*" she confessed. "Never has it been this way. Always has there been some left over for, for indulgences."

Indulgences. The word did not bode well, to Roarke's mind. And 'twas not the first time Roarke had heard the nobility complain of this same problem, but he suspected his mother would not find that revelation particularly reassuring. Instead, he took her hand in his, surprised to find it trembling slightly.

"Surely Rochelle and Denis could have managed this without selling your treasures," he said softly, completely unprepared for several of his mother's tears to spill. She bit her lip in a bid for control, and he slipped one arm over her shoulders, giving her an encouraging squeeze as he tried to fathom what had distressed her so.

"I had bought some cloth on credit," she confessed, shooting a glance to his face as if testing his mood, her fidgeting fingers revealing her nervousness. "It was for Rochelle, and I did not want to tell her about it. A woman needs new things for her wedding day, you know. 'Tis only fitting."

"And when Denis said there was no money to spare, you bartered your things," Roarke concluded heavily, not needing to see his mother's nod to know he spoke the truth.

"He tells her *everything*," she muttered mutinously.

Roarke sighed heavily and shook his head, scanning the solar once more and realizing the value of what she had traded. "Exactly how much cloth did you buy?" he demanded impatiently. Ermengarde pulled away from him, her features brightening as she tapped her chin with one finger and recalled her purchase with evident delight.

"Well, there was fine wool for two kirtles, one a lovely blue, that beautiful smoky blue dyed in England. Sure I am that you have seen it, dear, and 'tis indeed a fine color for Rochelle. Let me see, I finished the kirtle and folded it away, but certain I am that I could find it and show you." She would have risen, but Roarke placed a restraining hand on her shoulder.

"What else?" he asked flatly, and she blinked as she thought.

"The wool for the second kirtle is a pale pink, the very shade of the roses in the garden in the summer, and I think it, too, will flatter Rochelle's coloring. You know, I cannot help but think that her new husband will find her very fetching indeed, and—"

"And what else?" Roarke interrupted, certain that even two lengths of the very finest wool could not have been valued so high.

"Well…" Ermengarde looked away guiltily, and Roarke knew well enough to dread this confession. "Well, it seemed to me fitting that a new couple should have something new in the solar, not these dusty old rags that were here when I arrived." She gestured to the room, and Roarke groaned aloud when the cavalier motion encompassed not only the bed curtains, but the linens and the heavy drapes hanging over the shuttered windows, as well.

Fitting was a word that was beginning to get under his skin.

"Tell me you did not," he muttered as he dropped his head into his hands, but his mother continued undeterred, seemingly encouraged by the fact that he had not shouted outright in disapproval.

"Oh, aye, Roarke, and 'twas the most lovely design I commissioned. Certain I am that you will think it beautiful beyond compare," she trilled. Roarke's head snapped up, and he regarded her with outright horror.

"Commissioned?" he croaked, but Ermengarde merely smiled, completely oblivious of his distress.

"So lovely, it is. I simply must show it to you, Roarke," she insisted, efficiently putting her needlework aside and rising to hasten across the room. "You know, these weavers in Ghent are so wondrously skilled, no point is there anymore in buying cloth from afar, let alone troubling with weaving it ourselves."

Roarke watched numbly as she opened the largest trunk, her words running over him in a ceaseless and unheard torrent while she enumerated the virtues of the weaver she had chosen. Even as she spoke, Ermengarde victoriously hauled out a length of subtly striped wool in myriad shades of blue and white, echoing the standard of Aalgen, and draped it proudly across her arms.

"See?" she said challengingly, as proud as if she had wrought it herself.

It *was* beautiful, but as Ermengarde hauled ell after seemingly endless ell out of the trunk, Roarke's heart sank in despair. He could not summon a single word of praise for the work, watching helplessly as his mother dragged a goodly quantity over to the bed, evidently intending to show him the completed effect. All Roarke could think about was how much of the cloth there was, and he licked his lips carefully before he spoke.

"How did you imagine you would get the silver without telling Denis what 'twas for?" he asked quietly, unencouraged by the pert look his mother shot in his direction.

"Denis well knows that I have need of the occasional frippery," she supplied easily, stretching to her toes in a futile effort to push the cloth over the bedpost. "Mayhap you could drape this, dear, and then you will be able to see precisely how lovely it will be—"

Roarke shoved to his feet and closed the distance between them, summarily plucking the cloth from his mother's hands and compelling her to look up at him when he did not drape it as she had bidden. Evidently some of his disapproval showed on his face, for once she had met his eyes questioningly, she bit her lip like a guilty child. No surprise was there in her expression, though, and he knew that she fully expected his chastisement.

"Was this worth the loss of all your precious heirlooms?" he asked quietly instead, and her tears rose anew. She made a helpless motion with one hand, and Roarke saw that the sacrifice of her valuables had not come as readily as she would have liked him to believe.

"I just wanted to give her something fine," she confessed brokenly, and her tears spilled now in a torrent. Roarke made a growl of frustration deep in his throat and hauled his mother into his arms, the beautiful cloth crushed between them as she sobbed all over her purchase. "It seemed ..."

"Fitting," Roarke supplied when his mother's voice faltered, and she nodded against his chest. He shook his head as her sobbing increased in tempo, patting her back ineffectively and stifling a sigh of frustration.

Somehow he had to make this right, Roarke resolved, unable to bear the sound of his mother's crying. Impossible 'twould be to return the commissioned cloth, to be sure, but mayhap somehow, in some way, he could manage to regain her few treasures.

Roarke found the abode of the weaver in question in Ghent without much difficulty, although he lingered for several long moments outside, struggling to decide how best to present his case. When inspiration failed to strike and he had fussed with his steed's reins longer than was really appropriate, he grudgingly handed them off to Yves, squared his shoulders and entered the shop.

'Twas now or never.

The shop was much more pleasant than he had anticipated, the filth of the city streets outside having led him to expect a dingy hovel. The weaver's shop, in marked contrast, was unexpectedly bright, its whitewashed walls clean. A wood-topped counter was placed close to the door that Roarke had entered, and he was tempted to touch the smooth surface of the polished wood, seeing the subtle notches along its opposite side used for measuring.

The walls on either side of the counter were packed solid with lengths of folded cloth in every hue imaginable. It was quieter in here than out in the street, perhaps because of all the cloth, and Roarke felt some of the tension ease from his muscles as the muted sounds of the working looms filled his ears.

Behind the counter, in the shop itself, he could see the looms themselves, their light pine battens rocking back and forth, harnesses rising and falling in a ceaseless litany. Half a dozen looms were there, a weaver at each with sleeves rolled up, working in silence, hands moving like quicksilver as shuttles shot back and forth.

Despite himself, Roarke was fascinated by the gentle creaking of the apparatus, watching with wonder as a discernible increment of cloth grew on the closest loom. It seemed indeed that the cloth magically appeared before his very eyes, the weaver's hands and feet moving so quickly as to be virtually indiscernible.

"Perhaps I could help you, sir?"

The question brought Roarke back to the present with a start, and he glanced up to find an older man patiently waiting behind the counter. When he had appeared, Roarke had no idea, but he summoned his most engaging smile and nodded once in greeting.

"Indeed, I should hope so," he concurred, and the merchant smiled agreeably. "I believe my mother, the Lady Ermengarde of Aalgen, commissioned some cloth from you recently."

"Ah, yes." The man nodded understandingly, and Roarke wondered if he imagined the wariness that seemed to dawn in the other man's eyes. "A lovely variety of blues did she select." He granted Roarke a sharp glance. "Is there perhaps some complaint with the work?"

"Oh, no," Roarke confirmed hastily. "'Tis indeed lovely, and she is most looking forward to completing the sewing, that she might see it in place."

The merchant smiled again, this time with a measure of pride. "I am most gratified to hear it, sir. Mayhap you seek something else to match? I did have the remainder of the dye lot woven in a different pattern...." He turned to the shelf and ran one fingertip over the stacked cloth as he spoke, evidently intending to seek out the cloth in question, but Roarke quickly protested.

"Nay, in truth the reason for my visit concerns the previous purchase alone." As Roarke wondered how best to present the question he must ask, the proprietor shot an unencouraging look over his shoulder.

"Well I thought you said that there was no complaint with the cloth," he pointed out with an indisputable wariness in his tone. Roarke swallowed and frowned.

"It is as you say." He took a deep breath. "My concern is with my mother's means of payment," he admitted, his words falling in a rush. The merchant's bushy gray brows rose fractionally, and he turned to face Roarke anew, folding his arms resolutely across his chest.

"Well I thought that matter settled," he said flatly.

Roarke plunged onward. "She paid you in goods, I understand."

The proprietor nodded but once. "The matter rests between the lady and me," he said simply. Roarke leaned one hand on the counter, realizing that this was not quite going as he had expected.

"Well, 'tis not so simple as that," he began, summoning a measure of his usual charm. "As well you can imagine, many of those articles were heirlooms, and of sentimental value to both my mother and sister. It seems now that my mother regrets their loss."

"Indeed?" the merchant asked idly, and Roarke saw that the man did not intend to give him any assistance.

"Indeed," he repeated firmly, refusing to be deterred. "And seeing her distress, I have little option but to try and resolve the matter in another fashion."

"Do you indeed?" The man's eyes were cold now, his manner tending decidedly toward hostility. "And what solution would you propose, sir?" he demanded softly, the formal address sounding more than slightly mocking to Roarke. Hating what he had to say, Roarke stubbornly took a deep breath and forced himself to continue.

"Mayhap the cloth could be returned," he suggested, his attempt to smile engagingly cut short by the flash of outright anger in the man's eyes.

"Have you any idea what you ask?" he retorted, his quiet tone not fooling Roarke for an instant.

"Well enough do I understand that the cloth was ordered—" Roarke began, but got no further before the merchant interrupted him.

"Ordered?" he repeated with clear annoyance. "Aye, it was that, as was the dye and the fine woolen warp she demanded I use." He wagged one finger at Roarke to emphasize his point. "No small investment did I make in this matter, only to find that your mother had not seen fit to ensure that she had adequate coin with which to pay me! The best of a bad situation did I make with that exchange, and no intention have I of making it more to your benefit!"

"But my mother—"

"Deceived me flatly," the older man confirmed dismissively, drawing himself up straighter. "'Tis only a measure of the fact that I cannot bear to see a woman cry that we came to any arrangement at all, but having been made a fool once, I will not step into that trap again."

"But the goods she exchanged with you are valuable beyond question," Roarke protested, taking offense at the man's attitude. Truly he had done Ermengarde no favors by hoodwinking her out of everything she held dear.

"Valuable, mayhap, to the lady," the proprietor growled, folding his arms across his chest again. "Valuable, mayhap, to you," he mused as his eyes narrowed. "Were you perhaps expecting them as a legacy, and now find yourself with leagues of cloth instead?"

Roarke drew himself up angrily at that charge. "My mother seeks their return," he responded coldly, and the man snorted under his breath.

"'Tis not your mother I see before me begging their return," he pointed out dryly, and Roarke felt his color begin to rise.

"Well did she entrust me with the task," he shot back, and the older man actually smiled, though his expression was cold. He leaned across the counter and dropped his voice as he addressed Roarke.

"Then well might you tell your mother that I would gladly exchange her goods for the price of the cloth rendered in good silver deniers, as we had originally agreed."

At Roarke's questioning look, the merchant confided a sum that fairly made the knight's ears burn. He opened his mouth and closed it again, unable to think of anything with the knowledge of just how much money his mother had spent bouncing around his head.

"You still have the items, then?" he managed to croak, not in the least appeased by the deprecating smile that lit the merchant's lined face.

"Oh, aye," he confirmed with a wry shake of his head. "Little market is there for such trinkets, leastways not an adequate one to return the price *I* paid for them."

Too much was it that this merchant should imply that Roarke's family had taken advantage of him, and a burst of pride lifted the knight's chin defiantly again. Surely Denis could make some arrangement. Surely there was some other option, should the matter be explained in full.

"Certain I am that recompense can be made to you," Roarke insisted, with a blithe assurance he was far from feeling. The merchant granted him a wary eye, but Roarke simply smiled with accustomed ease. "Indeed, I shall be back before the week is out, and we shall see this matter resolved, one way or the other," he vowed glibly.

"We shall see," the merchant conceded skeptically, but Roarke let the retort pass unchallenged. Determination flooded through him as he left the shop, and he resolved to find some solution to restore his mother's tokens to her.

One way or the other.

Adela carried a length of freshly pressed and folded cloth out to the counter, hoping that the countess would find these colors to her liking. Her father was chuckling to himself, and she gave him a questioning glance.

"What amuses you so?" she asked, and he shot her an indulgent look.

"Just another young nobleman trying to assure his inheritance," he admitted with a slow shake of his head. "Indeed, if they paid more attention to the reason for their lack of funds than to the loss of a trinket here and there, mayhap they could resolve the problem more satisfactorily."

Adela smiled as she eased the cloth into a space on the shelf, more than familiar with her father's views on the nobility and their financial straits. "And what did you tell him?" she inquired idly, not in the least uncertain of his response.

"That he could have his mother's trinkets in return for the currency she owed me, of course," he supplied matter-of-factly, his skepticism evident in his tone.

Adela turned and regarded him with an affectionate smile. "You do not think he will manage it?"

Her father shrugged at the door to the street. "Unlikely it seems at best," he concluded, but Adela heard a thoughtful note in his tone as he scowled. He flicked her a glance and smiled thinly as he shook his head. "I must admit, though, that there is something persistent about that young man that truly gives one to wonder." He turned to Adela and granted her a grin. "And well you know that not a denier would I give for a man who readily abandons any task."

"Aye, well enough I know," Adela agreed, feeling the color rise over her cheeks as she recalled one particularly stubborn man.

She wondered guiltily for the hundredth time whether she had truly hurt that knight, or whether 'twas the fault of the spirits he had imbibed that he had fallen so readily beneath her blow. She yet again wondered whether she had acted aright, turning abruptly from her task as she wondered anew where he had gone.

But that was all idle thinking, and well she knew it, for 'twas unlikely at best, to use her father's favorite phrase, that she would ever lay eyes on that troublemaking knight again.

* * *

"So you see, Denis, something simply must be done," Roarke concluded easily, fully confident that the chatelain would have a solution to the problem now that he knew the tale. Denis pursed his lips and rubbed his brow in a most discouraging fashion, however, and Roarke knew a moment's trepidation.

"Surely something can be done?" he insisted, his anxiety growing when Denis shook his head and sighed.

"Sadly, they are both cut of the same cloth," the chatelain muttered, and Roarke's heart drooped.

"Of what do you speak?" he demanded impatiently, drawing Denis' glum gaze.

"Just this very morn, I learned that Rochelle borrowed an unholy sum from the moneylenders in Ghent," he supplied unhappily.

"How much?" Roarke asked with no small measure of dread, groaning when Denis supplied a number even greater than the sum the weaver required.

"And this is not the half of it," Denis continued grimly, flipping open the ledger for the château and running one finger down a column of figures. He tapped the scribble at the bottom that Roarke supposed was a tally, though he was himself incapable of deciphering it. "Each year for the past five, the château has shown a loss."

"Have the harvests been inadequate?" Roarke asked.

Denis shook his head. "In truth, we harvest more than ever before. The grain is worth less, though, for all are harvesting more, and on top of that, we have need to buy more goods than afore. We buy cloth these days, instead of making do with what we weave ourselves, for the workmanship is finer. As with wine, as with tools. And little need had we of sugarloaves, cardamom, saffron and silk in our grandsires' day, for naught did we know of them, or if we did, their expense was beyond our means and desires. Now all expect such luxuries, and the manor is hard-pressed to support our needs."

This news was not welcome in the least, and Roarke struggled to conceive of a solution. "What of Rochelle's betrothed? I had understood that he was an affluent man."

Denis nodded sagely. "Aye, that he is, and a good match 'tis, in that regard at least."

Roarke glanced up at the implicit comment in the older man's words. "But mayhap not in others?"

Denis shrugged again, leaning closer to confide in a low voice, "In truth, I suspect that Aalgen itself is the greater part of Rochelle's appeal to the man." He grimaced in acknowledgment of Roarke's wince.

"But Rochelle? Surely she sees this?"

"Rochelle is so enamored of the man that she desires naught to come between them. Indeed, she confided this very morn that she took this debt to ensure the château was in the black when he took the reins." Denis tapped impatiently on the ledger again, and Roarke did not miss the troubled light in his eyes.

"What ails you?" he asked softly, and the chatelain shook his head anew.

"She begged very prettily that I somehow conceal this loan and see that her betrothed never learn of its existence."

Roarke exhaled slowly, certain that two women could not have made such a mess if they had tried. And he certainly knew better than to ask after the fate of the cash settlement he had expected to receive as his own legacy.

"But surely he will demand to see the books?" he asked, earning a weary nod from Denis.

"Aye, I would expect as much," he conceded heavily. "And what right have I to hide them from him?"

"Could you not omit the debt from the ledger?" Roarke asked hopefully.

"Only should the debt be paid in short order, and not from the manor's coffers," the older man confirmed crisply, closing the ledger with a dismissive flick of his wrist. "Well indeed do you know that your sire trusted me because of my honesty, and I would not tarnish such a long-held reputation, even now." Suitably chastised, Roarke murmured an apology, and the chatelain sighed as he leaned across the table and patted the knight's shoulder.

"Ensure that you share with me any solution you might discover," he suggested wryly, and Roarke managed somehow to summon a smile.

"Aye, that I will," he murmured, lost in his own thoughts, as the chatelain excused himself.

Mathieu was surprised to find Lady Ermengarde's son in his shop again but two days later. Indeed, he had thought the matter resolved, for surely, if the silver had been available, the lady would never have sacrificed what were clearly sentimental treasures. And with Michaelmas past, the tithes would have been already gathered at Aalgen when she settled her debt. In truth, the pending tithes had been the reason he did the work on credit, assuming that a property the size of Aalgen would raise a goodly annual sum.

Regardless of the size of the sum, it had evidently not been enough, and despite his better judgment, Mathieu had weakened before the Lady Ermengarde's tears. Well enough had he known what the sacrifice was costing her, but business was business, and he simply could not afford to let the cloth go for naught, whatever his chivalrous leanings.

And now the son was back, his proud carriage not completely hiding his nervousness. Evidently he had learned that there was no silver available, and Mathieu grudgingly admired that the knight had even bothered to return. He had not spoken lightly when he praised perseverance to Adela, and it seemed that this man had that quality in more than adequate measure. He greeted the younger man and waited, wondering what solution he might propose.

"It seems my mother well overstepped her means," the younger man began with an expression that might have been disapproving.

Despite himself, Mathieu felt himself warming to the young knight, knowing only too well what 'twas like to return home to find things less than they should be. Indeed, it encouraged his sympathy with the younger knight's plight to know that he did not approve of his mother's behavior any more than Mathieu did. Mayhap he had misjudged him to so quickly assume that his manners were as frivolous as those of other knights.

"Aye, 'twould seem so," he said, clinging to his unencouraging tone. Business was business, after all, Mathieu reminded himself sternly, and he was out valuable coin for that order of the Lady Ermengarde's.

"It also seems that there is no surfeit of silver deniers at Aalgen," the knight admitted in a low voice, his embarrassed tone revealing what the admission cost his pride.

The son of Aalgen was a handsome man, Mathieu acknowledged as he watched the emotions play across his face and wondered whether his earlier assessment that all had come readily to the knight's hand had been correct. Ethics this young man seemed to have, and as a lack of such in the nobility was one of Mathieu's pet peeves with the blooded classes, he found himself feeling a curious empathy with the man before him. What would he have done in his place?

"'Tis a difficult year for many," Mathieu found himself conceding without intending to, and the younger man shot him a sharp look. He seemed to draw encouragement from that comment, holding Mathieu's gaze and straightening as he obviously prepared to make a suggestion.

"I would offer to work to honorably settle the debt," he proposed tightly. For an instant, Mathieu thought the knight was making a jest, but the resolve in those gray eyes told him without doubt that the offer was sincerely meant, for all its unconventionality.

"No need have I of a knight's hand," he countered carefully, still uncertain that he was not misjudging the younger man's intentions. A nobleman working for a bourgeois?

'Twas unheard-of, unthinkable, but Mathieu watched in amazement as the knight's lips thinned with determination.

Persistence this one had aplenty, of that he was sure.

"Then I would labor for you in another way," the knight insisted firmly, the way he fingered the hilt of his sword the only outward sign of his nervousness. "Have you not any debts that have proved difficult to collect?" he proposed boldly, his gaze locking with Mathieu's once again.

Mathieu felt his mouth drop open in shock, and he hastily closed it again, even as he tried to come to terms with the very concept.

"'Twould be highly improper," he protested, knowing how the honor of the house of Aalgen would suffer if its son was seen collecting debts. And not even the debts owing to his own home, but those due to a mere merchant. The knight looked unlikely to move, however, and Mathieu quickly sought another excuse. "And no debts are owing to me in need of such force," he concluded, hating that he was responsible for the disappointment that clouded those eyes.

"Have you not any other labor that I might perform?" the younger man pressed.

Mathieu could only imagine what 'twas costing the knight's pride to make such a concession to ensure the honor of his house—indeed, the very exchange was making Mathieu himself nervous. He cleared his throat and met the younger man's gaze once more, trying to show him that although he well understood his predicament, there was little he could do. Indeed, 'twas only right that he decline the knight's offer.

"Surely you can see that I cannot take a nobleman to labor in my business," he pointed out quietly, though his words appeared to have little effect.

"My rank is of little bearing in this matter," the younger man retorted. "Indeed, the honor of my family's word is at stake as long as this debt remains outstanding."

"Well indeed do I consider it settled," Mathieu argued, knowing it to be of little avail.

"But I do not," the knight countered evenly. "My mother desires both her cloth and her trinkets, and—" he shook his head despairingly as his lips turned unexpectedly upward at the corners "—in truth, I cannot bear her tears."

That admission struck a resonant chord within Mathieu as the two men's eyes met anew, and he found himself grinning despite himself. "'Twas those same tears that left me with an assortment of trinkets for which I have no use," he confessed, feeling a rapport between the two of them when the knight chuckled quietly and shook his head in frustration.

"But in truth, the only labor I have need of right now is that of an apprentice," Mathieu insisted firmly. "And 'tis indeed a task poorly suited to one of your experience." He glanced up and acknowledged the knight's frustration, wishing there was something he could do for the him.

But business was business, after all, and one had to maintain a demeanor appropriate to one's status. Indeed, 'twould reflect as badly on himself as on the noble house of Aalgen for him to take on the manor's own son.

One must know one's own place, despite any instincts to the contrary, Mathieu reminded himself flatly, just as the door opened once more.

Chapter Three

Roarke barely noticed the countess sweeping into the shop, ducking his head in respectful acknowledgment more out of instinct than from any particular awareness of the woman's presence. What was he going to do? How could he possibly settle these debts if the weaver had no need of his labor?

The tourneys, he concluded, barely stifling a groan. What irony that would be, that he who had so little interest in waging war would be forced to play at it to pay these debts. Roarke's lips twisted as he wondered whether he could even count on himself to be successful in such a task. Would it not just fit his luck to lose at the tourneys and come home even more shorthanded?

'Twas only when the countess' giggling retinue began to nudge him aside that he glanced up and realized the number of women who had managed to crowd into the small space. He found himself backed against one of the walls of cloth and glanced over the women's heads to see the weaver looking markedly less composed. Indeed, 'twould seem that that man was nervous, and Roarke watched the unfolding exchange with dawning interest.

"Oh, nay. 'Tis not at all the color I had envisioned," the lady declared waspishly as she ran one dimpled finger dismissively across an expanse of rosy cloth and the weaver noticeably blanched.

"Milady, mayhap you could describe for me again the precise shade you wished," he suggested. Roarke suspected there was more than a hint of frustration lurking beneath his controlled tone.

"More rosy," the countess asserted with a firm nod that set her chins to jiggling. The weaver swallowed noticeably, then appeared to straighten his shoulders as he made a decision. He reached for the shelf and took down another length of cloth, more rosy in tone than the length she was fingering.

"Here is the cloth we wove previously for you," the proprietor pointed out tactfully, but the countess merely pursed her lips.

She pouted. "Well indeed does it seem *too* rosy to me."

"But it did not seem thus when you saw the wool afore 'twas woven," he countered evenly. The countess' nose rose skyward in disdain.

"Well enough does *everyone* know that the woven cloth looks much different from the raw wool," she argued frostily. "Still is it too rosy."

"And the new cloth?"

"Not yet rosy enough," she complained, jabbing at the cloth with a disdainful finger.

Indeed, Roarke could see only a measure of difference between the two tones and could not imagine her difficulty. To his astonishment, the proprietor lifted yet another piece of cloth from the shelf that was, quite remarkably, precisely between the two shades.

"And the first is still inadequate?" he prompted. Roarke watched in silent amazement while the lady drew herself up to her full stature, slight though it was.

"Indeed it seems that one can little enough make a simple order of goods in this town," she snapped, gesturing dismissively to the three samples of cloth. "But a length of rose wool did I want, yet cannot acquire it for love or money." The proprietor's expression was one of such defeat, and truly he had striven heroically to meet the lady's demands, that Roarke felt compelled to intervene.

"I would not presume to interfere, milady," he said as he did precisely that, noting with satisfaction the effect of his most devastating and well-practiced smile. The plump countess positively preened before him, and her gaggle of ladies-in-waiting parted to clear a path before him. "In truth, I cannot help but wonder if this cloth is destined for a garment for yourself?"

The lady sniffed delicately. "Should the color not be matched to my desire, this cloth has no destiny with me," she stated tightly, and Roarke feigned astonishment.

"Indeed?" he demanded. "No idea have I what shade you seek, but this one—" with his unerring eye for such things, Roarke scooped up the darkest shade "—this one becomes your coloring most wondrously."

"Sir, you flatter me," she demurred, but, undeterred, Roarke lifted the cloth toward her face and cocked one brow at her ladies-in-waiting.

"Do you not think that the shade makes her eyes yet more blue?" he asked, favoring them with a smile.

The four women's color rose of one accord, and Roarke grinned as they quickly agreed with his assessment. He looked back to meet the countess' gaze, to find her watching him avidly, and managed not to cringe at her obvious thoughts. He even dared to wink, all the while certain of the audacity of what he did.

"And makes her lips yet more ruddy," he murmured, as though intending the words for her ears alone.

The countess flushed.

"Mayhap the shade suits as you say," she retorted with forced severity as she resolutely pushed the cloth away. "But the workmanship is shoddy beyond compare."

"Indeed?" Roarke lifted his brows high and glanced down at the cloth, more than adequately aware of the way the weaver had sharply inhaled at the insult. "The work seems most fine to me, although I am undoubtedly a lesser judge of such things than you, milady.''

He glanced up to find her gaze yet upon him, and feeling the weight of the proprietor's gaze upon him, as well, Roarke suddenly thought that he could indeed show himself useful to this weaver.

Before he could question the impulse, he boldly took another step closer to the countess, dropping his voice as though he would exchange a confidence. She inhaled quickly at his proximity as he leaned yet closer, but Roarke did not yet dare to savor a victory.

''Indeed, milady, I must tell you that high praise did I hear of this shop's labors when last I was in Troyes,'' he murmured in a low voice.

''Indeed?'' she asked breathlessly, her eyes widening as she unabashedly held his regard. Roarke permitted himself to smile in a leisurely, sexual manner.

''Indeed,'' he breathed, closing the space between them an increment more. ''The talk of the Hot Fair was their work, and although I would not dare to question your own opinion, it seems that possession of a piece of such reputedly good work might be admired by many who have a less discerning eye than you.''

He lifted the cloth again, holding it this time to the underside of her jaw. Her gaze softened as he deliberately let the wool slide over her skin in a slow caress, knowing she could feel the outline of his fingertips beneath the cloth. ''And indeed, a dress of such a fetching shade on a lady as lovely as yourself could only make a stunning sight.''

Roarke licked his lips deliberately, gratified when the countess echoed his gesture without thought. ''A sight that I, for one, would be most honored to look upon.'' He held her gaze for a poignant moment, then swiveled abruptly to drop the cloth back on the counter.

''Of course, if the shade is incorrect, as you say, then you had best leave the lot behind,'' he concluded flatly.

Roarke dared to meet the weaver's eyes for an instant, seeing mingled admiration and disbelief there before the countess' hand closed over his elbow. He winked quickly and secretly to the weaver in victorious anticipation of what she would say.

"In truth, the shade has grown in appeal while I tarried," she informed the weaver briskly, pressing her bulk against Roarke as she lifted her purse to count out the necessary coin.

Adela stopped in her tracks when she realized precisely who was flirting shamelessly with the countess.

It could not be! She panicked at the thought that the knight was here, in her father's own shop, and was unable to keep one hand from straying to her hair. What was he doing here?

The countess handed her purchase to one of her ladies and Adela barely had time to marvel that she had actually bought something before that same lady planted one beringed hand familiarly on the knight's chest. He smiled at her gesture, and Adela damned him for the sensuous promise in his expression, a promise that she had been the object of once and which was now directed at another.

Another who was married, both older and plainer than Adela, and quite decidedly plump.

The comparison pricked at her pride, and she wondered irritably if this knight chased anything in a kirtle. She virtually gagged as the countess leaned yet closer, tracing one finger across the knight's hauberk as she spoke.

"I would look forward to finding your presence at the château," she murmured seductively. As if that were not enough to thoroughly gall the observers, the knight captured her hand within his and stroked his thumb across her palm with an intimacy that Adela was certain was well practiced.

"Indeed I shall count the days," he vowed, and brushed his lips across her fingertips. The countess colored even as she smiled, flicking a coquettish glance over her shoulder as she and her retinue swept out the door. The knight grinned unabashedly and turned back to address Adela's father, no small measure of pride gleaming in those mischievous gray eyes.

Adela grimaced. Making another conquest he was, without a doubt, and right here in her father's shop. Disgusting it was, not only that he was such a wencher, but that he insisted on making his indulgences so public. Her ire rose anew that he had expected her to fall in with his schemes as readily as the countess apparently had. What kind of woman had he thought she was?

She listened, but her father apparently was undisturbed by the interval, merely thanking the knight for his assistance in closing the sale. Mayhap the knight should thank her father for supplying yet another opportunity to see his pallet warmed! Indignation flooded through Adela, and she stomped into the front of the shop without further thought.

"You!"

Mathieu glanced up as Adela stormed into the shop, barely having time to notice that she was far from her usual sweetly composed self before she slammed a length of cloth onto the counter.

"What manner of man are you that you would insist on assaulting clients directly in my father's shop?" she demanded indignantly of the knight.

"Adela!" Mathieu gasped, shocked that his daughter would comport herself thus. He spared a glance to the knight to find that man's shock only slightly less than his own.

"Noble blood you may sport, but still that does not give an excuse to such brazen behavior," she spat with an uncharacteristic venom. To Mathieu's amazement, the knight slowly began to smile with genuine amusement.

"Well enough should you understand the import of *assaulting* another," he charged softly. Mathieu frowned at the reference, glancing to his daughter to find her complexion flushed scarlet.

"Every right has a woman to use whatever means at her disposal to fend off relentless wenchers," she countered angrily, wagging one finger beneath the other man's nose, despite her evident discomfort.

'Twas a side of his daughter Mathieu had never seen before, and he was not entirely certain what to make of it. The knight, however, seemed merely amused by her attack. Was it possible the two had met afore?

The knight's eyes glinted wickedly, and he leaned closer to Adela. Mathieu was certain that the younger man had not missed her sharp intake of breath at the gesture, either.

"Mayhap you would prefer I *assaulted* you," he suggested with a wicked grin, and Adela's color deepened.

"You!" she sputtered, seemingly at a loss for words. "You are a pall on decent people everywhere. Little would you know a woman of value should she stamp on your very toe."

"Or spit on my tunic?" the knight inquired mildly, cocking one brow eloquently. Adela looked likely to explode at that, her normally tranquil topaz eyes snapping with fury.

"And well enough did you deserve that salute for your troubles," she asserted coldly. "Never have I been so rudely..." she floundered, searching for a word, and the knight smoothly interjected.

"Assaulted," he suggested calmly, earning himself a glare from Adela that might have pierced armor.

"Aye! Assaulted I was, and not in short order will that be forgotten," she finished in a breathless rush, stubbornly staring the knight down. Mathieu watched with interest, but the younger man did not rise to the bait, that same slow grin stealing across his features.

"Incorrigible you are," Adela muttered in unconcealed annoyance, spinning on her heel and striding back to the back of the shop. The knight watched her retreat with evident interest, flicking a mischievous glance to Mathieu that surprised the older man, though not as much as the words that followed.

"Indeed, I think she fancies me," the knight confided easily, sparing Mathieu a wink.

The weaver momentarily could find naught to say, the knight's assessment coming curiously close to his own. He glanced after Adela to find her fumbling with some warp in a most unusual manner, her heightened color evidence enough that she was aware of the knight's continued regard.

Mayhap... But no. Mathieu shook his head firmly. The man was of noble blood, far beyond Adela's station. But still. He glanced between the two once more, confirming that there was indeed something different in the knight's expression from when he had looked at the countess. And Adela was certainly more aware of this man than Mathieu had ever seen her be of another.

Mayhap.

He cleared his throat delicately, and the knight jumped guiltily as his attention returned to the matter at hand. The young man was more interested than he might like one to believe. Mayhap indeed there were possibilities here.

"You have met afore?" he inquired mildly, watching the knight slant a glance to Adela before he answered.

"Aye, at the Hot Fair." He struggled unsuccessfully to hide a rising smile. "I fear I did not deliver my compliments in a most suitable manner."

"And Adela?"

"Had no trouble then, as now, in conveying the fullness of her disgust," the knight responded readily with an unrepentant grin. 'Twas time enough to burst the younger man's euphoria, and Mathieu drew himself taller as he sternly looked the knight in the eye.

"As rightly she should, for my daughter is a most honorable woman," he stated firmly, gratified at the surprise that settled in the knight's eyes.

"Your daughter she is?" he asked weakly, and Mathieu barely kept himself from grinning at the other's obvious dismay. He had the sense that this knight was not often surprised, and he savored the victory for an instant.

"Aye, that she is, and no knight will I have playing frivolously with her heart," he continued, enjoying the way the younger man nodded quickly, evidently in fear of losing all he had gained.

"Indeed, sir, had I any idea, I would not have—"

"Indeed, the matter is past," Mathieu swept away the knight's words. "Now that you know fully the situation, though, I would have you show some regard for her position."

"Indeed, I could do no other," the younger man assured him earnestly. The glance he flicked to Adela without even realizing he had done so encouraged Mathieu's paternal heart.

"As long as we understand each other," he concluded briskly, before returning to the matter at hand. "I would thank you for convincing the countess to finally make her purchase, however unorthodox your methods." The knight nodded but once in acknowledgment, his very manner revealing his awareness that he was no longer in control of the situation.

"Indeed, your persistence makes me believe that you could well learn or do anything you set your mind to," Mathieu admitted carefully, seeing hope dawn in the younger man's eyes.

"Anything can I learn, should I have the need," he asserted quietly, and Mathieu noted once again that resolve in his eyes.

A notorious flirt this man might be, but the older man was sure that he did not sway his responsibilities when indeed he took them on. Was his very presence here not an indication of his dedication to his family and their honor?

Mathieu tapped the counter thoughtfully. Long had he been an admirer of persistence in a man, and still more a sense of honor. He spared a glance to Adela, feeling a twinge of guilt that one so lovely should have been left without a spouse because of his own demands on her time. He tapped the counter once more and decided to take a chance on this determined man before him.

"Still have I need of an apprentice," Mathieu conceded slowly, wondering if he was truly mad to make this offer. "A year of service would suffice to resolve your mother's debt and restore her heirlooms to her."

Instead of showing the pleasure or gratitude Mathieu had expected, the knight looked displeased. He cleared his throat hesitantly, and Mathieu frowned in turn. Did he intend to decline this offer and leave Mathieu looking like a fool?

The younger man must have noted something of that in Mathieu's expression, for he immediately shook his head.

"Your terms are most generous, and your offer is one I would do well to accept," he said hastily, that scowl pulling his dark brows together yet again. "There is but another matter that troubles me. Concerned I am that this service will have to be repeated elsewhere." His voice faded as he evidently considered the implications of that.

Mathieu suddenly, intuitively, understood the source of the younger man's difficulties. "More money is there owing?" he asked, and the knight nodded ruefully.

"Aye, well it seems that my sister has borrowed a sum and wishes her betrothed to know naught of it," he confessed with embarrassment. Mathieu inquired after the sum. His brows rose slightly as he scribbled it on a scrap of paper and made a few calculations.

"Unseemly 'twould be indeed for you to make a practice of working off your family debts," he agreed mildly, surprised when the knight chuckled under his breath.

"One could only hope that 'twill not be a practice they indulge in often," he jested, though his humor did not light his eyes convincingly.

Mathieu eyed his calculations and conceded that a half-trained apprentice was of little use to him anyhow. He could resolve this problem, should he choose to do so. His conscience pricked again at the knowledge of what Adela had sacrificed for him.

Surely he could take one chance in an effort to accommodate her. And 'twas not such a bad deal, for well it seemed that this knight would be a good worker. Had he not earned his spurs through labor every bit as arduous?

"Should I purchase the debt, two years of service would clear your obligation to me," he declared, and wonder lit the younger man's face.

"Verily you would do this?" he demanded incredulously. Mathieu nodded tersely.

"Several conditions must there be," he insisted in his most businesslike manner. "No one must know of your status, for word of that would bring shame upon both your house and mine."

"Of course, your thinking is most clear," the knight agreed readily, apparently still slightly shocked. "Abroad have I been for many years, so none are likely to recognize me."

"Good," Mathieu affirmed, and took a deep breath as he gambled. "And well must you leave my daughter alone," he said flatly, hoping the provision would simultaneously ensure Adela's chastity and yet increase her appeal to the knight. The younger man swallowed, his gaze seeking out Adela in the back of the shop once more.

"Agreed," he said, and Mathieu smothered a smile that the concession had not come easily to his lips. The knight's gaze flew suddenly to his, and Mathieu raised his brows.

"She alone knows my status," the knight confided in a whisper, and the older man nodded again.

"I shall resolve that matter," he assured him briskly. "Have we an arrangement, then—?" He hesitated, not knowing the younger man's name. The knight grinned and extended his hand.

"Chevalier Roarke d'Aalgen," he supplied.

"Mayhap simply Roarke is better," Mathieu suggested as he shook hands with his new apprentice, liking the strength of the other man's grip.

"Aye, that it is. And we do indeed have a deal, sir," Roarke agreed with an easy grin.

"Mathieu Toisserand," Mathieu said. "Take your mother's trinkets home with you this day and return at dawn on the morrow."

"And prepared to work will I be, sir," Roarke assured him. Mathieu did not doubt that 'twould be so.

Roarke found Denis perusing the ledger once again when he returned home, the chatelain's brow furrowed deeply as he scribbled in annoyance. Evidently a solution had not yet been found, and Roarke stepped firmly into the room to draw the man's attention.

"You bade me tell you if I found a solution," he said lightly, and the chatelain regarded him in something akin to amazement.

"Tell me that you do not jest," he urged, and there was no doubting the hopeful light in his eyes. Roarke grinned as he placed the rosewood chest of his mother's on the desk with a small flourish. Denis' eyes popped in recognition, and he opened the chest before he could stop himself.

His amazement seemed to grow when he spied the ivory casket, and he touched the two bundles of cloth as though to assure his doubting mind that the candlesticks did indeed rest within. Denis raised an astonished gaze to Roarke, and the younger man grinned anew, exuding a confidence he was far from feeling.

Indeed, he was beginning to worry just a little about the wisdom of his deal. Two years of service! 'Twas impossible to believe that he would labor two years under the weaver's hand and that he took the yoke willingly. But what choice had he?

And truly, what else had he intended to do for those two years?

But two years of working alongside Adela. Already he groaned at the thought, the very realization that she lived so close making him fairly itch to get back into town and taunt her until those topaz eyes flashed angrily. His first sight of her in the shop had dropped the bottom out of his stomach, but when she had commenced to give him a piece of her mind, it had taken every scrap of his control to not kiss her into silence.

But he had agreed to leave her alone. Little choice had he had, admittedly, but still the knowledge chafed at him, and Roarke knew that more would be chafing, should he be forced to work directly alongside her for any stretch of time.

He had made his bargain, though, and little enough could be done about it now. And there were certain to be any number of willing women in Ghent with whom he might satisfy his desires. Aye, for well enough had he sampled women to know that they were all interchangeable. Indeed, that comprised much of their charm, to his mind. Adela would soon enough be forgotten. The promise of numerous new conquests dismissed Roarke's lingering reservations, and he granted Denis a cocky smile as he took the seat opposite the desk.

"The tapestry and brass plate from over the fireplace are in the hall," he informed Denis nonchalantly as he lounged back in his chair, not surprised at the stern glance the chatelain granted him.

"And how might you have come by these items?" he asked archly. Roarke refused to squirm, doing his level best to simply return the other man's regard.

"In much the same fashion as I settled Rochelle's debt," he supplied easily. Denis looked suitably shocked.

"Verily you have done this?" he demanded sharply, and Roarke simply nodded. "But how? What have you bartered in exchange? What—" The older man halted his tirade to spare the young knight a suspicious glance.

"You did not steal them?"

"Denis!" Roarke recoiled in genuine horror. "What manner of man do you think I am?"

"A knight, to be certain, and surely that alone says enough," Denis muttered under his breath, shooting Roarke another glance. "Challenged someone, did you, then?"

"Nay, well you should know that I would not risk my life for even my mother's trinkets," Roarke countered amiably, managing to draw a chuckle from the reluctant Denis.

"Then how?" he demanded anew, evidently unwilling to let the matter rest. Roarke exhaled slowly and leaned forward.

"You need know no more than the fact that their return was honorably gained," he said firmly. The chatelain returned his regard for a long moment, then cleared his throat.

"And the debt, as well?" he asked softly.

"Paid," Roarke asserted, earning another wary glance from the older man.

"And you swear that you have done naught foolhardy?"

"Naught," Roarke swore readily, not in the least certain that was true. But his bargain was made and was hardly Denis' concern.

"But you will not confide what you have done?" the chatelain asked now, his tone revealing that he did not truly anticipate an answer.

"Nay," Roarke said firmly, shoving to his feet. "I depart early on the morrow and will be absent for some time."

"You will return for Rochelle's nuptials?" Denis asked hastily. Roarke wavered for an instant before he nodded, knowing the price his mother would exact should he not attend.

"Aye," he agreed reluctantly. "Mayhap you can find some labor for my squire while I am gone," he added. Denis' silver brows rose high, but he checked himself before asking any more.

"Well it seems that some task can be found for Yves," he conceded, his unspoken question hanging between the two, but Roarke did not intend to indulge him with an answer. Enough had he said already.

"The matter is settled then," Roarke concluded quickly, before the chatelain could ask him anything else. "I shall endeavor to bring you a receipt when I arrive for the nuptials."

"That would be most thoughtful of you, sir," Denis agreed quietly as Roarke nodded and strode away.

"Well it seemed to me that you knew that knight in the shop this morn," Mathieu commented idly as he sipped his beer after dinner, not in the least surprised at the hostile glare Adela fired in his direction.

"Certainly I made no claim to know him or any of his kind," she retorted, scrubbing at the pot with a savagery that seemed unwarranted.

"But you had met afore?" Mathieu persisted mildly. Adela sighed with exasperation, propping one soapy hand on her hip as she turned to confront him.

"'Twas so evident?" she asked, clearly hoping the opposite, and Mathieu had no need to even nod. She sighed again and returned to the dirty pot with less enthusiasm. "At the Hot Fair in Troyes, he saw fit to flatter me," she confessed quietly, and Mathieu's lips twitched. Indeed, his daughter had been working too much of late.

"Aye, a hanging offense that would be," he commented, and took another draft of beer. Adela gave him a glance that could have curdled fresh milk. Her mother's daughter she was, of that Mathieu was left little doubt these days, but he did not dare to smile.

"Drunk he was," she informed him self-righteously. "And obviously in search of something to warm his bed."

"Surely he was not so crass to assume you a whore?" Mathieu demanded quickly, but his daughter shook her head before his ire could truly rise to the occasion.

"Nay, not that." She frowned down at the pot. "But 'twas evident he made sport of me, and I fear I lost my temper."

Mathieu frowned in turn. "I confess I do not understand. Why would he make sport of you?"

Adela sighed and gave her sire one of *those* looks that told him eloquently that he had missed something completely obvious to the female gender. "By making such flattery to me," she explained patiently, her words doing little to illuminate Mathieu. She shook her head as his confusion remained, her blooming color visible even though she ducked her head to hide it.

"Well enough do you know that I am too old to be fetching," she confessed in a low voice, and Mathieu's heart was wrenched anew.

"But five-and-twenty are you," he protested. "And lovely as the dawn."

"Papa." Adela granted him an indulgent look. "You have but to look around the town. Most women of five-and-twenty have already spawned four or even five children, Wed they have been for a decade or more. Whereas I have but weaver's calluses to show for my years." She pulled one slender hand out of the dishwater and examined those calluses dispassionately.

"Well I thought that you enjoyed the work," Mathieu pointed out irritably, certain there had to be some benefit to be gained by the skill he had taught his daughter. She turned quickly, her features alight.

"But I do," she enthused. "Well indeed do I love it. But there are times..." Her voice faltered, and she shrugged. "'Tis mostly when Georges sees fit to take a wager with another to taunt me."

"Georges Desjardins does this?" Mathieu demanded, his anger rising now in truth. Adela nodded unhappily, and he felt, not for the first time, that he had allowed more to slip unnoticed beneath his nose than he should.

"Aye, he sees it as a great jest to so torment me," she admitted, sparing a glance to her father. "Be not angry, Papa, 'tis in itself a harmless thing."

"But cruel," Mathieu growled into his beer, knowing now why he had never liked that particular young man. "Good 'tis that you turned down his offer, for such a man could never have made you happy," he muttered, earning a wistful smile from his daughter as she returned her attention to the pot.

"Aye, Papa."

"Now, about this knight..." He returned to the original subject with ease, not missing the way Adela stiffened at the reminder. "Concerned I was that you might have met afore."

"And why is that?" she asked idly, but he was not fooled by her disinterested tone.

Mathieu took a deep breath and watched Adela's response carefully as he spoke. "The man will be coming to work here on the morrow, and none is to know of his rank."

"What?" Adela whirled in shock, disregarding the suds that flew across the floor. "Are you quite mad, Papa? What will he do? Why is he coming here? Of what are you thinking to take on such a man?"

Mathieu cleared his throat carefully. "It seems he wishes to learn the trade, and well you know that we have need of an apprentice," he supplied slowly, watching suspicion replace Adela's incredulity.

"Oh, likely indeed is that," she retorted sharply. "A *knight* he is, Papa, and a noble. Have you completely lost your senses? Why would you have this man here? What of all your ideas of the nobles and their ways?"

"Mayhap this one is different," Mathieu proposed gently, watching his daughter roll her eyes in exasperation.

"Different in that he sees the need to bed *every* single woman on the face of God's earth, not only those he finds alluring?" she demanded archly.

Mathieu almost laughed aloud at her disgust, wondering how much of her attitude was due to Roarke's skillful handling of the countess. He pushed to his feet, certain his instincts were leading him right, and fixed his daughter with a stern eye.

"Regardless of your thoughts on the matter, Roarke will be apprenticing here for two years." Adela gasped at this revelation, but Mathieu continued undaunted, his tone firm. "Make no mistake in this, Adela. You will be civil to him and treat him as any other. And you will forget his noble status and speak to no one of it. Are we understood?"

Mutiny flashed in her golden eyes for an instant before she quelled it, her lips tightening as she nodded reluctantly. "Aye, Papa." She tilted her chin and looked him in the eye. "He will be staying here?" she demanded quickly.

Mathieu nodded, encouraged that she was so concerned about the knight's presence in the house, but unwilling to give her any sign of that. "But, of course," he chided. "Well enough you know that all my apprentices stay here. He will take the pallet by the hearth, as is customary." Adela swallowed once as she came to terms with that piece of information, and then her challenging gaze met his once more.

"Is this Roarke not a little old to be taking an apprenticeship?" she asked coldly. "Usually you take on a boy."

"Well enough do you know that clever souls are never too old to learn something new," he replied calmly. "One can only hope that his age makes him both stronger for the task and more certain of his own will to take it." He could see that Adela wished to ask more on that score, but he hurried on so as to avoid telling her any more than she needed to know.

"And little have you to fear of Roarke's advances," he continued easily as he made his way to the stairs. "Readily enough did he agree to my condition that he not press you with his attentions."

With that parting shot, Mathieu started up the stairs to his chamber, smiling to himself at Adela's gasp of outrage, the sound of crockery being stacked in a most ferocious manner carrying in his wake.

'Twould indeed be a lively show, if he had his wager in the matter.

Roarke reined in his horse when they had ridden off the properties of Aalgen, feeling Yves' questioning gaze upon him even while he dismounted. He ignored the boy's speculative stare, nonchalantly handing off his destrier's reins and doffing his gloves.

The autumn chill in the predawn air made him disrobe more hastily than he had intended, his hauberk and tunic folded and dropped into his saddlebags as he donned the plain muslin shirt Mathieu had given him. Roarke's wool chausses were worn enough to suit, though he discarded his boots in favor of a pair of well-broken leather shoes, also granted by the weaver.

'Twas his spurs alone that gave him pause, or more likely what they represented, and he hesitated for a moment with them cradled in his hands before packing them away, as well. His knife alone did he keep, and he tucked it into his belt before donning a short hooded cloak. Roarke closed the saddlebags with finality and patted his destrier's rump. He slung a smaller pack containing a mundane variety of possessions over his shoulder and granted the dumbstruck Yves a cocky grin.

"Milord," the boy managed to breathe. "What is this you do?"

"Naught of your concern," Roarke countered blithely, feeling more lighthearted than he had in years. "Return to the château, boy."

"But your horse?"

"No need have I of it," Roarke said with a dismissive wave of his hand. "Well do I intend to walk from here."

"But, sir—"

"But naught, Yves," Roarke insisted firmly, closing the distance between them with a light step. "You have no reason to concern yourself with this matter. I but ask of you to return to this place, with these things, on the morn of Rochelle's nuptials.''

"Afore the dawn again?" the boy asked dubiously, and Roarke shrugged before he nodded agreement.

"Aye, that will suit as well as any." He grinned and stepped away, feeling filled with purpose as he began to walk toward the distant silhouette of Ghent's towers. Indeed, he would have to walk quickly if he was to be to work on time. The very thought made Roarke grin anew and he waved jauntily to Yves before he strode too far.

"*Au revoir,* Yves!" he called jubilantly. "Behave yourself while I am gone, and attend well to Denis!"

The boy nodded mutely, but Roarke had already turned away, lifting his nose to the scent carrying from the awakening town even as he hastened his steps. A new beginning 'twas, an adventure he was embarking on, and he could not stifle a rising sense of anticipation at what this day would bring.

Chapter Four

Sleep had not come readily to Adela, and well it seemed that she had spent the entire night tossing and turning, alternately fuming that the knight could so readily dismiss the idea of paying her attentions and puzzling over the reason for his intent to work here. No sense did it make that he should choose this working life over the leisure-filled days of the nobility, and Adela could not help but imagine that there was some greater scheme at work.

Was it possible that Georges had exceeded himself in his mission to bring her grief? Adela gritted her teeth and stared at the ceiling, wondering if she should have wed that man and personally ensured that he was tormented for the remainder of his days.

Though morning took endless hours to arrive, still it came too soon for Adela to manage more than a fleeting moment's sleep. She grimaced as she dressed, knowing she looked as dreadful as she felt, and wondered what the new apprentice would make of that.

Some reflection upon his presence, to be sure. Adela rolled her eyes and clicked her tongue as she spared her kirtle one last, completely unnecessary adjustment. The man thought too much of himself, of that she had little doubt.

He was already in the shop when Adela descended from the kitchen, and her heart stopped before it began to skitter nervously. He had his back to her, dark head angled for-

ward as he listened attentively to her shorter father, hands
folded behind his back. Adela recognized her father's old
shirt upon his back, the garment stretched to its limit to accommodate the knight's broad shoulders.

Indeed, he had already rolled up the sleeves as if they
might be too short, and Adela noted the scattering of dark
hair on his forearms with growing unease. She swallowed
carefully and composed herself before making her presence
known, reminding herself that he truly had not a scrap of
interest in her. The thought seemed to bolster her determination, and she stepped forward, certain he would not even
bother to acknowledge her.

Adela was wrong.

The knight spun at the first sound of her shoe on the
flagstones, and she quelled the impulsive thought that he
had been listening for her as his gaze collided with hers.
Adela fairly took a step back at the shock of his perusal, no
mischief in those gray eyes this morn, but then his expression dissolved into polite interest so quickly that she wondered if she had imagined that first glance.

"I believe you have met my daughter," Mathieu said
quickly, turning back after a cursory smile for Adela with
the obvious intention of continuing whatever he had been
telling his new apprentice. The knight's eyes twinkled with
humor now, and he spared Adela a quick grin that made her
wary of his next move.

"Not officially," he pointed out with slow relish, and
Mathieu glanced up with surprise. He looked then to Adela,
and she shook her head at her sire.

"Nay, not officially," she agreed reluctantly, in a voice so
quiet that it could not be her own.

Her father looked somewhat taken aback at this, and
Adela flushed, knowing that he was recalling her tirade of
the day before. A glance to the knight confirmed that he too
had followed the line of the older man's thoughts and found
that predictably amusing, though his smile seemed to crawl
more slowly across his features than she recalled.

Adela found that slow smile disconcertingly attractive, the very laziness of it conjuring the unlikely thought of mornings spent abed, and she straightened primly, that none might guess her mind. The knight smiled yet more broadly, and she knew a moment of hatred for his perceptiveness.

"Adela, this is Roarke," her father said matter-of-factly, taking her elbow with a proprietary gesture that she found curious under the circumstances. "As I told you last eve, he will be apprenticed here."

"Aye, Papa," she acknowledged, nodding once to the knight and realizing only when they stood so close that he stood a full head taller than she. "My pleasure." She greeted him with icy formality, suspecting that even this would not be allowed to pass unchallenged.

"Nay, the pleasure is indeed mine," Roarke countered, one brow arching eloquently as he spoke.

Though his response was typical enough, the way he murmured the words told Adela that he was used to capitalizing on a mere introduction. It well ought to be illegal for a man to consciously drop his voice so suggestively or fill his eyes with such a promise of intimacy, she concluded ferociously, wondering how she would survive two years of this.

How many times had he greeted a woman thus? Fascinating though he admittedly was, there was something loathsome about his ready manipulation of an ungodly amount of natural charm.

Adela deliberately cocked a skeptical brow. "Indeed?" she demanded archly. Roarke acknowledged her rebuttal with a minute inclination of his head, though his eyes twinkled mercilessly.

Mathieu cleared his throat deliberately, and Adela's eyes flew to her father, his stern glance telling her eloquently that she had already failed to live up to her promise to be civil to the knight. She colored, painfully aware of Roarke's observance of that gesture, and waited silently for her father's direction.

"I thought Roarke might start this morn with the stables," Mathieu stated firmly, and Adela nodded.

Always did her father start to train his apprentices with the most ignoble tasks, and this choice did not surprise her in the least. In fact, Roarke seemed more in need than most of having his pride cut to size, she thought waspishly, not daring to glance up lest her eyes reveal her thoughts.

"Mayhap you could show him," her father added, and Adela nodded again.

"Aye, Papa," she agreed quietly, summoning her nerve before she looked Roarke in the eye. "If you would," she said to him, indicating the back door with one hand.

Roarke nodded and strode to the door, swinging it open with a flourish that drew the attention of all the other weavers, who were just settling in at their looms.

"After you, milady," he offered gallantly, and Adela knew she was not the only one to hear the mockery in his voice. She tipped up her chin and gritted her teeth, refusing to make a performance before the others. She swept past him, studiously avoiding any contact with his hand, silently composing what she would say to him once they were alone.

Time 'twas that this Roarke understood exactly where he stood in her regard.

Plenty Adela had to say to him, of that there was little doubt, and Roarke fought a smile of anticipation. Should he tell her that her eyes betrayed her very thoughts? That he knew she was as aware of him as he was of her, despite her frosty demeanor? That 'twas only a matter of time, given that mutual awareness and their circumstances, before something happened? Mayhap before she begged for his attentions?

Somehow he suspected Adela would not take well to the news, which made the telling of it all the more appealing. She swept past him, and he caught an unexpected whiff of her scent. The response that triggered within him was a telling one.

'Twas the sweet scent of sleep that clung lingeringly to her, and Roarke immediately imagined her slumbering, his mind sketching in her hair loose, about her bare shoulders, and adding the vision of his own hands on her smooth skin. The image was a compelling one, all the more so because 'twas not the first time he had pictured her thus, and Roarke knew a moment's impatience that they were dithering so long with the chase, rather than getting down to the sport itself.

And why wait, after all? They were sure to be alone in the stables in but a few moments. That thought awakened part of him with a vengeance, and he hoped that his chausses were not snug enough that Mathieu had noted his response.

Barely had the thought formed in Roarke's mind when he glanced up and found Mathieu's stern regard upon him. The very sight recalled Roarke's vow to his errant mind, and he stifled a curse, even as he cast a longing glance after Adela's swinging hips.

Aye, he had promised. He nodded once to Mathieu as though to confirm that fact before ducking out the door, telling himself that there was no reason to be so disgruntled. Ghent was filled with beautiful blondes, most of whom undoubtedly had been spared a sharp tongue like Adela's.

But 'twas Adela he was following now, and Roarke found himself more aware of the fact that she was forbidden fruit than he would have liked to be. She was waiting for him impatiently in front of a small outbuilding, hands on her hips, and he could not help but note the delicious curve of those hips. Adela pursed her lips and frowned as he toyed anew with the idea of utilizing the stables for but a few moments, her expression telling Roarke that he was about to receive another sample of her bite. When she did not immediately speak, he could not resist taunting her.

"Cat stole your tongue?" he demanded impertinently, earning himself a glance so scathing that he was momentarily taken aback. Truly she was taking this much more seriously than he had expected, but he had not a chance to reflect upon this before she began.

"No idea have I what you and Georges are conspiring," she declared determinedly, "but I will not have you mock me within the walls of my father's own shop."

Roarke blinked, wondering whether any of that charge should have made sense to him. "Mock you?" he repeated hesitantly, seizing on but one of the things he did not understand.

"Aye," Adela asserted levelly. "Or are you in the custom of saluting common women so regally? Mayhap you expect me to swoon into your arms at being addressed as 'milady.'" This last was offered with unmistakable sarcasm, and Roarke felt that she had caught him when he was not at his best yet again.

"Indeed, I meant no offense," he pointed out, annoyed that she would make an issue of what had been a habitual use of the address. "'Twas a part of my upbringing that I learned to always address a woman thus," he added defensively, and Adela's brows rose.

"Oh, aye. A much *finer* upbringing have you had than the lot of us," she snapped, with a toss of her head that loosened her veil. A wave of blond hair struggled free, seemingly deliberately recalling Roarke's earlier image, and he bit down hard on his arousal, unable to comprehend why this woman, of all women, had to be fascinating and frustrating at one and the same moment.

He struggled to defend his position, though he knew it was far too early for him to successfully match wits with anyone. "I meant merely that the style of my upbringing required the adoption of such manners," he attempted to clarify, seeing before the words had fully left his mouth that he had only made matters worse.

"Whether 'tis an issue of your upbringing itself, the style of that upbringing or the loftiness of your manners, 'twould all seem to make the same result," she retorted. "Indeed, 'twill matter little whether I confide to anyone the status of your birth, should you be so determined to point out to all and sundry that you are better than all of us."

"'Twas not what I meant," Roarke argued irritably. "I called you thus simply because I did not spare the time to think afore I spoke."

"Implying what?" Adela demanded. "That if you had thought, you might have realized that I was unworthy of such an address?"

Roarke desperately tried to think of a means to make this right, but felt as though Adela had backed him into a corner from which there could be no escape. It occurred to him to tell her to hold her tongue for once, but he instinctively knew that that solution would prove of little merit.

"Had I thought about it," he endeavored carefully, then paused for an instant in an attempt to ensure that his next words would not land him even deeper in the mud. "Had I thought about it, I would undoubtedly have had to confront the conundrum of finding you worthy of such an address, but not wishing to insult you by inappropriately saluting you thus."

Roarke waited warily for Adela's response, and was gratified when her eyes but narrowed a slight increment as she regarded him. He exhaled slowly, feeling as though he had passed some sort of test, only to have her step quickly toward him and wag one finger angrily beneath his nose.

"Spare me any nonsense you and Georges have managed to contrive," she hissed. Roarke knew he looked confused, for he surely was so.

"Georges?" he demanded, but Adela did not pause to acknowledge his question.

"No prey will I be to any of your pranks," she continued vehemently. "You tell your friend Georges that he has adequately made his point these past few years, and no longer will I stand by while he torments me."

"Georges?" Roarke dared to ask again when Adela took a breath, intrigued despite himself when she turned those glittering angry eyes on him once more. Her breasts rose and fell indignantly and he could not help but watch the display.

"Play no games with me," Adela spat, her words drawing Roarke's gaze reluctantly back to her flushed face. "Well enough do I know that you have taken some wager with him to humiliate me yet again, but listen to me well." That finger shook beneath Roarke's nose anew, and he noticed the delicacy of her wrist.

"Adela," Roarke said, attempting to interrupt her, but she would have naught of it.

"I will not be mocked by the likes of you," she maintained in a low voice, as though he had not spoken. He was surprised to see a glimmer of tears in her eyes and was seized by an irrational urge to reassure her, even as she resolutely blinked them away. "I will *not* stand by while all the world is reminded yet again that Adela Toisserand is both frigid and old, and you can take *that* piece of news to Georges Desjardins with my blessings."

"And who *is* Georges Desjardins?" Roarke demanded in turn, wondering how he was supposed to know this mysterious man, and not at all certain he liked being lumped in common company with him.

Adela fairly growled. "Do not pretend that you know him not."

Roarke made a helpless gesture. "But in truth I do not," he confessed, watching Adela shake her head impatiently with a growing impatience of his own.

"But of course you do," she insisted.

"I tell you as surely as I stand before you that I do not," Roarke asserted hotly, the vehemence of his protest obviously taking Adela momentarily aback. She recovered quickly, though, as he had known she would, and Roarke felt a fleeting and grudging admiration for her spunk.

"Then why are you here?" she asked.

"What do you mean?"

"What other reason could there be for your presence here, if not for a wager with Georges?" she challenged with bright eyes. "Go ahead. I invite you to give me another explanation for your presence."

Roarke gritted his teeth, wondering when he had ever met a more annoying woman. "This I cannot tell you," he stated, producing a victorious "Ha!" from his opponent.

"Of course you cannot," she concluded blithely, "for you *have* no other excuse."

"I do not know any Georges," Roarke asserted in a low voice, but Adela merely lifted her topaz gaze defiantly to his.

"Prove it," she taunted, and Roarke knew not whether to kiss her or kill her.

Her challenge hung in the air between them, her gaze locked to Roarke's own even as he fought his instinct to trust her with the truth. But he could not endanger the honor of both their families, and knew he must hold his tongue.

Whatever the price this witch extracted from him.

"I cannot speak of this," he repeated tightly, his heart sinking as victory lit Adela's eyes.

"Aye, a man should well have the right to not condemn himself with his own tongue," she charged softly before turning to gesture to the stables. "A shovel and broom is there on the far wall, the dungheap on the far side of the barn." With that, she stepped past him, evidently intending to return to the shop.

But Roarke could not let her walk away thinking so ill of him. 'Twas not as she thought, and even though he could not confide the fullness of the tale, there had to be some way that he could clear his name with her.

He grasped her elbow and drew her to a halt when she would have passed him, holding her deliberately close to his side, even as he struggled to find some way to explain. Adela glanced up reluctantly, and he saw again that tentative awareness of him that set everything within him to tingling. Roarke adjusted his grip on her arm, letting his fingers curve around her proprietarily as he pulled her yet closer.

"I vow to you that 'twas not and is not my intent to mock you," he promised, willing her to see that he spoke the truth.

Adela stared up at him for a long moment, and Roarke watched, transfixed, as her lips finally eased their mutinous set. He thought briefly about kissing her until they were truly soft, but suddenly she twisted out of his grip, as though she, too, had followed the path of his thoughts.

"No more than you mock other women, mayhap," she charged flatly, her derision evident in her eyes.

How could she change moods so abruptly? Once again, he felt left in the dust, and, to his dismay, Roarke found no ready words of defense springing to his tongue. He could but return her regard until she turned quickly away. He watched helplessly as she strode away, the clinging apricot kirtle swaying gently in her wake, his frustration rising with every step she took.

When she had reentered the shop without so much as a single glance back, Roarke spun on his heel and slammed his hand against the wall of the stable, permitting himself the rare luxury of thorough profanity.

What was it about this woman that so frustrated him? Indeed, she turned every argument around, that he might have no honorable escape from her trap. She left him no way to show himself to advantage, always assumed the worst of him and made him feel the most bumbling of fools. 'Twas not a sensation he was used to feeling in the presence of women, and certainly not one to which he would become readily accustomed.

Two years. Roarke groaned and slammed the heel of his hand once more against the stable wall. Two years of Adela taunting him with her stinging words and sweetly swinging hips. The thought alone was almost too much to bear.

Unless the infamous Georges returned to stake whatever claim he had. That thought burned in Roarke's belly with more venom than it should have, to his mind, and he could only briefly consider the torment of watching Adela with another.

Another woman was what he needed to distract his mind, he concluded determinedly, resolving to visit the local tavern as soon as he was able. A blonde would he find, a buxom blonde with topaz eyes who would grant him a ride that would put the spurs for once and for all to this demon that tormented him.

After all, Adela was but a woman, one of many, to be sure. And plenty there were without the decided liability of her sharp manner. That was his trouble, he reasoned amiably. What with the problems at home to be solved, it had simply been too long since he had indulged himself. And well he knew that such denial could readily interfere with his usual good nature.

Certain that the matter could be addressed this very evening, Roarke shoved open the stable door and met the complacent gaze of the two workhorses calmly chewing there. A shaft of sunlight illuminated the interior of the barn, and Roarke saw that it had not been swept out for a few days.

Well, he had been in this position afore, he reasoned, even managing to summon a whistle as he pushed up his sleeves purposefully. And if Mathieu thought to intimidate him with this task, he evidently had not seen the extensive stables of Avigny. Roarke smiled grimly to himself as he found the shovel, certain he would not even break a sweat toiling over the leavings of these two old beasts.

The wink Roarke granted Mathieu when he excused himself after dinner that eve left not a scrap of doubt in Adela's mind as to where he was going, and she fumed inwardly as she cleared the table.

"I would thank you, *mademoiselle,* for the finest meal I have had in some time," Roarke said quietly, his low voice far too close for comfort. Adela jumped, not in the least gratified to see his expression of smug self-satisfaction. Not only had he stressed his address of her, but obviously he was making sport of her cooking skills. Adela's cheeks flamed, and she refused to look him in the eye.

"I am sure my cooking cannot compare with what you are accustomed to," she retorted, flashing him a dangerous glance as she poured hot water into the dirty pot.

"Make no mistake," Roarke offered with an easy grin, "it compares most favorably, or I would say naught."

Adela looked him in the eye then, fully intending to determine that he was in fact teasing her. His expression was one of complete sincerity, though, and she wondered how skilled a charmer he was.

"I would thank you for your kind words," she mumbled as she bent over the pot, well aware of her father's gaze upon her and conscious of the promise she had made to be civil. To her astonishment, Roarke laughed aloud.

"Thank me you might, but you would not believe me," he charged, and she met the mischief simmering in his eyes once more. "Be good this night, Adela," he whispered wickedly. "For well do I intend to be bad enough for both of us."

Before she could think of an adequate retort, Roarke had flicked one finger across the tip of her nose and jaunted down the stairs, whistling cheerfully.

"Indeed I cannot imagine what possessed you to have him in this house," she grumbled, not at all comfortable with what she knew Roarke would be doing this night. Her father chuckled, his mood doing little to improve her own.

"He is a young man with healthy desires, Adela. Already have I forbidden him to indulge himself here. You should be grateful that he so thoughtfully takes his attentions elsewhere."

"Grateful," Adela repeated disparagingly under her breath, bending to give the pot the thorough scouring it had long deserved. Her father cleared his throat, and she jumped guiltily, wondering if he had heard her.

"Well I thought that you intended to be civil to him," he reminded her, and Adela rolled her eyes, knowing he could not see the gesture, for her back was turned to him.

"Much easier that would be if he did not see fit to mock me at every turn," she replied tersely.

"Whatever do you mean?" her sire enquired mildly.

Adela sighed. "Since first I met him, he has made a point of ensuring I understand that he is of noble lineage while I am not," she explained. "Indeed, I weary of the telling, for the matter is hardly in dispute."

"Mayhap you see meaning where there is none," Mathieu suggested, and Adela glanced over her shoulder to him in ill-disguised despair.

"Papa! 'Tis as obvious as the nose on your face!"

Mathieu frowned and felt for his nose, as if doubting for a moment that 'twas actually there, and Adela laughed at his jest despite herself. "You thought his comment on your cooking was mockery?" he asked with that same tone of polite disinterest. Adela regarded his innocent expression with suspicion, wondering if he was not perhaps too innocent in all of this.

"Aye," she agreed simply, watching her father carefully.

He raised his brows and poked Roarke's trencher with one fingertip. "'Twas not mockery that made this meal disappear," he pointed out, openly assessing the slice of bread. "Indeed, I fear there is not even enough gravy left to merit throwing this one to the dogs. Likely they are to throw it back at us in disgust."

Adela laughed despite herself, and her father smiled indulgently. "Oh, Papa. Truly, you only see the best in people," she charged affectionately, brushing her fingertips over his cheek as she moved to finish cleaning off the table. Mathieu caught her hand unexpectedly within his, and she turned to meet his regard, only to find him uncharacteristically solemn.

"Mind that does not leave you only seeing their worst," he urged quietly, pressing her hand and rising from the board before Adela could think of a suitable response.

The tavern was easy enough to find, the distinctive blend of laughter and poor singing drawing Roarke as unerringly as a fish on a line. He straightened his shirt and ran one hand through his unruly hair, grinning in anticipation as he ducked through the doorway.

It was already crowded, and Roarke took a moment to shed his cloak on the threshold while he looked around. More women were there on the far side of the bar, he noted, and he headed purposefully in that direction without appearing to do so. Two blondes were there, and but a glance did it take for him to decide on which to lavish his attentions.

Seemingly unaware that he had paused directly beside the woman of his choice, Roarke leaned over the counter and ordered a draught of wine from the keeper. He busied himself with finding a silver denier in his pocket, fully aware of the perusal of the woman beside him. When he produced the coin and lifted the tankard to his lips, he glanced around as if doing so for the first time and met the woman's interested gaze.

And cursed inwardly that her eyes were cornflower blue.

But naught did that matter, he scolded himself testily. 'Twas a blonde he desired, no more than that, and blond she was without doubt. A vestige of annoyance remained, but he refused to acknowledge it further.

"Good evening," she purred, and Roarke recovered from his disappointment with what he thought to be remarkable aplomb.

"Good evening," he answered evenly, sparing her but a glimpse of his most winning smile. She inched closer.

"Not from around here, are you?" she demanded huskily, and this time Roarke grinned fully.

"Aye, now I am," he confirmed, lifting his tankard as though proposing a toast. "Apprenticed this very day I was, and this night I mean to celebrate." The woman's eyes narrowed slightly, and her gaze slipped over him once more.

"My congratulations," she offered, meeting his eyes speculatively once again.

Though she was not much older than Roarke, he saw even in the semidarkness that those years had not been easy ones for her. Though she was shapely, her eyes were cold, and not a doubt had he precisely what kind of woman stood before him.

But blond she was. He lifted his gaze to the thick tangle of her hair, his anticipation returning as he imagined it twined about him. Too long had it been, and well enough he knew that one busy night would cure him of this fascination with Adela. 'Twas simply a result of his own denial that a woman so intent on arguing with him could capture even a scrap of his attention.

This night would be busy, he promised himself, letting his own gaze slide over the woman beside him. She preened, that slow smile sliding over her rouged lips once more.

"An apprentice does not make much of a living, does he?" she asked, and Roarke saw that she understood he might not have the coin to pay.

"Naught but room and board," he confirmed merrily, reaching out to slide one fingertip up the length of her arm. When he reached the bare skin of her shoulder, he leaned closer and dropped his voice in that way that always guaranteed him results. He smiled leisurely as he stared into her eyes, and knew in that moment that she would be his.

"Naught have I to offer but my personal charm," he breathed, watching as she bit her lip and flicked another glance over him.

"Well might it be enough," she whispered, granting him a slow smile of her own. Their gazes held for a moment as each assessed the other. Then she flicked an impatient finger toward Roarke's tankard of wine.

"The night grows old," she urged, and Roarke grinned as he obediently lifted the tankard to his lips once more.

This night would surely cure him of the demons that tempted him.

Adela awoke with a start when the door to the shop squeaked quietly. She heard the latch click and rolled over silently, squinting at the faint pinkening of the sky and shivering at the early morning air.

Who was in the shop?

Stealthy footfalls climbed the stairs to the kitchen, and her pulse quickened as she imagined all manner of intruders. Surely Roarke would hear them from his pallet by the hearth in the kitchen. Adela strained her ears, but no sound of intervention could she discern, only the ever-advancing footsteps.

Just when she thought to charge down the stairs from the third floor and challenge the intruder herself, he apparently tripped on something. There was a clatter, then a resounding thud as he hit the floor. Adela held her breath in trepidation, a round of cursing in a familiar voice dispelling her fears in one swoop.

'Twas Roarke returned, and she giggled in relief as his swearing continued unabated.

"Well enough did I hear your mockery, witch," he growled in a stage whisper from below, and Adela could not check her giggles when she heard the outrage in his voice. She rolled out of bed and trotted to the top of the stairs, folding her arms about herself against the chill in the air as she confronted a very disgruntled-looking Roarke.

"Serves you right, it does," she charged softly. He held his shoes in one hand and rubbed his damaged knee with the other, looking every inch the dissatisfied child. At the sight of her, his expression turned rueful.

"And what would you know of what I deserved?" he demanded with a reluctant grin. Adela chortled despite herself.

"Think you that I cannot guess where you have been?" she replied, rolling her eyes eloquently at the foolishness of the very idea. Roarke shook his head.

"And much you have to say about that, I can well imagine," he commented dryly.

"Naught have I to say about it." Adela tossed her loose hair disdainfully, somehow not finding the ability to make her voice as frosty as she would have liked. "Should you wish to catch the pox, 'tis indeed of little interest to me."

"For one without an opinion, you certainly have a way of making your thoughts most clear," he commented acidly, glancing up at her anew. His eyes narrowed speculatively, making Adela abruptly conscious of their circumstances.

Suddenly she was aware that she stood before him clad only in her chemise, her hair yet unbound, and a flush stained her cheeks. What had she been thinking? She darted out of his view in alarm, not in the least relieved to find her hardening nipples making pert peaks in the soft cloth.

Roarke's muffled chuckle carried to her burning ears, and Adela needed not much imagination to guess what he thought of her modesty. She defiantly hauled a kirtle made of particularly thick wool over her head and laced the sides with a vengeance, certain she had never so thoroughly forgotten herself.

"Adela" came Roarke's soft call from the kitchen, and she braced herself for more of his teasing.

"Aye," she answered reluctantly when he seemed to be waiting for her to do so.

"Should I kindle the fire, could you see your way to make me something hot?" he asked, and there was not a trace of mockery in his tone. Surprised, Adela returned to the top of the stairs to glance down at him. He grinned crookedly up at her as he shoved one hand through his hair, and despite herself, she felt her heart softening.

"There is but a bit of broth left," she offered tentatively, and he shrugged.

"Even that would be welcome. I fear I am not at my best in the mornings, and this particular morning least of all," he explained, and Adela could not help but smile.

"Aye, 'tis readily evident," she confirmed with relish. "Though mayhap you have made enough mischief to deserve such a fate." He grimaced at her agreement, but did not seem inclined to take issue with her assessment.

"Have you not a scrap of compassion in your soul, woman?" he appealed, and Adela felt a mischievous grin curving her lips.

"Aye," she retorted. "But 'tis not for you as much as those poor horses whose stalls you must muck out."

Roarke's eyes gleamed unexpectedly, and in that instant Adela feared he might dash up the stairs to take his retribution for that remark. She made a little squeal in the back of her throat and dashed out of sight again, listening all the while for the sound of a tread on the stairs.

"I shall be there directly," she called softly when naught carried to her ears. "Please light the fire."

"Your very wish is my command," Roarke muttered from below, with no small measure of irony. Adela smiled, but to her dismay, when she raised her comb, she found her fingers shaking.

Chapter Five

The neatly attired Adela who appeared in the kitchen was naught compared to the vision that had greeted him mere moments before and Roarke bit down on his disappointment. Well enough he had known that she would not come downstairs in her tempting wisp of a chemise, but he had vainly hoped that that golden cloud of hair reaching past her hips might be left unbound at this early hour.

If anything, Adela looked more prim than she had the day before, and he chafed at the realization that he found her no less tempting despite the change. He sought in vain some glimpse of her golden tresses as she heated his broth, but her wimple and oft poorly fastened veil were this morn resolutely anchored in place. Not a single wispy curl escaped their trap, and he scrubbed his face, in a more disgruntled mood than he had been in when he returned.

'Twas true enough that he had not slept a wink the night before, due to his partner's enthusiasm, but the tension he had thought to dispel by such sport seemed to have been heightened, not diminished. He forced himself to acknowledge the fact that being denied another sight of Adela's hair was making him irritable, and shook his head sadly at his own state.

Evidently he would have to pursue this path with more enthusiasm.

'Twas when Roarke dunked his head in the washbasin that he caught a glimpse of her bare feet. A small grant 'twas indeed, but he fed on the sight of her feet as if 'twere a sight much more intimate arrayed before him. For a long moment, he could do naught but stare and feel his rising response. Then he scowled and shook his head at the path of his thoughts.

Of what was he thinking? This woman had no interest in him, that she had made abundantly clear, and truly, there was no excuse for him to have any interest in her. One woman was much the same as another, he reminded himself savagely, wincing as the soap found its way into his eyes. He growled in annoyance and scrubbed at the sting.

Sleep was what he needed. Sleep, and more companionship of the ilk of that blue-eyed blonde. But instead he had work to do this morn. And this afternoon. And this eve, likely, afore he had the opportunity to sleep or play again.

And he had survived but one day of the two years he had bound himself to serve. 'Twas enough to make a man violent. Roarke fingered the stubble gracing his chin and resolved to let his beard grow. Suited his mood well, it did, to be less fastidious about his appearance.

"Have you an aching head?" Adela inquired with no measure of censure in her voice. Roarke glanced up in surprise to find her regard upon him, her eyes lit only with polite curiosity.

"Why?" he demanded sharply, scowling as the soap leapt from his hand to hide in the depths of the basin. Would naught go aright?

"Something can I put in the broth to ease your headache, should you have one," Adela responded calmly.

Roarke shot her a suspicious glance before he peeled off his shirt abruptly. A regular lady of mercy she was, he thought sourly, and about as disinterested in him as one would expect a nun to be. He retrieved the soap and scrubbed his skin with a thoroughness that seemed unwarranted, despite the evidence of his labors that clung to him.

"Is it merely pity or a sense of superiority that makes you so pleasant to me this morn?" he demanded impatiently, glancing Adela's way, only to meet her innocent regard.

"Think you that I am so cruel as to kick a new puppy?" she asked mildly, strolling across the room to place the steaming mug on the table beside him.

Roarke might have been fooled by her nonchalant manner, if the tremor on the surface of the broth had not revealed her nervousness. He glared at her, thinking she made yet another jest of him, watching with dawning fascination as she swallowed carefully and kept her gaze averted from his bare chest.

She *was* aware of him, though that revelation did little to improve his mood, for her interest was so easily controlled that it could not be of the magnitude of his own. The tempting thought of gaining her attention thoroughly pricked at him, but Roarke forced himself to recall his manners.

"What do you mean?" he asked, and Adela flicked her wrist dismissively.

"'Tis evident that you are not capable of your usual sport," she charged with a quick smile of amusement that dismissed all his chivalrous leanings. Before he could consider the wisdom of his move, Roarke took a deliberate step closer to her.

Adela's fleeting expression of alarm at his gesture gave him tremendous satisfaction, and he dared to peruse her leisurely. By the time his bold gaze ambled back to meet hers once more, he had no doubt that she was thoroughly agitated by both his proximity and his partial nudity. Her cheeks flamed, but she resolutely refused to be the first to look away.

"Should you dare to look, *mademoiselle,* you will see that I am more than capable of my usual sport," he growled.

Adela's eyes widened, and she took a hasty step backward, her gaze flying briefly to his crotch, despite her efforts to the contrary. Roarke grinned wolfishly as he closed the space between them again, and she retreated anew, shaking one finger desperately in his face.

"'Twas not what I meant, and well enough do you know it," she charged breathlessly as she darted around to the other side of the table. "'Twas verbal sport I meant, and no more."

She braced her hands against the top of the table, evidently taking some reassurance from the expanse of wood between them, and the water in the washbasin sloshed at the movement. Roarke propped his own hands on the table, feeling suddenly that the odds had shifted in his favor, and regarded Adela intently. She trembled visibly, and his arousal redoubled at the sign of her awareness of him. He thought again of that tangle of hair and wondered how he might divest her of her wimple and veil.

"But the other sport was precisely what I meant," he asserted in a low voice, watching hungrily as Adela licked her lips.

"Aye, 'tis obvious to all that you think of naught else," she answered, and he marveled anew that she did not readily abandon a fight. He moved around the table, stalking her with a relentlessly steady pace, but she darted ahead of him, her breath coming quicker as she paused in gaining each side of the table. When they had circumvented the table twice, he stopped and braced his hands on the wood again.

"A word of warning have I for you, Adela," Roarke growled, leaning across the table so that their faces were but a handspan apart. Well it seemed that Adela stopped breathing. Her eyes were wide as she stared transfixed into his.

"Push me not this day," he breathed, toying briefly with the idea of sealing his assertion with a kiss. Adela seemed to sense his intent, for she danced backward and out of range once more, flattening her back against the far wall.

"Promised my father you did," she reminded him hastily and Roarke gritted his teeth against the truth of it. He glanced away for a moment, then impaled her once more with a sharp look, willing her to understand the truth in what he said.

"Aye, that I did," he agreed. "But you would do well to remember that a man can only bear so much."

Their gazes held for a long moment. Then Roarke muttered an expletive under his breath and turned away. He heard Adela's gasp when his back was turned to her, but did not see fit to enlighten her at this moment, scooping another shirt from his satchel by the hearth and hauling it over his head in frustration.

The woman would drive him mad in two years should he not find some relief. He shoved on his shoes and stomped down the stairs to the shop without a word, leaving his cup steaming on the board.

Adela let out the breath she had been holding and sagged briefly against the wall as the door to the yard slammed downstairs. She had not a moment to make sense of what Roarke had said, much less of the crisscross of healed scars she had glimpsed on his back, before her father appeared with a cheery smile. Somehow she forced herself to return his greeting amiably and lay out his bread and cheese as though naught had gone amiss.

But later, when Adela sat working at her loom, she had time aplenty to ponder what had happened that morn, and she wondered.

Was it possible that Roarke held her in some regard?

Impossible. She dismissed the thought before it could truly even form, shooting the shuttle through the warp with more force than was truly required for it to reach the other side. Impossible 'twas that that man could hold any woman in any regard different from that in which he held all of the fair sex.

He came into the shop in that moment, and though Adela was painfully aware of his presence, she feigned ignorance and made every effort to appear engrossed in her work. His voice rose as he bantered with old Bertha, his chuckle in response to that woman's good-natured teasing grating on Adela's nerves.

One and all the same to him, they were, and she, for one, would not fall prey to his charm.

And those scars on his back? Undoubtedly he had erred in chasing a woman some man of power held in regard and had been caught. Had that truly been the case, Roarke was lucky indeed to have only a few scars to show for his transgression, but Adela could not summon as much satisfaction with that conclusion as she feared she should have.

That evening, Roarke again complimented Adela on her cooking before excusing himself and leaving once more for the evening. Naught did she say, merely rose to clean the kitchen, though she could not fail to notice her father's brief frown of disapproval. She wondered at that, uncertain whether 'twas a comment on Roarke's activity or perhaps her own failure to be as civil as her sire might have desired, but no answer did she have.

And so the week fell into a pattern, Adela avoiding Roarke whenever possible and restraining herself to a polite response alone whenever it seemed required. Conversation at their evening meal faded to naught, and her father's scowl deepened with every passing day. Served Mathieu right, it did, Adela thought, for taking one to apprentice of whom he knew so little.

Although little complaint could be made of Roarke's work, and Adela reluctantly conceded that, at least. For always was he willing to do as he was bidden, regardless of the task. The barn was cleaner than it had been in years, and the horses were better groomed. He fetched and carried from the dyers, the combers and the spinners without complaint, and when it happened that he had a spare moment, Adela oft sensed his presence in the shop. She glanced up one day to find him watching the loom closest to him, seemingly mesmerized by the rhythmic working of the apparatus, and for the first time she wondered if he did truly have a hankering for the work.

For his part, Roarke grew quieter as the week passed, his sullen manner and the steady progression of his whiskers into a beard making him appear quite another man than the one who had crossed the threshold mere days before. 'Twas undoubtedly his lack of sleep, Adela told herself self-righteously, not having any desire at all to speculate on where he spent his evenings.

For 'twas evident he spent virtually no part of them on the kitchen hearth, the mornings evenly divided between those on which he returned only while she and Mathieu were breaking their fast and the others, when she heard him come home just as she was rising.

None of her business it was, and well Adela knew it, just as she knew the question troubled her more than it should.

'Twas Thursday when she learned what she would much rather have suspected and never known for certain. And, predictably, 'twas the dyer's daughter, Marie, who took especial delight in passing on the gossip to Adela.

Indeed, if Adela had had to choose one person on the face of the earth with whom she could well do without, Marie would have easily won her vote. Not only was her hair of an uncommon red color, but 'twas thick and straight, her complexion was as creamy fair as milk, and her eyes were as glittering a green as spring grass. But 'twas not the other woman's beauty nor her curvaceous figure that irked Adela, but her penchant for making trouble.

If a pot could be found to be stirred, Marie would be first to the ladle every time. Responsible she was for the dissolution of more than one set of marital vows and the disruption of many a betrothal. Suspicions did she feed with an expertise in innuendo seldom seen in others, and Adela took care to steer a wide path around the younger woman.

On this market day, however, her own wishes were of no import, for Marie clearly had something on her mind. She cornered Adela in front of the butcher shop, and Adela made the mistake of hesitating, forestalled by a genuine desire to not be rude. 'Twas all the opening Marie needed.

"And what have you done to so win the graces of Dame Fortune, Adela?" Marie purred unexpectedly, once cursory greetings had been exchanged.

"I know not what you mean," Adela replied cautiously, and was uncertain what to make of the other woman's throaty chuckle in response to that. Marie wagged one finger coyly and dropped her voice conspiratorially.

"'Twill do no good to feign ignorance, you know," she said, her words illuminating Adela little more. When Adela did not comment, Marie drew herself up, seemingly taking Adela's silence as a reluctance to exchange confidences.

"Come now, think you that no one else has laid eyes on that divine man?" Marie demanded, and Adela felt her color rise as she suddenly understood.

"You must mean my father's new apprentice," she said, watching the other woman's brows rise suggestively.

"Is that what you are calling him?" she mused, her gaze speculative. Adela knew then that her flush had not gone unnoticed, and she met Marie's eyes squarely, determined to lay any rumors to rest before they truly began.

"Roarke is called an apprentice, for that is precisely what he is," she stated.

"Roarke, is it, then?" Marie repeated cattily, a small smile playing over her lips. "So intimate you are for such brief acquaintance."

"Well enough do you know that all within the shop call each other by their Christian names," Adela responded, irritated at how easily Marie was irking her this day. "'Tis much the same in your father's shop, I would imagine."

Marie laughed once more and leaned closer. "Aye," she whispered, rolling her eyes with an eloquence that made Adela dread what next she would say. "But never has my father taken so fine a specimen under his wing."

"I should think 'twas not Roarke's looks that earned him the post," Adela retorted haughtily, distrusting Marie's easy smile.

"I suppose that would all depend on what precisely his post would be," she mused. Adela regarded her warily, certain she must have misinterpreted the words, but Marie continued so that there might be no mistake. "I hear he sleeps in your home. Others might assume in the kitchen, but we know better than that, do we not?"

"Marie! Truly you have overstepped the bounds of propriety by even thinking such a thing!" Adela was shocked at the other woman's insinuation. Marie's eyes glittered unrepentantly and, unwilling to hear any more maliciousness, Adela turned to walk away. To her astonishment, Marie grasped her elbow and dragged her to a halt.

"Come now, Adela, there is little to blame in your father's path," she insisted, and Adela shook off the weight of her hand, as though repulsed by her very touch. "Indeed, you are getting no younger, and should you not wed soon, the man may see no grandchildren." Marie lifted one slim hand suggestively as Adela stared at her in shock.

"Marie, I assure you that you are completely mistaken," she protested. "The man is my father's apprentice, no more and no less, and I guarantee you that he labors in the shop alone."

"So far," Marie concluded in a low voice, crossing her arms across her chest as she regarded Adela's outrage with evident satisfaction.

"Truly you see smoke where there is no flame," Adela retorted coldly after a moment's pause. The two women's gazes held, and then Adela turned to sweep away.

"Surely you know that I but jest, Adela, for 'tis not as though there is truly much doubt of your chastity," Marie called maliciously, and though Adela's ears burned, she determinedly continued to walk home. "Indeed, the man has made it evident enough by his exhaustion of the local 'working women' that there is naught to be had in the way of pleasure at the Toisserand household.''

Adela did not grace the other woman with a reply, resolutely gripping her basket as she felt herself the target of the entire town's mockery. Had she harbored any doubts about Roarke's intentions, Marie's words had certainly laid them to rest. The man was equally interested in all women, and truly only in one thing they could offer.

Well, she had not saved herself for this long only to casually cast her gift to a hopeless wencher. She gritted her teeth and swung her basket to her other arm, not even willing to speculate on what rumors Marie had spread. That was far beyond her control, and indeed she would do well should she manage but to control her response to her father's apprentice.

Aye, Adela resolved grimly. No doubt would Roarke have of her feelings on the matter. 'Twould not be long before he undoubtedly left her completely alone and reserved all of his attentions for these women in town.

Adela blinked back unexpected tears of self-pity, stubbornly attributing them to Marie's reminder of her advancing age. If the pity of an entire town had not moved her to tears afore, there was, after all, no reason why it should do so now.

By Sunday's dawn, Roarke was feeling markedly less than himself.

He groaned when he cocked open one eye warily and realized that the morn was already upon them. How long had he slept this night? Indeed, it seemed that it had been mere moments ago that he had dragged himself back to his pallet. He winced as he rolled over, his body complaining mightily of its labors of the past week.

Not only had he had little sleep, but he had toiled all of each day for Mathieu and labored long into each night in his quest to sample the charms of all the women Ghent had to offer. And plenty of twitching kirtles there were, legions of blondes, it seemed, vast numbers of whom seemed more than willing to give him a tumble. But some kind of curse Roarke had earned, in truth, for the more he chased and captured, the more sharply his desire for Adela rose.

And that witch had even forsworn arguing with him, from all appearances. Roarke had thought it annoying to be on the receiving end of her sharp barbs, but to have her ignore him when he was painfully aware of her was infinitely worse. He sensed her presence when she arrived and felt its loss when she left, found himself as self-conscious as a boy in those rare moments when he felt her regard upon him.

In those nearly nonexistent moments when he did sleep, he inevitably dreamed of the golden tangle of her hair. No doubt was there that this infatuation had risen to new heights. And 'twas all a result of Mathieu's cursed promise. Were Adela not forbidden to him, Roarke was certain he would find her less appealing.

Two years. Roarke ran one hand over his brow, reluctantly acknowledging that he had survived but a week already. And Ghent would run out of blondes before the next Sabbath, should he continue at this pace.

Indeed, Roarke knew beyond doubt that this bargain had been wrought in hell.

A bench scraped on the floor, and he forced open the other eye, only to gain a cheery greeting from Mathieu. None other than Mephistopheles himself, Roarke thought sourly, groaning anew as he sat up and propped his aching head in his hands.

"The morn comes early to those who would tarry late," Mathieu commented idly. Surprised at the lack of censure in the older man's tone, Roarke glanced up in surprise.

"So speaks a man who has been down this path afore," he observed, and Mathieu grinned.

"Aye," he agreed readily. "Young I was once."

"And still not in your dotage," Roarke pointed out, rising to take a seat opposite the older man. "And a widower, yet home you stay each eve." The implication of his words was evidently not lost on Mathieu, for that man pursed his lips thoughtfully.

"Aye, mayhap I have found another outlet for my energy," he conceded, and Roarke felt his brows rise in a silent query. Mathieu sighed and traced a path on the table with one heavy finger. "Long have I sought refuge in my work," he explained quietly, and Roarke could not check his irreverent chuckle.

"Even with the stables swept out, I would fear for my health to lose myself in mine," he quipped, and Mathieu grinned in turn.

"Not the last of your work is that."

"Nay, but I fear the sire of the sisters who spin for you would be unappreciative, should I find refuge in that aspect of my work," he retorted irreverently.

"Always is there gain to be made in giving the work one's full attention," Mathieu reminded him, and Roarke regarded the older man for a moment as he considered the concept.

True enough was it that his current path was gaining him naught, he conceded. Adela haunted him, but mayhap that was because he saw so little of her. Indeed, did not every woman's charm fade on closer association? Mayhap the best way to drive thoughts of Adela from his head was to get to know her better.

And the best way to do that was to work more at the shop. Two birds with one stone, as it were. Roarke cleared his throat, pleased with his solution, save for one matter. Always was he aware of the magic of the looms, and that alone was work he could envision pouring his attention into. Ample reward would there be in seeing the cloth grow beneath his own hands, this he knew without doubt, just as surely as he knew he would find it difficult to leave the loom each night.

Roarke found Mathieu's gaze still upon him and sought a diplomatic way to raise the issue. "In truth there is little in my work that would merit such attention," he remarked calmly, and the older man's brows rose speculatively.

"If truly you find your tasks so devoid of challenge, it seems others must be found for you," he said carefully. The very promise of learning to use those looms banished the last of Roarke's sleepiness, and he leaned forward enthusiastically, unable to disguise his interest any longer.

"Shall I learn to use the looms, then?" he asked, stunned into silence when Mathieu laughed aloud.

"Much have you to learn afore you touch one of *my* looms," the weaver clarified, and Roarke slumped in defeat. "Too valuable are they to be left in the hands of one so inexperienced," he added.

Roarke grimaced, wondering if he would ever have the chance to do anything even remotely interesting in this shop. He jumped when Mathieu's hand landed on his shoulder in a paternal gesture, and glanced up in surprise.

"Make no mistake, Roarke, 'tis better to learn one step at a time," he assured him in a low voice, and Roarke nodded reluctantly, well familiar with this line of logic from his days as a squire.

And eight long years that had taken to bear fruit, he reminded himself grimly. He squared his shoulders determinedly as Mathieu spared him another encouraging pat. Had he not survived those years of drudgery to earn his spurs? And the weaver threatened him with mere months of inconsequential labor. Well enough could he tolerate whatever Mathieu could dish out, as long as the bright promise of using the looms hung before him.

"But you will teach me?" he dared to ask, earning himself a small smile from the weaver.

"Aye, you will learn it all in time," the older man confirmed, his words setting Roarke's heart to singing.

Bolstered by that reassurance, Roarke poured water into the washbasin and commenced to wash for church, grateful that he had one shirt still clean enough to wear.

"Adela, make haste," the weaver shouted up the stairs, with a wink for Roarke. "Late shall we be for Mass, child, if you do not hasten yourself."

Despite her resolutions to the contrary, Adela could not completely submerge a thrill of pleasure when she took her father's arm to walk to church and Roarke matched her step on her other side. Though there was no mistaking that Roarke was in less than fine spirits, she found herself avidly aware of his masculinity, of the scent of soap on his skin, a jolt tripping over her skin when his knuckles accidently brushed once against hers.

'Twas a clear and sunny autumn day, there was an unmistakable bite in the air that warned of the cold months to come, and Adela felt unusually light on her feet. The church bell began to peal as they walked, others joining them on the cobbled streets as all made their way to Mass.

"In a fine mood are you this morn," Roarke commented, his low tone making Adela fancy that he spoke the words for her ears alone. She flicked a sidelong glance to find his speculative gaze upon her, and could not suppress her mischievous urge.

"'Tis but the contrast to your own mood that makes it seem so," she teased, smiling when her father chuckled under his breath and shot Roarke a look that spoke volumes. Roarke grinned himself, and his gaze dropped to meet Adela's once more.

"Aye, a sour houseguest have I been this week, indeed," he acknowledged. "But be forewarned that I intend to take your father's suggestion."

"Which is?"

"That I bend my attention to work and not frivolity," Roarke supplied, though his tone left Adela with no clues to how he felt about the matter. Until he winked mischievously and her heart took an uncharacteristic leap. "So cursed will you be with my presence this week that you will undoubtedly demand I resume my frivolity."

Mathieu laughed along with Roarke, and Adela joined them, unable to imagine what had sparked this change. Or was Roarke merely making jest of her?

Her euphoric mood was not to last, however, for no sooner had they reached the steps of the church than Marie appeared from nowhere to block their path. She smiled graciously, even as she determinedly hauled her own father into position, that the threesome might not continue without addressing them.

"Good morning," she enthused, the sparkle in her eyes leaving no doubt in Adela's mind what Marie wanted from them this morn.

"Good morning," Adela returned quietly, certain that she wanted no part of this play.

The two older men exchanged greetings, and Adela turned her attention to her shoe, ignoring Marie's obvious play for an introduction. The other woman cleared her throat when it became evident that their fathers intended to talk business, and Adela glanced up reluctantly, making the required introductions as quickly as she could. No satisfaction did it give her when Roarke did not immediately release Marie's hand.

Though she might have continued then into church, Roarke apparently felt no qualms about chatting with the voluptuous Marie. Forced to wait for both men, Adela stabbed her toe into the cobblestones in annoyance.

"Indeed, I feared we had been abandoned without an introduction," he commented smoothly, leaving Adela in no doubt of his censure. "But a pleasure it is to make your acquaintance, *mademoiselle*." Roarke's voice revealed more enthusiasm than Adela thought the situation merited.

"I had heard tell that the Toisserands had taken on a new apprentice," Marie breathed.

Adela dared to glance up and caught the end of the other woman's thorough perusal of Roarke, a perusal that made clear her conclusions about the man before her. Evidently they meant to make a show of it, Adela concluded acidly, bracing herself for further display.

"I know not your circumstance, Roarke," Marie continued in a confidential tone, her green eyes widening, as though her familiarity surprised even herself. "Oh. I hope indeed that you do not mind my addressing you thus, but already I feel a certain ease in your presence," she said, all in a rush.

Adela fairly gagged at the insincerity of Marie's seemingly innocent gaffe. Roarke, to his credit, seemed to fight a smile as he shook his head, but Adela wondered if she had imagined the gesture, for he responded with more than a healthy measure of warmth.

"By all means, I would insist that you do so," he urged, his voice dropping to that intimate timbre that Adela was beginning to recognize. She flicked him a venomous look, but quickly saw that he was too busy watching Marie to even notice.

Ogling, more like, she corrected irritably, surreptitiously squeezing her father's arm, that he might end his conversation in short order. Mathieu, to her dismay, continued undeterred his discussion of the rising price of woad, and Adela began to fume silently as Marie stepped closer to Roarke.

"Roarke, then," Marie continued agreeably, and even Adela could see the blatant invitation in her eyes. On the very steps of the church, no less. "Well enough do I know that an apprentice oft tires of the poor fare to be had, especially in the likes of a weaver's home." She gasped cleverly and covered her mouth with one hand, as if surprised at what she had said.

"No slight intended to you, of course, Adela," Marie added with a condescending smile. Adela managed to return the smile tightly.

"Of course," she agreed through clenched teeth, having no difficulty seeing where this proposal was headed. Well enough did she and everyone else know that the Taintenières were considerably more prosperous than most, and actually employed a cook.

"But I would be pleased to offer you the opportunity to sample from our board," Marie continued, batting her russet lashes before she gazed up at Roarke with a pretty pout. "It seems our cook always makes too much for just the two of us, and well I know that a man such as yourself must be famished by the end of the day."

"Your offer is certainly appreciated," Roarke said gallantly. Adela wondered waspishly which offer he referred to, for 'twas clear Marie was inviting him to partake of more than dinner.

"Then you must join us," Marie purred, seemingly sensing victory in the offing. "Mayhap this very night?"

"I would thank you for your offer, but must decline," Roarke replied politely. "Indeed, I would not want to slight my master so early in my term."

"Should you truly desire to eat elsewhere, certain I am that my father would not take offense," Adela pointed out tightly, disgusted that she was responsible for Marie's pout magically transforming to a beatific smile.

"Settled it is, then," she concluded, but to the surprise of both women, Roarke shook his head firmly.

"Nay, I say again that I must decline," he reiterated, and Adela sensed an undercurrent of determination in his tone. "Just this very morn, Mathieu and I discussed my responsibilities, and despite the assurances of you both, I would not offend him with such a move."

Adela knew not what to make of this, though as she puzzled over it, Marie attempted to change Roarke's mind.

"But surely you could be spared for one decent meal per week?" Marie wheedled. "On Sunday, no less?" Roarke smiled thinly, and Adela had a sudden feeling that he did not care for the other woman's persistence.

"Charming as your offer is, *mademoiselle*, I must profess that the fare Adela provides is more than adequate to satisfy," he countered smoothly.

Adela looked up at him in surprise, disconcerted to find his gaze warm upon her. "Indeed, your cook would have to be fair talented to surpass her skill in the kitchen," he continued, and Adela knew not what to say. She felt her color heighten and concluded that he must be mocking her yet again.

"No need have you to be so gallant," Marie charged with a chuckle, reaching out to tap Roarke familiarly on the arm. "Friends are Adela and I, and few secrets are there between us. No insult would she take, were you to confess the limits of her skill to me."

Friends? A cold day in Hades would it be before that was the case. Certain she had no interest in hearing any more, Adela drew herself up taller and gave her father a definite pinch on the tender flesh inside his elbow. That man jumped in a most noticeable manner, comprehension dawning in his eyes when his daughter flicked but one glance into the nave.

"What have we been thinking?" he asked good-naturedly, leading Adela up the steps and away from Marie. "The Mass will begin before we ever get inside."

To her relief, Adela felt Roarke's presence immediately behind her. Marie's sigh of exasperation revealed that he had ignored her intimation that he should escort her into the church. Indeed, 'twas only proper that her sire do so, but Adela smiled at the realization that Marie's plans had been thwarted.

For now.

"No jest did I make in complimenting your cooking," Roarke murmured under his breath as all were settling into the church.

Though the interior of the building was dim, the sunlight filtering through the stained glass and the flickering candles far ahead at the altar casting little light where they sat, he studied the woman beside him expectantly. Adela shot him the suspicious glance he had fully anticipated, but still he could not let the matter rest. He had paid her a well-deserved compliment, and it irked him that she had assumed he spoke untruthfully. What reason had he ever given her to think him a teller of tales?

"Think you that I was born yesterday?" she hissed, and he quickly shook his head.

"None could learn to cook thus in but a day," he retorted, feeling a surge of victory when she could not completely quell her smile.

"Well do you know that my sire would not object should you wish to eat at their board," she whispered, her low tone forcing Roarke to lean closer to catch her words. More than that did he catch, for a fragrant whiff of her skin rose to tease his nostrils, and he forced down his instinctive response.

"Mayhap I would object to being served as dessert," he replied pertly, and Adela's expression turned skeptical.

"Since when?" she demanded warily, and Roarke could not help but grin.

"Since I decided to work harder and inflict my presence solely on you," he retorted, and doubt clouded those topaz eyes.

"Never do I know whether to believe you," Adela confided with a quick frown. Roarke shrugged, thinking 'twas progress indeed for her to merely doubt his word, rather than to flatly disbelieve everything he uttered. No hasty progress would he make with Adela, of that there was little doubt.

Just as there was little doubt that he was even interested in making progress with Adela, he reminded himself sternly. Indeed, he had but to acquaint himself enough with her to see her faults and loosen her hold over his desires.

Like her sharp tongue. Aye, there was a liability, although admittedly of late she had shown a sweetness he had not expected. A sweetness he found intriguing indeed.

Roarke wrenched his errant thoughts back to the present, only to find her still awaiting his reply.

"Then I shall have to ensure I only speak the truth to you, that you might have no doubts," he replied easily, earning himself another most dubious glance. He returned her regard steadily, willing her to understand that he had meant what he said. 'Twas important somehow that she knew he did not lie, though Roarke refused to question the reason why he found this so critical.

"Make no mistake, Adela," he insisted softly as the congregation fell silent. "A fine cook you are." She held his glance for an instant, as though she were testing him, and Roarke felt a measure of relief when she looked to the altar with a single nod of acknowledgment.

"I would thank you for your kind words," she said quietly, leaving him marveling at how sweet she could be when she had no quarrel with him.

But little time had Roarke to savor that victory, for it soon became clear that Adela could well be sweet to another than himself.

Chapter Six

"Adela!"

Roarke felt his two companions turn even as he glanced over his shoulder at the masculine call. A tall, fair man with a tentative grin was approaching them. He felt Adela stiffen slightly, and was reassured by that, until Mathieu greeted the other man with an effusiveness that seemed forced.

"Georges. Good it is to see you again." He shook the younger man's hand. Georges' gaze slid to Adela in a way that left Roarke no doubt what was on the other man's mind, finding himself bristling just before those blue eyes speculatively met his own. Roarke glimpsed an assessing gleam in Mathieu's eye before the older man turned back to Georges with uncharacteristic enthusiasm.

Georges, Roarke repeated to himself silently. Where had he heard that name recently? Had he not known better, he might have thought Mathieu hatching some scheme.

"Adela, 'tis good indeed to see you," this Georges said, his manner reminding Roarke of a puppy that had been overindulged.

"'Tis pleasant to see you again," Adela commented politely. She tried unsuccessfully to extract her hand from the other man's grip, but Georges held fast. Roarke was annoyed at how readily she abandoned the fight and left her hand trapped within the other man's.

Did she not persist in fighting him with every scrap of defiance? Why then did she not do the same here? Was it possible she made the effort only for the sake of appearances? That she really wanted this Georges to hold her hand before all in the square? 'Twas outrageous and Roarke felt his ire grow.

Georges flicked another questioning glance to Roarke, and this time Mathieu seemed to notice. He introduced the men, and a derisive smile tugged at the corners of the blond man's lips when he learned that Roarke was but an apprentice. Apparently that was enough to make Roarke worthy of ignoring, and the blond man proceeded immediately along that path.

Roarke, for his part, assessed the other man's size and weight, and easily concluded that he could win a fistfight against him. Not that there was any reason to do so, of course, but something annoying there was about this Georges.

"Adela, oft have I thought of visiting you again," Georges said, beginning what was apparently to be a plea for her attentions. Roarke stifled a smug smile and waited, certain that Adela would make short work of that comment. Amusing enough 'twould be to watch her slice another to ribbons instead of himself.

To Roarke's dismay, Adela but smiled and glanced away in what seemed a most coy, feminine manner. What was this? Could she truly be enamored of this oaf?

"Indeed, Georges, it seems that you have oft favored me with your attentions," she commented quietly. Georges' fair brows rose in surprise, and he shook his head uncomprehendingly.

"In your wagers," Adela continued, her voice hardening ever so slightly. This was it, Roarke thought victoriously, wondering all the while what she was talking about.

Georges swallowed carefully and fidgeted with her fingers. "Of what wagers do you speak?" he asked awkwardly.

Adela inhaled sharply, and Roarke smiled in anticipation as he awaited her attack. "Your wagers that others
might taunt me," she retorted, her low tone revealing how
much the matter had hurt. "Your petty efforts to ensure that
I understood denying you was the greatest mistake I might
have made."

"I, ah..." Georges fumbled for words, evidently not the
quickest-thinking of souls, and Roarke glanced between the
two of them in amazement. Had he misunderstood Adela?
The accusation she had made afore leapt into his mind, and
he regarded the other man with astonishment. This was the
man she had accused him of being in league with?

"Play no games with me, Georges Desjardins," Adela
accused as she hauled her hand out of Georges' grip, her
eyes snapping furiously. "Well enough do I know that you
demanded others taunt me, that I might be made completely aware of my ripening age and undesirability."

Undesirability? There was a word Roarke had not asso-
ciated with Adela, but any disagreement was lost amid his
shock at the other man's lack of gallantry. Indeed, such behavior was cruel beyond belief. Truly, he had done this?

Roarke looked to the other man, his surprise redoubling
as the man positively writhed with guilt under Adela's eye.
And after such conduct, this Georges would maintain that
he held Adela in high regard? Impossible. Unworthy of her
he was, and Roarke had half a mind to point out that fact.

"Aw, Adela," Georges defended himself sheepishly. "All
over, that is," he argued, presenting Adela with an appealing eye. "Could we not leave the matter and move on?
Missed you, I have."

Surely Adela would not believe this nonsense?

"Over?" Adela demanded archly, much to Roarke's relief. "Did you not demand that this man do exactly thus at
the Hot Fair this year?"

Georges frowned and looked uncomprehendingly at
Roarke, shaking his head slowly. "Never have I laid eyes on
this man before this day," he said slowly, seemingly afraid

he had missed something. Adela spun to confront Roarke, hurt and anger flashing in her eyes, and his heart sank.

"Did he not wager with you thus?" she insisted, and he frowned in indecision. In truth, Georges had not, but Roarke was loath to confirm that fact. Too cruel was it that he should have to clear this man's name before Adela, even knowing him to be a knave, and Roarke cleared his throat with an effort.

"Well enough did I tell you that I had taken no wager," he asserted quietly, but Adela did not let the matter go at that.

"Know you this man?" she asked, and Roarke was forced to shake his head.

"Never have I seen him afore this day," he responded, watching helplessly as the tight set of her lips relaxed. Something flickered in her eyes that could have been regret, though that made so little sense and disappeared so quickly that Roarke was certain he must have imagined it. Adela turned back to Georges, her color deepening becomingly, and closed her fingers around his once more in a gesture that made everything within Roarke writhe.

"Well does it seem I owe you an apology," she murmured, and to Roarke's disgust, Georges positively beamed.

And where was *his* apology? Surely the earful Adela had wrongfully granted him in Troyes put this meager exchange to shame?

"As I owe you one, Adela. I know not what came over me when I took that wager," Georges declared earnestly. Roarke wondered if Adela was truly believing this swill, but she said naught in protest. "'Twas surely the prospect of being without you that made me lose my head, and well do I swear that 'twill not happen again."

Unlikely that was, Roarke fairly snorted, knowing that any man who would deliberately try to shame a woman would undoubtedly do the same again. He waited for Adela to put the misguided Georges properly in his place.

To his chagrin, she smiled sweetly and patted the other man on the shoulder. "Well enough is the matter forgotten, Georges," she said, with a docility Roarke had not known she possessed. Georges gazed at her with unabashed adoration, and Roarke marveled that he alone seemed to find the man's sincerity questionable.

"Well and good 'tis to see this matter settled," Mathieu declared, with a heartiness that rang false in Roarke's ears. "Mayhap this eve you would share our meal, Georges," he suggested. The blond man nodded quickly, his eyes bright as he regarded Adela, and Roarke struggled to think of some suitable objection to make.

But naught came to his mind, and he watched with growing dismay as Georges shook Mathieu's hand, then captured Adela's fingers once more before he turned away. The threesome turned again for home, Mathieu chattering about the good fortune of encountering Georges, and Roarke wondered what had happened to his earlier optimism.

The garden was fading with the chill of the autumn nights, the outer leaves of the cabbages turning yellow and most of the vegetables finished for the season. Adela sighed, thinking of the long winter ahead and the lack of variety in fare. Truly her culinary skills were sorely tested by the time Yule passed each year. Roarke would soon be dissuaded of his illusions about her cooking, she concluded sadly, still clutching those unexpected words of praise to her heart.

She could hear the low murmur of Roarke and her father chatting on the back step as they enjoyed the sunshine, her heart taking a little lurch each time she noted Roarke's deep tones. Adela wondered anew how much of Marie's sugar he had believed, pursing her lips in annoyance as she upturned a potato plant. And why had her father been so keen to greet Georges, even asking the other man to dinner, of all things?

Had her father finally noted her age and decided that Georges was her best and possibly only opportunity for

matrimony? Adela grimaced and dug the tubers out of the
soil with a vengeance. Half a mind had she to cook a
dreadful meal to terrorize Georges, but her father would be
furious with such churlish behavior.

And indeed, there was the matter of Roarke appreciating
her cooking. That thought made her warm inside, and
Adela stifled a smile of pride as she filled her pockets with
the dry pods of cooking beans. A rare treat it had been to
receive such a compliment, even from one who granted such
things so readily, and should she not mind the path of her
thoughts, she could easily let those few words go to her
head. Or, worse even than the words, Roarke's attention itself.

A sudden movement close to her elbow startled Adela,
and she jumped before she realized what it was. She grimaced when she paused to look, and turned to the men on
the step. Not for her, this task.

"Papa! A rabbit there is in the snare!"

Her father chuckled good-naturedly. "Well enough they
should know by now that our Adela will tolerate no losses
from her garden," he teased, and Adela flushed as she stood
amid the cabbages. He made to rise, but Roarke stayed him
and got to his feet instead.

"I shall tend to it," he insisted, and strode toward the
garden as the older man sat down again. Adela felt her pulse
accelerate as Roarke drew near, but she stood her ground,
even managing to return the smile he threw her once he had
glanced into the trap.

"Even two bold ones," he commented, and Adela felt her
brows rise.

"Are there?" she asked, and he looked to her in surprise
that she knew not their number. "Are they plump?" she
asked hastily, thinking they would make a better meal than
the rasher of bacon she had in the pantry.

"Will you not look yourself?" Roarke invited, but Adela
shook her head adamantly.

"I could not bear it, so soon before they die," she confessed all in a rush, knowing this to be a foolish weakness. To her surprise, Roarke did not laugh at her, though she could not read the thoughtful look he granted her.

"Well fed indeed do they look," he concluded easily as he knelt. "Mayhap they have been pilfering their meals in another garden of late."

"Mayhap." Adela nodded quickly, averting her gaze when Roarke pulled his knife from his belt, grateful that there was absolutely no hint in his cheerful voice of what he was evidently doing. She gazed blindly at the fruit trees behind the garden and tried desperately to think about anything other than those rabbits.

"Best 'tis that the task be done now, afore these two make three or four more to sample your cabbages," Roarke teased. Adela smiled at his jest, despite herself, and flicked a glance back in his direction to find him cleaning his blade.

"I can dress them," she offered weakly, and he shot her a sharp glance.

"Well I thought you had no taste for this task?" he demanded softly, and Adela swallowed with difficulty. In truth, she had none, but 'twas one that needed doing, and one that she had done often enough that it should not bother her as much as it did.

She managed to summon a thin smile. "Indeed, the worst is done," she asserted bravely, but Roarke was apparently not convinced. As she watched in amazement, he shook his head quickly.

"Nay, well enough do I think that the skinning is worse," he pointed out. "Will you not let me bring you the meat?"

"I could not ask this of you," Adela protested, wishing heartily that she could. "'Tis my task, truly, and I would not burden you with it."

Roarke smiled and shook his head with that resolution Adela was beginning to understand could not be swayed. "Enough have you to do this day, and naught have I to busy myself with," he argued, impaling her with his steady gray gaze.

"I will bring you the meat shortly," he said in a tone that brooked no argument, and Adela could only nod in relieved agreement.

Painfully aware of his gaze upon her, and that he apparently did not intend to start the task until she left, she gathered her potatoes and beans. She cast a longing glance to the cabbages, then to the step that her father had vacated. Knowing she could carry no more, but wanting the cabbage, she pursed her lips in annoyance. Roarke's chuckle drew her attention.

"Mayhap I could bring you a cabbage, as well?" he asked with obvious amusement, and Adela flushed.

"Aye," she agreed hastily, touching the biggest one with her toe. "This one, if you would, for 'twill get woody if 'tis left any longer."

"'Twill be my pleasure," Roarke returned smoothly. Adela wondered with annoyance whether there was anything that he did not mock. He stepped closer, touching the cabbage with his own toe as he unsheathed his blade again. "This very one?" he asked archly, that devil's twinkle in his eyes once more.

"Must you make sport of everything I say?" Adela demanded crossly. Roarke glanced up in surprise, but she could not check her words. "If 'tis not the cabbage I would choose, then 'tis my weakness in being unable to kill other creatures or—"

"Adela," Roarke interrupted flatly, and she halted uncertainly, hating herself for the tears rising to blur her vision. "No weakness is it to feel compassion for small creatures," he asserted softly, and she dared to look into his eyes, only to find those gray depths devoid of mockery.

"And, in truth, I do not mind cleaning the rabbits," he added in that same low voice, a mischievous grin transforming his features with an abruptness that startled Adela. "For well enough do I know that you will concoct something temptingly delicious. Should I not take care, I might well become plump and soft these two years."

"And dire consequences that might have for your nights of frivolity," Adela snapped, uncertain what lay at the root of that unmistakable twinge of jealousy his comment had tweaked.

"Aye, a bitter shame that would be," Roarke agreed unrepentantly, his eyes dancing as he glanced up at her once more. "Although, for a savory rabbit stew, the gain might well be worth the price."

Adela's lips twisted at his wistful expression, even though she would have preferred to stay cross with him. "I would almost guess that you knew of these rabbits when you turned down Marie's invitation," she teased, summoning a frown of mock disapproval. "Did you bait the snare, then?" she asked with false severity, but Roarke saw through her ruse and threw back his head to laugh heartily.

"Had I but known of the snare, I might have done so," he retorted, placing his hands on his hips as he regarded her indulgently. He stood but an arm's length before her, with those impossibly twinkling eyes, the autumn sunlight making bluish lights in his dark hair, and Adela felt her knees melt as though they were but made of butter.

"Would you have them for dinner, then, and indulge my fancy for rabbit stew?" Roarke asked in a dangerously soft tone.

There was that voice he used for intimacy again, and Adela panicked. Well enough 'twas to decide to spurn his attentions when his charm was not being lavished upon her, but uncertain indeed she was that she could maintain her resolve if he insisted on speaking to her in that sensuously low voice.

Did Roarke intend to seduce her, instead of all the women in town, despite his promise to her sire? No part would she have of this plan, but there was little enough she could do should he continue to speak to her thus.

Adela had to annoy him, and could think of but one way to do so.

"Aye, we shall have rabbit stew this night," she agreed easily, taking a wary step backward before she added, "Well enough do I recall that 'tis Georges' favorite meal. Had I but known he was coming this morn, I would have baited the snare myself."

Roarke's eyes flashed with something that could have been anger, but Adela pretended not to notice, sweeping down the row of cabbages with all the grace of a highborn lady, her pulse pounding in her ears at her audacity. He swore behind her, but she made no acknowledgment, smiling nonchalantly for her father as she approached the house.

And did it not serve Roarke right? she asked herself angrily when she gained the kitchen, feeling as low as a snail and furious with herself for that guilt. Who indeed was he to think that all maidens would fall swooning at his feet?

Adela's hands were shaking so badly that she spilled the water when she poured it into the washbasin. She wondered why her small victory had not left her feeling vindicated in the least. Had she not annoyed Roarke and forestalled his attentions, as she had wished?

The woman had a stone for a heart, of that there was little doubt. And a particularly small, hard and cold stone 'twas, indeed. Roarke skinned the first rabbit with expert gestures, finding the task he had proposed to do as a favor for Adela unexpectedly irritating. Not for him would she cook stew, but for the inimitable Georges.

And had Georges complimented her cooking? Not in Roarke's presence. Indeed, he thought viciously, the man looked not bright enough to tell the difference between good and bad fare.

How could it possibly be that his infallible charm gained him absolutely naught with this woman? She could not even be civil to him for more than an instant, and that presumably only because she forgot herself in that fleeting moment. Roarke gritted his teeth and gathered up the meat, pausing to cast the innards to the dogs.

Mayhap he should abandon his charm in dealing with Adela, he thought sourly. Mayhap she could only appreciate a heavy-handed oaf like Georges.

"Have you the skins?" Mathieu asked when he gained the steps, and Roarke handed them over, surprised at a certain reluctance to let them go. What was he thinking? That he would stretch them for Adela? And little enough would she appreciate his efforts. Well should he know that by now.

"A good size indeed they were," the older man commented, fingering the soft fur with a smile. "Adela will be fair pleased to have these," he remarked with satisfaction, and Roarke groaned inwardly. Never would he be able to guess this woman's moods.

"Indeed?" he managed to ask politely, and Mathieu nodded.

"Aye, stretching them she is, that she might line a cloak this winter," he confided, shaking his head indulgently. "More than likely she will sell the cloak once 'tis done, rather than keep it herself. Never does the woman think of herself, so like her own mother she is. Indeed, 'tis only taking her so long to make such a cloak as she keeps giving away the skins."

"Indeed?" Roarke asked, surprised yet again by another side to Adela that he had yet to glimpse.

"Aye." Mathieu grimaced. "Little matter did it make to her that I was concerned for her health last winter in that worn cloak she already has. She maintains that there are too many others who have less."

That confession sent an unexpected pang through Roarke and gave him an idea he would never have expected to have. "Mayhap we should stretch them for her, that she has not the chance to give them away," he suggested impulsively, but Mathieu shrugged.

"Truly, I have never troubled to learn how," he confided.

"Well enough do I know," Roarke admitted, earning a quick glance from the weaver.

"Mayhap if she were to receive such a cloak as a gift, she would be less inclined to pass it to another," Mathieu mused thoughtfully. For some reason, the thought appealed to Roarke, and he cast a glance over his shoulder to the garden.

"Well it seems that there are many rabbits hereabouts," he commented, and Mathieu rolled his eyes.

"Aye, that there are. And cheeky indeed will they get as the weather grows cold." The two men's eyes met, each seeing the sparkle of understanding in the gaze of the other. "I would not have her grow ill again this winter. Should you stretch the skins and I weave the wool, we could make her a cloak, mayhap for Yule. What say you to that?" Mathieu asked tentatively, and Roarke could not help but grin.

"A fine idea 'tis," he agreed, and Mathieu nodded with satisfaction.

"She must know naught of it," he pointed out, and Roarke nodded in turn as the older man tucked the skins away. "These will I keep until you can tend them," he whispered conspiratorially, and Roarke nodded again. His step was lighter as he climbed to the kitchen.

Georges would certainly never think of doing such a thing, he told himself with great satisfaction, smiling grimly as he gained the second floor.

Adela heard Roarke enter the kitchen, but did not turn to acknowledge him, so certain was she that she would give away the extent of her attraction. Woe could only come to her if he should discover that, for well she knew that he would relish the opportunity to tease her on that score. What mockery would he make of her then? Adela could not even imagine how cocky he would become in that case.

There would be no living in this house with him.

"Well do I hope that you can manage from here, as I am a poor hand in the kitchen," Roarke jested as he put the raw meat and the cabbage on the table beside her. He had a particularly adept hand with a blade, Adela noticed with some measure of surprise, for the meat was skillfully dressed.

"Aye, I can manage," she confirmed, feeling that 'twould be churlish of her not to make some acknowledgment of his work, but not needing much imagination to guess what he would make of any compliment she granted him.

"What have you done with the pelts?" To Adela's surprise, Roarke seemed momentarily taken aback by her question, but he recovered himself so quickly that she doubted her observation.

"To the dogs did I cast them," he said with an insouciant shrug, and she rounded on him, furious that he could be so wasteful of something of merit.

"Cast to the dogs?" she repeated in shock. "Have you no idea of their value?"

"Ridden by vermin, they were," he said, shrugging once more. "No value was there is such fur."

"Mayhap no value for you," Adela shot back, wagging her knife in his direction. "Mayhap the blooded classes have the opportunity to pick and choose which pelts they would keep, but we must use all that comes our way."

Roarke lifted one brow mockingly. "Shall I fetch the torn remnants from the dogs then, that you might patch them together?" he inquired archly, and Adela straightened angrily.

"I would only ask that you save any pelts for me in the future," she demanded, wishing her tone was not so harsh. Had he not cleaned the meat for her? Surely she should be more gracious, but the loss of two pelts vexed her sorely. Indeed, she would never get that cloak lined, and Papa would have her own hide if she grew ill again this winter.

Adela glanced to Roarke to find his lips tightened in irritation and felt immediately ashamed of her churlish behavior.

"I would thank you for dressing the meat," she began cautiously, glancing up in time to see that disconcerting warmth dawn in his eyes again as he looked down at her. He held her regard for a long moment, and the sudden lack of air in the kitchen make Adela panic. Without another thought, she plunged on, dicing the cabbage with unsteady hands as she spoke.

"Indeed, your skillfulness will surely be appreciated, for Georges has oft commented on the odd cuts I make," she confessed hastily. A painful silence followed her words, and Adela almost wished she could withdraw the comment.

"Aye, one must be ever certain that Georges' wants are satisfied," Roarke finally spat, with an acidity that surprised Adela. Always was he so even-tempered, and she glanced up in surprise at his words to find him fairly scowling. "Just who is this Georges to you?" he demanded impatiently.

"Courted me, he did," Adela found herself responding without hesitation, her tone rising angrily in response to Roarke's.

"And he thought not to ask honorably for your hand?"

"Nay, he asked," Adela confirmed flatly, slicing viciously into an onion as her lips thinned in recollection. "But I declined."

"And for this sage decision he chose to make sport of you?" Roarke asked, an uncharacteristically hard edge in his voice. Adela put down her knife deliberately and turned to face him, certain she had no interest in having him prying into the details of her life.

"No business of yours is this," she retorted coldly, hands on her hips as she faced him down. Roarke echoed her defiant gesture, drawing near her so that Adela was forced to tip back her head that she might hold his gaze.

"But after he so insulted your honor, both you and your father see fit to welcome him again to your hearth?" he asked with evident skepticism. "Evidently here is a man so worthy of merit that his favor must be courted with your cooking." The smell of Roarke's skin unsettled Adela, and she knew she took the bait more quickly than she should have, but she was powerless to check her response.

"Aye, it seems well enough that we have a weakness in taking men without merit to our board," she snapped, watching Roarke's eyes flash angrily.

"Should you think me of the same ilk as this Georges, you are sadly mistaken, *mademoiselle*," he replied icily. Adela lifted her chin yet higher.

"Indeed, I would not so insult Georges with the comparison," she parried. Roarke's jaw clenched, but Adela defiantly held his angry gaze.

"Insult Georges?" he demanded impatiently, his lip curling in a sneer. "And what know you of the manner of man I am, that you can make such a comparison?" As amazed as Adela was by his impassioned response, she stubbornly held her ground.

"A shameless wencher are you. I need not be a soothsayer to see that," she responded tersely, and Roarke shot her a venomous look.

"And what would you know of that?"

Adela inhaled sharply, outraged that he should think her so slow as to not know what he had been doing. "Well enough do all know that you have been taking your leisure in town with any woman who would have you," she spat. "For whatever faults he may have, Georges is an honest man, and would court only one woman at a time."

"Be not so certain that one who would so readily defame you is indeed a worthy man," Roarke shot back.

"How dare you presume to judge another?" Adela demanded hotly. "You who turn your charm on and off at your own discretion, that none might know the truth of your feelings. Do you think none saw how you readily manipulated the countess, or how easily you summon that smile that sends women falling at your feet? Insincere are you at best, a deceptive opportunist, if not worse, in truth."

Roarke's eyes narrowed, and Adela should have taken heed of how his voice dropped. "Make your accusation clearly, *mademoiselle*," he ordered smoothly, his features set to stone, and Adela was angry enough to do precisely that.

"Make my accusation? Aye, that will I do, but mind you do not blame me should you not like the way of it, for well enough did you ask," she retorted, the words tumbling from her lips in their haste to be heard. Not a doubt had she that Roarke was furiously angry, remarkable indeed for a man who was always in such good humor, but she was herself angry enough to take a deep breath and plunge on.

"Truly I doubt that you have ever had a scrap of regard for any other than yourself. So well pleased do you seem with your own endeavors that you have not any left for another," she snapped. "And surely it cannot be that you have ever approached any task with any measure of sincerity, for all of life is a joke to you. I shudder to think what jest you intend to make of us here for taking you under our roof. Little doubt have I that 'twill be a merry joke that none but you and your whoring knightly friends might enjoy at our expense."

"Enough!" Roarke shouted, his impassioned response doing naught to check Adela's disgust.

"Spare me the theatrics, indeed," she told him with a sneer. "No sincerity is there in your outrage, for well enough do I know by now that these words will roll directly off your back."

"Think you that I have no feelings, then?" he demanded angrily, looming threateningly over her.

"For any other than yourself, nay," Adela confirmed with an abrupt shake of her head. "Indeed it would seem that all you do is coldly calculated to serve your own ends." Adela fixed him with a bright eye, admiring how perfectly he had conjured the very stance and gesture of a wrongfully doubted man and believing not a bit of it.

"Indeed," she mused, fully intending to twist the knife in the wound, "I wonder if those women you so ardently court have any idea that 'tis impossible for your heart to be stirred." Adela would have turned away, but Roarke grasped her arm and forced her to face him.

"Think you that I have no sincere passion?" he asked in outrage, and she allowed herself a small, condescending smile.

"Certain of it I am," she asserted firmly, lifting her chin to hold his regard.

"And wrong indeed you are." Roarke's fingers flexed around her arm as though he could not check their movement.

So abruptly that she gasped in surprise, he hauled Adela close, and she had but an instant to note the flame in his eyes. Her own eyes widened in alarm as she guessed his intention, and she would have bolted, but Roarke's arms locked around her, imprisoning her against the hard wall of his chest.

"Fight me not, Adela," he whispered. Both the plea and the sensation of his breath against her lips proved her undoing.

While she hesitated to consider the merit of his words, Roarke's mouth closed over hers purposefully, and instantly she could think of naught but his coaxing lips. Her fingers slowly fanned out across his chest as he expertly kissed her. She was paralyzed by the fear that she was being manipulated, but knew all the while that there was naught she could do to fight his intoxicating touch.

Then her fingertips found the erratic pounding of his heart beneath them, its frenzied pace both an echo of her own and a denial of all her accusations. Adela gasped in surprise, and Roarke took advantage of the opportunity to slip his tongue into her mouth. She grasped his shoulders helplessly and closed her eyes against the tide of sensation rising hot within her.

"Adela," Roarke whispered against her throat, and she shivered at the soft flurry of his breath there.

"Adela, do you still find me dispassionate?" he murmured, and even though his voice was ragged, his words recalled Adela to her senses. Roarke's fingertips found her erect nipple, and the rage of desire that rolled through her when he caressed the peak through her kirtle made Adela shove him abruptly away.

"Nay!" she cried, watching Roarke's eyes flash. What was she thinking? Even knowing the kind of man he was, she had been foolish enough to permit him such familiarities.

Adela exhaled shakily, cautiously taking another step back from Roarke, who looked remarkably volatile. 'Twas an act, Adela scolded herself, unable to deny the signs of anger in the man confronting her and not knowing what to make of them.

Roarke, for his part, regarded her silently, the uneven pace of his breathing filling the kitchen, the bulge in his chausses unmistakable, the tightness of his jaw evidence that his teeth were clenched. His hands flexed, and she wondered if he longed to throttle her for interrupting his sport.

Adela retreated a hasty step farther away, and his eyes narrowed. 'Twas his fault she was on edge, she resolved wildly, certain beyond a doubt that he was toying with her again.

"Mayhap you should take your leisure in town this week," she proposed, not liking the sharp edge to her voice, or the way Roarke stiffened.

"Already have I told you that I have no intention of doing so," he responded silkily, and Adela swallowed carefully before she continued.

"Well you should know that no sport is there for you here." She felt her cheeks heat when Roarke's cold gaze swept over her.

"Well enough I see that you are saving all for the esti-mable Georges," he taunted and Adela shook one finger at him.

"Do not dare to mock the one honorable man that comes courting," she threatened, hating how high her voice had risen. Roarke cocked one dark brow and folded his arms deliberately across his chest as he regarded her.

"Surely you cannot be so hard-pressed for suitors that a man such as Georges—" Roarke barely concealed a sneer "—finds his bid uncontested?"

"Mock me not," she demanded unsteadily. "Only too aware am I of my woeful lack of allure, but 'twould be rude indeed for you to make the matter clear." To Adela's aston-ishment, Roarke looked genuinely surprised at her asser-tion, though well enough did she know that naught was sincere from him.

"Have you truly no idea how fetching you are, Adela?" he said softly, the warmth in his tone undermining her an-ger. Adela was appalled to find her tears rising yet again before this cocksure man who so disconcerted her.

"Do not mock me thus," she managed, the sight of him blurring with a veil of tears even as she spoke. "I beg you— do not do this here and now. Well enough can you see that I am not myself." With that, she turned away, unable to bear the sight of the pity her words were sure to bring. In-stead, the kitchen filled with an awkward silence, although Adela had no doubt that Roarke watched her carefully.

"Should my presence so distress you, mayhap I should take my leave," he finally said quietly, the very words send-ing another jolt of rage through Adela.

"Indeed, you have another pretty invitation for this eve-ning," she reminded him acidly, refusing to turn around. Again she felt his perusal, but she stubbornly folded her arms, resolving that mayhap he and Marie were well suited.

"Aye, that I do," Roarke concluded, though his voice sounded oddly strained to Adela. "And clear enough 'tis that my presence will be an interfering one here this eve."

By the time his words and tone permeated Adela's numbed brain and she pivoted in surprise, Roarke had already disappeared down the stairs. She darted to the window as he spoke to her father, her heart sinking as he strode toward town without sparing a glance back to the house.

Chapter Seven

Had any woman ever made him so angry? Roarke tried to quell the storm raging within him as he stalked along the cobbled streets, blind to all he passed.

His plan to lose interest in Adela by becoming more familiar with her could not be said to be working that well. He grimaced and sidestepped a bucketful of slops being tossed out of an upstairs window. Why could she not respond like any other woman to his compliments? Why did she always assume he was mocking her?

And who had planted this ridiculous notion in her head that she was unattractive? Roarke growled under his breath, more than a little tempted to show Adela just how fetching he found her to be. But he had promised Mathieu, and he forced himself to consider the other puzzles in her twisted thinking.

How could she possibly believe that he had no emotion? Truly it was ironic to have that accusation leveled at him by the most unfeeling woman Roarke had ever encountered, doubly ironic that she should be the one soul who could so readily rouse him to such anger. It seemed there was naught he could do to gain even a modicum of her attention, while Georges . . . Roarke gritted his teeth in annoyance.

Georges, it seemed, could do no wrong.

Was that the source of his fascination with her, then? The unflattering situation of being compared with the likes of

Georges and found lacking? Roarke frowned to himself, recalling that his interest in Adela had existed before ever he met the incomparable Georges.

Mayhap, then, 'twas simply the challenge. He nodded, to himself, pursing his lips as he strode and thought. Was she, then, the first he had courted who had not fallen for his charm? Roarke reflected and could think of no other.

Obviously, 'twas the challenge alone that motivated him. A matter of personal pride 'twas to never be denied by a woman he desired, Roarke reminded himself.

And desire he certainly had aplenty for Adela. His gut twisted in recollection of that kiss, and he wondered if he had imagined that Adela seemed affected by their embrace, as well. Had she not implied that she was less than herself when she begged him to leave the matter for now?

Roarke grinned. Mayhap her heart was not made of stone, after all, but merely heavily mailed. And mayhap he had discovered the chink in that armor.

It seemed to Adela that she could not refrain from touching her lips. The taste and feel of Roarke's kiss clung to her, and she found herself fingering her lips or running her tongue over them throughout the evening. Though her father glanced to her more than once with a speculative gleam in his eye, Georges fortunately did not seem to notice.

Indeed, Adela thought irritably, Georges seemed to notice naught at all. Her stew was consumed with matter-of-fact efficiency, making her wonder if he would have even been able to discern the difference had she indulged her impulse to prepare a horrid meal.

Too late she wished that Roarke had been here to share in the meal. Surely he would have found it to his taste, for Adela well knew that she had surpassed herself this night. And surely he would have made some comment about her cooking.

Too dangerous was that thought, and Adela rose abruptly to clear the table, certain she had no need to be missing the likes of Roarke. A ladies' man and a troublemaker he was, to be sure, and she would be a fool to grant him even a tiny corner of her heart. Sure he would be to leave it shattered, once he knew the treasure was within his grip. Her instincts fought against what she knew was the truth, urging her to trust him, but Adela knew better than that. Roarke was trouble, that much was sure.

And Georges was . . . what? She turned to watch him nod agreement with something her father said about the trade, and frowned with annoyance that the man seemed to agree with everything. Had he not a single thought to call his own? Adela sighed and shook her head, knowing without a doubt that he had not.

But what other possibilities had she? Time enough 'twas that she settled down to raise a brood of her own, and eligible men were not exactly beating down the door in their haste to offer for her hand. Georges and Roarke alone there seemed to be, and Roarke she knew was offering for a rather lower part of her anatomy than her hand. If that was the choice, well enough she knew which one she should make.

Adela summoned a polite smile when the two men glanced up. She placed the fruit and cheese on the table, surprised that her choice seemed not as easy to make as she thought it should be. The conversation flowed around her, but she was oblivious of its path, her thoughts returning unerringly to Roarke's kiss.

And his anger. Amazing it was that she had managed to provoke him thus, but she did not need long to ponder that before she guessed the reason behind it. Too accustomed was he to women falling in readily with his plans for sport, she concluded, her heart drooping a little with the certainty that he would surely find greener pastures in which to dally.

Indeed, he was probably with Marie even now.

That thought sent a chill along Adela's spine, and she straightened in her seat. Well enough did those two deserve each other, she reflected sourly, knowing she should be relieved at the prospect of Roarke finding another to satisfy his needs. Then would he leave her alone, she thought with what she hoped was satisfaction, but the idea only saddened her further, instead of granting her some respite.

When Georges finally rose to take his leave, Adela's emotions were in such a tangle that she could not think straight at all, and longed only for the escape of sleep.

"Mayhap you could walk Georges to the door," her father suggested idly, and Adela nodded without a thought. The two men shook hands, and she lifted a lamp, scooping up her kirtle as she made her way down the stairs. She heard Georges' heavy footsteps behind her and paused when she reached the door, turning to grant him a lukewarm smile.

"Good night, Georges," she said politely, unprepared for the heat in his eyes.

"Put aside the lamp, Adela," he urged. Adela frowned in confusion, her gaze dropping as she wondered what he was about, and landing on the bulge in his chausses. Her eyes flew back to his, and Georges smiled.

"A kiss would I have, after all this time," he asserted quietly, and Adela bit her lip in indecision.

Never had she kissed Georges, even when he had courted her before, preferring to maintain her dignity that there might not be whispers about her in church. Georges, she knew, would take her acquiescence as encouragement, but truly Adela could not find much harm in that.

Had she not spent the better part of their meal rationalizing why she should wed Georges? Indeed, it might be a wise investment in her future to show him some encouragement.

And should his kiss be as intoxicating as Roarke's, her problem would truly be solved. That unexpected thought dismissed the last of Adela's doubts, and her hands shook in anticipation as she set the lamp aside.

She jumped when Georges gripped her waist roughly and hauled her close, reminding herself that his lack of finesse was undoubtedly due to a lack of practice. Unlike some others she knew, who had bedded every woman from here to Paris. Reassured by that conclusion, Adela placed her hands on Georges' shoulders and lifted her face for his kiss.

His lips were wet and loose, and Adela could not help but think of the fishes lying in the market as revulsion rose within her. No warmth filled her belly, but rather a chill, and she braced her hands against him, tentatively trying to push Georges away, though he moved not.

She opened her eyes and found his blissfully closed, as he was evidently completely unaware of her lack of enthusiasm. Georges made an incoherent sound in his throat and backed her unerringly into the wall, his own arousal hard against her hip.

Adela wished only to flee, his kiss having proved more unappealing than she could have possibly expected, but her position left her little choice. She pushed Georges a little harder and, when he remained oblivious, panicked at the realization of how much larger he was than she. She pushed him hard, and finally he seemed to become aware of her protest, his eyes opening slowly. He lifted his head leisurely and gazed down at her with a satisfied smile, letting his hand slide lazily upward from her waist to cup her breast.

Adela twisted away indignantly. "Not that kind of woman am I," she murmured under her breath, flicking a telling glance toward the stairs. Georges raised his eyebrows and reluctantly dropped his hands away.

"On the wedding night, no such excuses will you have," he growled, and bile rose in Adela's throat at the promise in his voice.

"There will be no—" she began, then caught herself. What was she saying? No other options had she at this point. She flicked a glance to Georges to find him watching her carefully once again.

"Aye," he mused. "Well did I think that you were all bluster." He granted her another glimpse of that maddeningly smug smile, then swung out the door into the night.

"Good night, Adela, and worry yourself naught." He winked lecherously from the yard as Adela stood on the step, horrified at the words he uttered next in mock confidence. " 'Twill be soon enough we make our mating."

With that, Georges strolled off, whistling with a cocky self-assurance that made Adela long to wring his neck.

Roarke leaned back against the wall of the barn and watched the flickering light streaming from the kitchen window. Well enough could he imagine the intimate scene there, he thought sourly, pulling some of the hay over his knees against the chill of the night. And well enough did he know that his presence would not be welcome.

Hopefully Georges would take his leave soon, so that decent folk might get to bed.

Roarke smiled at that thought, trying to remember when, if ever, he had last thought of himself as "decent folk." But work had he on the morrow, beginning with the rise of the sun, if not sooner, and a good sleep was becoming a cherished commodity.

The horses nickered companionably, stamping occasionally as they perused the hay in their manger, and Roarke gave a glance their way, noting the stretched rabbit skins against the far wall. At least this evening had not been a total waste, he conceded, pleased with the size of the skins now that they were scraped and stretched. Mathieu had spoken aright, for they had been good-size rabbits. 'Twould be soon enough they would have enough for the fur lining of Adela's cloak, should all the rabbits hereabouts prove so large.

Provided she did not insist that he pass all the skins over to her.

He shook his head indulgently, knowing that he would find some way to pursue the plan he and Mathieu had made. No illness would she gain this winter for his neglect. This night, Roarke had baited the snare with Adela's kitchen scraps, that they might have companions by the morrow.

Mayhap he could convince Adela to make again the savory stew, the tempting smell of which was wafting across the yard to haunt his empty belly.

Mayhap Georges would not eat it all this night, and there might be some left for him.

Roarke scowled anew, disliking the place this man had acquired in the household in but a day. Mayhap Georges would commit some unforgivable gaffe this night, he thought, and wished heartily that it might be so. No wish had he to share the board with that oaf even once a week for the next two years, nor indeed to find himself often out here with the horses. 'Twould be too cold for such nonsense soon, and Roarke was surprised to find how much he resented the other man's dinner invitation.

Voices there were at the back door, and he looked up with interest, unable to keep from watching the two figures silhouetted by the light of a lantern. Roarke watched with dawning incredulity as Adela set the lantern aside and willingly stepped into Georges' embrace.

Too much 'twas that she should fight him, yet accept this other man's attentions, and Roarke found himself on his feet, his ire well and truly roused. To his disgust, the kiss went on much longer than he certainly thought proper, though if this was what Adela wanted, who was he to intervene? Had he not already tried to lift the scales from her eyes, to no avail?

But if she had already declined Georges' proposal, surely she could not hold him in any regard now? Roarke fidgeted restlessly, uncertain what to think when the embrace he watched covertly continued unabated. Surely such a kiss could only mean that Adela was interested in Georges' attentions?

Roarke shook his head in disgust, convinced that he would never be able to understand the woman. He stomped around the barn irritably, kicking loose straw every which way, telling himself that he was a fool for even bothering to stretch the skins for her, unable to dismiss the worrying thought that he was more troubled by the blond man's presence than he ought to be.

Roarke glanced toward the house once more, inexplicably relieved that the two lovers somehow had managed to tear themselves away from each other. Any ease he might have gained from this was summarily dismissed, however, by Georges' audacious parting words.

Roarke's head snapped up in shock at the man's confident assurance that he and Adela would soon consummate their match, and his blood boiled at the very idea. Adela could only be acquiescent for her part, though, he acknowledged with a measure of chagrin, for she—quite uncharacteristically, it seemed to him—made not a word of protest.

Well it seemed that she had made her choice, and indecision churned in Roarke's gut, along with a certainty that she would continue to haunt him should he not manage to banish her influence over his thoughts. His jaw set determinedly as her lantern bobbed out of sight, and he propped his hands on his hips as he considered the quiet house, as though it were his foe.

Would it not be for her own good to make her see the folly of her choice? Indeed, he could well kill two birds with one stone, should he steal but a few more kisses to ease his own mind and simultaneously strip her of this woeful illusion that Georges' was the rightful man for her.

Adela could do better than that oaf, Roarke was certain of it, and surely he owed it to the man who had done him such a favor to make the truth clear to his daughter.

Even if his means might be considered somewhat less than above rebuke.

Adela lay in bed and fought not to compare the two men's kisses, but her restless mind would not be stayed. Too readily did her memory turn back to Roarke's tempting embrace, and all the delightful little sensations it had launched within her. She tossed on the mattress, certain her pillow had been replaced by an uncompromising stone.

Unfair 'twas that she should have been haunted by that recollection even while Georges' lips were pressed to hers, and she fretted that Roarke's kiss would torment her for the rest of her days. And doubly unfair she found the realization that he had undoubtedly already forgotten the embrace. Indeed, whatever Marie had been prepared to grant him this night had apparently driven even the ability to find his way home from his mind.

Adela tossed again, not in the least satisfied to hear her father's voice rise in greeting and a familiar male voice respond. Well enough had Roarke eaten this night, she was sure, for Marie would have pulled out all the stops. Too late she wished that she had thrown the remaining stew to the dogs, and she pressed her fingers to her aching temples, wondering how she would survive two years of this man under her roof.

Or, worse, how she would survive the rest of her life enduring Georges' sloppy kisses.

Despite his best efforts to the contrary, it was late afternoon the next day when Roarke finally caught Adela alone.

He had been fetching and carrying for Mathieu all day, and his heart took a leap of anticipation when he drove the cart back into the yard, laden with the fruit of the spinners' labors, to find Adela in the garden. Well enough did he know that the snare had another occupant, but he feigned ignorance when he saw her start at the rabbit's movement.

Here was his chance to gain another telling taste of Adela and begin his campaign to convince her to abandon her plans to wed Georges. The very thought made his heart beat more quickly, and he schooled his response with difficulty, feigning a casual air as he greeted her.

"Have you another guest in your garden?" he demanded good-naturedly, and there was no mistaking Adela's relief when she looked up to find him laying the reins aside.

"Aye," she agreed, shooting a wistful glance down to the trap. "Though this one is indeed young."

Roarke closed the space between them with long strides, smelling the sunshine in her hair when he stood finally beside her. He fought briefly against a swell of affection as they both looked down at the young rabbit in the trap, sensing her reluctance to take the small creature's life.

"Eat more, they do, at this age," he reminded her softly, knowing full well that she was entertaining the notion of letting the little thief go free.

How like her 'twas to behave unexpectedly like this, to launch some warm feeling inside him and throw his careful plans into disarray! Roarke bit down on that persistent sensation that any sight of the sweet side of her nature invariably prompted within him, that one he refused to name, and forced himself to focus on his task at hand. Any tender feelings for Adela were definitely not a part of his plans.

"Aye," Adela agreed with a sigh as she fingered the hilt of her knife in evident indecision. "Aye, you speak the truth."

Roarke saw his opportunity and took not an instant to reflect before he acted upon it.

"Mayhap I could manage this task for you," he offered, gratified by the relief that filled those topaz eyes when Adela turned her gaze on him.

"Would you?" she asked hopefully, before she caught herself and shook her head determinedly. "What am I thinking? I cannot ask this of you," she amended hastily. "Indeed, 'tis my task, and you have much else to do."

"Mayhap we could make an exchange," Roarke suggested silkily, unable to believe his fortune that finally something was going his way with this infuriating woman. She shot him a glance filled with such suspicion that he was almost unnerved, but still he continued undaunted. "I will tend to the rabbit—"

"And I will make a stew from it," Adela interrupted hastily, as though she had guessed the direction of his thoughts.

Roarke shook his head slowly and permitted himself to smile in anticipation of the wager they would make. Her nervousness could only bode well for his plan, he concluded victoriously, knowing without doubt that mere moments stood between him and freedom from her spell. One more taste of her would loose him from her snare, of that he had little doubt.

"Nay," he said softly, leaning closer to Adela and noting with pleasure how her eyes widened slightly in awareness. "I will tend to the rabbit in exchange for a kiss."

Adela's eyes flashed furiously, giving Roarke adequate warning to grasp her flying wrist before her slap could reach his cheek. Her chest heaved indignantly, and her hand fairly shook within his grip, but Roarke could only marvel that yet again he had done something to earn her disapproval. Over a kiss? Surely she had come close to granting Georges more than that?

"Of all the unmitigated nerve!" she spat, undeterred by his grip on her wrist, and Roarke wondered wildly where his plan had turned wrong. Without a doubt, Adela would soon enlighten him, for she looked to be summoning her words for a lecture.

"What manner of knave would hop from one bed to another and expect a decent woman to fall readily in with his plans?" she demanded furiously.

Roarke knew his confusion showed on his face, and he interrupted her tirade impatiently. "Of what do you accuse me now?" he countered, savoring the flicker of surprise in Adela's eyes that he had retaliated before she regained her footing in the argument.

"Not enough is it for you to assault me on the Lord's very day and to continue your pleasures with another in town, but now you would return to insult me anew," she accused heatedly.

What was this? No pleasure had *he* continued the previous day, but she had had more than fair sample of Georges, for Roarke had witnessed the deed himself! Unfair was it indeed for Adela to accuse him of seeking pleasure elsewhere after that intoxicating kiss yesterday, when she alone had done so. Only too well did Roarke recall that kiss she had granted Georges so quickly after his own gain, and yet again the awareness that he had not similarly indulged chafed at him.

"Assault was it, then?" Roarke retorted irritably. "Quick you are indeed with that charge, though well enough did it seem to me that you enjoyed the embrace."

"Mayhap you have confused me with Marie," Adela answered sharply. Marie? The reference took Roarke off guard for a long moment, until understanding dawned. His anger was dispelled quickly as he grinned.

"Jealous, are you?" he teased, curiously pleased by the prospect, though his words proved soon to have been precisely the wrong ones.

"Jealous?" Adela repeated with blazing eyes, her voice rising. "Never would I be jealous of that tart and her liaisons, 'tis simply your assumption that I, too, will grant you such favors that stings." She leaned closer and prodded one finger into Roarke's chest, even as his victorious grin faded to naught. "A decent woman am I, and you would do well to remember that while in my father's employ," she hissed threateningly.

Roarke's sense of triumph disappeared completely at the disgust in her eyes, and he felt as deflated as he had after Denis had chastised him as a boy for pinching from the sugarloaf. Adela held his gaze for a long moment, as though expecting him to say something further, but, typically, he could think of naught to say in his own defense.

What had happened to that victory that had been so close within Roarke's grasp? What of his finely laid plans? What of his need to purge Adela from his mind? She glared at him in fury and, caught by that simmering topaz gaze, he could not summon a single word. With a snort of disgust, she evidently determined his guilt and spun abruptly away to stalk back to the house.

Suddenly it seemed that Roarke's tongue recovered itself, and he blurted out the first thing that came to his mind.

"Well do I wonder whether Georges thinks you a decent woman after that kiss," he mused aloud. Adela spun back to face him with no small measure of hostility, her kirtle swinging out over the cabbages in a wide arc at the speed of her movement and granting him an unexpected and disturbing glimpse of her trim ankles and calves. The vehemence of her gesture made Roarke feel like he had truly reentered the fray, and he granted her a cocky grin.

"How dare you?" she spat in a low voice. Undeterred by her indignation, Roarke stepped forward confidently. Once again he sensed that matters were aligned in his favor, and this time he did not intend to relax his grip on the situation until he had tasted Adela once more.

"Indeed, I wondered how you dared to kiss a man thus, right beneath your father's nose," he charged lightly, fascinated at the way the hot color flooded Adela's cheeks.

"No right had you to spy—" she began to protest, but Roarke interrupted her before she could truly begin.

"Spying I was not, merely coming home to my hearth," he denied flatly.

Adela fell silent, and Roarke marveled that for once she seemed to have naught to say. Well, now she knew how it felt, he thought with satisfaction, unable to stifle a soaring sense that he was getting better at sparring with her. Knowing the moment would not last, he pressed his advantage.

"Tell me, Adela, did his kiss make your heart beat faster?" he asked in a voice precisely pitched to gain results. Adela's gaze met his and darted away again, that very gesture telling Roarke that he had guessed the truth. Mayhap Georges was not as desirable as Adela would have him believe.

"Of no concern is it to you," Adela retorted, with somewhat less that her usual sharpness. Roarke took the last step remaining between them as stealthily as if he were stalking a wild boar, and though Adela glanced quickly up at him, he was encouraged that she did not move away. Indeed, it finally seemed that his previously reliable charm was providing results, and he nearly smiled at the prospect.

"Aye, but 'tis that, Adela," he murmured, leaning closer, that he might whisper right into her ear. Adela swallowed with difficulty, and he watched as she carefully licked her lips. Soon enough would he taste their rosy fullness, he reminded himself, lifting one finger to touch the softness beneath her chin. She exhaled shakily and shot him another sidelong glance, but, despite her evident desire to do so, she did not flee.

"Well you should know that I cannot easily forget our kiss yesterday," he whispered seductively into her hair, savoring the very scent of her. Roarke's errant mind summoned an image of Adela sprawled beneath him, and he could think of little else when his heart began to race in anticipation. Mayhap 'twould take more than a taste to eliminate this one's hold over him, he conceded, sliding that finger lazily under her jaw and toward her ear.

"Liar," Adela charged breathlessly, turning her head sharply so that his finger dropped away. Certain she intended to bolt, Roarke closed his hands around her waist, that she might not escape him now, and though she jumped at the surety of his touch, she did not fight him.

Roarke pulled Adela deliberately closer, the fear in her eyes when she looked up at him surprising him and giving him a moment's pause. Of what was she afraid? Of him? Roarke almost laughed at the very thought, certain that Adela could be afraid of naught, least of all a kiss from him, and pulled her into the circle of his embrace.

"Did Georges make your heart beat faster?" he demanded in an undertone, leaning down so that his words fanned her parted lips. "Like this?" he asked just before his lips closed over hers.

Adela melted against him, and Roarke's heart raced victoriously as her hands hesitated on his shoulders, then slipped shyly around his neck. He fanned his hands across the back of her waist, marveling that she could taste even sweeter but a day later than his first sample of her. Her touch was light as her fingers slipped into his hair, as though she were exploring him and uncertain of what she would find.

The realization that she was innocent, a decent woman, as she so vehemently claimed, launched a fiercely protective urge within Roarke that surprised him with its intensity. He found himself gathering her closer before he thought, as though he would physically keep any from hurting her. His hand slid up her back of its own volition, his loins tightening when he found that the cascade of her hair had wound its way loose beneath her veil.

He wanted then to see her hair, to kiss her and tease her until she cried out, to take her over and over again until this Georges and all others were permanently erased from her mind. Roarke nudged his tongue against her teeth, and when Adela immediately capitulated, her ready trust in him suddenly made him fear another would take advantage of her.

Not for Georges was this sweetness, Roarke resolved, knowing that oaf would scarce appreciate the marvel of Adela's embrace. And, indeed, he could scarce step away from her allure now. True enough it was that he would have to sample her fully to ease her hold over him, and everything within Roarke tightened in anticipation.

The barn, he thought incoherently, recognizing the chaos that Adela alone seemed to create in his mind. Naught else would there be but the two of them tangled in the hay, and he alone would it be who would show her the way of loving.

Roarke broke their kiss reluctantly, the promise of what lay just moments ahead the only thing that gave him the fortitude to do so. He nuzzled Adela's neck, pleased as the quick puffs of her breath against his ear revealed her own aroused state, and bent to scoop up her knees, fully intending to gallantly carry her to the private bower that awaited them.

"Nay!" Adela objected suddenly, her hand landing flat against his chest and stopping Roarke in mid-gesture. He met her gaze in confusion, further confounded by the fear he found there once again. Desire rose unchecked at her denial, and he bit down on the impulse to ignore her objection, stunned that such a thought would even occur to him.

"Adela, know that I would not hurt you," he said unsteadily, hoping to reassure her, but he only found that familiar anger lighting her features at his words.

"But you would readily dishonor me," Adela hissed. Helpless tears filled her eyes as she pushed Roarke resolutely away. "Think you that this would not hurt me? Think you that there would be no consequences for me to bear if you had your way?" she demanded when she stood stiffly straight, a safe arm's length away from him, her voice rising as she regained her composure.

Had he imagined that soft creature who had melted in his arms? Roarke could not honestly say, his own faculties of reason somewhat slower in their return to normal. Her assumption that he alone was at fault flicked him on the raw, however, for never had he taken a woman against her will. And Adela, as much as she might hate to admit it, and however briefly, had been willing. Roarke was certain of it.

"Typical of you it is indeed to lay all of the blame at my door," he retorted irritably. Adela's cheeks suffused with color, but she did not back down, her heightened color doing little to dispel Roarke's raging desire. Would she flush so when she reached her peak? Half a mind had he to toss her over his shoulder and make for the barn to discover the truth, but wrong would it be, and well enough did he know it, even without her reminder.

If only the taste of her did not so completely dismiss his recollection that he had taken a vow and meant to keep it.

"Well enough must it be your fault, for never has this happened to me afore," she argued heatedly, and Roarke felt the knave.

Truly he had sensed her innocence, though still it chafed him that Adela would imply that he was taking advantage of her. 'Twas *she* who had responded in such a tempting manner, he recalled savagely, she who had almost made him forget his promise to Mathieu, that promise that was only now easing into his recollection. He had only intended to kiss her once, to erase her haunting image from his mind. No intent had he originally to continue further, and 'twas only her unbridled response that had turned his thoughts in that direction.

'Twas she who was making him forget promises, cast aside chivalry, lose his manners. 'Twas she who tempted him, she who prompted this unfamiliar urge to take what he wanted and the consequences be damned. Never had Roarke come so close to losing control over a mere woman, and her charge that this was his doing alone did not sit well at all.

"Surely you cannot expect me to believe that," he charged angrily.

"Aye, 'twould be difficult for one such as you to believe anyone had ethics about such matters," Adela spat.

"And a fine accusation that is, coming from the likes of you," Roarke countered, refusing to let her win this match so easily. She looked lost for an instant at his accusation, but too well did he know the wiles of women and their mock innocence to fall for such a ruse. "Do not feign to misunderstand, Adela," he scoffed. "Well enough do we both know that you fully understand what I mean."

Adela propped her hands on her hips, a defiant glint lighting her eye as she stared Roarke down. "Mayhap you should make your charge perfectly clear," she insisted with a quietude that should have warned him of an impending storm. Roarke knew but a moment's dread before his annoyance urged him recklessly on.

"Too much is it for you to act the injured virgin, after the way you and Georges panted in each other's arms last eve," he pointed out hotly, fanning his face with an affected gesture. "Indeed, the heat of your embrace fairly broke a sweat on my brow."

"Why, you swine!" Adela breathed indignantly, eyes snapping, as she closed on him. "You *were* spying!"

"Hardly that," Roarke lied with a grimace, as though the sight had been particularly loathsome to view.

"No place have you to make such charges on returning from your own adventures," Adela pointed out coldly, and Roarke laughed humorlessly.

"Will you still not admit to being jealous?" he demanded, folding his arms across his chest as he regarded a clearly fuming Adela. She made a sound of frustration under her breath that might have been an expletive, had she not been such a decent woman.

"How indeed could I be jealous of what an immoral rogue such as yourself does with the likes of Marie?" she asked acidly. Roarke's ire redoubled that once again she had assumed the worst of him.

"Whereas you would only tempt a man with hot kisses, abandon him, then condemn him later for relieving himself elsewhere?"

"Georges, I am sure, did no such thing," she replied haughtily, and Roarke saw red.

"Then mayhap Georges is not much of a man," he sneered.

"Mayhap Georges is less of an animal," Adela suggested frostily, that particular charge hitting too close to home.

"Mayhap Georges was little interested in your kisses," Roarke responded savagely, surprising himself with the cruel accusation. Adela, however, merely smiled an infuriatingly coy smile and tossed him a look that spoke volumes as she turned coquettishly on her heel.

"Trust me," she commented with a low chuckle. "Georges was well interested."

That was enough.

Roarke stalked between the rows of cabbages in pursuit, grasped Adela by the shoulder and spun her to face him. Surprise lit her eyes just before he cupped her chin and kissed her hard, his other hand joining the first to slide into her hair and hold her captive beneath the raw possessiveness of his embrace. Adela sagged weakly against him, and he savored even this minute submission before tearing his lips away and glaring down into her eyes.

"Make no mistake, Adela," he fairly growled. "Should you kiss your Georges with such abandon as this, you are more likely to find yourself on your back than before the priest."

Adela opened her mouth to respond, but Roarke had little interest in anything she might say now. He released her abruptly and stormed away, feeling her gaze upon him as he bent purposefully over the snare, gritting his teeth at the realization that once again he had failed to slip free of the web she had spun around him.

Chapter Eight

Three days later, Roarke was still feeling dangerous.

Well advised was Adela indeed to grant him a wide berth and a wary eye, for even he knew not what he might do, should she tempt him again. Not a word did they exchange over those days, though oft Roarke felt her speculative gaze upon him.

And each night, before he left the board to pass the evening in the stables in his own sour company, he could not help but compliment her cooking. Though these days, his words were muttered and seemingly addressed to his empty trencher, that he might not have to see those haunting topaz eyes light with pleasure or watch a tempting flush stain those porcelain cheeks.

Never had Roarke been so completely enamored of a woman, and he knew not what to do. Every little glimpse of her fed his desire, the tiniest smile granted in his direction made his heart leap wildly, a similar smile granted to another sent jealousy raging in his chest. He even found himself glaring at Mathieu when she spared her sire a kind word or a laugh, but even knowing his foolhardiness, he was powerless to check his response.

And well enough did Roarke know what he would like to do to release himself from Adela's enchantment, his troublemaking mind teasing him endlessly with images of that possibility. But he had promised Mathieu. Not to mention that Adela would despise him if he made her less than a decent woman, and he was not quite ready to cultivate her scorn.

The only other option was unthinkable, and Roarke would not even permit the word to echo in his own mind, let alone allow it to pass his lips. A responsibility, a commitment, an entanglement, that he never intended to see a part of his life. Never. And if this agony was the price of remaining unfettered, Roarke would willingly pay it. The torment could not endure, this much he knew for certain, and he had only to ride out the storm.

If only his fascination with Adela showed some minute signs of fading, he might have been more encouraged as to the veracity of that particular theory.

Mathieu found him brushing down the horses in the barn after their run to the spinners' in the chilly autumn rain. The rain drummed on the roof of the barn, sending the dampness through Roarke's bones, but he lingered over his task, reluctant to go inside the shop and risk making a fool of himself yet again before Adela. Mathieu cleared his throat, and Roarke fairly jumped at the sound, turning quickly to find the older man in the doorway wearing a tentative smile.

"Bertha took the spinners' work from me," Roarke supplied, certain this was the reason for the visit. Mathieu shook his head and stepped into the barn, folding his arms across his chest as he leaned his hips against a bale of hay and regarded his apprentice.

"I know," he said matter-of-factly. "I came to have a word with you."

Roarke's heart sank at the words, and he turned back to his task, that his dismay might not be so clearly visible. Mathieu had guessed how he felt about Adela and, seeing the threat to his daughter, intended to cast him out. What then of Roarke's family's debts? Little more than a fortnight was it until Rochelle's nuptials. Would this throw all into disarray? He had failed his family, was all he could think, failed them because of his own lust. 'Twas hardly a noble confession to be forced to make, even to himself, and Roarke grimaced, not at all certain he wanted to hear what Mathieu had to say.

"Well it seems to me that you take your work quite seriously," the older man began, and Roarke closed his eyes against both the tide of failure filling him and the words he knew would carry to his ears next.

"I cannot help but think that your talents are being misused," Mathieu mused, and Roarke cursed him for taking so long to say the inevitable.

"Think you that you have time to learn another task?"

The words were so unexpected that Roarke turned immediately to face the other man, knowing his shock showed on his face when Mathieu smiled.

"Fleece there is to be sorted," he said. "I would see what affinity you have for the craft, should you be able to spare the time from tending these old beasts."

The craft! A test this was, that he might learn to weave! Roarke grinned outright and dropped the brush in his excitement at the possibility.

"Aye," he agreed, forcing himself to regain some measure of composure as he retrieved the brush. "Aye, I could spare some time." Mathieu chuckled, and Roarke knew the older man was not fooled, but he cared naught, barely able to believe that the bright promise of the looms was swinging within his reach so soon.

"This way," Mathieu ordered, gesturing back toward the shop, and Roarke schooled himself not to smile like an idiot while he followed his bidding.

They crossed the yard in silence, Roarke's gaze assessing the loose fleece piled in the small room at the back of the shop when they entered. Fresh from the sheep it was, uncombed, oily, and with pieces of debris caught in its whorls. He caught a whiff of the pungent scent of sheep wafting from the wool. Hard it was to believe that Mathieu would make this disreputable-looking pile into the beautiful cloth offered in his shop.

As Roarke watched, Mathieu lifted a chunk of wool, rolled it between his fingers and spread it out across his hand before he spared it a speculative glance. His offhand manner gave Roarke the unmistakable sense that he could have performed this task blindfolded with equal ease.

"Three grades of fleece are there, in my shop, at least," he said, handing the chunk of fleece to Roarke. "Of low grade is this." Roarke fingered the piece of wool himself, echoing Mathieu's gesture and striving to feel what was distinct about the fleece, even while the older man plucked another whorl from the pile. He repeated his fingering, nodded once and handed off the second piece to Roarke.

"Of high grade is this."

Roarke held one piece of wool in each hand and tried to discern the difference between them. Well it seemed that the one had a kind of silkiness that the other did not, and he peered at the two, wondering whether 'twas his imagination that the one Mathieu had deemed the higher grade seemed to have a dull shine.

Mathieu pinched, rolled and discarded several pieces of wool before his brows rose and he evidently found what he sought. He presented the third chunk of wool to Roarke with a flourish.

"And this is betwixt the two," he supplied simply, and Roarke fingered this third piece.

"'Tis the softness that differentiates them?" he demanded, but Mathieu answered him only with a smile.

"Many qualities are there that separate fine fleece from poor, but I would test your instincts alone this day. Feel the wool, smell it, listen to it, taste it if you must, but I would have you sort this wool—" he gestured toward the pile of fleece on the floor "—into the three grades. You may use those baskets." Mathieu indicated three baskets on the other side of the room, and Roarke frowned in thought.

"Most time-consuming does this labor seem to be," he mused, still fingering the three pieces of wool. "Always do you sort fleece thus?"

Mathieu chuckled and clapped him on the shoulder companionably. "Sorting is the breeder's task," he said firmly. "This is but a task contrived to test your instincts. And make no mistake, Roarke," he added as he paused on the threshold to the shop. "'Tis one you will repeat until you succeed."

Roarke barely had a chance to nod in understanding before the other man turned on his heel and abandoned him to what seemed to be a hopeless task.

When the others had gone home and darkness had fallen, Mathieu watched his daughter turn from the hearth in the kitchen, almost laughing aloud at her surprise at finding Roarke absent when the meal was ready. She looked to Mathieu, and he smiled as he pushed to his feet. Did he dare to hope that his instincts had been right about this man?

"I shall fetch him," he assured his daughter, and she nodded as he started purposefully down the stairs.

The shop was so dark and silent that Mathieu knew a moment's trepidation. Mayhap he had misjudged Roarke, he considered. Mayhap the man had fallen asleep or wandered into town to indulge in some diversion. Mayhap...

The sight of Roarke bent over the much-diminished pile of fleece in the back room abruptly dismissed Mathieu's thoughts, and he paused in the doorway to watch, knowing his presence had not yet been detected.

No need had the younger man of a lamp, for his eyes were closed, his brows pulled together in concentration, as his fingers moved though the fleece in his hands. Mathieu felt a surge of pride as the younger man split the handful, dispatching each piece to land unerringly in a different basket before him. He scooped up another chunk, his long fingers making quick work of that decision before tossing the chunk to its destination.

His decisions were quick, Mathieu concluded with a nod of satisfaction, hoping that they were also the right ones. Only too lucky would it be that Roarke might truly have an affinity for the work, as well as this debt to work off, but Mathieu could not completely quell his excitement as he watched the wool being sorted with more ease than he had expected after but one day.

He cleared his throat, and Roarke jumped, his eyes flying open in surprise. He frowned once more, quickly, as though startled by the darkness of the room, and looked to Mathieu with some measure of confusion. Concentration and perseverance, Mathieu thought with something like paternal pride. Good qualities were they for any craftsman, and he found himself hoping anew that Roarke might have an affinity for the work.

"Time 'tis to eat," he said quietly, and Roarke gave another surprised glance at the darkness outside the back door as he shoved to his feet. The younger man brushed off his chausses and shook his head.

"I know not where the time went," he mused, and Mathieu grinned, unable to resist putting his hand on his apprentice's shoulder as they made their way to the stairs.

"I will not be the one to tell Adela that even the smell of her fare could not distract you from your work," he teased, and Roarke shot him a mischievous glance as he chuckled.

"Nor will I," he agreed, and the two men laughed easily together as they gained the kitchen.

For someone who had supposedly been so tempted to roll her onto her back, Roarke seemed to have recovered from his infatuation remarkably well, Adela concluded sourly as she rose to clear the board.

And but a pile of dirty, unsorted fleece had it taken to replace her in his thoughts. Less than unflattering was that, and she blinked back her tears, wondering what she had expected.

Surely she knew better than to hope the likes of Roarke would hold her in enduring regard? 'Twas her cooking alone he appreciated, and though his praise was heady indeed, never mind his kisses, she would be wise to recall that her own appeal only rose when there was naught else to occupy his mind.

Fleece, she recalled, and cast Roarke a disparaging look, refusing to let her heart be softened when he passed one hand tiredly over his brow. Not the same man was this who had kissed her so ferociously, and even though her blood ran hot at the recollection, these past days she was evidently less interesting even than his evening meal. He even looked different as his beard grew thicker and fuller, its appearance seeming to echo the slipping of his more affected manners as he fitted securely into their household.

And 'twas not for lack of trying that Adela had failed to capture his attention again. Her offer to wash his shirts along with her father's had earned but a grunt of acquiescence; her attempts to coax a compliment by not only making a finer rabbit stew, but lavishing it with dumplings, had earned only a comment muttered in the direction of his trencher. Though Adela raised her skirts too high when she took the stairs, though one morning she had "forgotten" to fasten the neck of her kirtle and on another to bind back her hair, still Roarke disappeared in the evenings. Though she knew not where he went, her imagination was more than ready to supply alternatives.

How could he turn aside from her so readily? She stood and gazed out the window into the darkness silently as the men finished their meal, cursing inwardly when she heard the bench slide back from the board. Well enough should she have been relieved that Roarke had turned away from her before matters got out of hand, for inevitable 'twas that he would turn away at some point, but Adela could feel naught but regret.

* * *

Roarke held his breath the next day as Mathieu pursed his lips and checked his work. His thick fingers roved through the basket Roarke had declared of superior quality, his head shaking as he pulled out a chunk and wagged it beneath Roarke's nose.

"Feel this again," he demanded, and Roarke's heart sank as he did as he was bidden. It felt like wool, he was dismayed to find, all his ability to discern between the grades overwhelmed by the duration of the task. Now it all felt the same to him, regardless of the quality, and he raised his gaze to Mathieu's to find the older man's expression stern.

He had failed the test.

"Feel this again," Mathieu ordered. "Look at the length of the hairs. Only the longest can be spun into superior thread. Though this wool is soft and has the sheen of a fine grade, 'tis clipped too short. An error of the shearer, not of the sheep, but a telling one nonetheless." Roarke examined the fleece and saw that Mathieu spoke the truth, for the fibers were only the length of the last section of his thumb.

Mathieu dug in the "inferior" basket purposefully, producing a chunk from that basket with a victorious gleam in his eye. "Look at this," he ordered, spreading the fleece on his fingers beneath Roarke's gaze. "Tell me what you found at fault."

"The wool is stained," he explained tentatively, but Mathieu snorted impatiently.

"Think you that a sheep worries over the state of his coat when he chooses to roll in the dung?" he demanded impatiently. "No vanity has a sheep, and even the one bearing the finest fleece may be filthy beyond compare. Ignore the dung, and *feel* this fleece. Examine its luster, its softness, the length of its fibers, and tell me I am wrong about its grade."

Roarke did as he was bidden, nodding slowly as he felt the evidence of what Mathieu was telling him. He looked up with a start as Mathieu suddenly overturned the three baskets and bent to mingle the grades of fleece once again. He felt his eyes widen with horror, but Mathieu only granted him a cocky grin as he plucked the last whorl of fleece from Roarke's fingers and tossed it into the pile.

"Do it again," Mathieu bade him with twinkling eyes. "And this time, mind you get it right."

Roarke choked back his outrage and confronted the jumble of fleece anew, determination to succeed at the task flooding through him. Though he might have failed the test this first time, he would yet show Mathieu that he could succeed in this.

By Thursday, Adela could barely summon the will to go to market, so disinterested was she in food. Especially now that she suspected Roarke had turned not to another woman instead of her, but exclusively to her father's unsorted fleece. Only too clear was it now that he disappeared to the back room in the shop after their evening meal, not into town, and she had dared to peek once, only to find him frowning over the mound of wool.

That her appeal had been exceeded solely by a goodly quantity of dirty wool was not a revelation that would feed a woman's pride, and Adela felt herself scowling as she headed into town with her basket.

When she spied Marie, the other woman's expression revealed that she had been waiting for Adela. Adela's mood was such that she did not even try to avoid the encounter. Spoiling for a fight, she was, and Marie was as good an opponent as any. The dissatisfaction showing on the redhead's face redoubled her resolve.

"Good morning, Marie." She greeted the dyer's daughter with false cheer, taking warning when those green eyes narrowed to hostile slits.

"Happy indeed are you this morn," Marie commented, with an idleness that did not fool Adela. "One can only conclude that the rumors then are true."

"And what rumors might those be?" Adela demanded airily, refusing to be daunted when Marie smiled coyly.

"Why, everyone is saying that Mathieu's apprentice must have found something *easy* on his own hearth to so abandon his activities in town," she supplied, and Adela felt the color drain from her face.

"What are you saying?" she asked hoarsely, hating that her response evidently gave Marie such pleasure.

"No more than anyone else, I assure you," Marie said, dropping her voice conspiratorially as she warmed to her theme. "And considerably less than some."

"Surely you jest," Adela protested, but the other woman's smug smile told her she hoped for too much.

"Nay, Adela. Rumor is that Ghent's frosty virgin has finally thawed," she affirmed maliciously. "My only concern, of course, is what you will tell our Georges when the word that you have granted your favors to other than him reaches his ears."

Adela opened her mouth and closed it again, knowing only too well that any denial would be seen as confirmation of the tale. And well enough did she know that Marie would ensure Georges heard the tale, leaving no doubt in his mind that 'twas the truth.

No matter was it, evidently, that Marie's chastity could be doubted—indeed, did Adela not know herself that Roarke had availed himself of her hospitality the previous Sunday? The ready conclusion that Marie's charms, too, had fallen short of the appeal of the wool to Roarke bolstered Adela's confidence, and she lifted her chin proudly to face her opponent.

"Old enough should you be to know that gossip cannot always be believed." She satisfied herself with the comment, hating how ineffectively inane it sounded, even to her own ears. Marie smiled cattily, and Adela knew enough to dread her next words.

"And well enough should you know that the truth is oft beside the point," she pointed out smoothly, spinning on her heel to leave an astonished Adela in the wake of her swinging skirts.

* * *

Four times did Roarke sort the fleece before Mathieu pronounced himself satisfied, and he could not stifle the excitement that rose within him as he wondered what he might learn next. Could it be that he would be permitted to touch a loom?

But no. Roarke's heart fell when Mathieu led him to a large reel that reposed in one corner of the shop. Dowels were studded along a crossbeam at the top, and the entire mechanism stood about chest-high. The whisper of the working looms behind him filled Roarke's ears, tempting him with the promise of learning their magic, but he forced himself to listen to the older man's instructions.

One step at a time, he reminded himself. One step at a time, just as he had earned his spurs.

"A warping reel is this," Mathieu told him. "The thread that runs the length of the cloth is called the warp. See how 'tis wound onto the looms? The weaver adds the crosswise thread on the loom, which is called the weft." Roarke nodded his understanding, turning away from the looms reluctantly as Mathieu indicated the considerably less interesting warping reel once again.

"Well enough can you understand that each thread of warp must be the same length, that there not be waste," he said, glancing at Roarke until he nodded. "And inefficient 'twould be indeed to roll warp thread out on the floor to cut it. Hence the reel." Mathieu made a quick gesture with his finger, tracing a path from one dowel to another and then next in a convoluted pattern, then spiralling down to the base of the reel.

"In this way, a large length of thread can be measured without using a lot of space to do so. And the next can be cut to the identical length, by following the same path again. And should the threads be laid one next to each other on each peg and not overlapping, the thread has little chance to tangle." Mathieu spread his hands and turned to face Roarke with a smile.

"Simple enough 'tis, for the pegs are numbered. This old thread can you use until you learn the way of it." He touched his toe to a cone of undyed thread and left Roarke to his task.

Aye, simple enough would it be, if Roarke had had any idea what those squiggles called numbers actually meant. He frowned at the dowels, then picked up the end of the thread, wondering how he would make a convincingly good job of this without revealing his inability. Never had anyone expected him to be able to read, but evidently here that skill was taken for granted. He wished Mathieu had followed the path with his finger more leisurely, that he might have had the chance to memorize the motion.

From left to right must the path go, Roarke resolved firmly, for that was the way of most matters. And should the objective be to measure the most thread in the least space and keep it untangled, he reasoned carefully as he tied the thread to the first peg, it must always go next to the farthest possible peg without ever crossing its own path.

"Oh, Roarke, you have got it backward!" Adela chuckled, surprised when Roarke's shoulders seemed to stiffen at her laughter. Indeed, she had meant only to tease him, thinking he had deliberately made the error right before her, but his response made her wonder fleetingly if she could be mistaken.

But then he turned with a grin and dismissed her impression that he had taken insult.

"Aye," he admitted with a grimace. "Too concerned was I with not making the thread too tight."

Adela shook her head at him and stepped closer to his work, feeling that familiar tingling take residence within her when she stood close beside him. "But the numbers are there, as bold as can be," she chided gently, amazed when a sheepish flush colored his neck.

"Not used am I to looking for such small signs," he complained, and Adela spared him a sharp look.

"Have you trouble with your eyes?"

"Mayhap." Roarke shrugged complacently. "'Tis bigger targets one aims for with a broadsword." He winked mischievously, and Adela felt her own color begin to rise.

"Aye, evidently you were not paying attention at all," she teased as she unwound his work. "Your sight would have to be poor indeed that you could not tell a three from a seven."

To her surprise, Roarke did not make any comment, and his awkward silence prompted a thought to occur to her.

"You *can* read?" she asked quietly, and watched Roarke's lips tighten.

"Of course I can read," he confirmed hotly, shooting her a venomous look as he rewound the thread with a vengeance. "Simply unfamiliar with the task am I," he added, his very vehemence making Adela wonder if he spoke the truth.

"No shame is there in being unable to read, Roarke," she said softly. "Indeed, I meant no insult."

"I *said* I could read," he reiterated in a tone that brooked no argument. Adela's surprise at his insistence must have shown, for he shook his head and slanted her an apologetic glance. "'Tis just the pettiness of the task that feeds my temper," he offered as an excuse, and although Adela wanted to believe him, something in his manner made her suspect this was not the fullness of the tale.

"Aye," she agreed hastily, wanting to ease past the awkward moment somehow. "Well you should know that we all hate to warp." She dropped her voice to a whisper and dared to lean closer. "'Tis truly the only reason my father takes on apprentices, that we might pass off the task." To her relief, Roarke grinned, his shoulders relaxing as he tossed the thread in one hand and faced the reel yet again.

"Have you not the mercy to show me a quick way about this?" he asked in that soft, low tone that Adela could not resist, and she found herself winding warp onto the board before she knew what she was about.

"It can be neither tight nor loose," she advised as her fingers flew, needing to say something to cover her nervousness. "And the thread must not overlap."

"Aye." Roarke watched her path avidly, and Adela could not fight the sense that he was memorizing the order she used the pegs. Suddenly certain she had left her own task too long, she shoved the thread into his hand, shivering against the ripple that raced over her flesh when their hands touched for a fleeting instant.

"You had best continue yourself," she concluded breathlessly, her self-consciousness rising when Roarke's gray eyes lifted lazily to hers. He smiled slowly, and she was certain her heart completely stopped when his gaze dropped to her lips.

"Well it seems that I am in your debt," he mused thoughtfully. Adela took a quick step back, not needing much imagination to follow his thoughts as to how that debt could be repaid. The glimmer in his eyes sent her fairly flying back to her loom, even as he chuckled, but her trembling fingers made it impossible to work with any measure of effectiveness.

Adela breathed a sigh of relief when they managed to seat themselves in church that Sunday without crossing paths with Marie.

Immediately she saw that she had dared to be relieved too soon.

Several pews ahead, Marie cast a glance over her shoulder that could only mean trouble. The choir began to chant, the censers swung and cast the dim smoke of incense over all of them, but Adela was oblivious of the beginning of the familiar ceremony, her heart clenched in trepidation at what Marie might do.

'Twas not surprise that rippled through her when Marie leaned forward and tapped on the shoulder of a man in the pew ahead of her, though certainly Adela felt some measure of dismay. She inhaled sharply when Georges turned around, his gaze flying from Marie back over the shoulders of those who sat betwixt them to meet Adela's eyes. As she watched, his features hardened, his eyes narrowing as he glared at her, and she knew that, whatever Marie whispered to him, she had not heard the last of it.

"What is it?" Roarke murmured in her ear, and Adela glanced up at him, astonished that he had noted her distress. He cocked one brow, and she bit her lip, uncertain whether or not to confide her worries in him. But she could feel the weight of Roarke's gaze upon her as surely as if he touched her. Well enough she knew that she would not be able to hold her tongue should he continue to peruse her thus.

And what matter if she told him?

"'Tis Marie," she whispered. Immediately Roarke looked forward, then back to her. "Mischief is she making," she confided, glancing up in time to see Roarke's nod.

"Aye, that is clear enough," he agreed easily, surprising Adela with the piercing glance he shot to her. "Know you of what nature?"

Adela swallowed and looked down at her hands. Only too well could she guess what Marie had told Georges after their discussion in the market the other day. But what would Roarke think of such rumors? Mayhap it had not been such a good idea to begin to tell him the tale, for she should know by now that he would not stop short of knowing it in full. And too late did she consider his response to the telling.

Curse this man for the way he muddled her thinking.

"Adela," he murmured, and she dared to dart a glance to find him looking unexpectedly concerned. "Does she make trouble for you?"

Adela nodded quickly before she could think to deny it. Knowing that Roarke was waiting for a further explanation, and equally certain that having said this much she had no right to stop, she took a deep breath and leaned closer that she could whisper in her lowest voice.

"She means to tell Georges that you share more of our hospitality than our board," she confided, her words falling over each other in their haste to be heard. Roarke's sharp inhalation told her that he had understood, but Adela was not prepared for the way he stiffened, as though the charge angered him for some reason she could not discern.

It took but a glance forward to confirm to Roarke that Georges had indeed believed Marie's nonsense. Typical that was of that oaf, he thought with disgust, his resolve that Adela could do better than this man who held her in such low regard redoubling when he noted the angry set to the man's shoulders.

What manner of man believed the first rumor he heard of a woman he held dear? Especially if that rumor was passed by one of such character as Marie? Any fool could see that she was bent on making trouble purely for the sport of it, and Roarke could only conclude, once more, that Georges was more dim-witted than such as Adela deserved.

And what manner of men were there in this town, that they could not see the merit of a woman such as she? Roarke cast a scornful glance over the congregation, having half a mind to show them wrong in their whispered belief that Adela was cold. Should he kiss her right here and now, they would well see her passion. And should he take her to wife, he would be proud to ensure that her belly rounded with child in short order....

But what was he thinking?

Roarke drew himself up with a jolt and exhaled shakily, disconcerted that *that* word had even managed to filter into his thoughts. Had he not decided long ago that the marital path was not for him? Had he not resolved to live his life carefree and unfettered? He would not cast all those plans aside just to show the good people of Ghent precisely how misguided their thinking was with regard to one woman.

He glanced down to Adela and saw that she was trying to hide her dismay. Roarke watched as she twisted her slender fingers together, unable to look away as her brows pulled together, her teeth worried the fullness of her bottom lip.

One admittedly fetching and desirable woman, he corrected himself, feeling that protective instinct launch through him once again at the sight of her worry.

Roarke's jaw clenched when Georges cast a hostile glance over his shoulder. Nay, 'twas Georges who was responsible for the lack of suitors bidding for Adela's hand, Roarke was certain of it. Indeed, he would not put it past the man to have bullied all other contenders aside.

Roarke's lips set grimly, and he folded his hands carefully together, completely certain of what he had to do. Georges had to be dispatched from Adela's life, one way or the other, that the way might be clear for more suitable men. And it seemed that Marie was handing Roarke the perfect opportunity to show Georges for the oaf he was.

He slanted a sidelong glance to Adela and knew a twinge of guilt. Well enough did he know that she thought Georges her best marital option, but equally well did he know her to be wrong.

And he owed it to Mathieu to show Adela the error of her ways.

Without Georges interfering, who knew what eligible bachelors might come forward to offer for her hand? Roarke refused to acknowledge the cold lump in his chest that thought prompted and straightened his shoulders determinedly.

His only involvement in the Toisserands' life was the fulfillment of his family's obligation, and he would do well to remember that. The removal of Georges was but a favor to Mathieu, a gesture any decent man might make in his stead.

Yet again, Roarke's methods were unorthodox, but he hoped that this at least might show Adela the magnitude of the mistake she aimed to make in taking Georges to her side. Roarke nodded to himself in satisfaction and attended to the service once more.

Aye, once she saw the man's true character, she would scarce be able to show her gratitude to Roarke for making all clear. He stifled a smile, not permitting himself to visualize the demonstration of that gratitude while he yet sat in church.

Chapter Nine

"But a week am I away, and you cannot control your lust," Georges muttered from behind her. Adela spun on the steps of the church to confront him.

"I beg your pardon?" she demanded archly, knowing full well what he referred to. Marie had indeed been at work, and anger flooded through Adela that she had been granted no opportunity to explain.

Georges propped his hands on his hips, his scowl thunderous as he regarded her, and she tilted her chin defiantly, recognizing that she had already been condemned. If he meant to find her guilty so readily, then she would ensure he spelled out precisely his charge against her.

Several others stopped on the steps to watch the confrontation, and Adela felt immediately self-conscious, only her awareness that both Roarke and her father stood silently behind her giving her the fortitude to face Georges in such a public manner.

"Well do you know what I say," Georges growled. "Playing me for a fool are you, Adela, to tempt me so, then grant your favors to another."

Adela gasped at his audacity, but she had no chance to make a retort.

"So easy is it to make a fool look like what he is that I doubt Adela knew what she was about," Roarke interjected lightly, and a ripple of laughter rolled through the assembly of onlookers.

"Roarke!" Adela shot him a censorious glance and reprimanded him under her breath, taking a step backward as Georges' face turned a florid shade of red. She backed right into Roarke's hand in her haste to put distance between herself and Georges, and a shiver tripped over her skin when its warmth came in contact with the small of her back. Well it seemed that Roarke stroked her back once, as if to reassure her, before he stepped alongside her and the weight of his hand fell away.

"Calling me a fool, are you?" Georges charged, and Roarke shoved Adela unceremoniously behind him, his decisive movement belying his bantering tone.

"Not calling names am I, merely naming what I see," he countered amiably.

"No man calls me a fool to my very face," Georges roared. Adela could not help but note how like a disgruntled child he was. In contrast, Roarke appeared supremely self-assured, his expression that of one indulging a poorly behaved toddler.

"None but a fool believes malicious gossip so readily as you evidently do," Roarke pointed out calmly. His even tone did not deceive Adela, for she saw the tension coiled within him, the way he fairly balanced on the balls of his feet as he waited for Georges to move abruptly.

"This matter rests between Adela and I," Georges blustered, but Roarke shook his head.

"'Tis not so simple, should your accusation be what I suspect," he argued matter-of-factly and the surrounding crowd's ears perked up with interest. Adela's heart sank as they looked from one man to the other with avid curiosity, and she concluded woefully that this incident would be the talk of the town for weeks. The weight of her father's arm slipped over her shoulders, and she could only reach up to grip his fingers silently within hers in response.

"'Tis the business of none but the two of us!" Georges declared. Roarke shook his head indulgently.

"Then no reason had you to assault Adela in such a public place," he pointed out evenly, and Georges' eyes flashed.

"No intent had I to make a display," he growled.

"Either you intended or you thought little of your path before you trod upon it," Roarke argued in a reasonable tone, his manner evidently doing little to mitigate Georges' simmering anger. "Surely mine were not the only ears to hear your accusation."

"Too close are you to all of this for my satisfaction," Georges muttered irritably, and Roarke cocked one brow as the two men faced each other warily.

"Mayhap you should make clear exactly what is at issue," Roarke prompted silkily, the low tone of his voice the only sign that his patience was wearing thin.

"Well enough do you know the way of it!" Georges roared, pointing one heavy finger at Roarke. "For are you not the one who took what should have been mine?"

The crowd gasped as one, even as Roarke stiffened. "State your charge clearly," he suggested coldly. "Should there be an issue between us, I would have all understand what lies at the root."

Georges nodded vigorously. "Oh, aye, I will indeed, and no friends will you make with the telling. Three years have I courted this frosty bitch, and no sooner does she begin to thaw than *you* step in and take what she owed to me!"

Even expecting the accusation did not lessen the shock of hearing it uttered aloud for Adela, and she gasped in indignation, but when she might have stepped forward, her father's grip on her shoulder tightened slightly.

"Leave Roarke handle this," he advised in a low voice. "'Tis not your honor alone that rides in this matter." Adela was so surprised at his words that she followed his bidding.

"And you know this to be a fact?" Roarke demanded of Georges, his voice more still and cold than Adela could have imagined possible.

Georges snorted in disgust. "One needs not a soothsayer to see that you are well enjoying the Toisserands' *hospitality*," he said with a sneer, his words making Mathieu straighten beside Adela. The crowd of onlookers murmured to themselves restlessly, evidently not at all in agreement with this last statement.

"And one need not be a soothsayer to see that Adela is a decent woman," Roarke replied, to the approval of no small number of women in the group.

"Mayhap afore you touched her," Georges spat, and Adela had to hold her father back from joining the fray.

"Mayhap despite your attempts to blacken her name," Roarke countered sharply, his tone turning speculative. "Is that the trouble, Georges? Do you fear Adela to be too good for you? Must you drag her name through the mud to ensure that none but you will have her?"

"Why, you..." Georges growled out, his meaty fist flying in Roarke's direction.

"Nay!" Adela cried, but her father gripped both her shoulders to hold her back in turn. Roarke ducked in time, much to her relief, his eyes glittering dangerously when he spun to face his opponent anew.

"Missed me," he pointed out mischievously. The crowd tittered, even as Georges lunged forward in rage and Roarke sidestepped him yet again. The two men bobbed back and forth across the circle defined by the press of the growing crowd, as cheers erupted from the onlookers. Those cheers turned to jeers when Georges failed to land a hand on Roarke.

Adela entwined her fingers and watched nervously, convinced that 'twas only a matter of time before Roarke's teasing comments fell silent. Georges was too much bigger than him, although Roarke was light on his feet and somehow managed to stay a step ahead of his opponent. She felt her father's tension in the tightness of his grip on her shoulder, but not a word did the two of them utter as the calls of the crowd rose to fill their ears.

Finally Georges paused, panting as he fixed a baleful glare
on Roarke.

"So, you think to make sport of me," he rasped, his eyes
narrowing angrily. "Do not imagine that I will forget this,
you son of a whore."

Adela barely saw the silver flash of anger in Roarke's eyes
before he stepped out of the path of attack, the punch
Georges threw landing far from its mark. Georges grunted
when Roarke's punch landed square in his belly, and he
staggered backward, landing on his backside as Roarke
stood over him. The crowd applauded, but Adela saw the
anger in the taut line of Roarke's shoulders, and for an instant she feared what he might do. He leaned over Georges,
the blond man sparing him a wary look, and Adela strained
her ears to catch his low words.

"Should you continue to have trouble telling women of
quality from those of less repute—" Roarke gestured toward Marie, and the redhead's eyes widened when the crowd
snickered "—rest assured that I will be glad to show you the
way of things once more."

With that, Roarke stood and spun grimly to face Adela
and Mathieu, brushing off his hands as he crossed the distance, his movements insouciant, though the anger still
simmered in his eyes. Adela met his gaze and knew not what
to say, the intensity of his expression sending an unexpected jolt through her. Her mouth went dry, but Mathieu
stepped forward, shaking Roarke's hand heartily.

"And a job well done, that was," he said quickly, evidently trying to cover the awkwardness of the situation. He
offered Adela his elbow with a smile and ushered her toward home, Roarke falling in step on Adela's other side. "A
quiet dinner should we have this night, do you not think,
Adela?"

"Aye, Papa," she managed to agree, her mind furiously
trying to make sense of what she had just witnessed.

Roarke had defended her honor! Never would she have
imagined that he could take anything seriously enough to

fight for it, and this threw a whole new light on his character. She dared to glance to him through her lashes, only to find his jaw set resolutely.

Was it possible that he held her in regard? Such a thought was intoxicating and her heart took a little skip of anticipation. Was Roarke truly ready to commit to her in Georges' place? Adela's heart began to sing as she imagined him offering honorably for her hand. Too much was it to hope for, but... Why else would he have taken her side against Georges? Had he had no interest, he would have just let the matter rest. And surely now he knew that others in town would assume he had staked his own claim, that Mathieu had not intervened because he approved the match, as well.

Had Roarke known for certain that he could best Georges? She preferred to think not, and hugged his unexpected gallantry to her heart.

"Mayhap there are rabbits in the snare again," Mathieu continued cheerfully. "Well could I fancy some rabbit stew such as you made last week. Do you not think so, Roarke?"

Roarke seemed to exhale slowly before he chuckled under his breath, his good humor evidently readily restored, as he slanted Adela a glance warm enough to curl her very toes. Had she been mistaken when she accused him of holding naught in esteem?

"Aye, Mathieu, mayhap there are," he agreed with lazy ease. The way he cocked one brow as he held her gaze made Adela feel as though they shared a private joke. About what? The rabbits he had dressed for her? Or the irony of her making the same meal for him that she had made only a week before for Georges? She knew not, and did not truly care, especially when he smiled at her thus.

Adela felt her color deepen beneath his gaze, and she tentatively smiled back, audaciously slipping her hand into the crook of Roarke's elbow and savoring the warmth of his skin beneath her fingers. Well it seemed to her that Roarke smiled a little wider before he turned away, but she could not be sure.

* * *

That Adela was pleased beyond compare was readily discerned, but Roarke could not think of a good reason for her pleasure. He listened to her singing in the kitchen as he dealt with the pair of rabbits that had found their way into the snare, and though he grinned to himself at the sound, still he puzzled over it. The sunny smile she granted him when he reached the kitchen, although so fetching that he could not help but respond in kind, was another question to ponder. As was the fact that she did not even ask after the pelts of these two rabbits when she took the meat.

Should she not be dismayed?

Well enough did he think that she was better off without Georges sniffing around her skirts, but Roarke had not expected Adela to see that side of things for a few days at least. Indeed, he had been bracing himself for a verbal lashing for his interference, and these warm smiles that he was being granted instead were proving to be most disconcerting.

Only because he had not anticipated them, of course.

And Mathieu's manner was another enigma. His smug smile seemed to be almost one of satisfaction, though that made little sense at all. Roarke retreated to the barn and pondered the behavior of a household gone inexplicably mad as he stretched and scraped yet another pair of skins.

'Twas when Adela served the meal and brushed against him, not once, but twice, that he began to get an inkling of an idea of what was going on.

The second time Roarke felt the warmth of her press against him, he glanced up in surprise, only to find Mathieu smothering a smile. He glanced to Adela in confusion, and she hastily inquired whether the meal was to his liking, a little frown of concern worrying her brow. He reassured her and considered his meal for a long moment, his appetite waning as the truth dawned upon him.

Adela thought he made a bid for her hand in Georges' stead.

Panic rose within Roarke, and he struggled to control his response, thinking it inopportune to bolt from the board, when Adela had taken so much trouble. What had he done this day? Out of the frying pan and into the fire had he gone, without a thought, and now, too late, he heartily rued his impulse to defend Adela's honor. How else had he imagined she would see the deed?

He shook his head mutely and tried to eat some of the delectable stew, despite the dryness of his mouth, willing the moments to pass, that he might clarify his position with Adela.

Adela knew a niggle of doubt when Roarke did not clear his trencher as fastidiously as was his wont. The meal was good, and well she knew it. His lack of appetite made her wonder what troubled him.

Little enough time did she have to wait, for no sooner had her father abandoned the kitchen with some mumbled excuse than Roarke turned on her with bright eyes.

"Adela, this matter must be made most clear," he began with an uncharacteristically hesitant tone that sent her heart plummeting.

"What matter?" she asked mildly, refusing to jump to conclusions. Roarke swallowed nervously, and Adela knew she had guessed aright. He had taken on Georges that he might offer for her instead, and now that the moment was upon him, he was worried about her response.

Truly, how could he doubt that she would be thrilled to be with him? Had he not noticed that she was powerless against his kisses? Well enough she knew that her touch seemed to affect him. Did he not understand that it was only a fear for her honor that had kept her from him this long? And should that no longer be an issue, well, the very thought made Adela warm all over.

"This afternoon," he said hastily, shoving one hand through his hair as he glanced wildly about the kitchen, as though he might find salvation hidden in one of the pots or beneath the board. Adela watched him with bemusement, marveling that he could be so terrorized by such a simple matter, such a natural matter between man and woman, and felt a warm glow of affection begin to buzz inside her.

"You must understand that I did not mean to make a bid for your hand by challenging Georges," he added quickly, his expression imploring as his gaze locked with hers once more.

This was not what Adela had expected to hear, and for a moment she could make no sense of Roarke's words.

Then she was quite certain she must have misunderstood. Why else indeed would he have challenged Georges?

"I beg your pardon?" she asked in a low voice, determined to have the matter absolutely clear before she responded. Roarke threw her a look of exasperated annoyance, and Adela's trepidation grew in that brief moment.

He did not mean to offer for her hand?

"I would not want you to assume from this afternoon that I intend to offer for your hand," he explained carefully, and Adela saw red. Why ever not? Was that not what he had done?

"What then did you intend to do?" she demanded sharply, and some of her anger must have shown in her eyes, for Roarke took a tentative step backward. She folded her arms decisively across her chest and regarded him as her anger rose to a rolling boil.

"Defending your honor I was," he claimed wildly. "'Twas that and no more."

"And now I should thank you for dismissing the only suitor I have?" she asked coldly, watching as Roarke swallowed carefully.

"Not good enough for you was he," he stated carefully, evidently keeping a wary eye upon her. Was he concerned she might attack him? Adela almost laughed aloud at the thought, sorely tempted as she was to do just that. Curse him for meddling!

"And so you decided that I should die a spinster rather than wed the likes of Georges," she concluded acidly. "Truly, Roarke, you have done me an honor beyond compare."

"There will be others once he is known to be gone," Roarke insisted, his tone becoming cajoling as he continued to make his appeal. "Well enough will you see the wisdom of what I have done when you have time to reflect upon it."

"And time I shall have aplenty, from the look of it."

"Adela," he said firmly. "Time will show me to have been right. Why, any moment now there might be another, finer suitor at your door."

Adela could not help but laugh. "Oh, aye, there will be hundreds, once they hear that my father's apprentice aims to fight each one he finds unworthy of me." To her astonishment, Roarke colored deeply at her charge and seemed genuinely discomfited.

"Well I told you that I staked no claim," he reminded her through gritted teeth, and Adela had had enough.

"Well enough you might have told me, but rest assured that I am not alone in drawing that conclusion," she informed him, watching in amazement as he blanched. His expression was horrified when he glanced up to her. "Oh, and so sorry a fate is it to be matched with me as that?" Adela demanded, hurt that he could respond thus to the very idea.

And to think she had been stupid enough to think that he held her in regard.

"Adela, 'tis not you," Roarke said quietly, the lowness of his tone revealing his sincerity, and she shot him a suspicious glance. He looked noticeably uncomfortable, as though he would rather run to Paris than have this conversation, and she set her shoulders stubbornly as she waited.

"Do continue," she prompted impatiently and Roarke made a helpless gesture with one hand.

"'Tis any woman," he muttered, throwing her an imploring glance.

"Oh, spare me such nonsense." Adela scoffed at his confession. "Surely you cannot expect me to believe that you never intend to take a wife."

"Never," Roarke asserted, holding her gaze determinedly. "Never will I take that vow, never will one woman hold sway over me."

"Never?" Adela repeated skeptically but Roarke nodded with vigor.

"Never," he reiterated flatly, lifting one finger in her direction in admonishment. "And you would do well to recall that simple fact, should you even begin to have any other ideas."

Adela opened her mouth to protest, but Roarke was already halfway to the stairs, unsettling a sack of flour as he darted across the floor and leapt onto the top step. The sack toppled and fell, and he glanced over his shoulder in alarm, just before he disappeared below. The door slammed downstairs, and Adela stepped to the window, watching him stride across the yard as though the very hounds of hell were nipping at his heels.

For a long moment, Adela stood in amazement, unable to fathom what could make Roarke lose his artfully controlled composure, especially over such a simple discussion. Then, slowly, as the golden autumn sunlight slanted through the kitchen window, she began to smile in understanding.

Roarke had half lost the fight, and he did not even know it yet. Well, Adela would be more than happy to ensure that he fully understood.

Roarke's breathing was uneven when he reached the stables, and he paced their meager length and back restlessly before he knew what he was about. Everything within him bade him turn his back on this house and run as far as he was able, but he could not, and well he knew it. The honor of his family was at stake, and but two weeks of his task had he served.

Two weeks! Some macabre joke it was that this torment had scarcely begun, and he ran one hand through his hair in frustration. Had she truly ensnared him so completely in but a fortnight? Nay, 'twas at the fair, when she had not fallen prey to his charms as readily as he expected, that Adela had captured his attention with a vengeance.

And now he knew that only the fullest taste of her would suffice to ease her influence over his mind, and even that he was beginning to doubt. Had not every taste of her lips drawn him tighter into her web? His luck would be to find that bedding her only whetted his appetite for yet more.

Which led inevitably to the idea of commitment that he so abhorred.

For he had made no jest when he explained his view to Adela. Never did he intend to take a spouse, and he would cling to that objective as long as he was able.

If only his determination was not beginning to show a markedly feeble grip.

But what alternative was there? Well he knew that he could not simply take Adela and cast her aside for another. A disservice would that be to her, and a travesty of his respect for Mathieu, never mind the promise he had made. On the other hand, Roarke acknowledged a niggling concern that he would find no man who courted Adela adequate for the task.

That he should spend two years of his life fighting off Adela's admirers was fate enough to make Roarke groan aloud, and he paced the length of the barn impatiently yet again.

Indeed, they might not all be as slow as Georges. He could get hurt at this foolhardy task.

Roarke sighed in exasperation and cast a desperate glance across the yard to the house, his breath catching in his throat at the sight of Adela unbraiding her hair. He could not look away, whatever his will, for the dying sunlight etched her in rosy golden hues that readily recalled to him the softness of her skin beneath his hand.

She appeared unaware of him, hidden in the shadows below, and Roarke felt his arousal as she shook the gleaming cascade of hair out over her shoulder. Adela smiled softly to herself, and he fancied he could hear her singing as she began to comb out its length.

He easily recalled her standing at the top of the stairs in her wisp of a chemise, that same cloud of hair cast over her shoulders, her slender perfection outlined beneath the sheer cloth, and he felt his fingers clench. Too readily could he imagine her combing her hair thus each night, too easily could he recall the scent of her skin, the soft invitation of her lips, and his errant mind pictured her joining him thus each night in bed.

Roarke swallowed carefully, reasoning that he had indeed been too long without a woman, but knowing in the same moment that he wanted no other. None but Adela, with her gleaming hair. She put down the comb, and he held his breath as her fingers fell to the neckline of her kirtle. Adela unfastened the apricot wool, lifting it from her skin just as she turned away. Though he caught but a glimpse of her chemise, and no more than the sight of the falling wool when she stepped away from the window, his imagination was quick to visualize more, and he turned back into the dark barn with despair.

How indeed would he free himself from Adela's spell before something happened he would regret?

When Adela came down the next morning with her hair unbound and her feet bare, Roarke knew that he was in serious trouble. She yawned as leisurely as a cat before the hearth, and stoked the fire up carefully, as though unaware that he lay an arm's length away on his pallet, and he found himself watching hungrily through his lashes as she stretched lazily.

Her kirtle was yet unlaced, and he fancied he could see the shadowy outline of her full breasts, the round silhouette of a hardened nipple, and thought he would come completely undone. She rubbed the back of her neck as the glow of the rising flames illuminated her, and let her head roll back as her lashes fluttered over her cheeks. 'Twas all Roarke could do not to drag her down beside him and make her moan aloud.

He bit down hard on his desire, rolling over to face the wall as though he were yet asleep, so that he could stop watching her.

Two years, he thought, and closed his eyes in anguish. Never would he make it, and he seriously entertained the thought of finding Adela a spouse, that she might be wed and away from here. The very idea disturbed him deeply, and he could not even bear to think upon it. He shook his head in frustration against the addled state of his thoughts.

Adela strolled past him, and Roarke covertly watched her bare feet. The soft scent of her skin, wafting to him, made him writhe in anguish. His fingers flexed beneath the blanket as he realized that he could reach out and stroke that delicate arch from where he lay. One more taste, he promised himself before he regained his senses and pulled himself back from the precipice just in time.

"Roarke?" Adela asked softly, and Roarke could only feign sleep in the hope that she might go away. Should she spare a downward glance, there would be little enough doubt in her mind whether he was awake, he thought wryly, for he was certain he had never been so aroused in his life.

From the sight of her feet, of all things.

"Are you awake?" she whispered. The brush of something soft against his cheek, and the proximity of her voice, made Roarke's eyes fly open in alarm. Adela smiled, and he saw too late that she was leaning over him. Panic rose in his chest, and he made to bolt, but Adela stayed him by dropping one finger to his lips.

One petal-soft finger. Roarke swallowed carefully and dared to raise his gaze to hers.

"Shh…" she murmured, but before he could question her demand, that fingertip slid slowly across his bottom lip, its very movement doing dangerous things to Roarke's equilibrium. He closed his eyes against the tide of sensation, desperately trying to coax his sleep-dazed mind into finding a solution.

"Shh…" she murmured again, much too close. Roarke's eyes flew open, to find her lips but a finger's breadth from his and rapidly closing that space. Her fingertips slid gently through his beard when he might have protested, and the caress completely undid his resolve to move away. One delicious instant of temptation, and he tasted Adela's softness once more, her sleepy scent assaulting him and making him almost forget himself.

Roarke raised his hands to push her away, but the soft tangle of her hair twined around his fingers, and he was lost. He rolled to his back, his hands fitting around the neat indentation of Adela's waist as he drew her down on top of him, savoring the weight of her breasts on his chest. He swallowed her gasp of surprise when his hardness imprinted itself against her belly, delighting in the golden net of her hair spread over both of them and the way the firelight was trapped in its web.

A tread on the stairs brought Adela's head up with a snap, and she gasped under her breath as she recalled her place. What was she thinking? Indeed, she had thought only to tempt Roarke, but matters had gotten out of control.

Undeterred by her retreat, he was running a row of kisses down her throat, and Adela closed her eyes as the warmth of his mouth closed over her aching nipple. She could swoon beneath such a sweet embrace, and felt inclined to do precisely that, when another footfall brought her up short again.

"Roarke!" she whispered urgently, but he barely opened his eyes, the lazy intent in his sleepy smile making her bones melt like butter.

"My father!" she muttered, and he nodded for a heart-beat before his eyes flew open with shock. Adela found herself on her feet in a flash. Roarke squatted dazedly before the fire, as though he tended it, though he did not even pick up the poker. She drew her kirtle closed against the chill morning air with shaking fingers just before her father stepped into the room with a cheery morning grin. A glance to Roarke confirmed that he was more than a little shaken by their kiss, as well, a fact that set Adela's heart to singing even as she fought against her laughter that he looked so perplexed.

That was naught, Roarke, she promised him silently while she struggled to steady her own uneven breathing. Indeed, she had but begun.

Although Roarke had not been quite certain of it at first, by midweek he was convinced that Adela was deliberately trying to drive him mad.

Those first few kisses could merely have been a result of circumstances, opportunity and the thrum of attraction between them. And mayhap she truly had been sleepy Monday morn and forgotten to bind her hair, or mayhap she was more comfortable with his presence now that he had been in residence several weeks.

Mayhap.

Roarke tried to give her the benefit of the doubt. Struggled to do so, in fact, for he could not believe that Adela, of all women, would set out to seduce him, but the evidence was strong to the contrary. Well it seemed that he could not turn around without catching a glimpse of her in some fetchingly disheveled state or see the flash of a well-turned ankle or spy the glimmer of her hair.

And as if that were not enough, she was unbearably sweet to him, thoughtful of his needs beyond compare. Her cooking surpassed anything previous, though Roarke found himself so befuddled that he could barely touch his meal, which only prompted her wide-eyed concern for his health. Truly he had thought he might die of arousal the night before, when she had insisted on feeling the heat of his brow, the motion bringing her full breasts into tempting proximity and the scent of her skin close enough to tease his nostrils.

Then there were her kisses. Indeed, he could scarcely mistake her intent when she cornered him and teased him with those soft and sultry kisses. To his dismay, Adela had discovered his vulnerability in the mornings, and it seemed that each dawn he awoke to her feather-light touch against his lips, the sunlight filtering through her hair.

The fact that she hunted him might have been a source of mingled pleasure and wonder had Roarke not been pledged to refrain from touching her. As it was, she tempted and teased him until it well seemed he was living his life in a painful state of arousal. A state that he was not even certain eased when he slept, for he surely awoke in precisely the same condition.

And his conundrum was such that he had no desire to take his leisure elsewhere. This troubled Roarke deeply, for he knew it could bode no good. Indeed, he did try to go into town one night, only to find himself back on the Toisserands' hearth with but one beer under his belt before even Mathieu had retired.

Pathetic, he told himself, though the way his heart leapt whenever Adela gifted him with a smile belied his conclusion.

Roarke would not permit himself to fantasize about taking her, for that could only undermine his rapidly eroding resolve to keep his promise to Mathieu. Too easy would it be one morning when he awoke to find the soft press of her lips on his to simply roll over and have the deed be done.

But no, 'twould not be right, and well he knew it.

Roarke considered the warp wound on the reel and conceded that 'twas the best he had done yet in keeping the threads of even tension and smoothly in line. Remarkable, really, that he had done so well, considering his state, but he had forced himself to concentrate, focusing his attention that for a few hours, at least, he could keep Adela from his thoughts. He felt a presence beside him and glanced up to find Mathieu appraising his work.

"Your best effort yet, it is," the older man said with a nod. "It well seems you might have a talent for this work indeed." Roarke felt his chest swell at the unexpected praise, and dared to smile.

"I hope so," he said, unable to resist a covert glance to the gently rocking looms. Mathieu noted his gesture and smiled.

"Well enough do I know your interest that you need not try to hide it from me," he chided, and for one wild moment, Roarke feared he had guessed his desire for Adela. But no, Mathieu looked indulgently to the looms, and Roarke released the breath he had not realized he had been holding while he nodded agreement.

"Indeed, it seems to me that 'tis time enough your work was such that you could lose yourself in it," Mathieu mused, and Roarke began to hope. "Come," Mathieu said. "An old loom is there here that is not in use. Bring your warp, for 'tis time for you to begin to learn."

Roarke stifled a jubilant shout, almost grasping his carefully wound warp outright and ruining its fastidiously achieved order before Mathieu stayed his movement. The older man gripped the warp firmly in two places, showing Roarke how best to remove it from the reel, and he mimicked the gesture, his heart singing with delight.

He was going to learn to weave!

Chapter Ten

On Friday eve, Mathieu had a guild meeting to attend, and Adela drew a deep breath when he departed early, knowing that this was her opportunity. Tonight she would truly make her play for Roarke.

Although he had responded beyond her wildest dreams to her surprise kisses, and indeed seemed quite agitated by her new ploy to gain his attentions, she sensed he was trapped in indecision. Always did he put her aside or bolt for cover, should he spy her early enough, and this was far from satisfactory. Adela meant to wed the man, and this night she would drive him to the edge and ensure her goal was met.

She smoothed her kirtle carefully when she heard Roarke's tread on the stairs, his whistle making her smile despite her nervousness. Evidently he had had success this day in warping the loom, and she dared for an instant to imagine that already were they wed, that each and every night he came to her thus, that the evening would end with them abed together in loving and respectable fashion.

The very thought made a lump rise in her throat and redoubled her resolve to see this matter through. Not so easily would she let Roarke slip free of the marital snare, for they were blessed by an uncommon awareness of each other. And that could only bode well for the future.

Roarke gained the kitchen, and Adela felt her heart swell with love at the very sight of him, wanting to run her fingers through the unruly wave of his dark hair, wanting the thick prickle of his growing beard against his lips, his strong fingers curved around her breast.

Not yet, she warned herself. She must take this slowly, should she wish to gain the desired result.

She smiled in greeting to Roarke, not missing the quick glance he darted around the kitchen when he realized they were alone. She turned to stir the stew to hide her amusement.

"Where is Mathieu?" he demanded. "Shall I fetch him for dinner?" Adela glanced over her shoulder, not surprised to find Roarke looking ready to bolt back down the stairs.

"Gone to a guild meeting is he," she supplied in her most matter-of-fact tone, knowing that anything else would see Roarke gone. "'Tis just the two of us this eve, I fear."

Roarke seemed to hesitate for a moment at the head of the stairs at that bit of news, as if indecisive about his path, so Adela continued on, hoping to reassure him. No success would she have should he take it into his head to leave now.

"I heard you whistling," she commented with apparent idleness, fixing her attention on final preparations for their meal. "Have you had some success, then, this day?"

"Aye," Roarke admitted warily, and she saw that he took a more resolute stance, though still he did not move from the top of the stairs, his fingers tapping nervously on the rail.

"Warping a loom, are you not?" she asked, sparing him a cursory smile completely devoid of intent. Roarke's fingers stopped tapping, and he took a step toward the table.

"Aye," he agreed with more enthusiasm. "Mathieu has permitted me to warp up the old loom in the corner. It seems it is no longer used."

"Aye," Adela agreed easily, frowning at the board, as though the possibility that she had forgotten something occupied all her thoughts. Roarke stepped closer, and she smothered a smile of anticipation, unable to believe that this eve might go so well. "Too narrow is it for the cloth widths we are obliged to make these days, although 'tis a fine loom, and Papa is loath to discard it.''

"Well constructed does it seem to be," Roarke said as he took his seat at the board.

"Indeed, my grandsire hand-carved the reed," Adela contributed, and Roarke flicked her a surprised glance.

"No idea had I," he said, with no small measure of astonishment, and Adela smiled back, leaning closer to fill his trencher with stew.

"Aye, good with his hands was he. I suspect Papa regrets that he could never match the old man's skill with wood carving. 'Tis undoubtedly for sentiment alone that he keeps that old loom."

"Then I shall be doubly careful with it," Roarke vowed as she took her seat opposite him. "No small matter is it to be trusted with such an heirloom." He tasted the stew, apparently at his ease once more, and spared Adela a nod of appreciation. "'Tis good as always," he complimented her. "Indeed, Adela, your skills are wasted in feeding just the two of us."

"I think not," Adela disagreed in a low voice, drawing Roarke's gaze. He cocked one brow inquiringly and she smiled. "No finer task is there, I think, than to cook for those one holds in regard," she added softly, letting all she felt for him show in her eyes.

Well it seemed that Roarke could not look away, and Adela knew without doubt that she could not, the flickering lamp on the table bathing one side of his face in golden light and casting the other into mysterious shadows. He chewed the morsel of meat slowly, his gaze running over her as surely as if he touched her, and Adela wondered fancifully if he would devour her next.

"Know you what you have done to me this week, Adela?" he murmured, his gaze returning to lock with hers once more, and Adela could but shake her head mutely. She felt her lips part and the heat rise within her, a tiny flutter of trepidation making her wonder if she had somehow, in her naiveté gone too far.

Roarke pushed to his feet slowly, and she watched transfixed as he moved like a great cat around the end of the table. She tipped back her chin to hold his gaze when he paused beside her. He reached for her, and Adela closed her eyes, a tear rising inexplicably when she felt the heat of his fingers brush against her cheek. His hands were gentle as he divested her of her veil. She sighed when he unfastened her hair, powerless to protest the tug of his fingers sliding through its mass to spread it over her shoulders.

Roarke made an inarticulate sound in the back of his throat and Adela opened her eyes just as the weight of his hands fell on her shoulders. His eyes burned with an intensity she had not seen in him before, and she shivered in anticipation when his work-roughened hands slid up the length of her throat to cup the back of her head in their strength. Roarke leaned toward her, and Adela's heart began to pound recklessly as she strained upward in search of his caress.

His lips closed mercilessly over hers, and she reveled in the taste of him, the tickle of his beard, the grip of his long fingers, even as her hands slid up to lock around his neck. His tongue demanded entry, and Adela closed her eyes against the pleasure coursing through her, knowing she could deny him naught beneath his practiced assault. Of naught could she think, indeed she could not think at all, her entire being centered on the touch of those demanding lips, the caress of his tongue, the soothing circles traced by his fingers within her hair. She moaned, striving to match him touch for touch, feeling her blood rise in anticipation of a nameless goal.

Well it seemed that something snapped within Roarke at her moan, for his kiss became more urgent in its demand, one hand leaving her hair to roam down her back even as he pressed her back against the bench. He pushed aside her kirtle and chemise impatiently, and Adela jumped when his hand closed over her bare breast, the way he expertly rolled her nipple to a peak between his finger and thumb sending her writhing beneath him.

He tore his lips from hers, his hot breath tracing a trail of kisses down her throat until the wet hunger of his mouth replaced his fingers, his teeth teasing her nipple to such a fever pitch that Adela nearly cried aloud. The weight of that mischievous hand slid over her stomach in exploration, and before Adela's muddled mind could guess its destination, those fingers were beneath her skirts, probing the slick warmth between her thighs.

"Adela," Roarke murmured against her breast, seemingly surprised at what he had found. That thumb and forefinger closed together again, and this time Adela cried out at the jolt that tripped through her from that source.

"Easy, *chouchou,*" Roarke crooned, his lips returning to tease hers again. "Well you know that I will not hurt you."

Adela returned his ardent embrace, his words slowly sinking into the practical corner of her mind that was almost lost in her state. She frowned at the realization that Roarke intended to see their loving through on this very night and managed somehow to stir herself to protest.

"But Roarke..." she whispered when his lips gave her some reprieve. Fascinated by her breasts was he, and his kisses turned there again. Adela's fingers clenched in the darkness of his hair as she fought against the tide of sensation to utter her concerns. "Well I thought that we would wait until the nuptials," she managed to gasp before those teasing fingers made her bones dissolve anew.

Roarke spared her a bemused glance, and she watched with fascination as he outlined her nipple with his tongue. His breath was hot against her skin when he spoke. "Clear indeed did I make the fact that there will be no nuptials," he whispered.

Adela's heart took a jolt, but then his smile made her think he but teased her, and she ran her fingers up the corded strength of his neck to tangle in his hair.

"And clear indeed is it to all that you protest over-much," she murmured lazily, her back arching as his lips closed over her nipple and he suckled demandingly. She gasped and clenched his hair in both hands. "Only too well do I know that your intentions are honorable."

Roarke chuckled dangerously, his fingers sliding audaciously within her as he traced a row of kisses back to her lips. "You err, *chouchou*," he whispered against the corner of her mouth, and Adela's eyes flew open in shock to find a mischievous twinkle in his gray eyes, so close over her.

"Nay!" she protested, just before his lips closed decisively over hers. She struggled weakly within his embrace, despite the way his fingers and tongue persisted in wielding their magic. Roarke swallowed her entreaties, cradling her against his chest as Adela twisted, unable to tell whether she fought his touch or responded to it.

"Nay," she breathed when his lips moved to nibble her earlobe, and Roarke pulled back slightly to regard her, his eyes glittering now in the lamplight.

"You would turn me aside now?" he asked silkily. Adela could but nod silently, knowing in her heart that loving without commitment had no place in her life. Roarke's expression hardened at her gesture, and he pulled her fully against him.

"Even knowing my intent, you have struck the flint these past days, Adela," he growled. "Only fitting it seems that you should be forced to endure the flame." With that, he leaned over her, and Adela struggled in truth, knowing that Roarke would have her fully this night, should she be fool enough to stay.

"Nay!" She gained her footing in a tangle of skirts, sparing a glance to Roarke in time to see his lips tighten into a grim line before she turned and darted for the stairs. Adela choked back her sobs as she dashed up to her room, shoving aside her tears with shaking hands while she hoped desperately that Roarke did not pursue her.

Fool! she called herself in despair as she threw herself across her mattress and let her tears win the day. How could she have imagined that Roarke regarded her differently from other women? Had he not made his position clear as he maintained? No consolation was it to find him right, and she sobbed yet harder, unable to dismiss the whimsy that he wanted her above all, even though she knew it to be false.

Roarke stalked the perimeter of the kitchen, hating the muted sounds of Adela's sobbing that filtered down the stairs to his ears, and hating even more the knowledge that he was responsible for her tears. Almost had he taken her, despite her objections, and he called himself the knave even as he defended himself with the surety that she had deliberately tempted him.

No matter. He had promised Mathieu, and well enough did he know Adela to understand that she would not cast her virginity so cavalierly aside. He had known she had expected more of him when she had permitted him to touch her thus, but so enthralled had he been by her softness that his mind conveniently chose to ignore that fact.

Roarke's heart clenched when he considered what might have happened had she not deigned to speak, and he groaned aloud, shoving his hands through his hair in frustration. Some recompense that would be for the man who had taken him in, for the man who had consented to teach him to weave so soon after Roarke had entered his household. The man who trusted Roarke enough to leave him alone with his daughter while he joined his guild members.

What had he been thinking? Unnerved him, she had, with her quiet conversation, and well Roarke knew that she had slipped beneath his guard with her tales of her grandsire's skill. Too comfortable was he with Adela in the lamplight, too readily could he relax, too easy would it be to confide in her his troubles. Too quickly could he imagine passing his days as he had this one, his evenings with Adela in conversation, his nights with her writhing beneath him.

Roarke lifted one hand to his brow, the scent of her catching him unawares. His body tightened with predictable ease, his troublesome mind readily recalling the glorious sight of Adela moaning beneath his touch. Addled his thinking, she did, he thought with annoyance. Indeed, Adela *eliminated* his thinking when she responded thus, and even now some corner of his mind tempted him to run up the stairs in pursuit.

Even more disturbing was the corner of his mind that tempted him to make the pledge she so desired.

Too close was she to permit him to gather his thoughts and muster his resolve. Too close, indeed, for the haunting sound of her sobs filled his ears and made his heart ache sympathetically. Had she not tempted him? he reminded himself viciously, but the assertion did little to make him proud of his intent.

Mayhap 'twas better this way, Roarke resolved firmly as he slung his cloak over his shoulders. Mayhap she had been frightened by playing thus with fire and sustaining some minute burn.

Mayhap now she would leave him alone.

He gritted his teeth, knowing full well that he would miss the way she had set out to entice him this week past, desperately trying to resign himself to the fact that no gentle kiss would awaken him in the morn. Roarke spared a glance out the window, feeling a measure of satisfaction that it had begun to rain. The cold autumn downpour more than suited his mood.

And a long walk in such foul weather would be more than sure to cool his ardor.

They avoided each other studiously throughout the next day, and dinner was a silent meal on Saturday night. To Roarke's relief, Adela excused herself quietly once she had cleaned up after the meal, and he permitted himself to relax for the first time that day. Little relief was it to feel Mathieu's speculative regard upon him, but 'twas a far sight better than the evidence of Adela's tears, coupled with the knowledge that he was responsible for them.

When Marie approached them purposefully on the church steps the next morn and Roarke felt Adela stiffen beside him, he recognized the opportunity for a reprieve. He had to dissuade Adela of this notion that he held her in regard, no matter how true it might be, and Marie was likely to be the best means of doing precisely that.

For her own good was he doing this, Roarke reminded himself with a vengeance after his heart tugged at Adela's surprise when he greeted Marie with false warmth. Time enough was it that she saw him truly for what he was and abandoned these romantic notions of his chivalry. None had he of that quality, and should Adela not already know it, he well knew he could make her aware of it.

Marie cooed and flirted, Roarke barely managing to follow the thread of her words, so distraught was he at Adela's dismay. But Marie seemed to detect naught amiss in his agreement to join their board for dinner, however stilted the words sounded in Roarke's own ears. Adela drew herself up tall, bidding Marie good-day with icy hauteur, and he knew only too well how he had hurt her pride.

But he would not feel the knave, Roarke told himself firmly, though he felt exactly that, Mathieu's censorious glance when he led Adela into the church doing naught to persuade him he had done aright.

Aye, it took not much imagination to conjure a picture of what Marie was serving Roarke for dinner this night. Adela stomped around the kitchen in poor humor after he left in his clean shirt, a shirt that *she* had washed for him, and could not summon a vestige of interest in preparing dinner.

How could he do such a thing? How could he not see through Marie's obvious facade?

How could he spurn her in favor of one like Marie?

To none of these questions had Adela an answer, though little enough it would have soothed her, even if she had known one. The man was a rogue of the most scandalous order, a knave who would not know an ethic should it jump up and bite his nose. She regarded an onion dangerously and set her lips as she sharpened her knife.

"Mayhap 'tis best that you not cook this night." Her father's voice interrupted her thoughts, and Adela spun on her heel to find him watching her from the top of the stairs. He smiled mischievously when her eyes met his, and gestured tentatively to her knife.

"Mayhap 'twould be best even if you laid the blade aside," he suggested, feigning fear of what she might do, and Adela relaxed as an unwilling chuckle escaped her lips.

"Oh, Papa..." She sighed as she followed his bidding and wiped her hands on a cloth. "I know not what to do."

"Give me but an onion to chew on, and heat up some of that meat from last eve. 'Twill suffice for me this night," he suggested amiably as he sat down at the board. His eyes twinkled, and Adela shook her head indulgently.

"'Twas not what I meant, and well you know it," she chided, drawing a chuckle from her sire in turn.

"Aye, I know, child."

Adela peeled the onion for him, laid it on the table and lifted the pot onto the hook in the fireplace. She knelt and stoked up the fire beneath with practiced motions before she turned and confronted her father with her hands on her hips.

"Well?" she demanded, cocking her head to one side as he watched, a smile dawning over his lips.

"Well, what?"

"Have you no words of advice for me? Usually you are quick enough with those," she charged, and Mathieu grinned outright, even as he bit into the onion.

"Too old are you for my advice," he teased. Adela threw the cloth at him in mock disgust.

"Aye, there indeed is a welcome reminder," she retorted with a grin, and the two laughed aloud.

"Adela, you must do what your heart bids you," her father finally said. Adela shrugged eloquently.

"My heart is sorely confused," she admitted, watching Mathieu shake his head slowly in understanding.

"Your heart would do well to recognize that it is not the only one to be so troubled," he murmured. His bright gaze held his daughter's dubious one until hope slowly replaced her doubt.

Roarke found himself painfully aware of the difference in his surroundings that night, and struggled to remind himself that he was doing this for Adela's good. Indeed, there could be no other justification for his being here, for 'twas more than evident that as enchanted as Marie seemed to be with him, her father clearly thought him far beneath the rank of his daughter. The older man would not even deign to speak with him, and consumed his meal with surly and silent deliberation.

And well Roarke supposed the man was right, for a weaver, however skilled, could never aspire to a dyer's wealth and social position. And should he have been in the man's place, he might well have been seeking a match with the minor nobility had he a daughter as fair of face as Marie.

Although, Roarke conceded silently to himself as Marie's gossip washed over him unheard, he would ensure she never opened her mouth until that prospective suitor not only became her spouse, but had consummated the match.

Though Adela had a sharp side to her tongue, 'twas naught compared to Marie's, and Roarke could not help but make the telling comparison. Adela spoke sharply only to protect herself from the hurt of others, for she was indeed too tenderhearted and evidently recognized that flaw in herself, trying to conceal her softness with a quick wit. Marie, however, was openly malicious, seeming to delight not only in the misfortunes of others, but in the aiding and abetting of their downfalls, as well.

He found the delicious meal difficult to eat while she recited gossip with such glee, and indeed, Roarke was certain the food was too rich for him. And the concentration on courtly manners made him fear to stumble. Although he had learned to eat at a more gracious table than this, none there were so avidly watching for a slip as Marie and her sire.

The combination of glowering father, oppressive formality and Marie's relentless gossip exhausted Roarke long before the meal was even ended. The courses continued in a seemingly endless procession that he came close to pointing out would have been taken as a crass exhibition of affluence in even the king's court.

But that would have necessitated explaining to Marie how he came to know such things, and the revelation of his noble birth was one that Roarke was certain he did not want to ever reach Marie's ears. Her enthusiasm now was naught, he was sure, compared to what would transpire should she, or more especially her sire, learn the truth of his origins.

Even knowing the truth himself while he sat at their board seemed too close for comfort, and when the meal finally ended, Roarke made his excuses, complimenting the chef and thanking the brooding Monsieur Taintenière for his hospitality. He spared a polite kiss for Marie's knuckles at the door before he stepped out into the night, noting her dissatisfaction that he had not aimed higher with a barely noticeable shake of his head.

The door closed solidly behind him, and he fought the urge to dance in the street. 'Twas snowing, the first snow of the year, and Roarke took a deep breath of freedom, feeling his childhood enthusiasm for the snow flood through his veins. The night was still, the sky fathomless indigo above, one of those nights when one can almost hear the fat flakes of snow land on their brethren. He tugged his cloak closed and strode through the gathering whiteness, lightheartedly kicking some of it into the air and smiling as it sparkled and fluttered back to earth.

He wondered whether Adela liked the snow, and could readily imagine her laughing alongside him. Roarke grinned, knowing he would have ensured a snowball made its way inside her kirtle, had she been here with him.

And well he could imagine her retribution. The very thought prompted him to chuckle aloud. Mayhap he should take a snowball home to her. He scooped up a handful of snow and expertly packed it into a ball, fairly laughing aloud as he imagined her outrage should he awaken her with such an offering.

But no. Roarke sobered and reluctantly let the snow fall from his fingers. Was this night not about dissuading Adela of her illusions regarding him? Such a move would only encourage her fancies, and he exhaled in disappointment, turning his face up to the gently falling flakes of snow.

'Twould be best if he stayed out even later, to fuel her suspicions, he acknowledged with a growing and entirely novel sense of loneliness, unable to keep himself from sticking out his tongue to catch snowflakes and swallow them whole. Roarke smiled sadly at his own antics, refusing to admit that his pleasure in the snow was diminished by the fact that he was alone, and hunched his shoulders against the cold as he resolutely began to walk a circuitous path through the cobbled streets.

Despite her father's encouraging words, it took Adela the better part of the week to summon the nerve to approach Roarke yet again. No small matter was it that he had come home at all hours Sunday night, whistling cheerfully, of all things, so that Adela was awakened to realize precisely how late he had tarried at Marie's. Had she not known better, she might have thought he had done so apurpose, but little sense did that make.

His loom warped, Adela had covertly watched Roarke's barely concealed delight as Mathieu began to show him how to weave. Each step did he perform carefully in preparing the loom, but she could fairly taste his excitement, and all in the shop smiled to themselves at his evident impatience when he was forced to abandon the loom to perform some other task. But naught did he complain, though he was quick to return to the work that so fascinated him.

For a first attempt, his work was more even than most others she had seen, Adela noted once when he was running an errand, and indeed, the work became yet straighter as it grew. Each eve now he filched the lantern when she retired to her room, and when she lay back on her mattress and closed her eyes, Adela could barely discern the whisper of the treadles in the shop as Roarke worked late to learn his craft.

That she was so evidently and easily forgotten did naught to bolster her resolve, but by the end of the week, Adela was preparing to take a chance. She wanted Roarke and no other, this she knew, but when he spared her a wink as he took the lamp on Friday night, she realized that she was in love with him.

The revelation brought her up short, and she stood rooted to the spot for a long moment, watching him descend to the shop as her mouth opened once, then closed resolutely. Surely he would mock her should she choose to confess her feelings. Adela licked her lips and gazed unseeingly around the kitchen before she turned blindly and headed up to her room.

But then again, mayhap he would not.

Her heart began to beat a staccato rhythm, and she perched on the side of her bed in the darkness as her mind raced ahead. Only her own fault would it be if she let him slip away without telling him of what was in her heart. Only herself would she have to blame if indeed she was left alone, without him.

Adela took a shaky breath and struggled to imagine what she would say, how she would manage to introduce such an intimate topic into the achingly polite conversations they seemed only to have these past days, but could think of naught. Her father bade her good-night as he headed to his room, and Adela responded automatically, her mind focused on the matter at hand.

She knew not how long she had sat there, pondering her predicament, when she heard sounds in the kitchen below. The faint glow of lamplight carried up the stairs, and she tried to compose herself, knowing that Roarke must have returned to the kitchen. Mayhap to retire. It mattered not, for she had to take this opportunity while she yet had the nerve to do so.

And what would she do? What would she say? Her blood heated as she recalled his assertion at their last late encounter, and Adela squared her shoulders determinedly. What better way to show a man her regard than to grant him the gift of her virginity?

And even should Roarke spurn her love, this moment of passion she would have, this pearl of recollection to treasure in the cold nights after she was bound to another in a loveless match.

Roarke had spoken aright when he said she had struck the flint, and now, Adela thought as she discarded her kirtle with trembling fingers, now she would step willingly into the flame. A moment's consideration, and her chemise joined the kirtle. Adela shook out her hair, finger-combing its length before she closed her eyes for one long moment, then headed for the stairs.

Sadly, his beard had to go.

Roarke resented having to take the time from his work to shave, the task recalling that he would be home for at least two days for Rochelle's nuptials. Two days without the looms.

Two days without seeing Adela.

Roarke refused to let himself speculate on the import of that thought, preferring instead to believe that the looms were his only source of fascination in this household. His

mind drifted toward home, and he patted the pocket where
Mathieu's receipt was secreted away, reassured by the crin-
kle of parchment beneath his hand. That would set Denis'
mind at ease, if naught else.

And lavish food there was certain to be, he reminded
himself as he hung a pot of water over the fire to heat. Game
aplenty, to be sure, and all of it larger than rabbits. Roarke
grimaced to himself, confirming yet again in his mind that
he had hidden the pelts where Adela might not find them in
his absence. No merit would he give to the fact that every
thought of home seemed to conjure at least one element of
life here that he preferred. But two years would he be here,
and then he would return to his rightful way of life.

Roarke's heart wrenched at that thought, and he was unable to dismiss how comfortable he felt here after but a
month. Indeed, tearing himself away for but two days was
proving to be a test of his resolve that he had not anticipated, and he would not even speculate on the difficulty of
the task two years hence.

He sighed and looked around for the sharpening steel,
that his blade might be fresh to shear his beard. His heart
stopped when his roving gaze fell on Adela at the foot of the
stairs, as rosily nude as a newborn babe.

He blinked, convinced his mind was playing tricks on
him, and dared to look again, only to find her still there,
though now she smiled encouragingly. Roarke swallowed
carefully as she took a step toward him, her gleaming hair
swaying in her wake, and felt his desire rise to a crescendo.

Still he could not reach for her, could not touch her, could
not in fact move, for fear that any motion on his part would
dispel this magical and unexpected sight. Adela's smile
widened, her topaz eyes filled with a softness that could
have been understanding, and Roarke watched in amazement until she stood directly before him. He dared not look
to her breasts, seeing the dark shadow of her nipples even
out of the corner of his eye.

Transfixed, he watched her hands rise to frame his face as though in a dream, and he closed his eyes in pleasure as he felt her stretch toward him. Her kiss landed gently on one corner of his mouth and then the other with tantalizing slowness, and his hands flexed impatiently, even as he fought to maintain his self-control.

Forbidden to him she was, he would do best to recall, though her scent and the light imprint of her fingers on his face was quickly dismissing any ability he had to reason.

"Roarke," she whispered, her breath against his lips launching a tide of answering sensations within him. "Look to me, Roarke."

Roarke obediently opened his eyes, losing himself in the warmth of her gaze before he knew what he was about.

"I would taste again the flame we kindled," she murmured, and Roarke could not have turned aside from her in that moment to save his soul.

Her fingers slid into his hair, and 'twas so easy to incline his head that last increment that he might taste her fully, an unwilling groan escaping him when Adela opened her mouth to him immediately. Her tongue darted playfully into his mouth, and he cursed himself for having taught her so well, even as he reveled in her embrace. *Adela* was the only thought in his muddled mind, and he repeated the refrain until the chorus became a demand. His hands curled around her waist, and Roarke felt the press of her breasts against his chest, felt her strain to her toes to taste him more fully, and knew that he was lost.

Chapter Eleven

Adela found herself on her back with satisfying speed, the wonder in Roarke's eyes as he knelt over her doing much to bolster her dawning confidence in her own appeal. Roarke slid his hand over her, as though to reassure himself that she was truly there, and Adela arched against his touch, wanting to feel more of his skin against hers. The pallet was cold and hard against her back but she cared naught, the glow from the fire and the heat in his regard all she needed.

She tugged impatiently at his shirt, and Roarke smiled as she pulled the undyed linen free of his chausses. His hands abandoned her with apparent reluctance, and he hauled his shirt over his head, his eyes meeting hers silently when he cast the garment aside and waited. Adela swallowed carefully at the splendid sight of his bare torso and sat up to kneel facing him, reaching out tentatively to touch the sculpted curve of his shoulder.

Her hand slid lightly down over the warmth of his chest when he did not move away, her fingertips exploring the flatness of his nipple. Roarke inhaled sharply, and she glanced up to find his eyes closed. She slipped her hands through the dark thatch of hair on his chest, surprised at its wiry texture, and smiled impishly when he straightened as her hands slid ever lower.

But still he did not stop her, and Adela continued on.

She felt the outline of each rib, her hands following the tautness of his stomach where the hair met in a V, then beyond. Roarke's eyes flew open when her hands passed over his navel, his gaze burning into hers, though still he did not check her exploration. Adela licked her lips in hesitation, her fingers faltering when they encountered the tie of his chausses, but when Roarke seemed to stop breathing, as though he waited to see what she might do, she took a deep breath and untied the lace.

He did not move when she cautiously pushed the wool over his lean hips, his size and hardness surprising her. Fascinated, Adela touched him, gratified when Roarke shuddered from head to toe.

"Easy, *chouchou*," he advised hoarsely, and she spared a glance upward, only to be snared by the heat in his eyes.

"I should not touch you thus?" she asked timidly, painfully aware of her inexperience and fearing that she had done something amiss. To her relief, Roarke grinned with some measure of his usual mischief, the warmth of his hand closing around hers as he folded her grip around him.

"Nay, you should, *chouchou*," he assured her, his voice so low as to be but a rumble in his chest. "I would but ask that you be gentle with me."

Adela giggled at his foolery, tightening her grip in jest and noting with amazement how his jaw clenched and his eyes closed. Could she then affect him so readily? A heady thought was that, and, emboldened by the possibility, Adela leaned down and brushed her lips tentatively across him.

Roarke shuddered convulsively, his strong fingers tangling immediately in her hair and clenching her nape. "Adela!" he gasped unsteadily, and Adela found herself on her back once more, Roarke's weight pressing her into the pallet. "I bade you be gentle," he scolded with a ferocious mock frown, and she laughed as he discarded his chausses. His hand returned instantly to caress the indentation of her waist with a purposefulness that stopped her laughter short.

"I was," she insisted, her hand wandering between them and unerringly finding his hardness yet again. She clenched her fingers around him, letting him feel the bite of her nails as she caressed his length. To her delight, Roarke seemed even more affected by this touch, and she stretched to lick his earlobe. "Now, this is not gentle," she whispered, loving the way he shivered beneath her assault.

"It seems we must even the score," he murmured into her ear, and Adela barely had time to comprehend the promise in his words before his hands were once again making her body sing. She was drowning in his touch and savoring every moment of it, knowing without doubt that this night these mysterious urges that had haunted her since first Roarke had kissed her would be satisfied.

Well it seemed that his touch was everywhere, and Adela could but hang on to his broad shoulders and enjoy the sensation. Her blood quickened as he caressed her surely, and she knew not what to make of it, a restlessness stirring within her that she knew not how to still. She looked to Roarke, but he merely smiled and gathered her closer against him as his fingers continued to tease her secret spot, his other hand cupping her shoulder. The hair on his chest teased her aching nipples, and when he pulled her yet closer, Adela fancied she could feel the unsteady clamoring of his heart against her own.

"Ride out the storm, *chouchou*," Roarke urged, and Adela closed her eyes, trusting in him as he guided her down this new path. Her lips opened of their own accord against the warmth of his skin, and she pressed hurried kisses to his chest, her hands sliding up the strength of his back as she held him yet closer.

Heat rose beneath her skin till she thought she could bear it no longer, and she felt her nails bite into his back, as though they were not following her own bidding. Her breathing seemed to stop as she balanced on the crest of a fathomless void, and then she plunged suddenly over the edge, a glorious tide of release flooding through her and leaving her gasping in its wake.

Adela's eyes opened slowly in the breathless aftermath. Her breathing was erratic and her heart was racing unevenly as she struggled to comprehend what she had felt. She found Roarke looming over her, his elbows bracing his weight on either side of her as he gazed down with a warm smile, and she reached up to touch his cheek in wonder.

"I would have you look at me in this moment," he whispered. His fingers slid into her hair possessively, and Adela felt his hardness move against her thigh.

A lump rose in her throat at his meaning, and she could only nod in mute agreement as she helplessly held his gaze. The telling moment was upon them, and, though she wanted to give to him as he had given to her, she held her breath in trepidation. Her fear must have shown in her eyes, for Roarke immediately dropped to kiss her gently, his hands framing her face.

"'Twill hurt but for a moment, *chouchou*," he murmured reassuringly against her lips, and Adela blinked back unexpected tears at his familiar endearment. *Chouchou. Little cabbage.* Had they not first kissed among her cabbages? She twined her arms trustingly around his neck, knowing that she wanted this beyond all else, and ardently returned his kiss.

And this would be but the first time they mated, she knew, her heart leaping at the promise of loving this man. The very thought of a lifetime of nights like this, a string of pearls stretched out as far as the eye could see, each to be savored in turn, was more than she had ever hoped for, and her heart swelled with the knowledge that this man had granted her this most remote desire. A more opportune time she could not have imagined for what she wanted to tell him, and she dared to hold his gaze.

"Oh, Roarke, I do love you," she confided shakily.

It could well be said that Adela's words had not the effect she anticipated. Roarke immediately drew back and regarded her with something akin to horror. "What did you say?" he demanded suspiciously, and Adela could not imagine what troubled him.

"Only that I love you," she repeated quietly, surprised when he shook his head and shoved resolutely to his feet. A chill stole over her skin when he pulled away and left her bare to the night.

"Oh, nay, you will not trap me thus," he muttered with an inexplicable edge of desperation to his voice.

He looked around with what seemed to be panic, then fell upon his discarded chausses with evident relief. Adela noted that he had difficulties in donning them once again, his usual grace having abandoned him in this moment when he seemed to need such haste. He cursed under his breath as the cloth seemed to fight him, and Adela gazed upon him unabashedly, his color rising beneath his tan as though he could feel her perusal.

"I do not understand," she dared to say, earning herself a wild glance from the disheveled man who had moments before been the very image of the suave and experienced lover.

"You will not snare me, Adela," he reiterated, tugging desperately at the lace of his chausses, which stubbornly refused to follow his bidding. Adela propped herself up on her elbows, his loving having left her so lazily replete that she could not trouble herself to become angry with him for turning aside.

Especially with this fascinating discomfiture that her words had prompted.

Though indeed she could imagine what troubled him, for he had already made the matter more than clear, the way he fumbled with the most simple task would seem to indicate that his heart challenged his own resolve. And that could only bode well for Adela's dream.

Roarke spared her a glance when he finally won the battle against his chausses, his eyes widening at the sight of her, still reclining nude on his pallet. "For the love of God, cover yourself," he grumbled out between his teeth, casting her his shirt and turning to pace the length of the kitchen, as though he could not bear to look upon her.

Adela laid the shirt aside, enjoying the fact that her nudity bothered him, and sat up on his pallet to watch his agitated pacing. Should her bare breasts disturb him so, she had no intention of making his denial easy, and she waited expectantly for his expression when he turned and discovered her still bare to his gaze.

"Indeed I do not understand why you should be so troubled," she pointed out calmly, and Roarke dragged his fingers through the thickness of his hair.

"You said those words," he muttered darkly.

"Which words?"

"*Those* words," he repeated viciously, sliding her a sharp look, his eyes widening slightly at the sight of her, but he relentlessly continued on. "And well enough you know which words I mean. I will not repeat them."

"You mean, that I love you," Adela said yet again, enjoying the way he winced at the very sound. Oh, he was troubled by this thought, of that there was little doubt. His dismay when first they had broached the issue of marriage was naught compared to this. Was it possible that Roarke was questioning his own objectives?

"Aye, that," he agreed with a boyish scowl. Adela tilted her head to one side and regarded him with curiosity.

"And none have said thus to you before?"

"None who meant it," he offered savagely, refusing to so much as glance at her.

Well it seemed to Adela that she understood what troubled Roarke, and that her instincts in this matter were right. She got to her feet with deliberation, knowing all the while that he watched her warily and covertly, and strolled leisurely toward him. She paused but a handspan away from him and noted with satisfaction the quickening of his breathing, though undoubtedly he would have preferred to think that he had hidden his response.

"And you, of course, have never uttered those words to another?" she demanded softly, no question in her tone, as she tilted her head back to regard him. Roarke licked his lips and darted a glance to either side, as though he sought a means of escape.

"Never," he confirmed hastily. "And never will I, you can be sure, for they can only lead to the other…" He made a gesture with one hand as words failed him, and Adela could not help but smile affectionately.

"To marriage," she supplied pertly. The way Roarke's lips thinned was all the answer she needed.

"Aye," he agreed heavily. "And thence to homes and lands and knights and children and dogs, each and every one of them…"

His voice faded to naught, and Adela watched him carefully. "Each of them what?"

Roarke spared her a glance that left her in no doubt that he hated her for drawing this information from him and visibly gritted his teeth. "Responsibilities," he declared in frustration. "Each and every one a responsibility to be borne and an obligation to be met. *Never* will I be trapped by responsibilities," he repeated firmly, pushing past a dumbstruck Adela to agitatedly pace the room again.

"But little enough could I expect *you* to understand such an objective," Roarke charged, his words bringing Adela up straight.

"I beg your pardon?" she demanded coldly, and he shot her a scathing look as he wagged one finger in her direction.

"A great lover of responsibility are you. Indeed, it seems you draw your very purpose in life from taking on obligations. Should there not be enough of them available, no doubt have I that you would *invent* responsibilities, that you might assume their weight."

Adela folded her arms across her chest, suddenly feeling the chill in the room. "I know not what you mean," she said flatly, unable to fight a persistent sense that she knew precisely what Roarke meant, but unwilling to admit it.

"Do you not?" he asked skeptically, as though he, too, had spied that secret suspicion. "Unaware are you, then, of all you do in this house? Not only do you play the role of daughter, dutifully working in your father's shop, but also have you assumed much of the role of spouse in your mother's absence." He confronted her and began to tick off his fingers as he listed tasks. "You cook, you shop, you clean, you launder, you tend the garden. Well would you have tended to the rabbits and stretched their hides, had I not intervened in that one task, at least."

"My father has his business to tend," she protested, earning a glance from Roarke that was too perceptive by far.

"Aye, that he does. But little doubt have I that you could run it in his stead, for have you not also filled the role of heir? Have you not learned the way of his business, traveled to Troyes to buy and sell by his side, or even in his place? Do you not ensure that all runs smoothly in the shop in his absence, that minor scuffles between the weavers are settled without his intervention? Think you that I have not seen this?"

Adela pursed her lips, unable to form any argument in the face of the truth. Had she not simply done what was required of her? Had she not merely attempted to do the best she could to fulfill her father's expectations and make his way easier?

"And still 'tis not enough for you," Roarke continued with a sigh of disbelief. "Are you not so anxious for the burden of children and domestic matters that you would take the likes of Georges to your side to see that dream become reality?"

"'Tis the way of things for a woman to act thus," Adela managed to object weakly, but Roarke smothered a deprecating smile as he regarded her.

"Think you that Marie labors this hard?" he asked archly, and Adela could not hold his knowing gaze. "Think you that she troubles herself over the fate of those who have less than she?'' he added softly, and Adela turned aside, not knowing how he had come to know of this weakness of hers but embarrassed all the same.

"Think you that I would step so willingly into this trap?'' he asked in a low voice, and Adela spun on her heel, unable to listen any more.

Bad enough was it that he should turn away from her at the last moment, but this assault on her character was more than she could bear. Mayhap she had been right and the choice was not an easy one for him, but even though he might be sorely tempted, 'twas more than clear that Roarke had made his choice. No place had she in his life, and she resisted the urge to inform him that he had made the matter most clear, that at least he might stop.

"Adela,'' Roarke whispered urgently, and she paused in her flight, daring to cast a tearful look over her shoulder. "You must spare something for yourself.''

Indignation rose hot within Adela, and she glared at Roarke, her tongue momentarily unwilling to form the charge that raged within her at his words. How *dare* he tell her such a thing?

"Did I not try to do exactly thus this eve?'' she demanded finally, her voice uneven in her own ears.

"Nay!'' Roarke retorted with a rare burst of anger, his quick steps bringing him to her side in a flash. "This eve you strove not to take some pleasure for yourself, but to ensnare me with the pleasure you might grant. Only too readily can I see the direction of your thoughts, and rest assured that I will plant no seed in your belly, that you might trap me into sharing your circuit of responsibilities.''

Adela gasped indignantly and turned on Roarke with flashing eyes. "No such intent had I, and you would do well to know of what you speak before you make such charges,'' she retorted, seeing immediately that he was unconvinced.

"Of little import is your intent, or whatever you would claim it to be, for well you know now that I do not intend to play your game." Roarke leaned closer, his gaze softening unexpectedly when he evidently noted the tears brimming in her eyes. "Know but this, Adela," he said with sudden urgency, his voice low. "Not the right man for you am I, and should you look inside your heart, you will see the truth of it."

With that he turned on his heel, and Adela closed her mouth with a snap, her annoyance with his summary dismissal bringing her chin up high in defiance. She *had* looked within her heart, and well enough she knew that Roarke was mistaken.

Half a mind had she to tell him so, even as she watched him grimly fill a basin with hot water, though his stubbornly preoccupied manner brooked no interference. She hesitated on the stairs for a long moment, but he resolutely ignored her. Something within her was disturbed when he lifted his blade to his cheek and scraped off a strip of his beard.

"What do you do?" she demanded, but still Roarke did not grant her a look.

"Home must I go on the morrow," he said tightly, rinsing the blade and removing another swath in the same manner. "And unfitting is this growth."

Adela's heart began to pound at this news, and she frowned, unable to imagine what she would do without Roarke here, how she would find him, even, should he not deign to come back. Where was home for him, and would he stay there?

"Will you return?" she asked breathlessly. At that he did glance in her direction, though his expression was impossible to read.

"Aye," he confirmed flatly, and turned back to his shaving. "A promise did I make your sire."

A promise? Of what nature? Adela was aching to ask for details, but Roarke's manner was dismissive at best, and indeed the evening air was cool on her bare skin. She shiv-

ered and started up the stairs, resolving to get the truth from
her sire in Roarke's absence.

"I will see you on the morrow, then," she said, unable to
resist one last comment. Her heart sank when Roarke shook
his head firmly.

"I shall be gone afore you rise," he said coldly.

"Godspeed to you, then," Adela said in a small voice, not
daring to ask the grim stranger when he would return, and
Roarke but nodded once in acknowledgment. No other sign
did he give, though she waited hopefully, and Adela sighed
with dissatisfaction as she slowly climbed the stairs to her
chamber.

Roarke felt no small measure of his own dissatisfaction,
his body well aware of every step Adela made as she retreated with obvious reluctance. Indeed, he was certain he
could hear her settle onto her solitary mattress above, and
he bit down on the impulse to follow her up the stairs and
pursue his release.

But repercussions would there be from sampling Adela,
and well enough did Roarke know it. Not only was there the
matter of his vow to Mathieu and the possibility of her
conceiving a child should they mate, but increasingly Roarke
was certain that one taste of Adela would not be enough to
quench his desire for her.

Too easily did he recall the intoxicating sight of her
reaching her first release in his arms. And not reassuring was
the realization that he had called her his *chouchou,* not once
but a number of times. The very uncharacteristic use of any
endearment, not to mention one that clearly recalled to him
the first time he had tasted Adela in the garden, made him
writhe. 'Twas not a good sign at all. Then there was the unexpected wish in that moment that he might spend the rest
of his life pleasing her thus.

Dangerous indeed was that proposition, and Roarke felt
the bite of the trap closing in on him as surely as he knew he
was not fighting it as resolutely as he should. Images of

Adela as his wife and his alone were too frequent in his musings for comfort, and his traitorous mind had taken to slipping the forbidden word *marriage* into his thoughts when he least expected it.

A few days at Aalgen might well be the break he needed to collect himself.

Too readily did the image of Adela's nudity intrude upon his resolve, and Roarke fairly groaned as he recalled the tentative invitation in her eyes when she had first come down the stairs. How could the woman doubt her own allure? Mayhap he would fetch her a glass from Aalgen, that she could see the marvel of her own delights. His body was quick to remind him of what it had been denied, and he laid the knife aside for a moment until his fingers stilled. How had he turned her aside, that golden, soft and willing temptress that he so desired?

And *why* had he done so? For how bad could it be, truly, to be bound to a woman who enticed and enthralled him so?

Enthralled. The very word reconjured Roarke's resolve, and he reminded himself forcefully how Armand had fallen victim to Alex's charms. Was it not unnatural for a man to hold a woman in such esteem that she alone could control his desire? He splashed in the hot water as though to wash away those troubling thoughts, then ran the pumice stone through the water before rubbing it on his jaw to remove the last of his stubble.

And well enough did Roarke know that he did not belong here. Of noble lineage was he, his destiny entwined with other noble houses, with knights and battles and the waging of war. Roarke grimaced at the reminder, though his expression eased as he thought of the magical looms. He deliberately took the pumice to the other side of his face with a vengeance, flatly refusing to recognize that Mathieu's was the first house where he had felt at home.

When he donned his shirt forcibly once again and Adela's soft scent rose from the cloth to tease his nostrils, he closed his eyes and inhaled deeply, admitting only to himself in the softness of the night and the quietude of the kitchen that 'twas Adela alone who was responsible for that ease. His lips twisted, and he moved quickly to pitch the dirty water out the window, acknowledging the hard twist of fate that had rendered Adela forbidden to him.

Unless, of course, he changed his mind about "obligations."

The very idea was unthinkable, and Roarke reminded himself of that salient fact throughout the night as he tossed sleeplessly on his pallet before the hearth.

"Too bad Roarke is not here to savor what you have done with this ham," Mathieu commented amiably in the afterglow of their evening meal on Saturday, and Adela knew she would get no better opportunity.

"Where has Roarke gone?" she asked lightly, not missing the way her father straightened.

"Something he had to attend to," he said quickly, but Adela fixed him with one glance. Her father sighed expansively and shook his head indulgently. "His sister is being wed," he supplied reluctantly, and Adela felt her brows rise in surprise.

"I knew not that he had a sister."

"Well, he has at least one," her father conceded.

"At least?" Adela prompted, earning herself a censorious glance.

"Little more do I know of his family," he said gruffly, and something in his manner told Adela that he lied.

"Indeed?" she asked. She dropped to the bench opposite and noticed the wary eye her sire granted her. "You took a man under your roof, knowing so little about him?"

"Other circumstances were there," Mathieu admitted uncomfortably. More to this tale was there, and Adela intended to learn the way of things before her father slipped away this night.

"Such as?" she inquired.

Mathieu made a low sound of frustration and met his daughter's inquisitive gaze stubbornly. "No business is it of yours," he insisted, but Adela would not be so readily swayed.

"Oh, it must then concern the vow that Roarke made to you," she concluded matter-of-factly, and her sire's gaze flickered for a telling moment.

"What know you of that?" he demanded, and Adela shrugged.

"Only that he made a vow that compels him to return," she supplied, leaning across the table to her father to make her appeal. "What did he promise you, Papa?"

"No business is it of yours," he hedged, but she sensed that he was wavering in his resolve and pressed her advantage.

"Indeed?" she inquired archly. "Would you not have me know more of this man I mean to wed?"

"Adela!" Mathieu exhaled her name, and Adela thought for an instant she had gone too far. Mathieu's mouth worked for a moment, as though he knew he should rebuke her but could not find the words. His very indecision fortified Adela's resolve. "Speak not your mind so clearly," he chided weakly.

Adela smiled to herself at this sign that her father did not openly disapprove of her intent, and wondered a heartbeat later whether he could have had similar plans for Roarke. But nay, a quick glance to her sire found him looking as innocent as a new babe, and Adela flatly refused to acknowledge the notion that mayhap he looked too innocent.

"Tell me, then," she urged. Mathieu shook his head before he cleared his throat and tapped the table between them.

"The tale must go no farther, for I promised him to hold my tongue," he insisted, and Adela nodded agreement without another thought. Mathieu regarded her bemusedly for a long moment, a smile playing over his lips. "And what does Roarke think of your intent?" he asked with seeming idleness. His words prompted Adela to laugh, her very manner enough of an answer to make Mathieu's grin widen.

"Papa, you said you would tell me the tale," she reminded him, and he straightened his posture.

"Aye, aye. Remember you the Lady Aalgen?"

"And her blue cloth," Adela confirmed quickly, to her father's nod.

"Aye, and her inability to pay for that cloth," he added dryly.

"Truly?" This twist on the tale was one Adela had not been aware of.

"Aye. Well enough you should remember the trinkets I was forced to take from her in lieu of silver." He spared Adela a telling glance, and she recalled now the fine brass candlesticks that had briefly rested here in the kitchen, along with other goods that she had not had the nerve to explore. Indeed, they had been here a short enough period of time that her suspicion they belonged elsewhere, which had kept her from looking more closely, had been confirmed quickly.

"Hers, were they?" she asked and her father nodded again.

"Well it seemed that she could not bear with parting with the goods and sent her son to negotiate with me for their return. But neither had the house of Aalgen any deniers to spare, so the son, a man of considerable charm, I might add, persuaded me to take his labor for two years to repay the debt."

Mathieu paused when she expected him to continue, and it took Adela but a moment to realize his implication and work through the information he had presented. It could not be so, she thought wildly, though one glance to her father's patient countenance was confirmation enough.

"Roarke is the son of Aalgen?" she demanded incredulously, her father's curt nod making her wonder what she had been thinking to aspire to one of noble lineage. Mortification flooded through Adela at the way she had thrown herself at Roarke, a man so above her station as to make her

play for him laughable indeed. Well she had known Roarke
to be a knight, but she had never suspected that he might be
the son of one of the local great houses.

No wonder he showed no signs of taking her bid for his
attentions seriously. She felt a flush of embarrassment rise
over her cheeks. Surely he had already been pledged to some
woman with blue blood coursing through her veins. Surely
he laughed at her antics in her absence. Adela could not help
but wonder whether the tale of her pursuit of him was entertaining the nobles at Aalgen's board even as she sat here
in her humble home.

No wonder Roarke had tried so to dissuade her from her
path with his ridiculous talk of responsibilities. *Responsibilities.* Adela fairly snorted at the word, certain that a noble son would bear more than his fair share of such without
even considering the burden of their weight. An excuse that
was, and a poor one at that, for did he not readily take an
onerous responsibility by working two years to release his
mother's debt?

She supposed she should be grateful to Roarke for turning her aside when she would have known him fully, but as
it was, the knowledge of his status only rubbed salt in the
wound of his rejection. How dare he not confide in her?
How dare he concoct this ridiculous tale of his avoiding responsibilities to sway her resolve?

And to think that she had been fool enough to believe
him.

Adela gritted her teeth as a hundred options for revenge
came to mind and were discarded, her annoyance growing
as she pondered the fullness of Roarke's crimes. 'Twas his
refusal to trust her with the truth she most resented, and
Adela well knew it, although her pride was no more encouraged by the readiness with which he had turned her
aside. No less by the certainty that he entertained his friends
with the merry tale.

Adela barely noted her father slipping away as she stared
blindly into the flames on the hearth, struggling to deal with

the unfamiliar torrent of feelings Mathieu's revelation had released. At the very least, two years would give her plenty of time to get even with Roarke for the way he toyed with her, and she consoled herself with that knowledge, even as she tried to think of a suitable way to make her disgust with him clear.

Chapter Twelve

'Twas with mixed feelings that Roarke passed his sister's hand to the man who would very shortly be her spouse.

Not that he could put his finger on what troubled him particularly about Robert, for the man's manners were impeccable, his attire was tastefully understated, his conversation was intelligent and witty. And the man had silver, and to spare, that could be said unflinchingly in his favor.

Mayhap 'twas an instinctive distrust of the motives of those men without lands that plagued Roarke, mayhap 'twas that alone that had made him imagine Robert cast an appraising eye over the contents of Aalgen's hall on his arrival. Mayhap 'twas that distrust that prompted the feeling that Robert asked too persistently about the precise extent of the demesne when they stood on the roof and looked over the fields.

Mayhap 'twas only that cursed protective urge that Adela had awakened extending to his sister, Rochelle, evidently enamored of a man who did not appear to return her regard.

Mayhap.

Roarke gave Rochelle's fingers a squeeze just before he released them into the custody of Robert under the priest's eye, and she spared him a happy smile before turning to face the man who would be her future. Roarke hesitated by her side, uncertain what he wanted to say and unwilling to simply leave her there, but then the priest cleared his throat and shot him a heavy glance. Roarke nodded in reluctant understanding and stepped back beside his mother, that the ceremony might proceed, wishing he might have found the right words.

Mayhap 'twas simply too early in the day for him to articulate what troubled him.

His chest tightened as the priest's blessing wound its way into his ears, a familiar enough litany now seductive with possibilities when he could not empty his mind of Adela. Too late he wished he could have brought her here, wished irrationally that she might have met his mother and sister, wished she could have looked upon his home. Would she have been pleased? Impressed? Roarke could not say, and indeed knew not even what he could have hoped to achieve with such a move.

Mayhap 'twould have been better to part with her on easier terms, for well enough he knew that his conscience pricked at him for deliberately hurting her. And after she had risked so much by daring to believe enough in her own charms to try to seduce him, he truly felt the knave for turning her aside.

"Does she not look lovely?" Ermengarde murmured by his side as she slipped her hand into his elbow, and for an instant Roarke was not certain whether she meant Adela or Rochelle.

"Aye, she does," he agreed with a shake of his head, glancing down to see his mother smile mistily.

"And so happy," she mused, giving Roarke a bright look so abruptly that he was taken aback. "Was it not worth our sacrifices to see her so?"

How could his mother know what he had done? Roarke regarded her in amazement, but Ermengarde merely smiled secretively and laid her cheek against his arm.

"What are you saying?" he whispered, not trusting the innocent expression in her wide eyes when she peeked up at him again.

"Naught," she said, as though confused by his question, and Roarke stifled a frustrated sigh.

"To what sacrifices do you refer?" he asked again, then watched Ermengarde shake her head.

"Roarke," she chided under her breath, as though she were compelled to deal with a particularly slow child. "Think you that I cannot see what you are about?"

Roarke's heart fairly stopped at that assertion, but Ermengarde blithely continued on. "Something have you done to settle the debt. Indeed, I cannot begin to guess what, and though it seems to take you from home, well enough do I appreciate your seeing to the matter."

The little speech took Roarke completely aback, and he watched the priest for a long moment before leaning over his mother once again. "To Denis have you been speaking," he accused softly, wondering how much that chatelain had figured out, though little enough had Roarke told him.

"Nay!" Ermengarde retorted, meeting her son's gaze with alarm. "Well enough did I tell you that he tells Rochelle everything. Not safe is it to talk to Denis." She shook her head in quick denial.

"Then how—?" Roarke stopped short when his mother pinched the tender skin inside his elbow ferociously. He winced and glanced down to find her eyes sparkling with mischief.

"Think you that I am so weak of intellect as that?" she demanded impishly, the priest's terse *"Shh,"* and his sharp glance in their direction, saving Roarke from having to reply.

"To whom are you sworn these days?" Robert asked with apparent idleness during the banquet, and Roarke glanced up in surprise at his new brother-in-law's curiosity. Natural enough it was, he supposed, reasoning 'twas no more than his own desire to keep his doings secret that made him unusually suspicious.

"To none right now," Roarke confessed, watching the other man's brows rise in surprise.

"Indeed?" he commented, a wealth of censure in that single word, and Roarke thought he spied a new wariness in the other man's eyes.

"Indeed," Roarke confirmed flatly, returning to his meal with feigned enthusiasm.

"What then are you doing?" Robert asked but a moment later, his tone markedly less conversational. Roarke flicked him another glance.

"This and that. Traveling. Making myself useful," he supplied enigmatically, feeling the weight of the other man's assessing regard upon him.

"Have you no opportunities to swear your blade, then?"

"Aye," Roarke confirmed, refusing to be goaded by the insulting insinuation. "A post as marshal was I offered at one keep, the opportunity to swear to the service of the house at two others."

"But you declined?" Robert asked with clear skepticism. The man wasted no time making himself at home, Roarke thought sourly, for he was quick indeed to cast aspersions on those born and reared to this house.

"Aye." Roarke slanted the other man a glance that indicated his desire to end this line of discussion, but to his annoyance, Robert persisted.

"Why would you decline a post of marshal?"

"Too far abroad was it," Roarke prevaricated. "And well I thought it time to be closer to home for a while."

"Hoping for such a post at Aalgen, were you?" Robert asked with thinly veiled hostility. Roarke shoved his trencher aside, granting the man an icy look.

"No illusions had I that matters might change at Aalgen on this day," he asserted flatly, well and done with Robert's insinuations. "Though indeed it might seem that I had hoped for continuity in vain." Anger flared in the other man's eyes, and Roarke knew he had seen aright when he thought the man hungry for power.

"I would know where you go and what you do," Robert demanded, but Roarke merely smiled.

"Your nuptials give you no dominion over me," he informed his opponent coldly. "And similarly, my lack of inheritance from Aalgen gives me none over you," he added, that the matter might be most clear.

"Other ties are there between us," Robert stated in a low voice, and something clenched within Roarke at the veiled threat.

"Should I ever hear tell of Rochelle not thriving at your hand, you will indeed have the opportunity to assess my skill with a blade," he murmured, low enough that none other might hear the exchange. Robert's lips thinned, but he did not offer a quick reassurance that might have eased Roarke's mind.

"Roarke." Ermengarde's short fingers closed around his elbow. Roarke did not turn for a long moment, his eyes narrowing as he held Robert's regard in silent challenge.

"Roarke, I simply must show you what was done with the blue cloth before the newlyweds retire. Marvelous it looks, indeed, and Rochelle was most pleased."

"Aye, Roarke, we simply must show you. *Maman* has truly outdone herself this time," Rochelle chimed in, and Roarke's gaze flicked beyond his mother to his sister's flushed features. Happy she was, and that, he knew, should be enough for him, regardless of his evaluation of this she had taken to her hand. Guilt flooded through him, and he glanced back to Robert to find that man's regard softened, as well.

Mayhap they had something in common after all, he consoled himself, hoping indeed that Robert held Rochelle in esteem. His instincts rose to argue the assertion, but Roarke stomped down on them, determined to be happy for his sister, on this day at least. The wedding was done, she had made her choice, and her future would reveal itself in its own time.

Roarke summoned a halfhearted smile for his mother before he turned and helped her to rise from the table, then offered his other hand to Rochelle as she rose in turn. Only too well aware was he that Robert's gaze followed them as they made their way across the crowded hall, Ermengarde fairly skipping in her excitement as she chattered like a child. Rochelle stood as tall and regal of bearing as ever she had. Roarke watched her smiling in response to felicitations as she glided elegantly alongside him, as graceful and aloof as the swans on the pond behind the keep.

"Do not trouble yourself, Roarke," she murmured under her breath as she nodded to one of their oldest vassals with a polite smile. Her hazel eyes, so bright with intelligence, flicked to meet his, and her smile became knowing. "Well enough do I know the bargain I have made," she added softly, her confident words reassuring Roarke as naught else could have.

He grinned recklessly and gave her slim fingers a squeeze. "Ah, but has Robert an idea what manner of opponent he has engaged?"

Rochelle chuckled low in her throat, that rich sound revealing that Roarke's words had truly caught her by surprise, and the two grinned at each other as they gained the stairs.

"Soon enough will he learn," Rochelle confided, the mischievous twinkle that danced in her eyes giving her an unexpectedly strong resemblance to Ermengarde.

Robert fingered his chin thoughtfully as he watched the threesome duck through the assembly of friends, family and vassals. He did not at all like Rochelle's brother's attitude. A man with a secret was he, unless Robert missed his guess, and Robert had well learned that men with secrets could not be trusted.

Though once their secrets were known, they could well be manipulated, under threat of inopportune revelation.

And no pleasure did it give him to see his wife and mother-in-law dance attendance on this man, their affection for him indisputable, although from what Robert understood, Roarke seldom troubled to make an appearance here. And unfitting indeed did it seem that this man should steal the women's attention.

Was *Robert* not the one who brought newfound wealth to the manor? Was *he* not the one who would act as lord of the estates, now that he had wed the heiress? Would *his* children not inherit these lands? Too much was it that this cocky son, deprived of inheritance by family tradition, should so readily undermine Robert's position in the household, and no intent had he of letting the slight pass unchallenged.

He beckoned imperiously to the boy he knew had been Roarke's squire, resolving that he would soon know the truth of this matter. Quite harmless might it be—a woman, perhaps, judging from the young knight's flirtatious manner and good looks—but Robert would know for sure what forces were arrayed against him.

"Follow him" was all he said to the squire, and the boy's eyes widened as though he might dare to protest. Anger rose hot in Robert's chest at this sign of defiance, especially as the lad evidently favored Robert's rival, and he glared at the young boy, satisfied to see him quake.

"I would know where he goes within a week, or 'twill be your hide that tastes the whip."

To Robert's satisfaction, the boy hesitated but an instant before nodding, bowing deeply and turning nervously away.

Two days later, Roarke and Yves paused on the perimeter of Aalgen's properties to reenact their parting scene once again. The dawn was later now, the surrounding trees shrouded in shadows as the first glimmer of the winter sun climbed over the horizon. Was it but a month past that he had first stepped toward the distant towers of Ghent? Roarke could scarce believe it, and he glanced to the distant snow-dusted spires just catching the first light, as though they would confirm or deny the truth of it.

Yves looked even more troubled this time than the last, and Roarke grinned at the boy reassuringly, pleased when Yves managed to summon a cursory smile in response.

"When shall I meet you here next, milord?" he asked timidly, and Roarke paused, stunned that he had no answer.

When *would* he be going back to Aalgen? Indeed, he knew not, and it hardly seemed reasonable to set a meeting with the boy two years hence. Two years. Who knew what could pass in that time?

"I know not," he responded, hoping his tone managed to be carefree, as he hauled his familiar linen shirt over his head. The undyed cloth felt good against his skin, more honestly won than the taffeta tabard he had abandoned, and he filled his lungs with the scent of simple soap that clung to the cloth.

Soap Adela had wielded, he recalled with some measure of pleasure, and felt his anticipation rise at the promise of seeing her again.

"Do you not return, then, milord?" Yves asked tightly, his words drawing Roarke's attention back to the present. He looked up and held the boy's troubled regard, closing the distance between them with a quick step and laying a hand on the boy's head.

"A task have I to fulfill. 'Tis only the fact that I must do it alone that keeps you from my side," he confided softly, helpless to check Yves' rising tears as the boy nodded miserably and stared at the ground. "Denis does not keep you occupied?"

"Aye," Yves admitted heavily, scuffing his toe in the snow. "But 'tis not the same."

"Nay," Roarke agreed ruefully. "Well can I imagine for, 'twas not Denis who taught me the sport of drinking. Think you that he tastes a dozen wenches a week? Or mayhap two dozen?"

"Nay, milord." Yves chuckled unwillingly, and Roarke tousled his hair with affection, wishing he could indeed take the boy with him.

But naught could Yves do in Mathieu's household, for well enough did Roarke know that he was all thumbs with small tasks. And indeed, the boy's family had entrusted him to Aalgen to earn his spurs. No right had Roarke to deny Yves that opportunity. Yves would have to find his own way under the hand of Robert.

"I would have you be careful of what you say these next days," Roarke urged, the insistence in his tone prompting Yves to meet his gaze questioningly. Roarke frowned, seeking a way to warn the lad without alarming him, and wondering all the while if his fears were misplaced. "Oft do matters change when a new lord takes a household, and you would do well to follow his bidding and keep your own counsel until the lay of the land can be discerned."

" 'Tis what you would do?" the boy asked, and Roarke managed to smile thinly.

"Aye. Know well that knights who fail to live with caution seldom live long at all."

Yves seemed to ponder this for a moment, his smooth brow puckered, and then he looked to Roarke again and offered his hand. "I would wish you Godspeed in whatever 'tis you do, milord," he said formally, and Roarke did not dare to grin at his manner as he solemnly took the boy's hand.

"I would thank you, Yves. Mind your back as you ride home, and know that 'twill be soon enough that we shall meet again."

"Aye, milord," Yves affirmed. Roarke could not resist tousling his hair one last time before he stepped away and turned to face Ghent once more.

His heart might not have been so light had he known that Yves did not head back to Aalgen, though indeed the boy lingered indecisively in the road for a long while before he stealthily followed Roarke.

* * *

Adela knew the very moment that Roarke entered the shop again. Although her fingers faltered momentarily under the weight of his regard and her shuttle stumbled to rest on the warp with uncharacteristic clumsiness, she flatly refused to look up. Endeavoring to look unconcerned, she picked up the shuttle again, hoping it appeared that she had meant to drop it all along, and nonchalantly continued with her weaving.

"Roarke! Good 'tis to see you home." Mathieu's voice rose in greeting, and Adela heard the other weavers call a welcome, several getting up to amble over and chat. She dared to glance over her shoulder, as though only moderately interested in events on the far side of the room, hoping she looked supremely unconcerned.

Much to Adela's surprise, Roarke was looking directly at her. The impact of his gaze locking with hers across the room, as well as the unexpected seriousness in his expression, fairly made her heart stop. Somehow she managed to summon a cursory smile of greeting and look back to her work as though his return had not set her heart to pounding. She caught the barest glimpse of Roarke's lips thinning and bit down hard on the wedge of guilt that rose within her in response to her own callousness, but then he laughed at something someone else said, and she viciously shot the shuttle through the warp, knowing she had no reason to trouble herself so much over such a man.

Mayhap she should seek out Georges again, she thought, knowing she had no interest in doing so and that 'twas only the prospect of irking Roarke that even gave her the idea. Adela sighed at the veracity of that thought and blinked back stubborn tears. Indeed, she would do well to shake herself free of Roarke's influence.

"So glad am I to see you returned," Mathieu said, with no small measure of enthusiasm, and Roarke spared a half-hearted smile for the older man. And what had he expected? That Adela would throw herself at his feet at his return, when their last encounter had ended so poorly? Indeed, he should count himself lucky that she had acknowledged him as politely as she had, even though the careless nature of her acknowledgment stung. Did she no longer care? Or had he cut her too deeply?

An intriguing puzzle either way, but Roarke was forced to remind himself that it mattered not. No interest had he in cultivating Adela's attentions, for no intention had he of being locked into marriage with any woman. And regardless of her motivation, the end result was the same: Adela had little time for him anymore, and that had been precisely what he wanted.

If only she had shown some sign of missing him as much as Roarke had missed her.

"Well it seems to me that the stables must be in need of mucking, if you are so glad to see me returned," Roarke jested with Mathieu, wondering how long he could keep up this good-natured facade.

"More than that, more than that," Mathieu confided, clapping Roarke on the back as he led him out the back of the shop. With difficulty Roarke fought the urge to look over his shoulder for one last glimpse of Adela, irritation rising within him to fill the void created by his disappointment.

How could she not have missed him? How could she not have thought of him over and over again, as he had thought of her, the very image of her plaguing him, these past few days? Had the woman not been ready to allow him the greatest liberties with her only days ago?

Indeed, it seemed that making his feelings clear about matrimony had thoroughly cooled Adela's ardor. Was that her only interest in him, then? Roarke immediately felt a fool for having been captured by her charms so much more completely than she had evidently been enamored of his own appeal, and he stomped into the yard alongside Mathieu in poor humor.

How could he feel so at home in a place that seemed to often leave him in such a foul mood?

Roarke gritted his teeth and forced himself to listen to Mathieu, guiltily realizing that he had not been attending the other man's words. Curse Adela anyway, for the distractions she made in his mind.

"...with the canal being frozen from this uncommon cold and Pieter needing that wool from England, we at the guild decided to travel with him to Bruges. The road is no place for one to travel alone, as well enough you know, especially with the night falling so early these days..."

She could have at least smiled at him, Roarke thought with growing annoyance. One little smile was all he had been expecting, and a genuine one, not that politely reluctant excuse for a smile that never reached her eyes. Well enough could she save that expression for the likes of Georges.

Surely she had not turned to that oaf again?

"Has Georges troubled you again?" Roarke blurted out. The bemused expression on Mathieu's face told him that he had shown his hand too clearly. Roarke felt his ears burn, certain suddenly that he must have interrupted the other man. Had Mathieu not been telling him something? Indeed, Roarke could not recall one word the older man had said and Mathieu seemed to guess as much, shaking his head indulgently as he continued to the stables.

"I have not seen Georges this past week," Mathieu admitted. The twinkle in his eye told Roarke that his curiosity as to whether Adela had seen Georges had been guessed. He bit back the question, refusing to give the older man the amusement of hearing him ask it.

And little enough interest had Roarke in the matter, anyhow, he reminded himself firmly, pushing past his companion and into the darkness of the stables. Indeed, Adela could well pick any man she desired, he thought viciously, disliking his own recollection that she had desired *him* but a few days past.

Although brief enough had been the duration of that attraction, from all the signs.

"Would you go with me, then?" Mathieu asked, and Roarke spun in surprise.

"I beg your pardon?"

"To Bruges," Mathieu explained patiently, yet Roarke had no idea of what he spoke.

"Whatever for?"

"To accompany Pieter, that he might safely collect his wool."

Pieter? Who was Pieter? "Why is his wool not being shipped along the canal?" Roarke asked, feeling the question was quite a reasonable one. To his dismay, Mathieu chuckled and shook his head, though he could not guess why.

"The canal is frozen," he supplied, folding his arms across his chest and leaning against the doorframe with laughter dancing in his eyes.

"The canal never freezes," Roarke pointed out.

"This year it has. Cold, 'tis. As I said."

Roarke licked his lips carefully, realizing what Mathieu found so funny. Already had he been told all of this, but he had heard naught, so concerned was he with Adela. Typical enough that was, he thought with dismay, wishing he could yet find a way to loose her grip upon his heart and mind.

"Late 'tis for shipping," he ventured to suggest. The rise of Mathieu's thick brows reassured him that he had hit on some topic that had not been covered.

"Aye," the older man admitted with a shrug. "Well enough I told him only to deal with the Cistercians, for they alone are rigorous about delivery, but instead he bought from a convent. It seems it has taken the abbess this long to organize the shipping."

"Mayhap she has not done it afore," Roarke suggested.

"Mayhap. At any rate, the fleece is late, the weather poor and Pieter is in desperate need of his wool."

"How many of us to Bruges?"

"Pieter and his son, you and I, mayhap Gunther and his apprentice. Three wagons should be enough to both cart the fleece and dissuade thieves."

Roarke nodded, reviewing the distance to Bruges in his mind. "Even with the wagons, we could make it there and back in but a day."

Mathieu lifted his brows. "Likely we will take two, to ensure we travel in daylight. 'Tis safer thus."

One last question rose to Roarke's lips, and he could not check its path before it had spilled forth. "And Adela will be fine alone?"

"Aye," Mathieu confirmed with a grin. "Worry not about her here in town. Oft enough has she stayed home alone since her mother passed. 'Tis we who take the greater risk."

"Aye. When do we go?"

"Probably tomorrow, should Pieter be amenable. Awaiting your return, I was."

Roarke turned and assessed the horses, which calmly returned his regard, his gaze running over the trap on the far wall. "I had best be about making preparations here, then," he said, and Mathieu but nodded before he turned to leave.

"Aye. Should you need anything, Arnulf the smith will likely turn the work this very day for he is a neighbor of Pieter's and knows our intent."

Chapter Thirteen

The wind wound its icy fingers through all the layers of wool clothing Roarke had donned, and he found himself traitorously wishing for the fur-lined cloak he had surrendered to Yves.

Though 'twas safer to wish for that than for the soft warmth of Adela pressed against him.

The snow that had begun to flutter around them was falling with increased intensity, and he peered through the haze to the back of Gunther's wagon ahead, finding that he could barely discern the vehicle and forcing himself to focus on the difficulties at hand.

"Well I told him to buy from the Cistercians," Mathieu growled into his collar. Roarke was beginning to agree with the wisdom of ensuring a timely shipping schedule, but he merely clicked his tongue to the team, urging them to pick up the pace. No sense was there in falling behind at this point. Time indeed 'twas to be home before the hearth, with the persistent snow darkening the road around them and making it seem much later than the midafternoon Roarke knew it to be.

And he was so cursed cold after a day and a half of sitting out like this. He flexed his toes, hoping against hope they had not turned blue, wiggling his fingers as he sought something positive about their situation. At least 'twas poor weather for bandits, he thought, squinting against the white blur of the snow as it started to swirl before them.

"'Tis getting worse," Mathieu complained, and Roarke could not help but agree.

"We should be home soon enough," he pointed out, and Mathieu nodded in turn.

"Not soon enough for me," he returned, and the two men grinned at each other. "Think you that Adela has been cooking?"

"Well do I hope so," Roarke said, with no small measure of enthusiasm, his stomach fairly growling at the prospect.

"That meal at the inn last night left much to be desired," Mathieu commented.

"Sat in my belly like a brick, it did," Roarke affirmed, drawing a chuckle from his companion.

"Mine, too," he agreed, closing his eyes against a virulent flurry of icy snow. "Mine, too. Mayhap she made that rabbit stew with dumplings. Now there was fare for a king."

Any response Roarke might have made was stolen away by the indignant whinny of one of the horses.

"What the—?" Mathieu's words were stopped short by the emergence of a dark rider on the road ahead. His horse stepped out of the swirling snow like an apparition come to light, and for a dangerous instant, Roarke doubted the evidence of his eyes.

"All your coin," he demanded. Mathieu spat into the road in disgust.

"Brigand!" he charged. A sword glinted suddenly in the rider's grip, and Roarke laid a cautionary hand on Mathieu's arm.

"We had best do as he asks," he suggested in a low voice, hoping Mathieu realized they had but a small blade each. And these two old horses could never outrun the thief's highstepping charger, even without the burden of the wagon.

"No coin have I for a knight turned to oppressing those beneath him!" Mathieu protested. Roarke hissed a recrimination, even as the rider came closer.

"I would urge you to reconsider," the thief said smoothly, and Roarke felt his heart begin to pound. Naught had they with which to defend themselves.

"Give it to him," he muttered, but Mathieu only shrugged, pulling his pockets eloquently inside out.

"I have naught," he insisted with a calm air of defiance.

"Liar!" charged the thief. He spun his horse abruptly, and Roarke dared to hope that he might leave, but instead he shouted again, *"Liar!"*

Riders erupted out of the storm on either side of the road with startling speed. Their blades flashed, and Roarke had but an instant to draw his own short blade before they closed in on the wagon.

"Gunther!" Roarke roared as he seized the reins and whipped the elderly pair of horses, terror galvanizing the beasts into action. They surged forward on the rutted road, and Mathieu fell heavily back against the plank that served as a seat. The first rider cursed as his stallion danced out of the way, his blade carving a silver arc through the storm as he swung for Roarke's head.

Roarke ducked wildly and whipped the horses again, well aware of the shadows gaining on either side of the bouncing wagon. His heart stopped as silver flashed again, two blades making short work of the reins and harness. The horses whinnied in terror as they bolted and disappeared into the storm. Mathieu shouted as the unfettered wagon pitched forward and skidded sideways across the icy road. The front of the wagon hit the ground with a vengeance. Roarke tumbled forward, the impact of his fall sending his blade out of his hand and skating across the road.

He lunged for the only protection he possessed, but a booted foot abruptly blocked the space between his hand and the blade. Roarke looked up slowly, only to confront the coldest smile he had ever seen.

"Your coin," the bandit urged, but Roarke could only shake his head.

"None have I," he admitted, and that smile grew yet colder.

"Liar." The bandit lunged forward, intending to impale Roarke with one stroke. Roarke rolled at the last minute, feeling the road quiver as the blade was buried deep within it. The bandit swore, and Roarke took the chance to retrieve his knife.

Not a chance had they against five, six? Indeed, Roarke could scarcely count the swirling cloaks in the frenzy. Where was Mathieu? He fervently wished for his sword, jabbing out with his knife when his attacker spun around, sword in hand. A gash appeared suddenly in the back of his hand, blood staining his glove, but he could not feel the bite of the blade, so cold was he. The bandit leapt forward, but Roarke stepped aside, managing to bury his short blade in the man's shoulder and drop him to his knees.

Mathieu cursed, and Roarke spun in that direction, slashing at another cloaked figure en route. A blade rose over the defiant Mathieu, and Roarke leapt forward. He managed to divert one blow from the older man before sagging under the weight of a strike to his shoulder. His mail should he have, he thought numbly, knowing it was too late to matter.

"Gunther!" Roarke called again, raising his blade in a desperate attempt to defend himself. A man's scream filled his ears just as he was struck over the head from behind.

Mathieu! Roarke struggled against the press of darkness closing around him, only to be savagely punched in the jaw. His head lolled, and he felt alien fingers root through his empty pockets, but was too dazed to interfere with their quick work. A man muttered a curse, and all the wind left Roarke's lungs when he was kicked in the stomach. He rolled backward into a drift of snow, its chill slipping into his collar and helping him to revive.

Roarke twisted to look to Mathieu and saw three shadows bent over the older man's huddled form as his pockets were similarly dumped. The jingling of a few meager coins, another curse, then the quick kick of a booted foot caught Roarke's eye. He winced in sympathy when he heard it find its mark.

The riders muttered to each other in dissatisfaction, and Roarke barely dared to breathe as they mounted their horses. Trap jingled, hooves pounded on the road, their beat muted by the snow, and he rolled over with a groan to find himself alone with Mathieu.

The older man had fallen in a heap, motionless within the wagon, bundles of fleece scattered in all directions amid the snow, and Roarke crawled toward him with difficulty. If only he had had his sword, he might have given those bandits more than they had bargained for, he reasoned irritably, groaning as he hauled himself into the tilted wagon alongside his companion.

Roarke let his weight fall when he had climbed over the side, a shudder rolling through him at the cost of his efforts. He reached out and placed one hand on the other man's shoulder, giving him a minute shake.

"'Tis all right, Mathieu," he muttered. "Gone they are."

Mathieu did not stir, and a shiver of trepidation coursed through Roarke as he leaned over the other man with concern.

"Mathieu?" he asked hoarsely, closing his grip over his shoulder more firmly. He shook the older man again, but still he did not move. "Mathieu!" Roarke cried, not daring to believe his suspicions. He shook the older man heartily, and Mathieu fell bonelessly backward, his head lolling as he rolled into Roarke's lap.

Blood there was on his cheek, and Roarke wiped it gently away, cradling the older man as tenderly as a babe. It could not be. Not Mathieu. Not now, not here. He shook Mathieu again as tears rose to blur his vision. Where was Gunther? Why had they not turned back when he called? They

must have heard him, they simply must have, for surely he
had bellowed with all his strength. He shook Mathieu with
renewed vigor, unwilling to accept that this man had been
stolen from his side. Relief flooded through him when Mathieu shook his head.

Had he truly moved? Roarke's heart stopped in his
throat, afraid that it was merely his shaking that had made
the older man move, but nay, Mathieu's eyelids fluttered.
Roarke swallowed with difficulty, unable to summon any
sound in his relief, and Mathieu took a shaky breath as his
eyes opened. He looked up at Roarke and seemed to see his
distress, for he patted the younger man unsteadily on the
chest, as though to reassure him.

"You must take care of Adela," he rasped, wheezing unevenly with the effort of making the words.

"I will," Roarke reassured him quickly, pulling the older
man's cloak closed against the cold. "But soon enough will
we be home that you may look to her yourself," he continued, his words falling in a rush, as though he would convince both of them. Mathieu shook his head slowly, but
Roarke plunged on, unwilling to accept the other possibility. "And well indeed will she see to you, I can imagine—"

"Roarke." Mathieu's voice was low, but his tone so
compelling that Roarke could do naught but fall silent and
regard him. Too pale he was, and Roarke suddenly became
aware of the warmth drifting over his lap where he cradled
the other man. It could not be, he told himself wildly, for
what would he tell Adela?

Mathieu licked his lips carefully, evidently marshaling his
energy for what he would say. "I would have you promise
me," he whispered, and Roarke nodded immediately.

"My most solemn vow do I give you," he said quickly.
Mathieu stubbornly held his gaze until he clarified his
promise, swallowing at the import of the demand. "I will
look after Adela," Roarke vowed. The two men's gazes held
for a long moment, and then Mathieu nodded slowly, as if
with satisfaction.

"Aye, I trust you will," he murmured, and Roarke had to lean forward to catch the soft words. No sooner had he comprehended than Mathieu's grip tightened on his shirt, his fingers clenching against the cloth for an endless moment before he made a small gasp.

Roarke watched helplessly as Mathieu's eyes rolled slowly back in his head. He waited expectantly as the snow spun around the two of them in its endless dance, but the man in his arms did not draw another breath.

With one shaking hand, Roarke carefully closed Mathieu's eyes and straightened the other man's garments, as though somehow these gestures could refute reality. It could not be, he told himself, but the words rang hollow in his mind, for well enough did Roarke see the truth of it. Tears blurred his vision, and he pulled his companion into a friendly embrace, suddenly realizing how much he owed Mathieu.

The chance to regain his family honor, in defiance of the rules of society—this had been Mathieu's gift to him, and how had Roarke repaid it? By letting the horses fall out of sight of Gunther's wagon? By failing to defend the master to whose apprenticeship he had been sworn? A shallow bargain was that indeed, and the taste of defeat was bitter on Roarke's tongue.

Even worse was the realization that this would never have happened had he not surrendered his sword. With the arms and garb he had earned through his labor, Roarke could well have defended them both. He had glibly cast aside the rights of his social standing, had put aside his skills, in order to foolishly pursue some whimsy of his heart. He had been mad to think there would be no repercussions from flouting the social structure thus.

And Mathieu had paid the price with his life.

Roarke's fault it was alone, and he knew that fact without a shadow of a doubt as he sat in the drifting snow and stared down at the dead man held against his chest, the warmth stealing away from his body even now. Roarke's responsibility was this, for surely his selfish disregard for the rules had brought this fate upon them both.

Naught but his own impulsive folly could be blamed.

There was but one thing he could do for Mathieu now, Roarke resolved as he laid the other man gently aside and rose to his feet with difficulty. His vow must he keep to this man who had granted him such an opportunity. 'Twas the only way he could possibly repay this sacrifice, and even that was a poor offering.

With dry eyes, Roarke tore a strip from his cloak and tightly bound his aching ribs with it, squinting into the relentless white for some sign of the others while he worked. But there was naught but snow, as far as he could see, no sound carrying to his ears in the eerie silence.

Pieter would have to come back for his cursed wool, Roarke thought bitterly, bending to lift the weight of the other man. He could not leave Mathieu here, could not even think of what he would tell Adela even without the indignity of leaving her father by the side of the road. He grunted as he draped Mathieu over his shoulders, his knees bending under the weight, hoping against hope that they were not far from home.

When the snow began to fall in earnest and the men were not home, Adela told herself not to fret. Together they were, and with the others, surely naught could befall them.

When the horses charged into the yard with wild eyes and frothing mouths, she knew she was wrong.

Adela dropped her work and ran out into the yard without a cloak, the characteristically calm animals almost bolting at the unexpected sight of her. Their trap was cut, and her heart went still for a long moment, then began to race as she soothed the beasts and coaxed them into the barn.

What had happened? Naught good, that much Adela could surely see from the state of the horses. She pressed her fingers to her temples even as she trembled in fear, struggling to gather her thoughts, that she might make a wise decision.

There was only one road to Bruges.

Adela urged the older and more distressed mare into her stall, and raced back to the house for her cloak before she climbed astride the other. The mare protested the unfamiliarity of bearing a rider, but Adela whispered under her breath to the creature, hoping that she did not bolt, for Adela's perch was precarious at best without a saddle. To her relief, the mare settled and followed her bidding, this last intrusion seemingly naught compared to what the creature had already endured this day.

At first Adela thought she imagined the vague silhouette on the road before her, the flurry of falling snow and the resolute onset of darkness making it difficult to tell for sure. But gradually the man's form became clearer as he closed the distance between them with a slow but steady gait. Some burden he carried on his shoulders, that burden and the man's bowed head and shoulders heavily encrusted with snow.

Adela could not imagine what he was doing on the road in this weather, merely urged the horse forward with the hope this man might have some news of her men. He did not look up as she approached, so bent was he on his own travail, and she wondered what she might say. Adela realized suddenly that 'twas another man this man carried across his shoulders, and her eyes widened. Would he expect her assistance on this stormy night? And how could she decline? But then how would she find Roarke and Papa?

The exhausted horse stumbled in its gait, and the man glanced up in alarm at the sound, shock registering in his eyes when he saw Adela. He stopped and stared at her as her numbed mind tried to make sense of the evidence before her.

It could not be. Her hand rose to her mouth, and she shook her head, barely recognizing Roarke with his ebony hair covered in snow, his features drawn, his color drained.

A dark stain of unmistakable color had spread over his clothes, covering his chausses and shirt, the torn remnant of his cloak. The source of much of the blood was evidently the man he carried, the stain gleaming wetly on Roarke's shoulders.

But if this was Roarke, then—

"Papa!" Adela slid from the horse's back and ran to Roarke, her hands clumsy as she reached for her father's still form. Not Papa, not here, not like this. She would not permit this to be.

"Nay, Adela." Roarke shook his head and lifted one weary hand to stay her, but she easily evaded his touch.

"I must tend him," she protested, framing her father's cold face in her hands. She saw the truth the same moment that Roarke spoke, her tears rising to blur the beloved features before her very eyes.

"Too late, 'tis," Roarke said, and she barely noted the exhaustion in his voice through her own pain. She shook her head wildly, refusing to believe what even her own heart told her.

"It cannot be so," she whispered unsteadily, disregarding her falling tears. "But put him down for a moment, that I might see to his needs."

"Nay, Adela," Roarke insisted softly. She reached again for Mathieu's face, but Roarke captured her wrist, compelling her to look into his eyes.

Roarke was feeling no small anguish of his own, she realized with a measure of surprise, and she found herself reaching out to touch his face. His skin was chilled, and she noted his pallor, the sorrow in his eyes when he did not look away.

"Others must tend to him now," he said quietly, and Adela's tears rose anew. She fought against the tide, knowing that if she let her weeping begin, she would not so easily be able to check its flow.

Roarke was right, she resolved silently, taking a shaky breath as she dared to look to her sire once more. Matters there were to tend to, and not only Mathieu's body. Her thoughts faltered at that, but she forced herself to continue. Roarke evidently was not unharmed, either, the wagon must be abandoned somewhere with Pieter's wool, the horses needed to be tended ...

Time enough later would she have for her sorrow. Indeed, her father would have expected no less of her.

"You should ride" was all she could manage to say, and she was relieved when Roarke nodded weary acquiescence.

Roarke watched Adela warily as she fingered his ribs, her features composed and devoid of emotion. Eerie 'twas, the way she had straightened suddenly in the road and become so businesslike. One less familiar with Adela might have thought her cold and unconcerned with her father's passing. Indeed he might have thought so himself but a month past, but now Roarke knew better, and he marveled at Adela's stoic endurance.

Not much longer could she last, and truly he was beginning to hope she might soften her guard. Far easier would it be to explain his intention to her in that state than this one, for little did he believe that this frostily efficient woman would give his vow a sympathetic hearing.

Indeed, his tired mind fancied that the raging storm had turned her into a very ice maiden. Even her hands were cold where she gently probed his side, and Roarke winced when she found a tender rib. She poked it again, and he chuckled under his breath, even as the pain shot through him.

"Aye, that is the one," he commented wryly, feeling considerably more himself now that he was home, warm, dry, his belly filled. "Mayhap you should poke it thrice to be sure," he suggested, gratified when Adela flicked a quick glance to his eyes and away, a faint hint of color staining in her cheeks as she continued her exploration. Roarke grinned mischievously, reassured to see even that faint sign of the ice thawing.

"Aye, careful you should be that I not realize how much you like touching me," he teased. Adela's cheeks were suffused with color, and her eyes jumped to his, awareness heating the air between them.

"Naught do you take seriously," she charged in a voice low with emotion, and spun away.

Roarke caught a glimpse of her shaking hands before she folded them in front of herself. He sat up carefully, binding his own ribs once more as he watched her warily. The dam was breaking, unless he missed his guess, and he, for one, would be glad to see Adela confront her sorrow. All was attended to now until Mathieu's funeral, and Roarke was feeling hale enough to fulfill whatever she required of him. He braced himself for her tears and prepared to draw her out.

"More like the Adela I know does that accusation sound," he quipped, not surprised at all by the scathing glance she shot over her shoulder.

"Jokes do you make at this time," she muttered in disgust, and Roarke grinned cockily. Should she need to hate him to let down her reserve, she was welcome to do so. She had to be hurting, and should she need to hurt him in working through her sorrow, this night he would willingly bear the scars. Time enough would they have together for the balance between them to be restruck.

"You it was who pointed out that I took naught seriously," he charged lightly as he pushed to his feet, surprised at the toll the simple movement extracted from his body.

"And named it aright I did then," Adela retorted hotly, flinging out one hand toward him. "Look at you. My father's body is barely cold, yet you go on about your business as though naught is amiss." Her words faltered as the thickness rose in her throat, and Roarke took a step toward her.

"Let it go, Adela," he murmured, lifting one hand to her, but Adela abruptly brushed his gesture aside.

"How can you even think of touching me now?" she demanded impatiently, the shimmer of tears in her eyes. "Does naught else but revelry capture your attention?"

"Let the tears come, Adela," he urged, but she fought them still, glaring at him as she retreated across the room. Roarke followed her slowly, knowing full well that she meant naught that she said.

"Tell me not what to do," she spat. "As though you could know what I am feeling. As though you know what it is to feel anything at all for another."

"Well enough you know that I held your sire in high regard," Roarke asserted quietly, but Adela's eyes only narrowed.

"You were supposed to protect him!" she fairly shouted as she shook one finger in his direction. The accusation brought Roarke up short, so close was it to his own certainty that he had failed Mathieu, but Adela seemed not to note the change in his manner.

"Why else do you think he waited for your return? Younger you are, younger and stronger. A *knight*, if I recall correctly." Adela turned and looked Roarke up and down with a sneer. "Tell me not that another knight could not have ensured my father's safety."

"Mayhap another could have," Roarke admitted quietly, struggling to maintain his control, despite the maelstrom of emotions her charge had let loose in his gut. A failure he was, of that Roarke had little doubt and the one thing he had promised to do for Mathieu looked highly unlikely to occur at this moment. He turned to hide his discomfort with his thoughts and picked up a clean shirt from his belongings.

"What are those scars on your back?" Adela inquired coldly, and Roarke froze, having forgotten all about the marks. He straightened slowly and turned, wondering why Adela asked about them now.

"Evidently, I took a lashing," he admitted carefully, holding her gaze stubbornly and watching as Adela tipped up her chin.

"Some lord took offense at your sampling of his wife?" she asked archly, and suddenly Roarke longed to throttle her for her incessant accusations. Had she learned naught of him since the last time they had bickered thus?

"Nay," he said in a low voice. "'Twas for taking a stag on his lands."

"Oho...." Adela's fair brows rose in mock surprise as she folded her arms across her chest. "Stealing from the lord. 'Tis indeed a flogging offense. Did you at least have a good meal of it?"

Roarke's lips set in a thin line, and he folded his arms across his own chest as he regarded Adela. Would ever she stop pushing him? He rather thought not, and he conceded reluctantly to himself that that might indeed be a measure of her appeal. "Naught did I taste of it," he admitted.

"Caught too soon, were you?"

"Nay," Roarke shook his head slowly. "'Twas for the lord's own board, for he had taken an inexplicable aversion to the hunt."

Adela frowned. "No sense does that make," she argued, and Roarke could not suppress a dry smile.

"'Twas my thought exactly. Unfortunately, Guillaume did not see the matter in the same light as you and I."

Their eyes met and held across the darkness of the kitchen, and Roarke watched Adela struggle with what he hoped was her desire to believe him. Suspecting matters would not get much better, he decided impulsively to take a chance.

"My best was not enough this day, Adela," he said quietly, taking a step toward her even as she turned abruptly to face the fire on the hearth. "I know not even whether there were five or six of them. Knights they were, marauders without hearth or home, without doubt, and bent on mak-

ing trouble. No blade had I but that short dagger, and out-
numbered we were from the first."

Adela stared silently into the flames, her arms still folded
stubbornly across her chest, though Roarke saw tears shim-
mering anew in her eyes. He dared to take a step closer, but
still she did not look to him.

"I know not what happened to Gunther and Pieter. Right
ahead of us they were, though the storm made it hard to see.
I lost sight of them just before the brigands circled us, and
though I shouted for help, they evidently were too far ahead
to hear." A tear caught the light as it spilled over Adela's
cheek, and Roarke lifted one finger to tentatively brush it
away. Adela turned to him, her sorrow filling her eyes, and
he shook his head as his own eyes filled with tears.

"Naught could I do," he confessed heavily. Her tears
spilled in earnest, and she shook her head, her bottom lip
trembling.

"Not fair is it," Adela whispered brokenly, and Roarke
hauled her into his arms, needing the comfort of her touch
as much as he suspected she needed his. Adela did not resist, melting against his chest as she began to sob. Her tears
soaked his chest, but Roarke only gathered her closer, unable to understand the strength he was drawing by offering
her comfort. He discarded the veil halfheartedly clinging to
her hair and rubbed her nape, working her hair free from its
braid and smoothing the loose ends back from her cheeks.

Still she wept for her sire, her mumbled words incoherent against his skin, but the tiny fists on his shoulders slowly
relaxed, her fingers spreading to grip his neck. Roarke
pressed a kiss into her hair and gritted his teeth before
bending to scoop her up into his arms. He sat down on the
pallet before the hearth, cradling Adela in his lap, murmur-
ing soothing sounds to her as she curled against his chest like
a lost kitten.

Roarke knew not how much time had passed when the
chill in the kitchen awoke him. He made to roll over, only

to find Adela's softness cuddled against his side. Her tear-stained face made him smile as he braced himself on one elbow to look down at her, so vulnerable in sleep.

Mathieu had known the truth when he asked Roarke to take care of Adela. Too gentle was she to face this world without a protector. He dared to touch the curve of her cheek, amazed that skin could be so soft. She stirred in her sleep and turned against his hand, her trusting gesture making Roarke smile anew as he let his fingers fan out into her hair.

His Adela.

She would be getting cold, he scolded himself, rising reluctantly to rekindle the fire. When the flames leapt high on the hearth, he sought out the blanket, returning to the pallet to find Adela stirring. She reached across the straw mattress where he had lain, her lips pursing with a dissatisfaction that pleased Roarke enormously.

"Here I am," he murmured as he joined her again. Her eyes flew open, and she glanced at him for but an instant before looking demurely away.

"Cold, 'tis," she whispered, her gaze averted while Roarke settled back beside her. For a moment, he feared he was being too familiar, but she snuggled immediately back against him, though still she refused to meet his eyes.

"Aye, the fire had gone out," he whispered into the golden glow of hair at her temple, the firelight dancing among the curls so that they looked like spun gold. "And a blanket did we need." With that, he wrapped the blanket over her, leaving his arm where it fell across her waist. Adela did not pull away, and emboldened by that, Roarke slipped his other arm beneath her, pulling her back against his chest as they lay together facing the flames.

Adela merely purred at his warmth, the scent of her skin teasing Roarke's nostrils even as her hair tickled his nose. He smiled to himself in contentment, that contentment rudely nudged out of the way when Adela wriggled closer, the fullness of her buttocks rubbing most decisively against him.

Roarke's eyes flew open, his body responding immediately, and yet Adela still moved against him. Surely she knew what she did to him, he thought wildly, certain that she could not mistake the hardness pressed against her for anything other than what it was. She finally, mercifully, stopped, settling against him with a sigh of satisfaction.

Emboldened by both her trust in him and his own state, Roarke allowed his hand to slip and cup her breast, and watched in amazement as Adela rolled back against his arm. Her neck arched, and though her eyes remained closed, she smiled and made a muted sound that could only be one of pleasure. The nipple between Roarke's splayed fingers tightened to a point seemingly of its own accord, and he glanced from its hard outline back to Adela's face. Her lips fell into a soft pout, and he watched with dread as her lashes fluttered, thinking she would awaken and cast him aside.

Roarke froze in place, unable even to move the damning evidence of his hand resting on her breast, as Adela's eyes opened lazily. She regarded him for a long moment as the fire crackled beside them, something unfathomable in those topaz depths, before she smiled and slipped one hand up to his nape.

No further invitation did he need, and Roarke lowered his lips to hers purposefully, savoring the way Adela arched demandingly against his hand. His fingers closed around her taut nipple even as the taste of her flooded within him, the way she writhed beneath him making him want to devour her whole. Her tongue was in his mouth before he knew what she was about, and everything quickened within him, his body threatening him with an inability to take things slowly.

Her first time 'twas, he reminded himself with an effort, pulling back to brace himself over her on elbows and knees. Adela, though, wanted naught of his stalling and locked her arms around his neck, her tempting lips following his retreat.

"Adela," Roarke breathed, struggling against the weight of his desire. She framed his face in her hands, her expression serious, as her regard locked with his.

"Do not turn me aside this night, Roarke," she whispered, the undercurrent of need in her voice fairly undoing Roarke's resolve to wait until their nuptials.

"Not like this, Adela," he protested, fascinated when her lips quirked with amusement.

"Then mayhap like this," she murmured seductively. Before he could protest, she had hauled her kirtle and chemise unceremoniously over her head and cast them aside, her bare skin glowing as she reached for him once more.

Roarke shook his head, evading her kiss, knowing that if he touched her he was lost. Adela seemed to sense the same, for she captured his chin and pressed her lips to his. When he shuddered involuntarily, she lifted his hand determinedly to her breast again. His fingers curled instinctively around its weight, and he groaned, Adela's nimble hands at the lace of his chausses dissolving the last vestige of his resistance.

Certain he must be dreaming that this temptress would finally let him taste her fully, Roarke sank down on top of her, cupping the back of her neck as he hungrily plundered her lips. How long had he awaited this moment? An eternity or two, it well seemed, and heartily now did he wish he had the fortitude to savor Adela like the rare treasure she was.

But her hands, and her tongue and, Roarke groaned, even her toes, were conspiring against him. With a growl that made her giggle against his throat, he surrendered completely to her touch, his fingers unerringly finding her sweet spot in a bid for retaliation. Adela gasped at the surety of his touch, and Roarke chuckled in turn, bracing himself above her to watch. Adela moaned as he caressed her, her slender form writhing beneath him in a most bewitching manner. She opened her eyes, and it seemed she would appeal to him for something, but her words fell in an incoherent murmur that Roarke swallowed with a kiss.

"Ride the storm, *chouchou,*" he whispered reassuringly to her, and her lips traced a path along his jaw as she strained toward him. Her thighs parted, and Roarke shivered in anticipation as he felt her toes slide up the backs of his legs, the wet heat of her beckoning him onward. Adela opened her eyes again when her feet curved around his buttocks, and she smiled softly. A hint of hesitancy there was in her manner when she spoke.

"Would you not ride with me?" she asked, her very innocence filling Roarke with a tenderness he had not experienced before.

"'Twould be my pleasure," he murmured with a grin, fascinated to see Adela blush suddenly after such intimacy had already passed between them, and he passed one finger gently over her cheek. He thought to say something romantic, to make some vow of sincerity, but she captured his errant finger between her teeth before he could find the words, the way she suckled it returning his mind to more immediate matters.

He cupped the back of her neck and kissed her possessively, easing his way into her with his teasing fingers. Adela caught her breath when first he pressed into her, but he stopped and caressed her until she relaxed, moving on in careful increments. When finally he was cradled fully within her, he dared to look to her face, only to find his own wonder reflected in her eyes. She shook her head wordlessly and touched his cheek, her gesture prompting the sudden thought that he had finally found a way to strike her speechless.

"What?" she asked at his smile, evidently fearing that she had done something amiss.

"For once you have naught to say," he teased with a chuckle, and was gratified when Adela laughed aloud. Her merriment stopped abruptly when he moved within her. She gasped and gripped his shoulders, and Roarke smiled down at her. "Better does it get," he warned.

Adela shook her head quickly, biting her lip and arching back when he teased her sweet spot yet again. "It could not," she gasped, and Roarke chuckled anew.

"Trust me," he whispered wickedly, his heart swelling when Adela smiled and reached up to kiss him in acquiescence.

Chapter Fourteen

Adela felt the warmth of the sunlight falling on her face and turned so that the light flooded her vision with pink. Roarke grunted something in his sleep, and she eased closer to him, savoring the ache between her thighs.

Well indeed did they both deserve their sleep this morn, she mused, flipping through her recollections of the night before with a smile playing over her lips. She thought of Mathieu and shoved the pain aside, refusing to dwell on her loss in this moment when she had gained so much.

Although—a realization brought her eyes wide open— Roarke had yet to confess his love for her. Adela slanted a look to the man sleeping contentedly beside her and knew a niggle of doubt.

Surely, knowing full well how she felt, Roarke would not have availed himself of her willingness unless he loved her, too?

Adela nibbled her lip dubiously and wondered whether she had leapt to conclusions. Indeed, not a single endearment had passed his lips, other than the *chouchou* she was sure she was not alone in having heard before. She had not noticed the absence of anything last night, so overwhelmed had she been by the tender tempest of Roarke's lovemaking, but now his lack of sweet confessions troubled her.

Adela sat up abruptly, rubbing her bare arms against the cold and noticing that the fire had burned down to embers again. She moved to get up and rekindle it, only to feel Roarke's strong hands lock around her waist from behind.

"Not so quickly," he protested with a sleepy chuckle, and Adela let herself be coaxed back into his arms, though she studied him carefully, waiting for those words that would mean so much to her. Roarke, however, seemed content to tuck her against his side and settle back to sleep once more.

"Roarke."

He stirred slightly at her utterance of his name, his hand sliding up to cup her breast. His thumb slipped drowsily over her nipple, and Adela sat up abruptly once again, but his hand did not fall away.

"Roarke, we must talk," she said flatly, and he frowned without opening his eyes as he rolled to his back with a mock groan.

"Well I knew that 'twas too good to last," he muttered, only the twinkle in his eye when he cocked it open saving him from Adela's retaliation.

"Serious am I," she insisted, and he heaved a sigh, rubbing his eyes before forcing them both open with some difficulty. Adela waited while he adjusted to the light, his eyes brightening as his gaze landed on her bare breasts. He lifted one hand, and she felt the nipple contract in anticipation before even he touched her. The way he lazily smiled told her that he had noted it, as well.

"So I see," he mused thoughtfully, and Adela shivered as his warm hands closed over her. Roarke sat up, his hands sliding to brace her back as he leaned forward to leisurely lick one pert nipple and then the other. "But what possibly could we have to talk about more important than this?" he murmured against her skin, the feel of his breath almost making Adela forget her intention herself.

"Roarke," she gasped, desperately trying to cling to her line of thought as he tasted and teased and suckled.

"Aye, Adela," he whispered, her name sweeter than the finest wine when he said it in that low voice that so weakened her resolve. He nuzzled her neck and sampled her earlobe as she melted against him, her ability to resist his allure eroding quickly.

"Come back to bed, Adela," he breathed invitingly into her ear, and she shivered, pulling back with her last vestige of resolve. She ran one hand into the thickness of his hair as she faced him solemnly, watching the path of her fingers in those ebony waves, and slowly met his eyes.

"Why did we do it?" she asked softly, only to see Roarke's eyes narrow speculatively.

"Because we both wanted to," he replied easily, his words doing naught to ease Adela's concerns. "Why else?"

"Why else indeed?" she demanded, hot tears rising as she realized the extent of her own foolhardiness.

Roarke had used her, just as she had always known he would use her, and she had been fool enough to fall for it. Adela shoved him away and stumbled to her feet, refusing to acknowledge the confusion dawning in his eyes. A game 'twas to him, no more than that. Aye, 'twas all a game. She found her discarded chemise and pulled it over her head, cursing at the knotted laces in her kirtle as she fought to don it, as well.

"Adela, I do not understand," Roarke began cautiously, and Adela shot him a venomous look to find him tentatively standing up. Little need was there for *him* to act as though the world had suddenly become a strange and hostile place, she thought viciously. Had he not had his pleasure? Would she not be the only one to bear the repercussions of this night?

"Adela, pray do not stop talking now," he urged, the thread of humor in his voice doing little to hide his uneasiness. And reason enough had he to be uneasy, she concluded with a savage tug on her laces, for little did even Adela know what she might do in this dangerous mood.

"No point is there in discussing something you have little ability to understand," she spat, a pang of guilt shooting through her when Roarke visibly cringed at her tone. As defenseless as a new puppy he looked as he ran one hand through his hair and regarded her with a frown, his hair disheveled and his gaze not as clear as 'twould be later.

"Of what do you accuse me this morn?" he asked wearily, but Adela had no sympathy for him.

"No other reason can you conceive for two people to do what we have done than that they both *wanted* to?" she demanded acidly. Roarke looked truly perplexed by her question.

"There are those who do it for coin, I suppose," he suggested uneasily, his manner revealing his lack of confidence that this was the right response, either, and Adela stamped her foot in frustration.

"Roarke," she said flatly, gratified when those confused eyes met hers. "What do you mean to do, now that this has happened?" She gestured toward the pallet, and he followed her motion, that frown deepening on his brow.

"Indeed you must give me some better idea what you seek from me, for no soothsayer am I in the morn," Roarke grumbled, rubbing his eyes once more before propping his hands on his hips and scowling at the floor. "Well I thought that you knew this by now." He sighed and spared her a glance that might have been resentful, had he been more awake. "Wed we will be, though I confess I have not thought much more beyond that." Adela gasped at the word *wed* but Roarke evidently had not noticed as he puzzled aloud over her question. "One could expect, I suppose, that there might be children one day, but that matter can be addressed when it occurs. I would think that betwixt the two of us, we might keep the shop running—"

"Wed, you said," Adela repeated breathlessly when she had found her voice.

"Aye," Roarke agreed carefully, his gaze growing more intense as he seemed to divine something of her meaning. "You mean, you thought that I had taken you last night without any intent to make you my wife?" Roarke demanded indignantly, and Adela could but nod, a thrill running through her at his response.

"What manner of knave do you take me for?" he asked impatiently, stalking purposefully across the room toward her. Adela grinned at his dismay, her heart unbearably light when he gripped her shoulders and gave her a playful little shake.

"Surely you did not think that you had left any doubt that you were a decent woman?" he teased, and Adela laughed, locking her hands around his neck and gazing up at him adoringly.

"Say it," she urged, but Roarke looked blank.

"Say what?" he asked mildly.

Adela refused to be daunted by his reticence to talk of tender feelings, reaching up to tap him pertly on the end of his nose. "Tell me why we will be wed," she insisted with a smile, and Roarke smiled with understanding.

"Ah. Because your father wished it to be so, of course," he responded happily, bending to nuzzle her neck once more.

His lips but grazed her skin before Adela stepped back in shock, shoving his arms away once more. "What did you say?" she asked warily, and Roarke shrugged.

"Your father bade me pledge to take your hand. 'Twas the last words he spoke."

"And this is why you would wed me?" Adela demanded in disbelief, anger rising hot within her when Roarke nodded in quick agreement.

"Aye," he said simply, his eyes darkening with intent as he closed the distance between them once again. "Come back to bed, Adela," he urged, though the low tone of his voice proved to have an unexpected effect this time.

The slap Adela dealt Roarke echoed resoundingly in the small room. The astonishment in his eyes when he met her gaze, his hand rising to his flaming cheek in disbelief, did little to dispel her fury.

"Get out," she spat, shaking as she retreated against the far wall. "Get out, and never come back."

"Adela," Roarke began to protest, but no chance would she grant him to cajole her into agreeing to his plans.

"I bade you get out of my home," she reiterated coldly, watching something set in Roarke's jaw before she turned her back on him, that he might not see her tears. Too vulnerable was she to his very touch right now, too vulnerable to anything, and Adela could only think that she had to be alone.

Mayhap for good, but she refused to let herself dwell upon that as she pointed imperiously to the door without turning.

Bad enough 'twas that she had given herself to a man who did not love her, but she would not redouble the error by wedding him, as well. She felt Roarke's presence as he hesitated behind her, but she refused to turn or make any acknowledgment of him.

"I can explain," he whispered, his voice too close for comfort, and she closed her eyes against the tears that threatened to spill over her cheeks.

"No interest have I in the tale," she managed to say, folding her arms across her chest as though to brace herself against Roarke's appeal.

He sighed heavily, and when she saw his hand rise in the corner of her eye, she panicked that he might touch her. Then his gesture faltered and his fingers dropped from sight. She listened to the sounds of him dressing, heard his leather soles brush the stone floor as he turned, felt his gaze heavy upon her as he hesitated yet again.

Another heavy sigh and resolute treads on the stairs, the solid sound of the back door closing, and Roarke was gone.

'Twas only then that Adela leaned back her head, letting her tears break loose to run in torrents over her face at the magnitude of what she had lost.

Roarke leaned against the house, desperately trying to collect his thoughts. What had happened in there? What had he done amiss? Indeed, he had no idea, and his sleep-fogged mind could make little sense of the change in Adela. Truly, he was having a hard time integrating the fact that he was standing shin-deep in snow, exiled from her home, after the marvel of their loving the night before.

He had failed Mathieu when the man had needed him most, and now he had failed to fulfill that man's last wish, as well. And he had left Adela alone, without her maidenhead that she might find herself another spouse, though indeed the choice to leave was not his own. Could his day grow any darker than this? Could he make any more of a mess of his life or the lives of those he held dear?

Had he not already done enough damage?

Mayhap 'twas time he went back where he belonged, Roarke resolved with a heavy heart. Something wrenched deep within him as he walked away from the muted sounds of Adela's sobs, knowing he alone was responsible for her misery, but powerless to ease her troubles.

Likely 'twas that he would make things worse, should he even endeavor to try, Roarke concluded sourly, kicking snow aimlessly out of the way as he trudged out of town.

"You! No beggars in the keep this day!"

Roarke turned at the gatekeeper's cry and folded his arms irritably across his chest, thinking the man would do well not to press his luck. Cold he was, his thin shoes no match for either the snow or the walk from town, and naught did he want but a hot bath and something warm to eat. Once he had slept, the inadequacies of merely tending to his body's needs now that his heart's desire had been denied would become most clear, he was certain, but no mind had Roarke to dwell on the matter now.

The burly man approached him with solid steps, his chest puffed with pride in his authority, and fixed Roarke with a professionally discouraging eye.

"Alms on Tuesdays and Fridays, and then only in the morn," he informed Roarke briskly without ever truly looking into his face.

"Time was you looked to whom you addressed, Wolfram," Roarke said coldly, drawing the man's gaze to his with a start.

"Sir!" he exclaimed, clapping one hand over his heart in surprise. "Indeed I did not recognize you in this garb. My pardon, sir!"

"Well it seems to me that times have changed at Aalgen," Roarke muttered, watching the color rise over the gatekeeper's jowls.

"Tighter security have we now, sir, for I have been so bidden," he confirmed with a defensive air. "Please understand that no offense was meant."

Roarke held the gaze of the man who had tended Aalgen's gates for as long as he could remember, noting with interest the flicker of fear that danced there. "No harm done, Wolfram," he finally said quietly, his exhaustion claiming him more tenaciously in the wake of his irritation. "Mayhap you would know where I might find Denis."

"At his books until dinner, sir. 'Tis his way these days."

Roarke tapped on the door to Denis' office, and summoned a weary smile when the older man glanced up. Remarkably, no surprise flickered through the chatelain's eyes at his appearance, though Roarke had little strength left for pondering such petty inconsistencies. Denis smiled thinly in return and waved his quill invitingly in the direction of the other chair.

"You look in need of a seat," he said without preamble. Roarke ran one hand through his hair as he stepped into the room, wondering if 'twas merely his imagination that Denis seemed less friendly.

"I should fear to sit, that I might not stand again," he jested weakly, closing his eyes as he leaned back in the chair. "But indeed, I care not at this point if I sleep on this very spot."

"Walked from Ghent, have you?" Denis inquired mildly, dipping his quill with businesslike ease as Roarke's eyes flew open in surprise. How could the chatelain know that? Denis wrote across the ledger, apparently undisturbed, and Roarke frowned.

"Taken up divination, have you?" he asked, but the chatelain shook his head with a faint measure of amusement.

"Told I was of your whereabouts," he replied enigmatically. " 'Tis some risk you have taken, young man," he added, though the censure in his tone was lighter than Roarke might have expected.

"You *know,*" he breathed, earning a curt nod from the old man. "How long have you known?"

"Since yesterday" was the terse reply, though still Roarke could make little sense of it all. Apparently sensing his confusion, Denis pierced him with a bright eye. "Yves was sent to follow you."

News this was, and Roarke worked through the implications as best he was able, but found himself returning to the same question. Why would any care where he had gone? He threatened no one—indeed, he worked off a family debt.

"But why?" Roarke demanded with a deepening frown. "Surely where I go is of concern to me alone."

"Not when you disfigure the honorable reputation of your house beyond recognition," Robert answered coldly.

Roarke looked up in surprise to find his brother-in-law framed in the portal, hands braced on his hips as though he expected a fight. Dazed at this turn of events and its import, Roarke could only return Robert's regard, watching as the other man shook his head disparagingly.

"Apprenticed to a weaver," he said with a sneer as he stepped fully into the small room. "Surely even *you* could find more worthy ways to spend your time."

Roarke looked to Denis' carefully composed features and then to the floor, even now uncertain how much Robert knew. Was it best to play along that 'twas impulsiveness alone that made him do such, or should he explain about the debts he sought to erase? Surely he did not want to draw

Rochelle into this discussion, for she indeed was most vulnerable, should Robert turn against them all.

"The moneylender confided that he sold Rochelle's note to the weaver," Denis supplied flatly, as though he had seen the direction of Roarke's thoughts, and Roarke lifted one hand to his brow. 'Twas all out in the open, evidently, and the fat would shortly be in the fire, if 'twas not burning there already.

"Working as a common laborer," Robert said with no small measure of disgust, his attitude finally rousing Roarke's ire. Had he not endeavored to make the best of a bad situation? Was it not love and respect for his family that had motivated him to make this sacrifice?

And what was the matter with common labor? No deceit had he practiced by working with his hands. Indeed, the work in Mathieu's shop satisfied him more than any task he had turned a hand to as a knight. It irked him sorely to be judged on the name of the task alone, not his ability to perform it or the merit of those labors in society.

"I sought only to defend the honor of the house," Roarke protested hotly, earning himself a derisive laugh.

"By shaming yourself and your lineage in town?" Robert scoffed. "Please spare me the tale. Your folly will make us the laughingstock of the province. 'Twill be all the talk at the countess' court, to be sure, that a knight of Aalgen has taken to shoveling the leavings of a weaver's two old mares."

"But unpaid debts would not have injured the reputation of the house?" Roarke challenged, rising to his feet. He had decided he had heard enough.

"I would have settled the debts," Robert claimed.

"Would you have?" Roarke demanded. "My sister was not so quick to pledge your purse. Indeed, she wished you to know naught of this matter, so certain was she that such financial issues would curb your ardor."

"Do not lay the blame for this whimsy at her door," Robert retorted coldly.

"Naught of my choice to work did she know," Roarke clarified, fighting the urge to point a finger at the arrogant man facing him. "Denis I told only that I had resolved the issue of the debt, and no more. But make no mistake, more than half of the debt was Rochelle's. Did she not beg you to conceal it, Denis?"

"Aye, and well enough I told you, sir, that the debt could only be cleared in the books if 'twere paid," the chatelain confirmed matter-of-factly.

"And I saw that it was paid," Roarke concluded. "Surely there is no shame in that?"

"To see a debt paid is one matter, to bend to the whims of women another. But what you have done—" Robert's gaze swept contemptuously over Roarke's garb "—what you have done is a betrayal. A betrayal, plain and simple, of the worst order, for in doing this, you have made a denial of your lineage and of your status. Folly 'twas, Roarke, no more and no less, and well shall I ensure that you pay dearly for your crime against this house."

"What crime?" Roarke demanded indignantly. "Saw to the family's debts by the labor of my hands is all I have done."

"Precisely." Robert bit out the word with satisfaction. "'Tis not your place to labor with your hands, and well enough you know it. No matter what the price."

"Mayhap I enjoy working with my hands," Roarke retorted.

Robert's brows arched high. "Then indeed you are a greater fool than even I imagined," he said. "And little choice have I—to preserve the honor of the house, you understand—than to ban your presence from Aalgen."

"What nonsense is this?" Roarke exclaimed furiously, something going still within him at the resolve gleaming in the other man's eyes. "This you cannot do."

"Nay?" Robert inquired, with the air of one who knew the opposite to be true. "Indeed, 'tis simple for me to do precisely thus. Already is it specified that you inherit naught, by Aalgen's own tradition.

"There remains naught but the matter of your stipend," he concluded to Roarke's astonishment, snapping his fingers impatiently at Denis. Denis lifted a small sack from the casket that reposed on his desk, refusing to meet Roarke's eyes as he counted out the coins within the sack and slipped them back within.

'Twas the amount of Roarke's stipend, not a denier more or less, and he numbly took the sack from Denis. Well it seemed that this scene had been planned, and he knew not what else to do but play along, so astounded was he by what was happening around him.

Cast out of his home, paid off years before he had anticipated. Treating him like some common thief, they were, a blackmailer or similar, to be granted his due and sincerely hoped never to be seen again.

"Simple, as I said," Robert noted with a chilly smile. "The gates close shortly. I would suggest that you not find yourself within Aalgen's walls this night."

With that, Robert spun, his surcoat fluttering in his wake as he stalked down the shadowed corridor. Roarke watched him leave in silent amazement, then turned to Denis with a cocked brow, seeking he knew not what from this man he had trusted for so long.

"There are many indeed who would see his side," Denis conceded apologetically, his fingers nervous as he moved his ink pot aimlessly across the expanse of his desk. What did *he* think? Roarke knew not, and evidently Denis was not tempted to say, his loyalty to his liege lord unswerving. "What you have done is irregular, to say the least," he added. "And foolhardy at best."

Roarke frowned at the sack in his hand, knowing he could not make his feelings about his choice to work for Mathieu more clearly understood than he had. He had done what he thought to be right, had endeavored to save his family from shame. Indeed, it seemed he had gained little other by his sacrifice than the disgust of those at Aalgen.

'Twould be long indeed before he matched the feat of this day, this much Roarke knew, for he had been cast from not one but two households since the sun had sleepily risen. Things could scarcely get worse, but at least he owed Denis the truth of the matter.

"The weaver died, Denis," he confessed in a low voice, grief at Mathieu's passing welling up within him with unexpected intensity. Roarke cleared his throat, feeling the other man's expectant look, though he could not glance up to meet his gaze. "Two years had I sworn to serve to erase the debt, and just over a month of it completed. His heir has cast me out, and I know not what will become of the remaining debt."

A heavy silence filled the office, and then Denis cleared his throat in turn. "I see" was all he said, and Roarke stifled a desire to laugh aloud. Indeed, Denis saw precious little of the reality confronting Roarke, and he considered momentarily the prospect of enlightening the older man.

But for what purpose? Naught could be gained by such an outburst. Roarke fingered the sack again, glancing up abruptly to meet the older man's thoughtful regard as he decided what he must do before he left the keep.

"Responsibility did I take for this debt," he affirmed softly, tossing the sack of coins across Denis' desk with a sudden and cavalier gesture.

Denis jumped in surprise as the cord loosened and the coins spilled forth. The silver reflected the flickering light of the candle as the coins danced and fell to rest, though neither man moved to pick them up.

"You cannot do this," Denis protested quietly, but Roarke shook his head.

"'Tis done," he said flatly, blinking back his tears as he turned away. "Betwixt Aalgen and me, the slate is as clear as ever it will be."

With that he stepped out of the familiar office, oblivious of the sounds and sights of the hall as he strode out to the bailey and crossed the snowy expanse to the château gates.

'Twas late the next morning before Adela could stir herself from her mattress. The house was cold, and she shivered at the sight of the barren hearth in the kitchen, wondering that no whisper of looms rose from the shop below. She folded her arms about herself to ward off the chill as she went downstairs, then paused on the bottom step to look over the silent ship.

Mathieu was here, in her mind's eye, at least, his portly figure bustling here and there, those bushy brows rising in acknowledgment of a comment or a jest. Adela sighed, the sight of three baskets of sorted fleece prompting her errant mind to sketch in Roarke, and tears rose unbidden to blur her vision.

Alone she was, and she dared not think overmuch about that. Alone, with few prospects. Mayhap the guild would let her continue to run the shop. She had the skills, they well knew, although undoubtedly they would prefer her to have a spouse to run the business. 'Twas the way of things, and practical enough, but without her maidenhead . . . Adela expelled a shaky sigh and tapped her fingertips on her elbow.

Well, she could but ask.

A tap at the back door brought Adela out of her reverie, and she was surprised to find Bertha on the step, the sympathy in her eyes bringing Adela precariously close to weeping yet again.

"So sorry we were to hear, love," she said, and Adela nodded quickly, hoping she would not be expected to say much. "'Tis said that Gunther is beside himself," she whispered, but Adela had naught to say that might reassure the other man.

"An accident," she managed to mumble, and Bertha patted her consolingly on the shoulder.

"That 'twas, love, and a tragic one, to be sure." She gestured to the pot she carried, which Adela noticed for the first time. "A little something did I bring along to tide you over. Well enough do I recall that I could not bear to think of cooking those first days after my husband passed away, God rest his soul, but men, you know, are seldom ones to forget their meals. And the last thing you are needing is that devil Roarke pestering you to cook."

Adela accepted the pot with some measure of amazement, so uncertain what to say that her words stumbled out clumsily. "Roarke is not here," she confessed abruptly, but Bertha only smiled.

"Back he will be when 'tis time to eat, you can be sure of that, love," she said blithely, then frowned when Adela stubbornly shook her head.

"Nay," she said with quiet resolve. "This time he is gone for good."

Bertha regarded Adela with shock, then shook her head with businesslike assurance as she evidently dismissed the words. "Not yourself are you, love, that much is clear. Feel your skin—chilled to the bone you are." The older woman tucked Adela proprietarily under her arm and steered her toward the stairs.

"Naught have you to fear about Roarke's return," she chided maternally, and Adela could only mutely follow her lead. "That boy will be back. Have we not all seen how he looks at you? Love, you have had him in a tangle from the start, but make no mistake. Despite his frivolous manner, that young man is one who knows what is right and does it. Back he will be, for anyone can see that you need him now."

So astonishing were Bertha's words that Adela had problems absorbing them in her mind. Could Roarke truly care for her? Was it possible that Bertha was right?

Had she made the biggest mistake of her life by casting him out?

"What you need is a hot blaze and something warm to line your belly," Bertha concluded as she hustled Adela up the stairs to the kitchen and tut-tutted at the cold hearth. "What is that boy thinking, leaving you without starting the fire? A word will I have with him, you can be sure of that," she muttered darkly under her breath, turning to give Adela a perky smile once more.

"A little something, and then you will be able to think straight, love," she informed a confused Adela as she bent purposefully over the hearth. "No worries have you about the funeral, at least, for the guild will take care of that. Indeed, I have oft said to the others that 'tis worth the dues for that assurance alone, for funerals can be a costly and troublesome business, love...."

Chapter Fifteen

"Roarke d'Aalgen! Where do you go?"

Roarke turned reluctantly back at the gate at the sound of his mother's indignant voice, avoiding Wolfram's sympathetic gaze. He stifled a groan, despite the pleasure that rose within him at the sight of his mother's characteristic fluster, knowing he had not the heart to tell her his tale right now. She slipped on a patch of ice, regaining her footing before any could assist her, and came to an ungainly stop before him, only to look him pertly in the eye.

"Never did I think to see the day that you would come home and not take the time to at least speak to me," she charged good-naturedly. When Roarke did not immediately respond in kind, her eyes narrowed and she seemed to notice for the first time his simple dress.

"Where is your cloak?" she demanded impatiently. "Too cold 'tis for this sort of garb, and well enough do I know that you have better." Roarke could not summon an answer, for then he would be condemned to tell the fullness of the tale, and so instead he dropped his gaze mutely to the ground. "Wolfram," she commanded, "fetch Roarke's fur-lined cloak from the keep, and his proper boots."

Wolfram shuffled, but did not move, and Roarke shot the other man a knowing glance.

"He will not, *maman*."

Ermengarde regarded her son with shock. "Why ever not?"

Roarke sighed and curved his hands around his mother's shoulders, not knowing how to tell her this piece of news. Best 'twas to just blurt it out simply, he supposed. "No longer welcome am I at Aalgen," he informed her quietly. "Little doubt have I that Wolfram has been ordered to watch my back pass his post, and no more."

Ermengarde's shock faded quickly to dismay, and she cast a suspicious glance to the gatekeeper, who, to his credit, looked not at all comfortable with his situation.

"Verily?" she inquired of the gatekeeper, who shuffled his feet sheepishly.

"Aye, milady."

"And who gave you this order?" she asked archly. Roarke smiled despite himself in admiration of his mother's regal manner. Only too well did she know the answer to that, he would wager, though her very tone made Wolfram fidget all the more.

"Milord Robert, *madame*."

"Fetch him here, if you please." Ermengarde bit out the command.

"But, milady—" Wolfram managed to protest before Ermengarde silenced him with a single look.

"'Twas I who recommended you for this post, and well you know it," she reminded the gatekeeper, and Roarke watched the man's ears grow ruddy.

"Aye, milady," he agreed awkwardly.

"Please fetch Robert," she repeated, satisfaction dawning on her face as the man scurried off. She turned a remarkably sharp glance on her son, who met her gaze warily. Rare indeed was it for Ermengarde to show resolve, but when she did, Roarke knew better than to object.

"What is this about?" she demanded in a low voice, and Roarke shrugged.

"Complicated, 'tis, *maman*, and I would not burden you with the tale," he said in an effort to avoid repeating the lengthy story, only to have his mother snort under her breath in a most unladylike manner. She wagged one finger at him indulgently, the humor glinting in her eyes belying her stern words.

"Well enough do I recognize this pose of the martyr, for your sire oft felt sorry for himself when he alone had made a mess of matters," she charged, her voice dropping to a confidential tone as she leaned closer. "Have you made a mess of matters?" she asked, and Roarke could not hide his embarrassment at being so readily discovered.

"Aye, it seems so, *maman*," he admitted reluctantly, feeling all of five summers old.

"But no assistance will you plead," she muttered under her breath with an eloquent roll of her eyes. She straightened her shoulders to turn and face the arrival of a disgruntled Robert before Roarke could respond.

"Well I hear that my son is being cast from his family home," she said by way of greeting, her tone openly challenging. Roarke regarded her in amazement, stunned that his mother, of all people, was going to champion his cause.

"Shame has he cast upon the house," Robert retorted defensively. "'Tis a blessing to all of us to see his back turned upon us."

"A matter of interpretation is that," Ermengarde countered, with a directness that reminded Roarke unexpectedly of Adela.

He frowned, though none noted the gesture, and tried to decide yet again if she had really wanted him to leave this morn. His conscience pricked at him, making him wonder if he had misjudged the direction of her mind once more, and whether she was cursing his sorry hide even now. Roarke fidgeted with the sense that he should return to Ghent to keep an eye on her, even if still she spurned him, for Adela was not as hardy as she would have one believe.

"For I indeed do not look with favor upon the prospect of seeing my only son naught again," Ermengarde continued frostily.

Robert stiffened at this charge, but stubbornly held his ground. "He will make us the laughingstock of all these petty provincials."

"By doing what?"

Robert sniffed with disdain. "He is laboring for a common weaver."

"Truly?" Ermengarde turned on her son with evident delight and fairly clapped her hands in excitement. "You did this thing? Let me see your hands. Have you calluses yet?"

"Aye, *maman,* I have done this," Roarke admitted heavily, well aware of Robert's scorn. Ermengarde looked up at him brightly, no disappointment glazing her eyes at finding his flesh as yet untarnished by calluses, and he knew he had to supply some additional explanation. "I sought to work off the debts of the house, but Robert finds my means of doing so abhorrent."

"'Twas your folly to choose such a means, and I would not see those under my responsibility suffer for it. The tourneys would have been a much more appropriate choice," Robert interjected, but Ermengarde pointedly ignored him.

"You did this for me," she whispered mistily. Roarke shifted awkwardly on his feet, more than a little disconcerted that his unworldly mother was the only one who saw the merit of what he had thought to be a reasonable plan.

"Aye, *maman,*" he agreed. "Well you know the power of your tears."

Ermengarde grinned recklessly at that. "'Twas just as your sire oft said," she said mischievously. Trepidation grew alarmingly within Roarke when his mother spun abruptly to face Robert in a sweep of skirts.

"This you find reprehensible?" she asked with surprise, and Robert nodded vigorously.

"Naught else can it be for one born noble to bend his hand to labor," he spat, encompassing Roarke with a sweeping gesture. "Regard his dress, regard the growth of stubble on his chin. No manner is this for one of such rank as he, and well enough should he know the difference."

Ermengarde drew herself up tall in indignation, the top of her proud head still not reaching Roarke's chin. "Do you question his upbringing?" she demanded, as haughtily as one of her stature could manage.

Robert considered the question for but a moment, then plunged back into the fray. "Aye, *madame,* that I do. How else might he have learned these degenerate beliefs?"

"Degenerate?" Ermengarde repeated hotly, and Roarke took an unwilling step back. "'Tis *you* who are degenerate! 'Tis you who do not understand what honor means!" She advanced on Robert with a well-placed jab of her finger, and Robert had the grace to look moderately alarmed.

"My son upheld the honor of Aalgen by covering its debts as best he was able and in the manner he found most fitting. *That* is honor. *That* is what it means to be nobly born. To conduct oneself with pride and honor. But you—" her gaze swept disparagingly over Robert "—*you* could not be expected to understand something so simple."

"*Madame,* you overstep yourself," Robert informed Ermengarde stiffly.

"*Maman,* Denis says he is right," Roarke murmured, earning a scathing glance from his mother.

"*Denis* never understood anything of merit, either," she hissed, jabbing her chin into the air as she faced Robert defiantly again. Roarke could not even begin to imagine what she might say, but he had no chance to interrupt her before she was addressing the other man again.

"Honor of the house," she repeated with disgust. "And what would you know of the honor of Aalgen? Raised here, I was, and what I know of honor will I show to you, for evident 'tis that you have the need of such a lesson. Honor of the house means not the reputation of the family among petty neighbors, but the nobility to make the fitting choice, no matter how difficult such a choice might be for he who makes it. That alone is honor, that alone is our birthright and responsibility, for the house that follows this path finds their reputation blossoming in response."

Ermengarde paused to assess the effect of her words, and Roarke wondered if 'twas as evident to her as it was to him that Robert remained unconvinced.

"One who has courted such shame cannot remain among us," Robert stated flatly, and Ermengarde's lips thinned impatiently.

"So, you choose to spurn my words," she charged as she folded her arms across her chest. "Well will you learn of honor this day, one way or the other, Robert, make no mistake. For should you wish to cast out the son of my own womb, the son of the woman whose inheritance you govern, then also shall you have to cast me out."

The dangerous words lay in a tense silence between the two, and Roarke barely dared to breathe at his mother's audacity.

Ermengarde risked too much, though, and he suspected Robert would not fear to call her bluff. And he would not see his mother turned out of her home for something he had done.

"*Maman,* I agreed to go," he reminded her quietly as she and Robert continued to glare at each other in silent challenge.

"No right has he to take this from you," she muttered, her words sparking something in her opponent.

"*Every* right have I to do this!" Robert asserted boldly, seemingly regaining his tongue so that the words spilled over themselves in their haste to be heard. "Every right have I, and this right will I take. As lord of this keep and administrator of these estates, my decision stands."

"Then I will leave," Ermengarde stated without missing a beat, spinning on her heel and tucking her arm into Roarke's elbow as though they but took an afternoon stroll.

Robert seemed struck speechless by her move, and Roarke looked between the two of them, uncertain what to do.

Surely his mother did not intend to walk back to Ghent with him?

"*Maman,* you cannot do this. I will not let you cast everything away," Roarke protested, but his mother waved his arguments airily aside.

"Time enough for a change, 'tis," she said with a pert smile, tugging impatiently on his elbow. "Come along, Roarke, the day grows old."

Roarke frowned, not knowing how to word his objection that his mother might not be offended. "*Maman,* understand that I take naught but what is on my back. We shall have to walk, and no food have we—" Ermengarde fixed him with a bright eye, the corner of her mouth twitching as though she fought a smile.

"Think you that I would make a poor beggar?" she asked, and he knew not what to say when she leaned over to tap him firmly on the chest. "Talents have I of which you know naught, my son," she assured him confidently. "A wager will I take that 'twill be I who gains our lodging and first meal."

The very thought of his mother begging on the streets struck Roarke as so ludicrous that he could not help but laugh, though the glitter of determination in her eyes left him little doubt that she would succeed. Her choice had she made, and well enough did he see that 'twas not his place to further try to change her mind. He laughed aloud at her expectant air and led her out the gate with a light step, fully aware of the incredulous expressions on both Wolfram's and Robert's faces.

"Do you dare to laugh at me?" she charged gaily as she picked up her skirts, and Roarke chuckled anew.

"Of an old friend was I suddenly reminded. 'Twas your talk of 'honor' I think," he confided and his mother smiled victoriously.

"A wise man is he, then?" she asked laughingly, and Roarke felt his grin widen.

"I know not, but well it seems you two might agree on matters of the nobility."

"Then most assuredly he is a wise man," Ermengarde concluded, giving Roarke's arm a little shake. "You must introduce us, for long indeed has it been since I spoke to a man with a whit of sense."

Roarke's smile grew sadder, and he shook his head, even as he eyed the distance to Ghent and the lengthening shadows. "Would that I could, *maman*," he murmured, giving her hand a squeeze. "Would that I could."

Bertha did indeed help Adela collect her thoughts, so much so that by the late afternoon she was restless within the confines of the house.

She studiously avoided her father's belongings, not yet ready to face the task of touching his clothes or straightening out the amiable disorder of his room. In the shop, she had discovered quite by accident a length of cloth, already cut and half-stitched, the familiarity of the colors making her smile wistfully.

A cloak 'twas, a woman's cloak by its length and cut, and one evidently for her, judging by the way 'twas secreted away with the books of the business that she was not to touch on her own. And well enough did Adela recall this topaz wool, the richness of the color one that she had admired when it came back from the dyers.

She buried her nose in the wool and caught the faint scent of her father's skin, savoring the sweet reminder of his thoughtfulness. Warm she felt suddenly, the realization that somehow she would and could go on without Mathieu filling her with quiet resolve. Adela carried the length of wool back upstairs with her, cradling it in her arms like a child, suddenly determined to finish this work he had started for her and wear his craftsmanship with pride.

After all, there was no one to nurse her back to health should she fall ill this winter, and well enough did this intended gift recall his scolding of the winter before.

Mayhap 'twas that realization that fueled her desire to escape the memories of the house, the pallet on the hearth in the kitchen that she dared not even look at, let alone touch, and Adela donned near everything she owned before heading outside into the cold. The horses needed tending, and after their fright two days past, 'twould be cruel indeed for her to neglect them.

The work of mucking out the stalls made her warmer even than Bertha's soup, and the pungency of the manure teased her nostrils and reminded her of the vibrancy of life. Adela forced herself to inhale deeply of the crisp, cold air, the scent of the manure, the taste of someone's distant fire. She doffed her gloves and ran her fingers appreciatively through the thick winter coats the horses had grown, gazing about the barn with new eyes.

She liked it out here, she realized, intuitively understanding why Roarke had felt so at home in the barn. An honesty there was about matters here in the stables, the horses' needs straightforward, the links of trap pure in their function and design. Adela trailed her hand over the heavy leather harnesses hanging on the wall, sleek with years of wear and the accumulated sweat of the horses, kicking aside the straw as she walked.

Something out of place caught her eye, and she bent, the softness of the fur that enveloped her cold fingers surprising her with its unexpectedness. Adela crouched and dug carefully scraped and stretched rabbit hides out of the corner where they had evidently been hidden. With amazement, she spread them carefully across her lap, as though they might vanish before her very eyes.

Tears rose in eyes that she had thought could never manage to squeeze out another tear, and she stroked the soft fur, unwilling to believe the thought that assaulted her mind.

It simply could not be thus.

Adela counted the pelts with shaking fingers, knowing how many there would be before she started, biting her lip at the confirmation that the hide of every rabbit Roarke had dressed for her rested in her lap.

She recalled the way Mathieu had left the edges of the cloak destined for her unfinished, and easily guessed the destination of these pelts. Not just her father, but her men, had planned this surprise for her. A gift of their own labors it was to have been, and in the face of this she could not believe that she had been so cruel to Roarke. Adela pressed one trembling hand to her forehead at this new sign that she had erred in casting him out.

Curse that devil, she thought with a reluctant smile as she buried her nose in the fur. Flea-bitten. Thrown to the dogs. Unfit for use. Each of Roarke's disclaimers rose in Adela's mind, even as she saw his earnest expression when he had made the tale. As though he had not expected her to believe him. She chuckled unevenly, biting her lip as her tears threatened to spill, and gathered the soft pelts to her chest.

He did care, he simply must, for why else would he go to such trouble? Briefly Adela toyed with the thought that he had stretched the hides for another, but no. Her heart knew the way of it—indeed, that organ always had.

If only she had had the sense to listen to its claims.

Adela sat back on her heels in the quiet barn, fingering the pelts and shaking her head at her own foolishness. He was gone. She had sent Roarke away and bidden him never return, she recalled with dawning dismay.

And if Roarke followed her dictate, how would she ever find him again?

"Who is she?" Roarke's mother demanded in the darkness, and Roarke stiffened on his pallet before he turned nonchalantly toward the mattress his mother occupied. To his dismay, she had in fact obtained lodgings for them that night, and a hot meal, as well, in the home of a villein on the outskirts of Aalgen. Roarke had been considering their path when his mother's question interrupted his thoughts.

"Who?" he responded mildly, certain that his mother could not have guessed his secret, though his heart raced nonetheless.

"The woman who has you in such a muddle," Ermengarde responded pertly. "Who is she?"

Roarke felt his color rise, and was grateful for the cover of darkness as he desperately sought some reasonable response. "No woman is there," he managed to protest, only to hear yet again that unfeminine snort of derision.

"Truly you do not hide your feelings so well as that," his mother chided, and Roarke's heart sank. "How many times this evening did you lose the thread of what I told you? How many times did I find you gazing into naught?"

Ermengarde's words sent a ripple of dismay through Roarke, and he nearly sat straight up. Was it true? Was he acting like some besotted calf? Had Adela divined that he held her in regard, as well? His panic was short-lived, for he quickly recalled her refusal of him and scowled into the shadows.

"And so certain you are that 'tis a woman who distracts me?" he asked crossly, his mother's light chuckle doing naught to assuage his pride.

"With your turn of mind, what else could trouble you so?" she retorted blithely.

What else, indeed? Roarke folded his hands resolutely behind his head and glared at the dim silhouettes of the rafters.

"Oh, Roarke," his mother said softly a long moment later. "Certain I am that you can win the heart of any woman you desire."

"Not this one," he responded, more sharply than he had intended, and felt his mother's surprise. Naught did she say, and he sighed heavily, knowing that she would not be content without an explanation. "She refused me when I asked for her hand," he confided, his voice low with embarrassment.

"Well," his mother said indignantly, and he heard the rustle of bedclothes as she sat up purposefully. "Evidently this woman needs the benefit of some common sense."

Roarke smiled despite himself, unable to imagine his mother as a fount of common sense. Then his smile faded as a sobering thought occurred to him. "Mayhap 'tis common sense that bids her refuse me," he suggested slowly, not at all comfortable with the prospect. But had he not himself told Adela that he was not the choice for her?

"Nonsense," his mother concluded flatly. Her tone became speculative as Roarke felt her peering through the darkness at him. "You did, of course, tell her how you felt?" she asked, and Roarke fidgeted.

"Evident enough is my regard by my very proposal," he hedged, hating the way his mother tut-tutted to herself at that.

"But did you tell her that you love her?" she insisted, and he turned to face her in the shadows in shock.

"Tell her *what?*"

"That you love her," she repeated calmly.

"Nay, nay," Roarke stammered, disliking that he sounded so discomfited by such a ludicrous idea. *Love* her? Ridiculous. And even if he was enamored of Adela, on the most remote chance, never would he tell her so. What manner of man would freely tighten the noose around his neck? "Never would I tell her such a falsehood," he said firmly.

"Falsehood?" Ermengarde challenged quietly, and Roarke fancied that she chuckled under her breath again. "Falsehood," she repeated, and audibly laughed.

"You think 'tis not so?" Roarke demanded impatiently. "You think I could not hold a woman in regard, yet not be in love with her?"

His mother stilled her quiet laughter with an evident effort and cleared her throat carefully before she spoke. "I think you protest the charge overmuch," she maintained, her words silencing the last of Roarke's protests.

Was it true? Was he in love with Adela? Was that why she troubled him? Was that why he could not rid his thoughts of her?

It could not be. Never would he permit a woman to hold him and his heart in thrall.

Roarke's heart began to pound as he reflected once again on Adela's refusal. Had she truly turned him down only because he had failed to make a sweet confession?

Nonsense 'twas, and surely she was practical enough to see the matter clearly. Hope surged through Roarke, and he tossed on the hard pallet, suddenly impatient for the morning to arrive. Should he seek out Adela and set her straight on these inconsequential confessions of the heart, mayhap she would change her mind.

At the very least, he owed it to Mathieu to try.

The press of familiar faces surrounded Adela in the churchyard, and her heart swelled with gratitude that her sire had been so loved by those in his employ. The priest's words drifted over her unheard, untold memories filling her mind to overflowing as the coffin was lowered into the ground.

Godspeed, Papa, she thought. The hollow echo of the priest's handful of dirt landing on the coffin drew her back to the present. She felt the priest's expectant regard upon her and fingered her own handful of dirt, uncertain she was quite ready to bid a final farewell.

Adela glanced over the assembly of mourners, seeking support of some kind, but found only expectancy on those well-known faces. Until she spied Roarke.

He stood on the far side of the group, his expression somber, his gaze holding hers unflinchingly. Relief that she had been granted this unexpected opportunity to see him again flooded through Adela and so weakened her knees that she thought she might fall. Bertha's arm closed resolutely around her waist, the older woman evidently having seen her waver.

"Always will he be with you in your thoughts, love," she murmured reassuringly, but Adela could not tear her gaze away from Roarke, feeling for a confusing instant that Bertha referred to Roarke, not Mathieu. "Come, 'tis time we all got out of the chill," she urged.

Adela felt her eyes fill with tears. The last thing she saw was Roarke's nod of encouragement. She cast the dirt into the grave and turned quickly away, embarrassed that she should make such a public display of her grief. Bertha patted her once more on the shoulder, and the assembly began to disperse, the gravediggers purposefully setting to the task of filling the grave.

Countless hands offered solace in their own way, a pat on the shoulders, a handshake, but Adela was oblivious of them all. When her vision cleared, she dared to glance back to the spot where Roarke had stood, her heart sinking when she saw he was not there.

He had only come to pay his respects to Mathieu, she realized dully, taking a ragged breath in an effort to compose herself. Indeed, she had dared to hope too much.

"Adela, I would like you to meet my mother." His voice came unexpectedly from before her, and Adela looked up with a start.

"I thought you gone," she whispered unevenly. Roarke smiled, his eyes as warm upon her as the finger he gently touched beneath her chin.

"Not without speaking to you, *chouchou*," he teased in a low voice. "Surely you do not think me so ill-bred as that."

Needled by the reminder of his noble birth, Adela turned abruptly away, folding her arms across her chest. "Call me not that," she urged bitterly.

"Why ever not?" Roarke demanded, and she glanced up to find his brow darkened in a scowl.

"No flattery is it to be addressed so, when you have doubtless coaxed countless other women with that same

endearment," she retorted, refusing to be softened by his
evident displeasure.

"Doubtless not," he said flatly. Adela looked up once
more and saw that Roarke's earlier scowl had been but a
promise of the one that he wore now.

"I do not understand," she said warily, barely daring to
hope in her foolish dream yet again.

"None have I ever called *chouchou* but you," Roarke said
so resolutely that Adela could not doubt he spoke the truth.
Her heart quivered, but she refused to give it rein to soar, so
certain was she her hopes would be dashed yet again.

"I do not believe you," she lied, delighting in the exasperation that flickered across those beloved features.

"How like you 'tis to think the worst of me," he growled,
and 'twas all Adela could do not to laugh aloud. She
thought of the rabbit pelts and hugged herself tighter, certain 'twould be mere moments before she heard the telling
words. "Mayhap 'tis because no other woman has kissed me
so sweetly amongst her cabbages, but never have I whispered that endearment into a willing ear before you."

Roarke took Adela's hands in hers, and she was sure he
would feel her trembling, but he simply stared down at her
slim hands, trapped within the breadth of his. Nervous he
was, and she longed to kiss away his dismay, to tell him he
had to say naught, for she was his. But nay, 'twould trouble her later if she heard not the words, well enough she
knew, and she would wait out his declaration.

"Adela, I would ask you again to consider my offer,"
Roarke urged in a low voice, some of his trepidation evidently easing when he tentatively met her eyes. A smile
pulled at the corner of his mouth then, and he dropped his
voice to that even lower tone that so unnerved Adela.
"Chouchou," he added seductively, and 'twas all she could
do not to fall into his arms and kiss him breathless.

"Say it," she demanded impatiently, uncertain how long
she could manage to wait.

"Say what?" Roarke asked suspiciously, his eyes narrowing as he pulled back minutely, but Adela barely noted his dismay.

"That you love me, of course," she chided him gaily, unable to avoid noticing the way he gritted his teeth and his expression cooled.

"Adela, can we not dispense with these sweet confessions?" he asked, and Adela drew back to cast an assessing glance over him.

"You do not care," she whispered hoarsely. She could not believe that she had been so foolish as to believe in her dream once again.

Roarke grimaced, his gaze intent as he held hers, his grip tightening on her hands as though he feared she might flee. "Of no import is such a confession, and well you know it. I hold you in regard, I would wed you and do honorably by you, 'tis truly all you need to know."

"Nay!" Adela protested hotly, shocked that he would play her for a fool. "Nay, 'tis not enough, and well you know *that*."

"I will not say it, *chouchou*," Roarke vowed, and Adela stared back at him, aghast.

"Then naught else is there to say," she whispered brokenly, pulling her hands free from his grip with an effort. Her tears rose yet again, and she blinked them back impatiently, unwilling to give this impossible man any evidence of how strongly he affected her. She looked for the first time to the older woman beside Roarke and recognized the Lady Ermengarde, her hazel eyes filled with sympathy.

"Adela . . ." Roarke began again, but Adela would not permit his cajoling voice to work its magic upon her. She was spared the trouble of a reply by the interjection of an all-too-familiar feminine voice.

"Lady Ermengarde?" Marie cooed with an affected awe that had all three of them turning to face her. "Mayhap you do not remember, but you were in our shop last summer."

Roarke's mother smiled. "Ah, aye. Well do I remember. The Taintenières, was it not?" she responded with a social ease Adela knew she could not have summoned in this moment to save her life.

"Surprised am I to see you at such a local funeral," Marie commented once greetings had been exchanged, and Ermengarde gestured to Roarke.

"My son wished to attend—" She got no further before Marie's eyes brightened with a mercenary light that Adela hoped she was not the only one to note.

"Your son?" Marie asked excitedly, her gaze raking over Roarke. Adela did not dare to look at the expression on his face, certain he would be more than pleased to have another willing prospect so shortly after she had turned him aside.

And mayhap they were better suited to each other, she thought, suddenly feeling lightheaded from the events of the day. Adela murmured her excuses and stumbled from the churchyard with an aching heart, interested in naught but the silence of her house and the solitude of her mattress.

Chapter Sixteen

Even though she knew all the men at the guild meeting three days later, Adela felt somewhat awkward as the only woman in attendance. But time 'twas to make her appeal, and should she be successful, this situation would be one she would have to grow accustomed to. She folded her hands carefully in her lap, fighting the impulse to check her veil yet again in her nervousness.

No favors did it do her equilibrium to see Roarke slip into the meeting. He flicked a glance over the room, and she bit down hard on her irritation that his freshly laundered shirt made him look yet more handsome than she had recalled. Well she knew she had not been responsible for his cleaning, and ugly thoughts began to ferment in her mind. Evidently he had had little trouble making himself at home in the Taintenière household, Adela concluded bitterly, telling herself that Marie was more than welcome to his deceitful hide.

Roarke seemed to straighten when he spied her sitting quietly to one side, and Adela schooled herself not to let her excitement show when he cut an unerring path toward her. Playing with her he was, no more than that, and she was so distraught at the loss of both him and her father in such short order that she knew herself ill-prepared to defend against his advances.

"Adela," he murmured as he took a seat on the bench beside her, the master of the guild tapping on the table for everyone's attention at that same moment. Adela shot Roarke a scathing glance, cursing him silently for taking the seat when 'twas too late for her to politely move away, and he seemed taken aback by her expression. "Talk we must," he muttered, but she jabbed her chin into the air.

"Naught else have I to say to you," she declared between her teeth. "And certain I am that you have naught to say that might interest me."

"Adela," Roarke growled in frustration, but she shook her head stubbornly once.

"Leave the matter be, Roarke," she whispered tersely, shooting him a look that brooked no argument as the master raised his hand in a final bid for silence.

Roarke held her gaze for a long moment, his gaze sobering slowly. He shook his head, and, fearing he might make another appeal, one that she might not be able to turn aside so readily, Adela turned abruptly to face the front. Roarke sighed beside her, and her heart wrenched at even the possibility that she might have hurt him, but she forced herself to redouble her resolve.

It could not be so. Time and again he had shown that she could not wound him, that she was just another in a long and seemingly endless stream of women. Had Roarke truly held tender feelings for her, he would have confessed to them by this time, and to continue hoping for such a confession was foolhardy at best. Adela straightened her shoulders and fixed her attention on the master, knowing that somehow she had to dismiss Roarke from her heart.

Even if she was achingly aware of him so close beside her that she could feel the warmth rising from his skin through her kirtle. Even if she could not help but watch his hand from the corner of her eye, those strong fingers tapping impatiently on his knee.

Had he not warned her that he was not the man for her? Well it seemed that Roarke himself had seen the matter aright from the first, and she only teased herself by pretending matters could be different between them.

"A special meeting is this, as all we know," the master began, nodding once in Adela's direction, and she braced herself for the inevitable reference. "Long did Mathieu Toisserand have a place among us, and I speak for all of us in extending our sympathies to Adela."

The men nodded around the room, several making gruff comments, and Adela could but nod, the lump in her throat making it difficult for her to speak. Roarke seemed to ease closer, but 'twas her mind playing tricks on her again, she was sure, though intuitively she felt that he offered his support. But little interest could he have in offering her support, with Marie certain to be tending to his needs, she reminded herself forcefully, and did not look to him.

"Adela has applied to the guild for the right to continue to run Mathieu's shop," the master continued, flipping through several papers resting before him. Adela clenched her hands more tightly together, well aware of the approving glances shot her way by her father's former employees. The master glanced up and met Adela's gaze soberly, the considering expression she found there sending her heart plummeting.

"Though indeed Adela has the skill to run the shop and shows an adept hand with the books of account that does credit to Mathieu's lessons, still there rests the matter of her marital status." The master paused, and Adela knew in that instant that they intended to deny her request.

And what then would she do?

"In truth, the matter would be more clear should Adela be wedded or even widowed, but as the matter stands, the council has concerns." The men murmured to each other, and Adela had no doubt that they were agreeing with the wisdom of this concern. Her hands began to shake as the master gestured to her, that she might make her case.

Adela rose to her feet and surveyed the faces turned to her, surprised to find that not all were closed against her.

Mayhap there was a chance after all, she hoped, and her voice carried with a clarity and determination she had not expected when she began to speak.

"Well enough do all of you know me, and most know that I learned to work the looms as soon as Papa could coax me to hold a shuttle."

The assembly chuckled approvingly at this reminder of Mathieu's enthusiasm, and Adela allowed herself to be encouraged. Everything rode on this matter for her, for without the shop, she could not afford to keep the house and would be forced to labor for another. And well she knew that that path was not for her.

"Travelled to the Hot and Cold Fairs with my father have I these last eight years, as well as to England to buy fleece at the Saint Ives fair. Long have I been a full journeyman and worked daily in the shop. My sire also showed me oft the ways of the accounting, that I might manage the shop should he be forced to be away or fall ill." Adela scanned the attentive group once more and knew not what else she could say in her own favor. She drew a deep breath and continued in an even tone.

"I would ask the permission of the guild at this time that I might make my master work and thus gain the status to continue to run the shop my father began." There, she thought, 'twas out in the open for the guild to affirm or deny.

Adela exhaled shakily into the terse silence that followed her request, hoping against hope that she would gain the right she needed to continue. At least let me have the shop, she pleaded silently. Even if she was denied the comfort of Mathieu and the love of Roarke, at least with the shop she could maintain herself and keep her hands from falling idle.

"But should you wed, the responsibilities of hearth and home will oblige you to give up time in the shop," protested one man finally, making the argument Adela most dreaded to hear.

"Nay," she replied with a firm shake of her head. "My father's household have I managed since my mother's death, and the tasks there do not take time from my work." She forced herself to summon a small smile before she continued. "Well enough do you all know that I am getting older, and in truth marriage has little appeal for me."

It seemed Roarke fidgeted beside her at that, but no time had Adela for his sensibilities. Too much lay at stake this night. The men discussed the matter among themselves for a moment while Adela stood silent, painfully aware of her flushed cheeks.

Then the master held up one hand again, reaching for one of the sheets of parchment before him and lifting it to read. Adela's heart began to pound, for she knew not what news the parchment bore, fearing that some other guild member had already lodged a protest against her request.

"A petition from Mathieu have I here," the master supplied, and Adela straightened with a frown. Had her father already anticipated this instance? "But a fortnight old is it, and concerning a different matter, though indeed I suspect it to be relevant to this discussion." He raised his gaze to meet Adela's and held out the parchment. "Adela?"

Adela stepped forward to take the proffered document. Her eyes widened as she scanned the text. "I do not understand," she confessed in confusion, her nervousness rising yet again as she lifted her gaze to the master's once more. "What has this to do with this matter?"

The master smiled a thin smile and turned to address the assembly again. "The document concerns a recommendation from Mathieu that a man of his acquaintance be permitted to join the guild. There is no mistaking his esteem for the man's character, and I would suggest to you all that such a man might be one a man might choose for his daughter to wed."

"Nay!" Adela protested in shock, but the tide of the meeting swept on, undeterred by her objection.

"Solves the matter of leaving a woman alone to run a business," affirmed one man with satisfaction, and Adela felt her eyes widen in horror at the very suggestion.

She would not be compelled to take a spouse at the dictate of the guild! And *this* man! 'Twas too much. She cast a hot glance down at the incriminating document, written in that achingly familiar hand, wondering if her father had ever imagined the havoc his simple praise might unleash.

"Is the man a master?" demanded another, and the master leading the meeting shook his head.

"Nay, but Adela could well teach him," he suggested. Over her dead body, Adela thought mutinously, wishing she could crumple up this document and make it cease to exist.

"The shop cannot be run by a novice" came another argument.

"But Adela could complete her masterwork in short enough order, I am sure, for I have seen that she is indeed skilled. Then she could master the shop until her spouse gained his training and completed his master work."

Sounds of approval broke out over the crowd, and Adela sank into her seat in disbelief. They were going to do this, with or without her agreement. Truly, this could not be happening to her, that she would be compelled to make the one match that would rend her very heart in two.

"Who is the man?" Roarke whispered tersely, and Adela barely noted the outrage in his tone. She numbly handed him the document without a word of explanation, more than willing to let him see the capricious hand of fate himself. He made some sound of disgust under his breath, and she nodded silently at the confirmation that his assessment so closely echoed her own. Only too sweet was this vengeance of some malicious angel.

"Adela, what does it say?" Roarke whispered in annoyance, and she gave him a look of disdain.

"You will not convince me to read you news such as this," she informed him, surprised at the way his lips tightened in frustration. He glanced quickly to the master and leaned closer to her, his gaze burning into hers.

"Well you know that that is the only way that I will learn its contents," he muttered, and Adela felt her eyes widen in shock.

Suddenly she recalled how Roarke had confused the pegs on the warping reel and how defensive he had been when she teased him about it. She eyed him carefully, noting now the signs of his discomfort.

"Can you truly not read it?" she asked quietly. Her question was adequately answered by the hostile look Roarke shot her.

"Never has anyone cared whether or not I could read," he confessed in an undertone that made clear his reluctance to talk about his inability. "Yet here, you seem to think *all* should read, as though 'twere perfectly natural to do so." He gestured with the piece of parchment, and Adela plucked it from his fingers, unable to deny him the knowledge of her father's praise.

"In the name of the Father, the Son and the Holy Ghost, I greet the esteemed masters of the weavers' guild of the fair town of Ghent." She read her father's words tonelessly, without looking up. "This day I would appeal to your wisdom in granting an apprenticeship to a man recently taken into my employ. A willing worker is he, and a man with nimble fingers, a man one can rely upon to fully shoulder his responsibilities and keep to the letter of his word. Although he is older than any apprentice I have yet taken, he seems already to have a manner of bearing fitting to one of our esteemed association, a sureness with business transactions not oft seen and a talent with the thread that seems indeed to have been born within him. I do, then, respectfully ask the guild to honor my offer and grant permission for Roarke d'Aalgen to apprentice in my shop for two years in preparation for journeyman status.''

Adela smoothed the parchment across her lap before she dared to glance up to Roarke. He looked somewhat stunned, and he frowned momentarily before looking down to her.

"Truly your father said thus about me?" he asked hoarsely, and she smiled as she nodded. Roarke took the parchment with surprisingly unsteady fingers, tentatively touching the black outline of the text. ''Would that I could read it for myself,'' he said, so quietly that Adela barely caught his words. She softened toward him, catching herself just before she offered to teach him to read.

A sweet mess that would make, and a situation that would be sure to torment her yet further. And no place had she to even make such a suggestion, Adela reminded herself, her resolution fading with Roarke's proximity. She turned back to the master, only to find him smiling too smugly for her taste.

"Roarke d'Aalgen are you, then?" he demanded genially, and Roarke stood up smoothly.

"Aye, sir," he responded, and as Adela recalled the direction of the master's thoughts, her cheeks began to heat. Surely they did not truly intend to compel her to wed Roarke that she might keep the shop?

"And would you consider the option outlined?" the master asked, his concession making Adela want to stamp her foot in frustration. *Roarke* was being granted the option of denying her, but she would not be granted any choice? Unfair, 'twas, for the shop was hers and hers alone, and no interest had she in welcoming a man to her hearth who did not hold her in regard.

"Aye," Roarke responded evenly, his voice growing more resolute as he continued to speak. "Already did I vow to Mathieu that I would do this." The men nodded to each other in approval at their former comrade's clear thinking.

They evidently considered the matter settled, and Roarke turned back to Adela with a satisfied smile to offer her his hand.

Too much was it that *he* thought the matter so readily settled, when she had already made her objections clear. And too much was it that they all expected her to acquiesce without any consideration of her opinion. Adela ignored Roarke's hand and swept to her feet, raising her chin anew as she confronted the master.

"Roarke has neglected to tell you that already have I declined his offer," she informed the dumbstruck master coldly, and all eyes turned as one upon her.

"Adela, your whimsy has no place here," Roarke warned under his breath, and Adela shot him a venomous look.

"My *whimsy?*" she echoed in amazement. "No whimsy is it that bids me take only a man to my hearth and home who holds me in some measure of regard. 'Tis my hearth, my home, my shop, my skill, that will make the business thrive. Not even as an apprentice are you sworn, and here the guild offers you the full assets of a business on a silver platter. Should I not be skeptical? Long have I waited to take a spouse, and should I take one who would step into such a fine situation, I would at least have one who would make the pretense of holding some tender feelings for me alone."

"I would not lie to you about such a matter," Roarke growled, bracing his hands on his hips as he faced her, as though he would much prefer to give her a shake. Adela was not dissuaded by his anger, and she held his gaze angrily, placing her own hands on her hips as she stared him down.

"Nay, you would not spare me any sweet words at all," she spat. "Should my bed be devoid of love, I would rather it be completely cold."

"What is this nonsense you spout?"

"Having waited this long, I will not take a man to husband who does not love me," Adela affirmed hotly. "Do you love me, Roarke?" she challenged, and it seemed all in the room held their breath.

Roarke gritted his teeth, though he said naught, and Adela spun away from him in disgust. Curse him. If he did not care for her, then she was better without him.

"Then naught more is there to say," she concluded crisply. "I would take my leave from the meeting now that you might continue your business." She addressed the master, and that man nodded mutely in response.

"Adela." Roarke's voice was low with anger, but she did not turn, well aware of the other men watching her progress as she picked her way between the benches, back to the stairwell. A plague on Roarke and all his tempting glances! A small thing she asked of him indeed, yet he could not even manage to form a lie for his own gain. Truly he must find the thought of being bound to her repugnant, and she fought against tears of self-pity as she wound her way across the room.

"Adela." Roarke's voice rose slightly, as though he were growing distressed, but still she ignored him. "Adela, well you know that I love you," Roarke muttered, and though her heart leapt at the confession, she was not prepared to let the matter go so easily. Not even a halfhearted lie would suit her after all of this humiliation. A resounding declaration, no less, or she would remain a spinster for the rest of her days.

Knowing Roarke awaited her response, Adela paused and made a pretense of listening, meeting Gunther's eyes speculatively where he sat before her.

"Is that the wind I hear?" she asked innocently. The older man stifled an unwilling chuckle as he nodded mischievously.

"Noisy in the chimney 'tis this time of year," he replied, the two grinning quickly at each other before Adela nodded matter-of-factly and continued to the stairs.

"Aye, I thought as much," she concluded, sweeping around the last bench as the guild members chuckled behind her.

"Adela!" Roarke called in annoyance as she gained the staircase. Adela smiled to herself as she heard him curse roundly.

Served him right, it did. More than enough chances had she given him, and 'twas time enough she gave him food for thought. An anxious scuffling on the floor above revealed that he headed in pursuit, but Adela continued walking leisurely, raising her nose to the cool air when she gained the street as though she took but a relaxing stroll.

"Adela!" Roarke called, and she turned slowly, tilting back her neck to find him leaning out the window of the room they had met in over one of the other shops. His shirt had come untucked and flicked in the cold winter wind, his hair was tousled, his expression was anguished. Indeed, he looked more agitated than she had yet seen him, and she savored the sight.

"I love you!" he shouted furiously, and Adela smiled yet wider as she stared up at him. 'Twas true, then, she thought, and her heart began to race at the prospect. Roarke loved her! Adela permitted herself to grin outright, knowing she could not have checked the happiness bubbling within her for anything.

Oblivious of her response was Roarke, though, for he was well and thoroughly annoyed. "Loved you I did from the very start, and well enough you should know it, for I showed all the signs," he yelled. "All the journeymen in the shop knew. Your father knew. My mother laid but one eye upon me and knew the truth. Why must you alone be blind to what I feel? I love you, *chouchou!* Would you have me tell all of Ghent before you take my hand?''

''Well do I think you already have,'' Adela responded mildly, laughing at the shock that crossed Roarke's face when he glanced around and realized what he had done.

His eyes glinted dangerously when they landed on her again, his wicked grin ample warning of his intent before he leapt up to crouch on the base of the window. Adela made a little squeal of anticipation and began to run for home before he jumped, knowing full well that Roarke intended to make her pay for his public declaration.

And the closer she was to home and her—nay *their*—plump mattress when he caught her, the less time she would have to wait for his retribution.

Adela heard Roarke land on the stones behind her, his footsteps quick in pursuit, her anticipation rising at the knowledge that she would not get far before he caught her. Still she gathered up her skirts and ran down the cobbled street in the cold night air, her heart racing at the sound of his breath right behind her. Then, suddenly, his hands closed around her waist.

Adela laughed as Roarke swung her into his arms, her laughter silenced when his lips closed possessively over hers. She twined her arms happily around his neck and pressed herself closer, unable to restrain her delight. He was truly hers and hers alone! Adela poured her response into their kiss, endeavoring to show Roarke her relief and joy without words, and he groaned as he lifted her closer.

With a visible effort, Roarke finally tore his lips away from hers, and they stared wonderingly into each other's eyes for a long moment, their breath mingling white in the winter air.

'' 'Tis true,'' she whispered in amazement, and Roarke grinned.

"Aye," he confirmed in that low voice that turned her knees to butter. "I do love you, Adela."

"I love you, too," she murmured, reaching up to brush an unruly lock of ebony hair back from his brow. Roarke's eyes sobered, and his hold on her tightened slightly before he spoke.

"Marry me, Adela," he urged, and she was amazed that he was yet uncertain of her response.

"Gladly," she declared softly. Adela watched the heat flare in his eyes before he claimed her lips once more, and barely noticed the sound of the guild members' applause carrying from the window far behind.

* * * * *

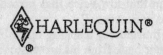 **HARLEQUIN**®

The proprietors of Weddings, Inc. hope you have enjoyed visiting Eternity, Massachusetts. And if you missed any of the exciting Weddings, Inc. titles, here is your opportunity to complete your collection:

Harlequin Superromance	#598	*Wedding Invitation* by Marisa Carroll	$3.50 U.S. ☐ $3.99 CAN. ☐
Harlequin Romance	#3319	*Expectations* by Shannon Waverly	$2.99 U.S. ☐ $3.50 CAN. ☐
Harlequin Temptation	#502	*Wedding Song* by Vicki Lewis Thompson	$2.99 U.S. ☐ $3.50 CAN. ☐
Harlequin American Romance	#549	*The Wedding Gamble* by Muriel Jensen	$3.50 U.S. ☐ $3.99 CAN. ☐
Harlequin Presents	#1692	*The Vengeful Groom* by Sara Wood	$2.99 U.S. ☐ $3.50 CAN. ☐
Harlequin Intrigue	#298	*Edge of Eternity* by Jasmine Cresswell	$2.99 U.S. ☐ $3.50 CAN. ☐
Harlequin Historical	#248	*Vows* by Margaret Moore	$3.99 U.S. ☐ $4.50 CAN. ☐

HARLEQUIN BOOKS...
NOT THE SAME OLD STORY

TOTAL AMOUNT	$
POSTAGE & HANDLING	$
($1.00 for one book, 50¢ for each additional)	
APPLICABLE TAXES*	$ _____
TOTAL PAYABLE	$ _____
(check or money order—please do not send cash)	

To order, complete this form and send it, along with a check or money order for the total above, payable to Harlequin Books, to: **In the U.S.:** 3010 Walden Avenue, P.O. Box 9047, Buffalo, NY 14269-9047; **In Canada:** P.O. Box 613, Fort Erie, Ontario, L2A 5X3.

Name: _____

Address: _____ City: _____

State/Prov.: _____ Zip/Postal Code: _____

*New York residents remit applicable sales taxes.
Canadian residents remit applicable GST and provincial taxes.   WED-F

This holiday, join four hunky heroes under the mistletoe for

Christmas Kisses

Cuddle under a fluffy quilt, with a cup of hot chocolate and these romances sure to warm you up:

#561 HE'S A REBEL (also a Studs title)
Linda Randall Wisdom

#562 THE BABY AND THE BODYGUARD
Jule McBride

#563 THE GIFT-WRAPPED GROOM
M.J. Rodgers

#564 A TIMELESS CHRISTMAS
Pat Chandler

Celebrate the season with all four holiday books sealed with a Christmas kiss—coming to you in December, only from Harlequin American Romance!

CHRISTMAS STALKINGS

All wrapped up in spine-tingling packages, here are three books guaranteed to chill your spine...and warm your hearts this holiday season!

#302 THE KID WHO STOLE CHRISTMAS
Linda Stevens

#303 I'LL BE HOME FOR CHRISTMAS
Dawn Stewardson

#304 BEARING GIFTS
Aimée Thurlo

This December, fill your stockings with the "Christmas Stalkings"—for the best in romantic suspense. Only from

HARLEQUIN®

INTRIGUE®

On the most romantic day of the year, capture the thrill of falling in love all over again—with

Harlequin's

Bachelors

They're three sexy and *very single* men who run very special personal ads to find the women of their fantasies by Valentine's Day. These exciting, passion-filled stories are written by bestselling Harlequin authors.

Your Heart's Desire by Elise Title
Mr. Romance by Pamela Bauer
Sleepless in St. Louis by Tiffany White

Be sure not to miss Harlequin's Valentine Bachelors, available in February wherever Harlequin books are sold.

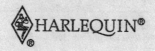

VB

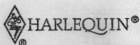

HARLEQUIN®

Don't miss these Harlequin favorites by some of our most
distinguished authors!
And now you can receive a discount by ordering two or more titles!

HT#25483	BABYCAKES by Glenda Sanders	$2.99	☐
HT#25559	JUST ANOTHER PRETTY FACE by Candace Schuler	$2.99	☐
HP#11608	SUMMER STORMS by Emma Goldrick	$2.99	☐
HP#11632	THE SHINING OF LOVE by Emma Darcy	$2.99	☐
HR#03265	HERO ON THE LOOSE by Rebecca Winters	$2.89	☐
HR#03268	THE BAD PENNY by Susan Fox	$2.99	☐
HS#70532	TOUCH THE DAWN by Karen Young	$3.39	☐
HS#70576	ANGELS IN THE LIGHT by Margot Dalton	$3.50	☐
HI#22249	MUSIC OF THE MIST by Laura Pender	$2.99	☐
HI#22267	CUTTING EDGE by Caroline Burnes	$2.99	☐
HAR#16489	DADDY'S LITTLE DIVIDEND by Elda Minger	$3.50	☐
HAR#16525	CINDERMAN by Anne Stuart	$3.50	☐
HH#28801	PROVIDENCE by Miranda Jarrett	$3.99	☐
HH#28775	A WARRIOR'S QUEST by Margaret Moore	$3.99	☐
	(limited quantities available on certain titles)		

TOTAL AMOUNT	$	
DEDUCT: 10% DISCOUNT FOR 2+ BOOKS	$	
POSTAGE & HANDLING	$	
($1.00 for one book, 50¢ for each additional)		
APPLICABLE TAXES*	$_____	
TOTAL PAYABLE	$_____	
(check or money order—please do not send cash)		

To order, complete this form and send it, along with a check or money order for the
total above, payable to Harlequin Books, to: **In the U.S.:** 3010 Walden Avenue,
P.O. Box 9047, Buffalo, NY 14269-9047; **In Canada:** P.O. Box 613, Fort Erie, Ontario,
L2A 5X3.

Name: _____

Address:_____City: _____

State/Prov.: _____ Zip/Postal Code: _____

*New York residents remit applicable sales taxes.
 Canadian residents remit applicable GST and provincial taxes.

HBACK-OD